DINER Guys

by Chip Silverman

FOREWORD BY BARRY LEVINSON

A Birch Lane Press Book
Published by Carol Publishing Group

Editorial Offices
600 Madison Avenue
New York, NY 10022

Sales & Distribution Offices
120 Enterprise Avenue
Secaucus, NJ 07094

In Canada: Musson Book Company
A division of General Publishing Co. Limited
Don Mills, Ontario

Library of Congress Cataloging-in-Publication Data

Silverman, Chip.
Diner guys / by Chip Silverman : foreword by
Barry Levinson
p.   cm.
"A Birch Lane Press Book"
1. Chip Silverman. 2. United States--Biography.
I. Title
1989   [B]
ISBN 1-55972-009-3

TO MY MOM—MY GREATEST ROOTER
AND STRONGEST SUPPORTER

Author's Note

I've changed a lot of names, places, and some dates, etc., in order to protect both the guilty and the innocent. I've embellished some of the stories, but most of what you'll read in this book really took place. I mean, the dust and drugs of the '50s, '60s and '70s played havoc and killed a number of Diner Guys.

There are some of you, for a variety of reasons, who will see yourselves at the Diner or in some of the other places in the book you think you'd want to be.

That's natural, just as it was natural for half of Baltimore to say they saw pro-football Hall of Famer Jim Brown score seven goals in an all-star lacrosse game at Johns Hopkins Homewood Field, when the actual attendance that day was 4,000.

Four thousand is about the same number of people who were in Hershey, PA, one night and saw Wilt Chamberlain become the only player ever to score 100 points in an NBA basketball game. Yet, everyone you meet in a Sports Bar anywhere swears he was there that night, and that the game was in Madison Square Garden.

In any event, any resemblance between you and the Diner Guys and the other guys and gals in the book—growing up, coming of age, finding your place somewhere—it's all intentional. Have Fun!

Chip Silverman
April 1989

Contents

FOREWORD BY BARRY LEVINSON   xiii

1. THE PLAYGROUND   1
2. THE WANDERING JEW   7
3. THE NEIGHBORHOOD   17
4. THE FIFTIES: THE ERA OF MALE BONDING   23
5. THE SIXTIES: THE AGE OF ENLIGHTENMENT   87
6. THE SEVENTIES: A PERIOD OF INDIVIDUALISM   201
7. THE EIGHTIES: A TIME OF DISCOVERY   269

    Appendix A: ALUMINUM SIDING: ANNALS OF THE TIN MEN   309
    Appendix B: NORTHWEST BALTIMORE'S FAMOUS GRADUATES   337

Gimme the beat boys and free my soul,
I wanna get lost in your rock and roll,
  And drift away.

—Dobie Gray

Foreword

Queensberry Playground was located in Northwest Baltimore about two miles southeast of Brice's Hilltop Diner on which I based the film *Diner*. The playground and diner were but two of a number of hangouts for a group of very unique guys who grew up in Northwest Baltimore. For them, the mid-'50s to the mid-'60s signified the zenith of a lifestyle of endless knockings, sarcastic put-downs and bull sessions that lasted from early evening to early morning seven days a week.

Chip chose to write this book simply because he chronicled events. He keeps the memories better than anyone else, and just loves to tell stories. In this book he's followed the lives of dozens of us over four decades through anecdotes that are almost complete stories in themselves.

Chip and I attended Forest Park High School in the late '50s along with Ken Waissman, creator and producer of the Broadway hit *Grease;* Bill McAuliffe, a professor at Harvard; pop star Mama Cass Elliot (née Ellen Cohen); and many more you'll read about in this book. These include a surprisingly high number of famous students from Forest Park in fields of entertainment and politics (such as novelist Leon Uris and former Vice-President Spiro Agnew), even though they may not have been full-time playground and/or diner guys.

Playground and diner terminology, humor and characters were unique to Northwest Baltimore, and Chip has accurately defined them in the stories. Although Chip wasn't as funny as Ben, as good-looking as Hud, as smart as Bill, as tough as Boogie or the Gripper, or as uniquely odd as Fenwick and Yussel, he still impacted on the guys. This was because he had a good memory and instigated and initiated a lot of things that happened.

And he finally put it all together in one book, whose underlying theme is the camaraderie of the guys, and whose style is uniquely different and wonderfully documented. It's an easy read and enormously funny. I loved it!

—Barry Levinson

The backyard led to the playground, and the playground led to the street corner, and the street corner led to the pool room, and the pool room led to the Diner, and the Diner led to . . .

1

The Playground

The playground was a melting pot. When you left the confines of the backyards and the back alleys and ventured into the playground, you met people from other backyards and back alleys, and other streets and other neighborhoods which surrounded some of the lower Pimlico area. Pimlico was located in Northwest Baltimore.

Queensberry Playground was centered in the middle of the back alleys and backyards of four streets. Officially opened in 1949, the playground was bordered on the east side by the fifty-hundred block of Queensberry Avenue. West Garrison Avenue was the southern border, Spaulding Avenue was the northern side, and the western border was Palmer Avenue.

It was very, very small for a playground and had strange rectangular dimensions. Whichever end of the field that a softball game was played on, there was always a very short fence for either a right- or left-handed home run to be hit. The playground had a hill on which sat a bunker-type small building that housed the recreation center. Inside was a pool table, a ping-pong table and a Coke machine (which served the coldest Cokes I ever tasted), and in one corner were round tables where you could mess with some clay if you were really young. There was also an office for the playground director, Mr. Fisher. Outside to the right of the building was a baby playground (sand box, etc.) and to the left of the building were larger swings and a sliding board for older kids. There was a grassy

1

hill which led down to the ballfield that was made of red clay, and at the far end of the ballfield was a fenced-in cement basketball court.

If you weren't playing softball, basketball or stickball, you would be up on the building porch playing Pitch or pinochle until dark.

Many softball games ended when the ball was hit over the long or short fence breaking somebody's window, or disappeared high over the houses. Other times the ball would sail into the backyard of Melvin Gross. He was a very powerful, strong, silent type who, as soon as he saw the ball or heard it break something, would come rushing out of his house with the softball held high over his head and the players would scatter. They would resume the game the next evening.

At the playground you met guys who had somehow acquired the strangest of names. There was Monk, Boards, Mole, Bug, Tool, The Gripper, Climbing Bercy, and Whitey the mailman. There was Fat Pete Tringolly who owned a fruit and vegetable stand in the Hollins Street Market in Southwest Baltimore. He used to take us down to play teams from around the market, and when we went to a city championship series, he was one of the guys who drove and helped coach the team. There was Joel Sherman who became very adept at basketball and was one of the better players to come out of the city high school system in the late '50s. He would shovel the snow off the basketball court in the dead of winter to practice shooting foul shots. And there was also Bull Losover who was so tough that he once beat up a car.

There was Stan Diamond, a good ball player but a better gambler, who used to bet on the outcome of the games. He couldn't pay off a bet with Sonny Stern one time and went into hiding for six months. The Diamonds lived next door to us and one day Sonny approached their backyard for his money or revenge, screaming for Stan to come on out. "What are you doing?" he yelled, "Hibernating? You must be a bear!" Thus, Stanley became known as Bear Diamond. His brother Louis shortly became "Middle-Sized Bear," and the youngest brother, Steve, was eventually dubbed "Completely Bare."

The playground became the center of life for many. Those of us who were young would wait for our chance to get into the organized games of basketball or softball, knowing what an honor it would be to play with the older guys from 13 to 35: those like Fat Pete Tringolly, who had such strong hands from working his fruit and vegetable market that he could squeeze a softball into a piece of mush when he was pitching, and Whitey the mailman who was ever so swift.

One evening, a tense game was in progress. No one had ever thrown a no-hitter during these "older guys" games and "Don" Hank, an engineer at WBAL-TV, was working on one. It was the bottom of the last inning and two were out. The batter was Bug, a notoriously weak hitter, and the crowd sensed they were viewing history. True to form, Bug hit a dribbler back to the pitching mound and the game seemed headed for the playground record books. In his haste to retrieve the ball, "Don" Hank lost his balance and dislocated his knee. As Bug streaked to first base, "Don" Hank spastically crawled in the red clay after the ball, but it was too late. Bug reached first on an infield single, and the "Don" never returned to Queensberry Playground.

It was strange, but there were guys from certain streets who you knew if you walked into their neighborhood, or they walked into yours, there was going to be a fight. Yet, when they came up to the playground there was an unwritten rule: you were friendly, nobody started anything with anybody. It was only off the grounds where there was trouble.

Meyer's Deli jutted out where Palmer and Spaulding Avenues met at a point. It was a short walk from the back of the playground on the Spaulding Avenue side to Meyer's. Meyer's had great hotdogs, bologna, corned beef sandwiches, coddies (cod fish cakes) and a great soda fountain. He also had pinball machines in the back room which you weren't really allowed to play until you were 14, but which you began playing when you were 10. Meyer later sold the deli to Nat in the late '50s. Nat was a refugee from Nazi Germany who came from the concentration camps with his family and parlayed "Nat's" into three or four other delis when the neighborhood's racial composition changed in the early '60s. Nat was slick. He could catch us stealing the coddies and other goods, but we continued to do it, and we also tried to sneak out without paying the bill, but he'd always spy us and collect.

The Newmans lived on Spaulding Avenue, which was the northern street whose yards backed up to Queensberry Playground and where the main entrance to the playground was situated. (Those of us from the southern streets came in on Garrison Avenue's back entrance through the alleys.) The youngest Newman brother was Joe, who by some odd reason owned a Cadillac convertible when he was 16 years old. Joe also never wore socks. (Maybe he was one of the earliest preppies but didn't realize it.)

Joe became the manager of the Queensberry softball teams from an early period on. Although he knew very little about the sport, the team was so good that he took the credit for managing it to many city championships. Joe actually became manager because he had a car. We always needed somebody to drive the guys to games since there was very little transportation back in those days for those of us who played eight- to 10-, 10- to 12-, and 12- to 14-year-old ball. Anyhow, "The Coach," Joe Newman, became so legendary that the playground later took on the informal title of "Newmanberry."

The patriarch of the Newman family ran a newspaper stand on the corner of Belvedere and Park Heights Avenues which bordered the southwest point of Pimlico Race Track. It was, for a time, one of the busiest newspaper stands in the Baltimore metropolitan area. He was married to a short, fat, pug-faced woman and they had three sons. Aside from Joe, there was Howard or "Reds" Newman, who had lost all of his marbles and was continually in and out of mental institutions, and there was Bernard Newman, who initially took on the phallic nickname "Tool" (supposedly due to his sexual prowess, or so he said), and then later "Doag," which was a takeoff of Mad-Dog since he was reputed to be a tough fighter (although he lost most of his fights and had false teeth from the time he was 17). The Doag used to lay out back behind his house and lift crude weights in the hot sun, day after day after day.

Joe and Doag used to torment their older brother "Crazy Reds." They used to send him out to buy ice cream at Nat's and carefully instruct him to make sure that none of it melted before he returned. He would rush to the deli, and when he would return home, the brothers would lock the doors and not let him in. Terrified, not wanting the ice cream to melt, Reds would try to break into the house using a ladder to reach the high second floor windows just below the roof. But after he would climb up, Joe and Doag would also lock the windows and remove the ladder, and Reds would remain on the roof or in a nearby tree for days; the remnants of sticky ice cream lodging in his clothes.

Doag Newman and his mother always tried to sneak into the racetrack. Once, when they were caught, a security guard engaged them in an argument and then tried to sucker-punch Doag. He missed and knocked out Mrs. Newman. Doag replied in his daily newspaper jargon, "The *Sun* is out, the *News* is out, and soon you're gonna be out!"* And then he knocked the guard out.

Some guys couldn't cope with being away from Queensberry. Two actually went AWOL from military service to come back to the playground. One guy ended up living in the bathroom behind the playground building for weeks. Another guy, AWOL from the Navy, just spent his time in Nat's back room playing the pinball machine. His name was "In Again—Out Again" Finnegan. About eight months later, the Shore Patrol came by and caught him in Nat's. He had to serve some time in the brig, but after his discharge Finnegan returned to the pinball machine.

Once a month, there would be a dance thrown on the basketball court at the playground. Usually there was a Victrola which played early rock and roll music, and everybody would stand around and watch one or two real good dancers. Doag Newman decided to form a musical group to play at these dances. He persuaded softball star Nino Seltzo, who played the accordion, to join him. Doag played the comb fairly well but was a fair-to-poor vocalist. The guys were received well in a humorous vein, but, taking himself seriously, Doag advertised in the *Jewish Times* that his group could play Bar Mitzvahs and weddings. No one ever hired them.

---

* *Sun* was the *Baltimore Morning Sun; News* was the *Baltimore News American.*

The Wandering Jew

By playing ball for Queensberry Playground, we got to wander quite a bit. Usually we traveled to other playgrounds in the Northwest Baltimore corridor, but if we won the Northwest regional title, we also got to visit other areas of the city during the playoffs.

Northwest Baltimore was comprised of the following areas:

Forest Park	Hampden
Pimlico	Roland Park
Upper Park Heights	Howard Park
Lower Park Heights	Gwynns Falls
Mt. Washington	Park Circle

With the exception of Howard Park, Roland Park, Hampden and parts of Mt. Washington, Northwest Baltimore was predominantly Jewish until the late '50s when the "blues"* began moving uptown. During the next five years, different buffer zones emerged as the Jews once again became the wandering Jews and our "nomadic" instincts became "paranoidadic"—the instant a blue broke the block, the Jews scattered like wildfire.

The poor blues; some had finally attained middle-class status and moved into a nice neighborhood to get away from the crime-infested ghetto, and immediately house prices plummeted. When the Jews

---

*Blues was playground and Diner terminology for blacks.

moved, the speculators rented the homes to poor families and within a couple years re-created the ghetto and its problems. The first demarcation line became Park Circle after the blues took over Mondawmin Shopping Center and its surrounding neighborhood. Forest Park fell next and beautiful homes that were sold to upper-class Jews for the unheard of price of $50,000 (30 years ago) dropped to the teens. Then Lower Park Heights went blue. My widowed mother sold our Pimlico home in 1960 to old refugee Jews at a decent price (we bought the house in the late '40s for under $4,000 and sold it for $10,000) and we moved uptown to Millbrook near Reisterstown Plaza, which today has become a mall that is ready to fall to the blues.

After Pimlico fell, the new "demilitarized zone" became Northern Parkway just beyond Pimlico Racetrack. Following Rommel's Panzer Division tactics in Africa in World War II, the blues, instead of moving straight up Park Heights, swung out to the left (Liberty Road) and the right. It was at that point that Mom sold our Millbrook rowhouse, which she bought for $12,000 in 1961, for almost $50,000 in 1980. She could have broken the block and received more money but she became guilt-ridden, although she cursed herself when a former neighbor sold her home for $1,000 more to a family of Koreans two years later.

We were unaware then that, just as Napoleon had been stopped by the Russian winter, so would the blues be held off by an influx of Hasidic Jews who bought the homes in the upper reaches of Park Heights at the cheap rate originally established for the blues. The blues had to regroup since they were unable to deal with this strange sect that they had never been exposed to before—Jews who would not move or be pushed around. Today the Jews occupy the northern-most part of Northwest Baltimore (the goyim never did leave Hampden and Roland Park). Most Jewish families could not go any further north since the homes are too expensive; the south is closed off by the blues; the west is occupied by upper-class blues and the Jews who refuse to move, and they can't cross to the eastern part past Falls Road since it's too Gentile. They've met "their" Stalingrad and now any time they see a blue jogging down their street they call the police. (The best part is when the cops are blues.)

Jews do wander a lot. Take my mother for instance. When she was almost two years old, right before the outbreak of World War I (and during the periodic pogroms in Russia), she took part in one of the great wandering exercises of our time. She lived in Pinsk in Minsk (or was it Minsk in Pinsk), a large city in a large state located in Bielor or White Russia. Mom lived there with her parents, my Bubbie and Zaidie (Yiddish for grandma and grandpa), her sister Rose and her brother Albert. To make a short story long, I'll dispense with telling it in Yiddish and give the rough translation.

Actually, the family wasn't really from Pinsk proper. They lived in a very small *shtetl* (pronounced shtetel) or town outside of the city of Pinsk which was in the state of Minsku Guberne or Minsk. The shtetl was named Laheshin and was so small that the townspeople had a funny rhyming saying for it in their native Yiddish that went, *"Laheshin vu de hiner pishen."* It meant, "Laheshin where the chickens piss." Oh well, I guess you had to be there.

It was important back then that the Jews all live in their own shtetl so that if the pogroms got out of hand, some goy's property, heaven forbid, wouldn't accidentally get burned or looted or his daughters raped. Anyhow, nobody remembers any other distant relatives on my mother's side except that some blonde blue-eyed Cossack raped one of my great-great grandmothers and that's how we inherited our coloring.

Around the time my mother was six months old, my Zaidie decided that he would go to America and make it big, start a new life, and then send for the family. Since he and Bubbie had relatives and *landsleit* (friends from your home village) who had gone to America and were living in Chicago, Zaidie said that he would go there. He promised to send money and bring everybody over as soon as possible, and, if he couldn't earn the money, there was still the Jewish Welfare Services who sponsored families coming to America.

Soon after Zaidie leaves, World War I breaks out and the Germans are moving toward Russia. Russia, in the meantime, is going through a little internal turmoil with rabble-rousing guys like Lenin and Trotsky causing a lot of grief. So the first thing my Bubbie does is to send her daughter Rose to a town further east inside of Russia to prevent the Germans from doing bad things to Aunt Rose who was 15 years old and pretty good-looking. After Rose departs, Bubbies takes my mother, Uncle Albert (who turned out to be a real prick) and her own mother (who was 84 at the time) and heads toward Moscow.

Aunt Rose developed dysentery on her way east, and the relatives she is sent to join decide that they don't want anybody in their family catching whatever she has. So, they just throw Aunt Rose out in a wheat field and say, "See you later." Now here's Aunt Rose laying out in this field, a gorgeous teenager with dysentery, and the Germans come marching through. The Germans get hold of Aunt Rose but instead of raping and beating her, or putting her in an oven, they say, "We'll wait until World War II for that," and they nurse her back to health, give her some food and money, and send her on her merry way.

Meanwhile, the wandering Jews of the Beguns*, my Zaidie's family name, arrive in Moscow and write Zaidie of their whereabouts. Nothing's really happening in Moscow except scary rumors that the Germans are fast approaching. The authorities send Mom, Bubbie, great Bubbie and Uncle Albert to Arzamas in the state of Novograd, which is in Siberia, and that's where they're to start their new lives while waiting to hear from Zaidie. The Russian bureaucrats tell my grandmother, "Don't worry, we'll let you know when Zaidie writes." Sure!

Three years go by in the coldest climate in the world. They're suffering from starvation, barely surviving, great-Bubbie has frozen to death, they haven't heard from the Russian bureaucrats or Zaidie, the White Russians are fighting the Red Russians, and Aunt Rose is still missing. So my Bubbie goes to the officials in Novograd and demands they send her back to Moscow. Bubbie is one tough woman, even though she's only 4′10″, and she raises so much hell that the authorities pack up my mother and Uncle Albert (now maybe five and nine years old) and ship them all back to Moscow. It's pretty crazy there when they arrive—like in the Warren Beatty movie *Reds*—and they can't find out what's going on. Instead of getting an audience with Czar Nicholas or Rasputin—as though they could find Zaidie—Bubbie gets a rifle butt up the ass and is almost sent back to Siberia. Somehow she gets money from the Jewish Welfare Services before it's dissolved, and the family boards a train headed for Vladivostok, which is only about 6,000 miles away on the Trans-Siberia Railroad. (A comfortable ride in 1917!)

During this time, Bubbie was writing letters to America but nobody seems to know where Zaidie is. He hasn't been heard from in about four years. Nobody knows where Aunt Rose is, either.

---

* The author of *Roots* would have a field day tracing my family tree. It seems the Beguns from Minsk later shortened their name to Begin (made a lot of sense, right?). The famous Israeli prime minister's family was considered a relative.

They decide to give her up for dead and naturally blamed the Germans for raping and killing Aunt Rose. Rather than bore you with the difficulties of that trip,* they arrived in Vladivostok, a seaport town on the east coast of Russia, some months later, and from there they boarded a big boat sailing toward Japan.

They get to Yokohama all right but can't go on since they've run out of money and have to wait for another Jewish Welfare Service (in Japan?) to take care of them. The Japanese, of course, are amazed at the Beguns because they haven't seen this many short white people together in a long time. After six weeks of speaking Yiddish to the Japanese, they still can't locate Zaidie, but they do get money from another Jewish Welfare League (The Hias)—which was probably financed by Sony in order to get all of these White Russian Jews out of their country.

Bubbie et al. board a tramp steamer headed for the U.S. and, a few hundred miles out of Japan, they hit either a mine or a torpedo. Naturally, my family is riding "first class steerage" and figure they're history; but the ship doesn't sink and luckily it limps into port in San Francisco several weeks later. How they made it from Minsk no one knows.

In San Francisco, wrapped in rags, with no money and no inkling of where Zaidie is, Bubbie somehow contacts the landsleit or "lantzmen" (shipmates of sorts or travel mates of your relatives, or fellow villagers) from Chicago who send her money to take the train there. This is only a short 1,500 mile trip—the Beguns already are used to such fun train rides. When they get to Chicago, it takes about a week to locate the lantzmen. (What did they do to exist for the week?) The lantzmen recall Zaidie, complain that he didn't bathe, and tell Bubbie that they haven't seen him for over two years.

Poor Bubbie is dejected but still very much determined to find Zaidie. She is still a tough woman but now only 4′9″ tall since she has lost an inch in her height due to the rigors of the trip. Bubbie was no weakling, however. She was 54 years old when she had my mother, lived to be 102 and died with all her faculties intact—except she was only about 3′6″ tall when she passed away. Mom laments that Bubbie would be alive today if we kept her and hadn't put her

---

* Remember this wasn't exactly AMTRAK with club cars and dining and toilet facilities; and I know they weren't wearing goose down coats and hats or Gucci boots. I mean, how the fuck did these three little unprotected Jews survive the people, the turmoil, the elements? What did they use for toilet paper?

in a nursing home 20 years ago at age 100. Caffeine and paregoric were Bubbie's diet the last 20 years of her life, thus making her the first refugee junkie.

Bubbie checks around Chicago and finds out that Zaidie might be in Baltimore. She goes to the Jewish Welfare Agency and is once more sponsored with Mom and Uncle Albert to "train it" to Baltimore—another short trip.

Bubbie et al. are in Baltimore a couple of weeks before they finally run into some Russian Jews who think Zaidie is in Meade, Maryland, working as a carpenter in the nearby military facility. So Bubbie goes out to Camp Meade and finds Zaidie, whom she hasn't seen for about five or six years now, and she says, "Hey, schmuck, it's me! Where the hell have you been?" Zaidie calmly replies, "You know, Rebecca, I meant to contact you but I never did learn to read or write, and I haven't had a chance to get somebody to do it for me." Bubbie probably sucker-punched him at that point but who knows. He did end up with his wife and two kids, and about a year later Aunt Rose shows up. How the hell she found these people or got to America is uncomprehensible. I have no idea because I don't ever remember her ever speaking English or talking about the trip before she died, but if that isn't wandering, I don't know what is.

As it turns out, the Beguns made their home in East Baltimore around Patterson Park, and Zaidie continued to wander. He used to wander from Patterson Park up to visit us when we lived in Pimlico, which was about a 20 mile walk. He would be missing for a couple of days, but my father or Uncle Albert would eventually find him. He died when he was 75. He had completely lost his mind by then, but he was a Jewish carpenter so what could we expect.

Now bear with me since my mother says it's important that you understand where we first-generation "greenhorns" (that's what our nasty neighbors used to call us) came from.

My father's side of the family was a little more difficult to trace, since after Dad died, his family stopped talking to my mother, and when they finally spoke to me, they'd forgotten everything or were dead. What we do remember is that the name Silverman was given to my paternal grandfather when he entered the United States in the late 1800s; sort of like the blues who received the names of the families who owned them or the plantations where they worked. But not exactly.

My maternal Zaidie's was nothing compared to my father's father's wanderlust. Words like restless and shiftless were much more appropriate to Dad's dad, and Zaidie Begun, no paragon of virtue or example of dedicated husband and father, was a saint in contrast to Zaidie Silverman—a real asshole, according to family legacy.

Unlike the Beguns, I never met granddad or grandma Silverman since Zaidie died in the late 1920s and Bubbie died in 1940. She, according to the family, was a wonderful and giving woman.

Anyhow, my paternal Zaidie (whose original name was Yushewi Shpritz) and Bubbie were also from Minsk—which had a helluva Jewish population back then—and, soon after they married (around 1895), he decided to split for America. After giving Bubbie a similar pitch like Zaidie Begun, he took the European route to the nearest seaport, steaming into Locust Point, Maryland, several months later.

The job of an immigration officer wasn't real easy in the late 19th or early 20th centuries. Here were all these "homeless, tired and poor" sailing into Ellis Island, Locust Point and numerous other ports by the thousands and speaking numerous languages and dialects to some underpaid, over-worked civil servant who hated foreigners. The guy's trying to process everyone quickly while checking for people with smallpox and other diseases, and having to record names, country of origin and destinations.

Now up steps my paternal Zaidie who announces, "Ich bein Yushewi Shpritz!" The immigration officer looks at him quizzically and asks him to spell his name, but granddad just stares ahead and repeats his name. The immigration officer brings over a Yiddish interpreter who asks Zaidie one more time to spell his name. Zaidie answers that he can't spell the name, but can the immigration officer spell it? This goes back and forth for awhile while the line keeps getting longer, and the immigration officer finally blurts out a name beginning with "S" and says to granddad, "You'll be Samuel Silverman, refugee. Now get lost!"

He stamps the official seal to the name and, bingo, we're all Silvermans from that time on. So Samuel Silverman, nee Yushewi Shpritz, is now off on his own in Baltimore to find his lantzmen. It takes him a couple of days but he finally locates some former villagers, stays a few weeks and then returns to Minsk to bring back his wife Rebecca* and his brother Naucham.

---

*Same name as my maternal grandmother. They were so poor in Minsk, I guess they had to use duplicate names.

When they return to America after a few more months and go through the immigration line, Rebecca Shpritz becomes Rebecca Silverman, and Naucham, who knew how to spell and speak a little English, is Naucham Shpritz. So now, for over 80 years, one half of the family is Silverman in America and the other half is Shpritz. I mean it's okay with me since Chip Shpritz would have sounded a little strange.

Zaidie Silverman goes into the cap-making business and, since he learned his trade from his parents in Minsk and there're few quality hat makers in Baltimore, he becomes quite successful. He then proceeded to implant in his wife Rebecca seven children, and each time she became pregnant, Zaidie went off and wandered. He traveled throughout the United States, but most of the time he would return to Europe and Minsk to visit his parents. It wasn't that he was homesick, he was just restless, and besides he was kind of a schmuck since he never gave Bubbie Rebecca any of his money, using it to pay for his travel and fun.

Since granddad was sensitive about his image, he blamed his negative reputation on the U.S. Immigration Service for defiling him when he entered the country, thus causing the devil to fuck with his "goodlines." When the immigrants came to America they had to be inoculated, and many Jewish settlers reacted violently to this action. It seemed that Orthodox Jewish law forbids the defilement of the human body, and a needle puncturing the skin is an unpardonable sin. Zaidie Silverman said it was this nefarious act that had defiled him and resulted in his selfish and shiftless behavior. (I guess he's the one I inherited my bullshit from.)

By the time my father Ben is born in 1910, Zaidie Silverman has made at least a dozen trips across the Atlantic and numerous other ones throughout the South, mainly to Atlanta where he must have kept a blue hooker. He isn't going for the time of day and treats his kids like shit. He even used to get a kick out of hurting family members emotionally (with the exception of his oldest daughter Ida who for some reason he always took care of.)

In the meantime, the oldest son Charlie became the main worker in Zaidie's cap business and opened up a couple of stores called "Sil's Cap and Hat King." Now Uncle Charlie was very successful but he was considered a dishonest business genius and he flaunted his wealth. He had full-time maids, drove big Buicks (comparable to driving a big Mercedes today) and used to do lots of traveling to New York.

My father idolized Uncle Charlie and used to work for him in his Washington Boulevard store. Unfortunately, Dad was too honest, and one day, unbeknownst to my father, Charlie set fire to the store in the backroom and came out and told Dad he was going to lunch. My father nearly burned to death before he realized what was going on. He almost had a nervous breakdown and actually tried to kill Charlie for not telling him that he was torching the store for the insurance money.

Charlie eventually lost all of his money. While down on his luck, he got into a hassle with some guy whom he criminally assaulted, and he was put into jail. During the same time, the next eldest son Frank, whose nickname was Folly, became addicted to narcotics and committed a series of burglaries and muggings to support his drug habit. It's obvious that, unlike his pseudo-ultra religious father, Folly was not averse to defiling his body. One day, downtown in front of S&N Katz Jewelers, he broke the store window, grabbed all of the diamonds and fled. He sold them off one by one for dope but never gave the family a dime, claiming that he didn't want them to get into trouble for it. Sure enough, Folly finally got arrested and put into jail, joining Uncle Charlie.

It's the late 1920s now and granddad Samuel Silverman, who is really Yushewi Shpritz, comes up with a toothache and goes to the most expensive dentist in Baltimore to have the tooth pulled. While the dentist is trying to do his job, granddad's tooth breaks off in his mouth. The tooth becomes infected and it poisons granddad's body. He's put into Johns Hopkins Hospital, but it's too late and he dies. At the funeral, two days later, the family convinces the authorities at the penitentiary to bring Uncle Charlie and Uncle Folly. A guard takes them in handcuffs to pay their last respects and go to the cemetery. This is a wonderful family tree—two uncles are hoods and my Zaidie dies of a toothache at Hopkins.

My Bubbie Rebecca is now a young widow without any money, and her oldest sons are in jail. My father has to support his mother and his sisters at home. Dad, meanwhile, meets the woman he intends to marry, but is opposed by his sisters. They didn't know who's going to support them if Ben gets married. As a matter of fact, one day my father wanted to bring my mother over to meet the family for dinner but my Aunt Sally said, "I don't think that will be possible, Benny, because I had an accident today and fell down the steps." My father, stunned, said to her, "When did this happen?"

and she quietly replied, "Now," as she tossed herself down three flights of stairs.

Anyhow, Dad married Mom and shortly afterwards had my sister Harryette. When she was a year old, in 1940, my grandmother Rebecca fell ill. Bubbie was an Orthodox Jew and their beliefs follow some very unusual practices. It was said that if you're near death, or it looks as if you may die, you should go and change your name, so that perhaps the former name only dies and you can live on. So my grandmother Rebecca Silverman, whose real name was Rebecca Shpritz, goes to the shul (synagogue) and changes her name to Anabelle, which didn't help a whole lot because she died about a month later.

In the fall of 1939, Mom, Dad and Harryette moved to Queensberry Avenue, purchasing a large row home for $3500.

I was born during a World War II blackout in 1942 at Franklin Square Hospital in West Baltimore. It's a shaky birth and I almost lost my left arm, but the doctors saved it. When I was brought home to the house on Queensberry Avenue, the first thing that met me was a toy truck thrown in my right eye by Harryette, a tad annoyed at the attention I was receiving.

And a few years later, in January of 1948, some 15 months before Queensberry Playground opened, my younger sister Nancy was born. We realized she'd become the favorite when Dad named his installment business Nancy Jean Sales.

Somewhere around 1954, I discovered sex and began to masturbate with great regularity. Two years later, Aunt Frieda from New York, the widow of Dad's brother Charlie the ex-crook, died and I somehow correlated it with my jerking off. I'm sure it caused her death and I ran away from home determined to wander forever. After three hours I returned home, deciding instead to secretly swear to God never to masturbate again. Within a week I was doing it like crazy. I have no self-control.

The Neighborhood

Queensberry Playground was a stone's throw south of the Pimlico Race Track—that is if you could throw a stone over 250 yards. I lived about a block from the playground on lower Queensberry Avenue, and just around the corner from us was Chalgrove Avenue. My sister, Just Harryette,* once told me that a struggling writer who resided on Chalgrove created his first novel as I was growing up, but I was paying no particular attention at that time to anything associated with the written word. His name was Leon Uris and, according to Just Harryette, he wrote *Battle Cry* when he lived around the corner, and shortly thereafter moved on to fame and fortune.

But Uris didn't become an accomplished writer overnight. In the ninth grade at Forest Park High School, he received a deficiency slip in English, and then transferred to City College, an all-male school located about a half-hour streetcar ride south. He happened to flunk English three straight times at City and eventually dropped out of school.

The teacher who gave Uris the deficiency slip was Virginia Schaffer. She began teaching English when Forest Park opened in 1924 and retired the year I graduated in 1960. She was a very strict

---

* When Harryette first separated, I introduced her by her first name to some friends in a restaurant. When they asked for her last name, she responded, "It's *Just* Harryette."

teacher. Ms. Schaffer never discussed any of her "poor" students, who numbered in the thousands, and continually refused to reminisce about 1937 grad, disgraced former Vice President and current author Spiro Agnew, and Leon Uris. The only person she deigned to pontificate upon was an obscure international poet named Wilbur Isaac (Forest Park 1932) who now publishes his works out of Japan, that is if you are fortunate or unfortunate enough to locate a copy of his poetry. Ms. Schaffer said that he was her brightest student; they corresponded until her death in 1985.

Despite scholastic difficulties, Uris relished his high school days and immortalized Forest Park and City in the pages of his first novel *Battle Cry*. Uris's later works, *Exodus, QBVII, Mila 18, Trinity*, etc. still failed to have an impact on Ms. Schaffer.

At about the time Uris was flunking out of City, another would-be writer, Russell Baker, was graduating from that school and embarking on a quest that would lead to success as a *New York Times* columnist and Pulitzer Prize-winning author of the book *Growing Up*, chronicling his years in Baltimore.

Being a city of neighborhoods, Baltimore was split into regions, and, if you lived in a certain region or catchment area back then, that designated the high school you attended. However, there were exceptions. There were open schools such as the all-male City College which had a good academic program; the all-male Poly, a bitter rival of City, which was mainly an engineering and math school and enjoyed an excellent reputation; and two all-female schools: Eastern High, across the street from City College, and Western High, which changed locations from time to time and enjoyed an academic reputation over Eastern.

Those of us who grew up in the Northwest corridor, and were white, went to Forest Park, which was a co-ed school, or to City. A small number of Jews went to Poly, none went to Eastern and only a handful to Western. Very few Jewish girls dared venture away from the Northwest area back in the late '50s and early '60s.

Forest Park, too, enjoyed a reputation of academic excellence and achievement, and during that era it sent over 90 percent of its graduates to four-year colleges—a remarkable record. In the '50s, Forest Park was at least 90 percent Jewish and remained that way until the mid-to-late '60s when the racial composition of the area changed and the majority of Baltimore City schools became predominantly black.

What happened at that one little school in Northwest Baltimore was unique—a little enclave at Eldorado and Chatham Avenues where an unusually large number of graduates excelled in sports, political science, and especially, the performing arts. Since it would take several pages to detail the names and credits of all of these students who went on to achieve excellence and recognition for their work, I've lumped them together—in the best sense of the word. See Appendix B.

From Broadway to night clubs and live entertainment, from radio to records, and on to Hollywood for movies and television, dozens of Forest Park graduates have distinguished themselves.

How did it happen?

Out of what confluence of social ethnic-educational factors did one mid-century American high school produce so many individuals who have reaped show business success?

The school seemed ordinary enough. Its students were those newly moved to Baltimore suburbia. Many were middle class and Jewish. A lot were high achievers.

Back in the days when Baltimore was in (but not aware of) its golden era, an energy and vitality pervaded all quarters and all ages. The high school in general was central to the life of all Baltimoreans, and later, Forest Park High School in particular was to have an incredible impact on the national performing arts scene.

And what muses inspired these purveyors of the performing arts? What sparks, ignited at the impressionable adolescent years, sent these talents on the road to Hollywood, New York and Motown? Most of those currently making impact on the media came out of a '50s mentality. These were the Eisenhower years when the energies of the young turned inward and were less involved with social issues. The Forester of the '50s was pushed hard by parents and faculty whose sole mission was to produce star quality academic performances. Under such pressure there seemed few escape valves but humor on an interpersonal level, and the legitimacy of the public school stage. It was generally a period of sexual repression, and the dichotomy between those with and without a "reputation" is very clear in Forest Park graduate Ken Waissman's *Grease.* There was a kind of "crinoline criteria" for what were deemed healthy outlets. School productions were guaranteed to be endorsed by parent and faculty alike. Drama was encouraged by being included just for the over-achieving elite under the guise of a fifth major. In the '50s, Forest Park was the only high school which offered a drama elective in the junior year and a theater elective in the senior year. It was considered the ultimate in progressive education.

The drama and theater courses were the equivalent of those in college, and in the school plays, everyone wanted the lead role. There was a general awareness about what was going on in the New York theater on Broadway.

The students were very mature for their age. They were interested in the arts just like their parents, and they did a lot of reading. The neighborhood was very stable. Its residents were interested in culture, and they supported culture and the arts in Baltimore.

The students were so bright that they actually ran the school, in a positive way. They were very active, they could monitor the halls properly, and they could give tutoring without having to be told. They also had more power than they realized at the time. When the school administration wanted to force Frank the Candyman off the school grounds, the students actually boycotted the cafeteria for a week, forcing the administration to cave in and let Frank remain.

There was great pressure to be funny or witty. Without a sense of humor, Forest Park was a tough place to be. So you were forced to develop wit. There were continuous knock sessions, behind the school or at "The Cross" (where the hedges met) in front of the building.

You'd practice at home, at night, standing in front of the mirror. It was important. You got that first knock in, you were "in" for the day. Guys would sit in class thinking of knocks. It was a matter of survival. The scholastic thing came easy for most of us. Breaking guys up was how you got status. Maybe show business was just the logical extension of it.

To put it into perspective, Baltimore is a big, small town. It goes at a nice easy pace; it's not expensive; it's a great place to raise a family (even if you're not married), and its centralized location on the eastern seaboard places the City in the unique position of having its cake and eating it too.

However, until Baltimore's most recent renaissance (we've had a couple) under Mayor William Donald Schaefer, and the national media's realization that there is urban rebirth taking place, and that Baltimore most typifies it, this city on the Chesapeake Bay was viewed strictly as a blue collar, dusty, backward, upper-southern town situated between mature Philadelphia and sophisticated Washington, D.C. The City's reputation around the country was based on the professional football Colts (before the team moved), baseball's Orioles, steamed crabs, and the infamous adult entertainment zone known as The Block.

So, although I may have arbitrarily stretched the boundaries of Northwest Baltimore, the students and/or their families for the most part still grew up only a couple of miles south and east. But, the area is miniscule in relation to the national impact Forest Park grads (and non-grads) have made upon our country's political, entertainment, cultural, sports, literary, health and educational life. Remember now, I'm just talking Northwest Baltimore, not other areas of the city which produced Babe Ruth, Eubie Blake, Billie Holiday, H.L. Mencken, Henrietta Szold (founder of Hadassah), Wallis Warfield Simpson (The Duchess of Windsor), Frank Zappa, David Byrne (Talking Heads). . . .

I attended Forest Park High School. It was a 15-minute streetcar ride and a brief walk from Queensberry Avenue.

Forest Park looked like a school straight out of an old Andy Hardy movie. Located on a tree-shaded street, this impressive and beautiful structure had ivy crawling up its front and immaculately cut hedges adorning the sidewalks and entrance ways.

It was, by many measures, a placid time. The most significant political issue for those '50s students was the designation of a smoking area outside the school cafeteria. Everybody wore hummers (tennis shoes) and madras shorts that had to bleed.

It was blossoming for most. A very unobtrusive type of upbringing. Psychologically we just felt terrific. We had very few detrimental urges. There was no friction. The atmosphere was so middle class that you just kind of drifted. And these were positive influences.

Most of the kids at Forest Park were also strictly middle-class. Just a few were from wealthy families, in business or the professions. The Jewish study ethic was pervasive, not only because of the parents but also because of the kids.

Smart was hip. A girl with an "A" in trigonometry had as many dates as a girl who was top heavy, but the girl who could tutor you in French and who had great legs was worth getting a part-time job for.

The school was a microcosm of the neighborhood whose kids it educated. Nobody ever stole anything (except from Read's Drug Store). Everyone always wore clean clothes and brought nourishing lunches, and enjoyed the little enclave that moved them between the arms of their parents and the reality of college like a herd of well-dressed antelope.

School days had plenty of breaks and your reputation as a

funnyman had to be sustained every day. Trying to get fresh laughs with stories you stayed up late inventing and practicing was harder than memorizing Spanish idioms. The crowd would turn on you in an instant if your material was tired or boring, or if you wore the same shirt two days in a row. The sole example of planning ahead was to try to get the car for the weekend, or to get up enough nerve to buy prophylactics.

The student body of Forest Park High School took the school motto to heart—"Enter to Learn, Go Forth to Serve"—and moved out into various walks of life with these words as guidelines. Many of us took longer to "go forth to serve" than others.

The Fifties:
An Era of Male
Bonding

> . . . wish I didn't know now
> what I didn't know then.
> —Bob Seeger,
> "Against the Wind"

1.

Reputations, 30 years ago, revolved more around one's fighting prowess or zaniness than anything else. Sexual prowess and relationships with girls, for the most part, were categorized under zaniness since our comprehension of women, over the decades, would only warrant the heading ZANY; especially when we did (and still do) hide behind an intense camaraderie which, for better or worse, molded our characters.

Even today when Diner and playground guys get together to reminisce—which is what we do best—the highlight memories always drift to the tough guys or the crazy ones. Not discussion about who received an "A" in science in the eighth grade, or who had the lead in the senior play. Even sports, which prompts a lot of debate, takes a back seat to now-epic battles, colorful plays and smiles. The guys of my era weren't even remotely aware of the famous graduates of their high school or neighborhood. We're much more concerned with what happened to the Gripper, Fenwick, Neurotic Nat, Third, Boogie, Charlie-Bo-Death-Straight-Twelve.

Playgrounds, poolrooms, fraternities and "far-away" bars were the basic devices for measuring status in Northwest Baltimore from the age of eight to 22.

In the '50s, there were five playgrounds in our area— Queensberry, Towanda, Cahill, Lucille and Pall Mall—that were extremely competitive and won a majority of city-wide softball and track championships. Cahill was predominantly Gentile, Pall Mall and Lucille seldom fielded representative teams, and Towanda and Queensberry were the biggest rivals. Good athletes at Pall Mall and Lucille affiliated themselves with either Queensberry or Towanda.

For example, Lucille Playground's Sylvan Feldman (he later shortened his name to the more romantic—and less Jewish—"Van" when he worked the door at the Rhapsody Bar) was brought up to Queensberry one day after school to participate in a choose-up game. His first two times at bat, he hit home runs over the fence which were observed by Coach Joe Newman from a pinochle game on the playground building porch. Following the game, Coach Newman "signed" Feldman to play for Queensberry by buying him a Coke and telling him to show up for Saturday practice or never cross Park Heights Avenue again. To Feldman it was the crowning achievement of his adolescence.

Winning our area title was an opportunity to travel outside our ethnic boundaries, be called dirty Jews and kikes, get into fights, and meet Italians and Poles and call them names. A guy wore his playground affiliation proudly and it was his first experience with social acceptability. Not all Northwest Baltimore guys hung around at playgrounds. Middle and upper-class kids from Upper Park Heights and Forest Park spent summers at overnight camps in Western Maryland and Maine and were regarded with distain by playground guys.

There were two gangs of Gentiles from streets which bordered Queensberry and Towanda playgrounds—the Maple Avenue or Skeets' gang and the Oswego Avenue gang, respectively. The playgrounds were neutral turf and truces existed there. But on asphalt it was everybody for himself.

Nobody ever sustained permanent injuries during gang fights but there were embarrassing moments against the Skeets' gang. We used to mess around in this wooded area called Track Oval near Pimlico Racetrack and every now and then we'd be attacked. All the guys would quickly shin up the trees and taunt Skeets, a heavyset bully who couldn't climb a stairway. Neither could I, so Skeets and his boys inflicted some serious beatings on me as my buddies watched from the trees.

The playground experiences wore off when, in our mid-teens, we discovered poolrooms. If you could prove you were 14, you were granted entree into a world of low-lifes, gamblers and drug addicts, along with a chance to get acquainted with your old playground, gang and school rivals.

Our mid-teens provided lasting social position when a majority of guys was selected into the high school fraternity system. Many were also blackballed. The selection process varied according to wealth, popularity, neighborhood, toughness and the like. The unofficial title of best frat shifted depending upon the make-up of the newest pledge class. Thirty years later, country club selections, business deals and friendships are still determined largely by what fraternity a guy pledged in high school. There were exceptions which allowed for some guys to better themselves by renewed athletic ability, looks and personality. (This changed between high school and college and permitted a guy in no frat or in a "bad" frat to enter a real good college fraternity or later in life a top country club or social group. The latter depended largely on accumulated wealth or a good-looking wife.)

The final social status to guys at the end of adolescence (did it ever end?), which formed initially their rank at the Diner, was their access to "far-away" bars.* The one or two local bars had a mostly Gentile clientele and no entertainment. (One of the most recognized and least discussed avenues in the assimilation of the Jewish community today into American society is the increase in drinking,

---

* Although the age requirement in Maryland was 21 for admittance into a bar, from the age of 16 most of the group had fake I.D.'s.

alcoholism and number of bars in Jewish neighborhoods.) Back in the late '50s and early '60s, very few Jews ventured outside of their neighborhoods to go bar-hopping except for playground, poolroom and Diner guys. At first only a couple braved this new world. The best places to go were, naturally, the ones farthest away—easier to brag about and more difficult for most guys to verify. There were two main bars then with great rock 'n' roll entertainment: the Rhapsody on the far west side of town and Hollywood Park on the far east side. Recognition in these places was hard to come by, and the first few times we showed up we got some real bad looks. But the music was great and the girls, basically lower-class, were good-looking in a cheap sort of way. Better yet, they were easy. (We were also lower-class, cheap and easy.) We befriended the toughs from Northwood and, in a matter of months, became regulars—that is, Wednesday night, Rhapsody, and Thursday night, Hollywood Park, regulars. And when other guys finally discovered they had the balls to come out to the far-away bars, our status was assured.

2.

A great deal of the stories and terminology of the guys who hung out at the playgrounds, poolrooms and the Diner were the creation of Ben Jensky.

Ben was a witty, sarcastic, often hilariously funny individual. He was cute to the point of being good-looking, especially when you threw in his personality, which you couldn't avoid doing. Curly-haired, with a beautiful complexion, Ben was medium in height, and you could see that he could develop a paunch if given the opportunity. However, during junior and senior high school, he remained good-looking, and his personality and wit charmed everyone. Ben was a Don Rickles character, except that it was hard to get really angry at him no matter how badly he knocked you, despite the fact that Ben was quite two-faced and would turn on you at any time. It didn't matter. He was very, very funny.

My initial encounter with Ben happened while I was waiting for my father to come out of the Vice Principal's office when I was in the ninth grade. Dad was called up to the school because of my occasional disciplinary and truancy problems during the first few months of the school year. Ben needed a late slip and was parading around the office like he owned it. Everyone there knew him as he had zingers for the office staff and anyone he observed, including me.

"What are you here for kid? First degree murder or for being too tall?" Ben asked as he stuck a pencil up his nose.

I bit my tongue but still couldn't help from laughing just as my father and Vice Principal Kaufman emerged. Dad looked sternly upon my behavior and smacked me a glancing blow on the back of my head as he pushed me out of the office.

Ben didn't soften his routine at all. Mr. Kaufman approached him. "Nice shoes Mr. 'K,' I didn't know there was a sale on used shoes at the Good Will Store." You could hear the Vice Principal's laugh from the hallway.

Ben had a friend named Rifkin who had a terrible acne condition which extended down his back. Ben made up names to call him, never in front of Rifkin, but to break up the guys—names like pusman, pimpleman, craterman, skinman and oozeman. He also coined the term "get off my Rifkin," for "get off my back." Or, if a car was following too closely behind. Ben would say, "This guy is driving on my Rifkin," meaning right on his back.

Ben began "amoeba faces," creating an obnoxious expression by distorting his mouth and nose when someone wasn't watching. He would usually do this to some guy who was a poor slob, either behind his back, and sometimes to his face. Sometimes he'd scream out, "Amoeba face!"

Ben used the word "toast" to mean a really sorrowful type of individual—"Hey, see that guy over there, what a toast!" Or, if he saw a jerk walking into the Diner, "Hey, Toast, what's happening?" If you didn't know what the term meant or if you weren't on the "inside," then you were ignorant of why Ben and the guys were laughing. However, those of us in the know would get hysterical when Ben would call someone "toast." Thirty years later, guys still say it. Ben also played on the word "dibs." At one time "dibs" used to mean that you wanted to share something that someone had. You would say, "Dibs on that." Ben took it a step further and "dibs" came to mean something terrible that you would use in a negative fashion, which was what most Diner sarcasm centered around— negativism. If a guy had a bad complexion, Ben would look at the guy's face, point to it, and say to everyone, "Dibs." Or if somebody in school had a deficiency slip or a bad report card, Ben's comment would be "Dibs on your report card!" The same if a guy had an ugly date, Ben would say, "Dibs on your date!"

Negativism was behind most of our sarcasm. If you were with a very pretty girl and a guy asked you if she was your date, you usually responded, "No, she's *your* date!" Or if you wore an ugly shirt or a terrible pair of pants, Ben or somebody would look at you and say, "Hey, nice pants!" This was also appropriate if you had an ugly date. Guys would say, "Hey, nice date!"

When Ben was 15, he won a contest called "Royalty" in which members of the top Jewish fraternities and sororities would put up their best-looking pledges for king and queen of the Royalty Dance. After Ben won, and for years to come, whenever he wanted to knock somebody he would say, "Hi Royalty!" or "You're Royalty!" or "Hi *Me!*"

Another great-looking guy a couple years older was Gary Huddles, a former Baltimore County councilman. There were rumors that he had turned down a Hollywood screen test when he was in high school. He was the quintessential Clark Gable of his time in Northwest Baltimore. Ben started calling guys "Hud" who were ugly, and from then on, if a guy was feeling too cocky or too happy sometimes, or too egotistical, you could always bring him back to earth by saying, "Hey, Hud, what's going on?" or, "You're Hud!"

Ben would also use the word "death," for meaning great looking or outstanding; such as, if you were describing a beautiful girl you would say, "She's death!"

There were some un-Ben-like terms—untraceable, but widely used in Northwest Baltimore—like squares and drapes. Squares were Ivy League, or preppies. Drapes were greasers, dirtballs or Fonzie-type guys without a conscience. Nobody feared blues in those days, but everyone was scared of drapes. Drapes wore their collars up and rolled their cigarette packs in their T-shirts's sleeves.

The etymology of the word blue, originated by Diner guys in the early '70s (or so we thought), stems from the black baseball player Vida Blue. Blue was so black he looked blue and thus "blues" became Diner guys' jargon for blacks—rather than using words like spade, jig, etc. We were always conscious not to offend people who could overhear us, unless we wanted them to.

Actually, blues was used to describe black people by the tin men (aluminum siding salesmen) who hung at the Diner in the early '50s.

3.

The Diner was located in the center of Northwest Baltimore and was called Brice's Hilltop Diner. It was L-shaped, had a rather huge parking lot, and was directly across the street from the Hilltop Shopping Center which had two main attractions: The Crest Movie Theater and Mandell and Ballow's Deli. The shopping center had a parking lot in front and on the side. Parking lots were big in those days although their primary function served as a staging area to show off your car and/or race it. A lot of pedestrian traffic flowed back and forth from Mandell's to the Diner, although it slacked up as we got older and "leaned" (hung-out) primarily at the Diner. It was an unspoken rule in the late '50s that you never took a date or a nice girl to the Diner—only to Mandell's. As we aged, the rule gradually softened.

Guys in my generation usually hung out in front of the Diner or sat in the first booths on either side of the cash register as you entered. An old Greek guy, George, was the manager and "maitre d'" at the Diner. He also served as the cashier. George was a complicated person. When we entered the Diner he would graciously greet us, take us to an empty booth, and hand us the menu. Since we usually ordered only Cokes, coffee or french fries with gravy, or occasionally went without ordering anything, it was just a matter of time before an indignant George threw us out. He would scream at us in broken English saying, "C'mon yu bums, geddouta here! Hurryup yu trash!" After being herded outside, we would go across the street to Mandell's and then return ten minutes later and lean against the Diner window. We would then re-enter the Diner and, surprisingly, George would greet us as graciously as he had before, walk us to a booth, hand us a menu and return to the cash register. This normally happened several times a night, seven days a week until we went home in the early hours of the morning.

The rear of the Diner was normally occupied by the Tin Men.* They were older men who sold aluminum siding, although hustlers

---

* See Appendix A.

from different variations of the home improvement business were among this group which often included degenerates and derelicts. They were mostly confidence men and free spirits whose lifestyles consisted of gambling, drugs and booze, good times, very little work, and getting in and out of "jackpots" [trouble]. "Anything Goes" was the motto of that era of the aluminum siding business, at least before the consumer advocate and Home Improvement Commission days.

4.

Harold Buxman, known as "The Gripper" or "Bux," used to hang around the playground, the poolroom and the Diner. Although universally feared, Bux always drew a crowd since he was also very amusing. He developed the reputation of being an extremely strong, agile and scary individual who loved to grip people. His hands were vise-like. He literally trapped you in a submission hold. His grip became legendary. He could grip a person while shaking a hand or sometimes he would do it while fake-tackling like a football player. Other times he would throw one arm around a person's waist and grip his side and then grip his other arm while making him walk on his toes. When you were gripped, you did whatever Bux wanted you to do.

Bux was not always as big and tough as he seemed to be. I remember him as an extremely good athlete at the Queensberry Playground where he was the butt of a lot of jokes and abuse, as were many of us growing up in that period wanting to be accepted by the older guys. Although the smallest playground in the City of Baltimore, Queensberry was developing a reputation as being one of the best playgrounds for athletes in softball, football and basketball. Our eight to 10-, 10- to 12-, 12- to 14-, and 14- to 16-year-old teams constantly vied for or won city championships.

One year we didn't win the 14–16 softball championship and it was because of Bux. It occurred during a semi-final game between Queensberry and Towanda Playground (Towanda, our chief rival, was the largest playground in the city, and was approximately three miles south of Queensberry). The game took place on Queensberry's distorted diamond which had a very short left field fence of about 150 feet, and a right field fence of about 400 feet. Queensberry was leading 3–2 in the last inning, there was one out and the Towanda "Grand Boys" had the bases loaded. The batter hit a grounder to the third baseman who threw to Bux, who although being left-handed was playing second. Bux took the throw, touching second for the force-out, and then made the pivot to first (a very difficult move for a left-hander playing second base). As he wheeled around to make that quick throw to first, he threw the ball over the fence and into the garages behind first base. Two runs scored and Towanda won 4–3.

Suddenly realizing what he had done, Bux knew he had to leave the playground in full flight. The coach of the team, Joe Newman, immediately took off after Bux wanting to kill him because the championship was lost. Bux ran out of playground gate toward Park Heights Avenue and didn't stop until he was at the Coast Guard Recruitment office at Park Circle, four miles down the road. While there, he enlisted and left for four years.

Bux felt certain guys always picked on him when he was younger and he had a dream when he enlisted that when he returned he would be able to get back at them. Perhaps it was a fantasy when he first thought of it. He never did exact revenge, but he did return with enormous strength, gaining a reputation based on fear, and respect beyond his wildest dreams.

While in the Coast Guard, Bux would squeeze rubber balls in his hands day in and day out and digest enormous quantities of milk and bread. He grew to the height of 6′1″ and weighed about 200 pounds. He would grip other sailors during long voyages on the Coast Guard cutter, and refined his grip in ports like Hong Kong and Sydney, Australia, on men as well as women. Bux had a strange and often cruel sense of humor. He once told me that in Hong Kong he was in a bar where "Australian party girls" performed with such dexterity that they could squat down on the bar top and pick up quarters and half-dollars with their vaginas. Bux would sadistically throw pennies, dimes and nickels on the bar and watch them strain as if they were contortionists to try and lift these small objects. They never could, even though Bux would egg them on, holding up and waving dollar bills that he promised if they picked up the change.

Bux was stationed in Hawaii, and one night he walked into a bar at the precise moment that a guy from his ship, rowdy and drunk, climbed on top of a table and bellowed that he could "lick any Jew in the place." Looking around, Bux to his dismay realized that he was the only Jew in the bar. Instinctively, he leaped up and pulled the guy down off the table and they began to fight, but Bux was eventually subdued when the guy's buddies broke a bottle over his head.

Out for revenge, Bux waited to get the guy from the bar as they were steaming into various ports in the South Pacific. On one long voyage the guy found himself walking through one of his ship's passageways carrying a crate of milk to the galley. (It was very important on board in those days for milk and other drinks to get to the galley as quickly as possible and not be spilled, slopped or dropped.) The passageway was very narrow and Bux eyed the guy coming toward him. He had been waiting for this moment since the Hawaiian incident two months earlier. Bux saw an exposed part of his adversary, his heart, since the guy was carrying the crate up high in his hands with his arms raised. The guy gave Bux a kind of quizzical look and smiled, knowing that he was in for trouble. As they came close, Bux nodded, drew back his arm, and with his powerful fist punched him in the heart. The guy's knees buckled, he went down and almost passed out. The pain was excruciating, but he didn't drop the milk. "Ah," said Bux, "the heart punch," which he had "invented." (Bux later refined the heart punch when, according to legend, he was scratched by an alley cat on his way to the playground and punched it in the heart, killing it.)

5.

Nat Smertz, whom the Gripper gripped a lot, was a bright, articulate and ultra-neurotic guy who hung around the Diner—literally. He only rarely came into the Diner or even stood out front with most of the other Diner guys. He usually sat in his car on the Diner lot, or on Donnie Burger's car, listening to Burger's portable record player blaring out folk music and jazz. Occasionally, they'd belt down four-ounce bottles of codeine-laced cough syrup, swallow a "red bird" (seconal), and get very high. Every now and then, Nat brought out his stick-ball bat—a shortened broomstick—and would play Turko at the corner of the Diner lot around 3:00 A.M. for money. He always lost.

A short, slightly-built young man, Nat wore thick-lensed Woody Allen-type glasses, and shirts and pants that always seemed to be one size too big. His hair was crew-cut and he got a haircut twice a week, whether he needed it or not. Nat suffered from the ultimate anal complex and was so organized he knew if a paper clip was moved a half-inch on his desk. Being very set in his ways at a young age didn't exactly help him with social interactions, nor did his inferiority complex, which caused him to create a superiority complex that he eventually believed. He looked down on everyone and considered himself vastly more intelligent than all of his peers.

In high school, Nat was in the Boys' Opportunity Club and Boys' Leaders Club, two prestigious organizations concerned with a person's academic ability as well as his dedication to school activities. He also became a student judge in his senior year which, at the time, was quite an honor. He took this job quite seriously, although one time he did sentence a student to hang for going up a down stairway. He almost carried it out.

In the '50s, athletic ability was vital to social acceptance, and though Nat's forte was more in the realm of sports knowledge than physical ability, he did consider himself talented in the field of stick ball and basketball. However, since he excelled in neither sport, he eventually settled on scorekeeping as his safest and surest bet in high school, and being a squad leader in physical education class. Actually, Nat did play fresh-soph basketball one year when he was a junior. He averaged one point per game with his favorite fade-away driving lay-up. Nat faded away every shot since he was terrified he would get hurt. In his junior year, he also got into trouble with the physical education staff when disciplinary action resulted in his dismissal as squad leader, relegated to backing up the goal for loose balls at lacrosse games. Nat's "crime" was making a mistake in logging the time of his running of the 440-yard dash during gym class. After scoring everyone in his squad, he took the lowest time of the fastest member, approximately 61 seconds, and wrote in his own time, around 12 seconds less. Since it was 1958, his 48.6 time became the existing world's record which the gym teacher, Mr. Zollet, found difficult to believe. The entire Physical Education Department came out the next day to observe Nat repeating this remarkable world class feat by running the 440 again. A very nervous Nat "ran" it in just under two minutes.

City. He came up to Queensberry Playground wearing an Ohio State sweatshirt and walked onto the basketball court to see if he could get into a game. Immediately, Bux the Gripper approached and said, "The Buckeyes are fairies," and instigated a fight between Nat and me. I promptly beat the shit out of Nat, not because I was so tough, but because Nat was so weak. It was the beginning of our friendship.

The second time I met Nat was when I was coming up to the playground one day and I saw him in the alley hiding behind some trash cans and bushes. He told me that a few of the guys had been chasing him, trying to make a fool out of him and beat him up, and could I please not say where he was. Just then three or four guys came by. They were older guys and included the Gripper. Instinctively, I gave Nat up and along with the guys dragged him to the playground where we threw him against the fence and made him sing "Teddy Bear" in Elvis Presley's voice. He never forgave me for it.

6.

I met Fenwick in September of 1954 in Ms. Spencer's seventh grade home room 105 at Garrison Junior High. Actually, Fenwick didn't acquire the name until two years after being dubbed that by George Burnham in the spring of 1957 when we were playing lacrosse for the Mt. Washington Pee Wee's.

George named him after the Jackie Gleason TV character, "The Poor Soul," Fenwick Babbitt, and it stuck. Before graduating from high school, he was calling himself Fenwick. He later shortened the name to "Wick."

Wick was wealthy by 1950s standards but in reality looked like the Poor Soul. He dressed sloppily, and was forever living the life of a loser. He never bathed, splashing Canoe or other colognes upon his body to keep from emitting odors. He had a rather sick way about him, and when he would get upset or was ecstatic over something, he'd actually bite his wrist and arms.

I befriended Fenwick—we'd become punchball buddies at Garrison Junior High—and even brought him to the playground. I was rewarded by his mother with trips to New York with serious pocket money—$85! An enormous sum to a poor lower Pimlico boy.

Fenwick's Aunt Bodney was the owner of the prestigious Algonquin Hotel in New York City. It housed the famous early television round table of Jack Paar, Alexander King, etc. These were the pre-*Tonight Show*/Johnny Carson stars. Fenwick's mom would send us to New York for culture—and we would check into the Algonquin before going out on our quest for the whores on 42nd street.

One night in front of Nedick's, the foot-long-hot-dog stand, we overheard a blue promising us a wide range of white, black and yellow hookers. Although both only 14 at the time, Fenwick and I secured assurances of truth from the blue, who described in beautiful detail an adolescent's wet dream. We ran back to the Algonquin for enough funds to purchase the pimp's promises. Failing to heed the warnings of the night manager, we taxied with the pimp to Harlem, oblivious of our destination.

We climbed several flights of a huge row house after walking a number of blocks, identified by the pimp as the front for the whorehouse, and paused at the fourth floor landing to undergo a rigorous pseudo-examination before entree by both the pimp and the manager in charge. We were told that to guarantee our belongings from being stolen by unscrupled sluts, it was house policy to place our valuables and money inside of a sealed envelope, adorned, of course, with our initials. We complied, gladly informing the pimps as to what each of us had, although Fenwick and I argued over his use of false initials. The pimps even let us lick and seal the envelopes. How thoughtful of them.

They instructed us to wait for the other customers to depart and then disappeared upstairs. After a long ten minute wait, it dawned on us (hell, we were only 14 years old) that we had been taken, and we ran upstairs only to hear their footsteps scurrying across the roof. Reality hit! We're across 110th street (darkest Harlem) without money and looking extremely white. We rushed outside and hurdled towards the subway station where I proudly announced that I had enough change to get us aboard. Fenwick went berserk—"How could you hold out when the spade told you to give up all of your money? You could have been robbed by the whores!"

7.

As Swartzie was shimmying his pudgy body down the north fence at Pimlico Race Track, having been hoisted up by Fenwick, Mr. Heeps, their ninth grade Latin teacher, approached. The brand new Pimlico Junior High School was only two blocks away.

"Can I help you, Mr. Swartz?" he asked sarcastically.

"No thanks, Mr. Heeps," replied Swartzie.

"How about you, Fenwick?" Heeps joked, "Need a boost over?"

Propelled by fear, Fenwick was up and over the fence within seconds. In a more serious vain, Heeps advised, "It's 12:00 boys. I do hope this is your lunch hour."

Swartzie was now very antsy. As he and Fenwick moved away from the fence, he called back, "Mr. Heeps, we'd love to stay here and chat about Caesar's Gallic conquests and verb tenses, but it's more important to make the daily double. So if we win, we'll see you in class tomorrow!"

Swartzie was short and plump with slick, black hair and chipped front teeth. From junior high school on, he was the consummate hustler and gambler, continually cutting classes to sneak into Pimlico Race Track. He was gambling serious money from the age of 12 and would engage in ludicrous pool games, bowling matches and card games just to have the action.

8.

"Closet scenes" was a term which originated in Northwest Baltimore. You hid in a closet and watched two people get laid. My first closet scene occurred when I was dating this girl in high school after having become very friendly with Fenwick. Still quite sloppy and not too good looking, Fenwick was rather oversexed. He had all kinds of "French" films and dirty books at home, and he would sneak into the Gayety Theater on "The Block" or anywhere else to observe women naked or partially dressed. He was known to spy on neighbors, friends, even relatives.

Fenwick asked if he could watch me with this girlfriend whom I was banging. He tried to convince me that he just wanted verification of whether I was really screwing her. I told him that I would do it only if he swore on his parents' life that he would not make a sound or come out of the closet, or ever hint about it to this girl. He agreed and, I guess as a result of ego or status, I relented and let him watch. True to his word he did not utter a sound, and at one point, I didn't even remember if he was there or not.

Later, during the early '60s, strict closet rules had to be established since the closet scenes grew in numbers along with an increase of individuals hiding in the closet. Sometimes guys hid outside of the room, by the bed, or out by a window, but it was still termed a "closet." The rules were simple: You could not make a sound or movement, you could not talk to anyone in the closet, you had to hold a towel to bite on if you got too excited, and you had to have some hard candy to suck on so your throat would not get too dry and cause a cough. By all means, if you were heard you could never give yourself up, and if you were caught you had to swear that the guy who was putting on the show had no knowledge of it. We even tried to go a step further one time and told guys they should bite a cyanide pill in case they were caught since this was a more serious offense than a downed U-2 pilot's, but to our knowledge no one ever killed himself.

There were instances where guys got caught. Snyder and I were once caught in Fan's closet but refused to come out. We held one of those sliding doors as tight as possible and fake-slipped out the names of two wimpy guys who eventually got into trouble since the girl swore it had to be them. And we never did "give up" the closet.

There were some very funny closet incidents. We all got caught one time down in Yussel's cellar. About six of us were in the closet when this girl found us and each guy came out of the closet with a different excuse. Some grabbed hangers and "confessed" they got delayed hanging up clothes and weren't aware anyone was in bed until too late. Another guy said he was brushing dandruff off his jacket, got to bullshitting, and dozed off with all six guys. Later, the girl turned up at the Diner with the guy with whom she had put on the "show" and received a standing ovation. She broke into tears and ran out into the street never to be seen again.

There was a time once in Atlantic City in an integrated closet where I, a girl I was dating, and Dude and Mart were watching Fan with some girl from Philadelphia. The guys putting on the show also had certain responsibilities. They had to see to it that they didn't try to break-up anyone in the closet, or put on a show or an act for the benefit of the closet, and that they would either turn water on or a radio or TV so loud that no closet sounds could be heard. It was also the responsibility of the performer to allow enough light to shine on the sex act.

Another term was "late-date." Sometimes a guy took a girl out who insisted that she had to be home by a certain time. After he came up to the Diner, he'd find out that somebody had "late-dated" him. Someone had picked her up and had taken her out from midnight to two in the morning. Some guys were perennial late-daters who wouldn't go out on a regular date. They would only late-date girls who were dating other guys. Others were kind of Romeos who would go around late-dating or early-dating girls in different parts of town.

Still another term, attributed to Ben (or so he said), was "Great Posts," which meant showing up with a great-looking date. The date was for show only—which meant that you were lucky if you even got a handshake goodnight from the girl. But it didn't really matter since you gained increased status showing up with a great post. The quintessential great post was a blue-eyed, blonde shiksa, at least 5′6″, that no one in Northwest Baltimore had ever seen.

To this day, some 30 years later, great posts are still spoken of in awe. Perhaps the best great post date ever was Mary Miller, a blue-eyed blonde, straight hair, 5′7″, perfect body, always tanned, beautiful smile. She even went to a Catholic high school and wore those uniforms that the clergy never realized were unbelievably sexy. Or did they? There was no way for guys to imagine that these girls could piss, shit, or even fart. Unthinkable. These girls never slipped or stumbled, they never sweated, and they never had bad breath. They were goddesses. No one ever asks what happened to these girls. We just can't face up to admitting they may have actually took a turn for the worse, got married, aged, had babies, or even got fat—yiii!!! not Mary!

Another word which Ben coined, in concert with Stern and Snyder, was "blows." In Northwest Baltimore it meant that somebody had given you a great compliment, a "blow," and this led to "blow sessions" in which guys would sit in a car on the Diner lot or get together in a booth and give each other compliments. The compliments or praise centered around athletics, what girls said about you, or what guys who counted considered you. For example, a great blow would be, "I saw Susan and she really thought you were cute," or, "In that game against Poly, the coach couldn't believe how strong you looked, the way you were throwing body checks and playing." Or they could say, "I talked to this guy at Hopkins and he really thinks you're a mensch!"

The opposite of blows were "downs," which guys would give at times just to get on somebody's nerves or to knock. I remember returning from a sorority party at University of Maryland and everybody was giving different "blows" to each other, like, "This girl said this, that girl said that." One of the guys in the car named Dave Garp had not received any "blows" and he inquired if anyone had complimented him. Snyder turned to him in a mock serious vein and said, "Dave, you received no blows and seven downs," which of course broke up the car.

9.

Many a night, a group of us would sit in the Diner or Mandell's Deli and play "pennies up." Everyone laid a penny on the table and then we went around the booth trying to break up one another until one guy said something funny enough to make the entire group laugh hysterically. This wasn't accomplished easily since the guys prided themselves on keeping a poker face no matter what was said. Certain guys were so fanatic about not laughing that they'd secretly dig their fingernails into there skin or hit their knuckles against the table and chair. Fenwick would actually bite his wrists raw.

To win you had to be the master of quick one line sarcasms and negative knocking. Jensky, Snyder, Turns and Dude usually won— the object, of course, was status, not the pennies. Although Jensky was the acknowledged maven of funny guys, Snyder and Stern were held in high esteem at knocking or "killing." They knocked each other relentlessly; but only when the knockee wasn't around.

One time in Ocean City, for example, Snyder was on a roll about Turns that wouldn't quit. Turns was a nice looking, stocky intelligent guy and considered a great local athlete, although he couldn't swim and was terrified of the water. It was very humid and we were sitting on the beach when Turns strolled down toward the ocean. Hesitantly, he bent over the smallest of waves to splash water on his shoulders, ready to back up quickly should any wave above six inches come crashing towards him.

Snyder calmly pointed and said, "Look, Turns just swam to Europe and back." One of the group answered back, "Really?" and Snyder started rolling. "Yeah," he began, "It took him 10 minutes."

"You're kidding," the guy mused. "No," said Snyder, "the undertow slowed him up and he was unable to complete a full racing turn against the French continental shelf."

"Besides," Snyder continued, "Turns had a cold and had to surface every 750 miles for air."

Everyone was giggling now and watching Turns who had unwittingly inched closer to the ocean while daintily splashing his face. Suddenly a small two-foot wave washed around his knees and he frantically sprinted a few yards up the beach.

"You guys know, of course," lectured Snyder, "that Turns is banned from swimming events in the Olympics. The doctors who examined him found that he had gills." Snyder wouldn't let up. "He used to do the stunt work in the swim segments for Buster Crabbe and Johnny Weissmuller in the Tarzan movies.

We were holding our sides now since everybody knew Turns's head had rarely ever been underwater and that he was even fearful of taking showers preferring baths with very weak streams of water.

"I'll tell you guys a secret," Snyder deadpanned, "but you've got to swear never to reveal it or Turns will get very mad and embarrassed." Snyder paused, savoring the concluding knock. "He actually is the real life pattern for the serial *Aquaman!*"

Snyder's wit was dryer than Ben's and geared to a somewhat higher intellectual level, although his sarcasm was universally enjoyed. At 6′ tall and well built, he was a physically imposing athlete, but it was his smarts and finesse that projected him to a high school basketball and lacrosse standout.

10.

If you saw the movie *Diner,* you'll recall a brief, very amusing scene of a very fat man stuffing his face practicing for an eating contest in one of the booths. His name was Earl Maget and he was one of the unique Diner guys. At 5´8″, weighing over 400 lbs., he was so fat that he couldn't get laid until he was 33 years old and lost 175 lbs. It seems that even with an erection, his enormous stomach made it impossible for him to penetrate a woman. So, he depended on oral sex until he lost the weight many years later.

Earl owned a taxi, was an accomplished pool player and card shark and a very humorous fellow. He would hang out at the Diner from late in the evening until early in the morning, and when he wasn't there, you could find him at Benny's Poolroom. He loved to gamble and would bet on just about anything, as would the people who backed him. This was especially true when it came to eating contests, events Earl never lost. I met my wife at one of the last great eating contests at the Lotus Inn Restaurant when Earl bet that he could eat *five* "dinners for six" at one sitting, drinking two pitchers of water with each dinner. Earl, of course, won that bet but he did lose an unrelated side bet to a guy named Matt Hammond. Hammond bet Earl that Bruce Hawk could eat the small dish of hot mustard sauce that came with the Chinese egg rolls. Bruce scooped it up in four spoonfuls, went outside and vomitted for the next three hours, but was elated that he won ten dollars, his share of the bet. Earl didn't care. He split his sides laughing at Bruce's "illness." He never liked Bruce.

Bruce was always making strange bets—such as racing on foot against cars in the Diner parking lot. He seldom won but neither did the guys in the cars since they constantly dented their front ends on the fence at the edge of the lot.

Bruce Hawk attended more high schools than anybody, and, after being expelled from most Baltimore public and private schools, he received his diploma from Staunton Military Academy in Virginia. It was the only way they could get him to leave.

Bruce was tall and sleek with a ruddy complexion. He not only had a penchant for getting into trouble but also he was always getting caught. Hawk had the largest 45 RPM record collection of all times. Bigger even than Mason's or Bartz's, two guys who bought and/or traded for outstanding collections. They actually knew every rock 'n' roll song, singer, label, and color of all of the records made from 1955 to 1965. But Hawk's collection dwarfed theirs. He accumulated it by stealing records from homes and parties up and down the east coast.

Earl's eating contests soon became legendary. There was a time at Benny's Poolroom when a group of card players bet Earl that he couldn't eat 80 Little Tavern hamburgers. Back in those days, the Little Tavern made a hamburger about as big as an oversized biscuit. It contained a hamburger patty, onions, mustard, ketchup and relish. We used to call them "death balls," yet they were sometimes fairly digestible. Earl not only ate 80, he ate 85, so one of the bettors asked him, "Hey Maget, didn't you forget the bet was over when you hit 80?" Earl calmly replied, "I know that sucker, but by the 73rd hamburger I actually got hungry; that's why I ate the additional five! Pay up!"

Two weeks later, Earl won another bet when he ate 12 Harleyburgers. A Harleyburger was a submarine or hoagie sandwich that had about six hamburgers with every ingredient imaginable on each sub. Back in the '50s, a submarine sandwich was awfully big, probably twice the size of today's subs. Earl ate the 12 subs so fast that the guys who bet him almost refused to pay off thinking that they had been conned, which they had since it was ridiculous to bet against Earl.

Another time, Earl saw a sign in the window of a place called Champs over on the west side of town. The sign said that if you could eat one Big Thing and one Little Thing that you would win $10. The Big Thing was this enormous three-foot-long submarine sandwich made up of so many cold cuts that you couldn't get two hands around the sub roll. The Little Thing was a sundae made up of 18 different scoops of ice cream—bananas, cherries, walnuts, whipped cream, etc. Earl went there on a Monday, ate the Big Thing and the Little Thing and won the $10. He came back the next day, ate the Big Thing and the Little Thing, and the guy said that he didn't have $10, so he gave Earl $7.50. Earl returned the following day and ate the Big Thing and the Little Thing once more. The owner came out and told Earl that all he had was $3.00. He handed him the $3.00, took the sign out of the window, and gave that to

Earl too, telling him never to come back as long as he lived.

It was, of course, at the Diner where Earl continued to amaze spectators. He once ate the entire left side of the Diner menu. Also, Earl never had to buy breakfast in all of the years he came up to the Diner. There was always a sucker waiting to bet Earl that he couldn't eat the entire breakfast menu made up of every type of egg, omelet, pancakes, cereals, biscuits, creamed chip beef, sausages, bacon, juices and coffee. Every morning one or more guys would bet him, and every morning Earl would eat the entire breakfast menu. And George, the Diner's manager, loved the contest more than anyone.

Fenwick once tried to emulate Earl. He also loved to bet on anything but he rarely won. Mandell's Deli was across the street from the Diner. They used to make great kosher hot dogs, which were very, very greasy, and stayed on the grill for hours. They would place the dog in a greasy roll and add hot fried bologna, along with mustard and onions. Swartzie bet Fenwick that he couldn't eat 10 of them at one time. Fenwick ate the first four, threw-up, ate the second four, threw-up, ate the next one and passed out. Swartzie revived him long enough to get paid off. Fenwick gave up eating contests forever.

11.

A dining associate of Earl Maget was Jeff Hall. I first saw Jeff in junior high school. He drove a car to school in the eighth grade. I thought this was an awesome display, and I asked my father if I could drive his car to school. He enlightened me that since most kids in the eighth grade were 13 or 14 years old, I should consult the motor vehicle laws.

Jeff was a little old for junior high school. He was heavy set, with a bulldog-like face. Although he was pretty rough, Jeff was also a very sensitive and quite funny guy. He knocked himself so much about how he looked and dressed, that he very seldom was knocked by other guys either to his face or when he was absent. Nobody could knock Jeff better than himself.

Jeff always hung out in the poolrooms and the Diner. He was

self-sufficient. In high school, he was driving a taxi while his fellow "students" were attending classes, something which Jeff himself did with great irregularity. He eventually bought his own cab, then a couple more, and had several drivers working for him by his early 20s. He also liked to gamble and to eat. I don't really remember if he did well with girls because there was another facet about Jeff that was very unusual. He only had one testicle and guys usually resorted to rhyme with Jeff: "Jeff Wall has one ball." Cute.

12.

My dad died at 49 of a heart attack. He had his first one at 42. A combination of stress, improper diet and smoking four packs of Camels a day may have contributed to it. He and his four brothers each died at about the same age of heart attacks. I've got a lot to look forward to.

His death makes me more bitter than sad. I feel sorry for myself and my mother. I'm also somewhat ashamed that I'm fatherless, although at least half a dozen of the playground guys are also father-less. Somehow I keep thinking he's coming back. In my dreams, it's so vivid, his bouncing up the front steps, that I awake believing he's still alive.

13.

In the '50s, The Ezrine Family (four brothers) sold tires. Every so often, they'd go out of business, but would recover and quickly reo-pen. Their business eventually caught on and they cautiously expanded throughout the Baltimore Metropolitan area. Milton Ezrine was the titular head of the business. He initially lived on West Garrison Avenue a few blocks from Queensberry Playground where his two sons, Charlie and Alan, spent time. Charlie, the older one, was more gregarious and a better athlete than Alan, and enjoyed popularity at Forest Park and the University of Maryland.

One summer, a freak accident while working on a snowball truck cost Charlie the first joint of his right trigger finger. He was cleaning out the ice from the snowball machine with a wooden spoon when someone accidentally turned it on. Thus, the Gripper later dubbed him Charlie Three-quarter Finger, or Three-quarter Finger Charlie.

Alan was tall, dark and handsome, outwardly cocky and somewhat crude, but actually extremely self-conscious. We became very friendly at the age of 11, originally meeting at the playground. Ez, as we called him, was stubborn and seldom, if ever, faked-blew or kissed ass, with the possible exception of avoiding getting gripped by the Gripper.

Ez, Fenwick, and I went to Ocean City in July of 1958. We envisioned screwing dozens of shiksas as we were motoring down the Eastern Shore in Fenwick's '54 Buick, without reverse gear. On the way, Fenwick stopped at a root beer stand to quench our thirst. He bought the biggest container of root beer for the three of us, not realizing it was warm; then, insisting that we drink it immediately, he began to pour it into our cups while he's speeding along, attempting to make the Ocean in record time. Naturally, the warm root beer spilled all over Ez and me, and our clothes, arms and legs.

We parked a block from the beach and froliced in the surf until dark. Ez and I begged Fenwick to drive over to the public showers (since we couldn't afford a motel) to clean up and dress for the night, but he screamed, "What're ya, princesses or something? We'll change in the back seat!"

The back seat contained the remnants of the root beer and a ton of beach sand.

We dined at Melvin's Steak House, all you can eat for $1.99, and fortified ourselves with beer. We bribed a hillbilly to buy it at the Ice House, and then proceeded to the Pier Ballroom for a Buddy Dean Bandstand Record Hop.

It was Saturday night and mobbed with more girls than guys—our lucky night. Every third dance was a ladies' choice and we fantasized rubbing up against some firm young girls during the slow numbers. We called this the California Press.

Ez got asked to dance as every ladies' choice for two and a half hours while Fenwick and I suffered inside. Naturally, we knocked each girl who picked Ez. Finally, I was chosen—she originally picked Ez but he rejected her and motioned her to me. My heart rose as this short plump farm girl led me to the dance floor. If she'd have danced any further away from me she would be back in Baltimore. By the middle of the song, I attempted to pull the girl closer but she was resistant and whispered, "Look, don't take this personal, but you're sticky, you smell of root beer, and you've got sand and seaweed in your hair. I've got cleaner farm animals."

I was devastated and told Ez. We both verbally assaulted Fenwick who got pissed off, ran out into the night, and drove back home. Quickly, we located Ez's brother, Three-quarter Finger Charlie, at the Beach Club on Ninth Street. Reluctantly, he drove us back to Baltimore the next day.

14.

A mensch in Jewish is like an All-American boy. Main men were similar. There were a few mensches who emerged from the '50s and '60s among Diner guys in Northwest Baltimore. A mensch had to have these attributes: he had to be tall (for a Jew); he had to be a good student; he had to be good-looking; he had to be popular, and he had to be a good athlete. All mensches became successful in college and in their careers.

Mensches always had a following of guys who came to be known as "blowers." Playing off the definition of "blows," blowers were guys who idolized or hung around, for status, the mensches, or main men as they were called at a later time. Blowers were early-day groupies. The only non-Jewish main man who drew a number of Jewish blowers was a guy named Ernie Betz, an All-American lacrosse player at the University of Maryland in the late '50s. Betz was blonde haired, blue-eyed, a great athlete, and a B.M.O.C. [big man on campus] at the University of Maryland.

Three-quarter Finger Charlie promoted and dubbed Betz "The Lord." Some considered him the Lord's main blower, but Ezrine reaped the rewards of being the Lord's chief lieutenant. He created the Lord's legend and enjoyed amazing popularity. Charlie eventually became an original and the first Jew to be an editor of an underground newspaper on campus called the "The Four T's" which criticized everything and everybody—knocking guys and gals throughout

College Park. This highly secretive, crudely written tabloid survived for 25 years—cautiously annointing succeeding editors.

Dark-haired Stu Harrison (there was a light-haired Stu Harrison nicknamed Goose) promoted Gary Huddles the same way Three-quarter Finger Charlie promoted the Lord. Hud turned every girl's head on campus at Maryland with his great looks and, as his roommate, Harrison took advantage of it. He told eager co-eds that he could get them a date with Hud but, because Hud was in such demand, it was his responsibility to take out, select and recommend girlfriends for Hud. Of course, if they were a good lay this would greatly influence Harrison's recommendation; and for the next two years, Harrison got laid more than the Lord, Three-quarter Finger Charlie, and Hud together.

The original mensches, three or four years older than the Diner guys, were Eddie Bernstein and Larry Becker. The mensch of the Diner guys' generation was Ray Altman. Ray was an All-State high school basketball and lacrosse player, an All-American lacrosse player at the University of Maryland, and an excellent student.

In order to be a mensch, you had to have a minimum entourage of five blowers adoring you, picking you up, and being at your beck and call night and day. One of the greatest blower/mensch stories centered around Duke Lane who was Larry Becker's [better known as "Face"] main blower. Duke had one of the first foreign sports cars back in the early '50s. One night in Atlantic City, he was showing it off, gunning the motor by the Ambassador Hotel up by the Boardwalk. Almost 200 people were there watching and actually "blowing" Duke. Duke was in seventh heaven—couldn't believe the adoration of the crowd. Just then Becker showed up and told Duke, "Come on, let's go, cut off the motor!" Incredulous, Duke couldn't believe what Face had just told him. He immediately turned to Becker and cried, "But Face, look at all of these people, look how they're idolizing me." Becker, somewhat shocked at Duke's reluctance, sternly replied, "That's it Duke, turn it off." Duke promptly turned the car off and they left. The crowd was stunned. It carved a place in the annals of all-time blowing.

15.

A guy who was never mistaken for a mensch was "Third." Third was not an original regular at the Diner, although he had the status at Mandell's Deli. He was at one time viewed as an outcast and frequently chased away by Ben Jensky, but eventually became a returning anti-hero during the later pinnacle years ('65–'68) of the Diner.

Since nicknames were then mandatory, accepted or not, they stuck. Third was a take-off of *The Rise and Fall of the Third Reich*. His real name was Steve Reich, and his karma rose and fell with stunning regularity.

He grew up around Druid Hill Park [northwest of what was then Center City] and later moved to the upper lower and lower middle-class neighborhood north of Pimlico Race Track, as opposed to playground guys who lived south of the track. Third was never a guiding light of tact and diplomacy. His mouth and attitude always getting him in and out of jackpots. You either loved or hated him, there was no middle ground. If you loved him you usually turned. He was tall for a Jew, and his rugged Aryan good looks and natural athletic ability enabled him to excel in lacrosse for over 20 years.

Although he never had a dime in his pocket, Third enjoyed great popularity in his teens because of his looks, athletic prowess and self-confidence. He pledged Mu Sigma (Mu Sig), a somewhat wealthy elitist fraternity in high school which was considered the most consistently top frat in the '50s and early '60s, although other fraternities survived on specific pledge classes. Most guys disliked or were jealous of Mu Sig. The true litmus test of fraternity status was popularity with girls, and a guy in Mu Sig usually had easier access to the ladies.

I pledged S.E.D. (Sigma Eta Delta) instead. S.E.D. threw the best dances, bringing to Baltimore Bill Haley and the Comets, The Shirelles, and Ray Charles in succeeding years in the late '50s. The dance was called the Carnival Hop and was held in the Dixie Ballroom at Gwynn Oak Amusement Park, not far from the Forest Park neighborhood.

Third's personality was such that he became one of the few guys who was openly, sometimes brutally frank with girls. Most loved it. He was the king at one-on-one dialogue with women, enjoying an almost mystical rapport.

And so he did great with the ladies in spite of gaining a rapidly expanding Women's Hate Club, due to his tactless verbal abuse of many early day Jewish princesses. He dated and scored with the prettiest girls throughout Baltimore, regardless of religious affiliation or social class.

Third went to City and I to Forest Park. I initially disliked him and we didn't become friendly until our senior year. We were rivals on the lacrosse field, although it didn't matter much since City usually beat us by wide margins.

For a couple years, Third dated Sue who was a classmate of mine from the ninth grade to graduation. She grew from Pollyanna to star overnight, was an excellent student, and one of the prettiest girls ever to attend Forest Park. We had a platonic relationship, although I didn't know it was platonic at the time, and I was always hoping for a chance "spite make-out" with Sue when Third was nasty to her, which was often.

Sue was the consummate princess, sheltered and never allowed to befriend people from lower Park Heights. She was, however, an excellent female jock for that era. Her brother Lenny played world class tennis in the late '60s before a shoulder injury shelved his career. During one of Sue and Third's occasional split-ups, she promised me $10 and free lunch until June if I would injure him in the annual City-Forest Park lacrosse match. Opportunity presented itself and I threw a once-in-a-lifetime vicious check on Third during the game. Although I fantasized additional amorous rewards, Sue only gave up the $10 and a week's free lunch before going back with Third. And if that wasn't enough for my crushed ego, when I later confessed the bet to Third, he demanded and received payment of half it.

Sue's family moved to Baltimore from Atlanta. In the tenth grade, she was befriended by Joyce and they became very close, with Joyce introducing her to a lot of popular guys to date.

Joyce was an Audrey Hepburn clone. She had a very pretty face with a bubble hairdo, and she wore clothes that looked a size too big because she was extremely skinny. Since she had no shape of any kind, there was occasional knocking addressed her way, although I don't think that she ever realized it to any great extent. For example, every time Ben Jensky was in a room with her, he'd turn around to the guys and then immediately hit the floor, screaming, "Duck!" The guys would look around astounded and then Ben would get up laughing and say, "Pshew, you guys are real lucky. You almost got knocked over by Joyce's tits when she turned around just now."

In the 11th grade, Sue made a critical error. She became friendly with Sandy Barr who lived across the street from Joyce. As a result of Sue's new relationship, Joyce stopped talking to Sue for the next seven years. Sue was shocked, but not as shocked as she was a month and a half later when Sandy dropped her because Sue was dating Third, of whom Sandy didn't approve.

I was marginally friendly with these girls who were all in my year. We usually had lunch together but they treated guys their age like younger brothers. They would only go out with college guys two or three years older than they. Some even went out with guys out of college.

After Joyce stopped talking to Sue, I stopped talking to Joyce. It was during the spring of our senior year and I had a good reason for it. We all went to take the entrance examination at the University of Maryland at College Park. This was the exam to determine what English and math class you would be in at Maryland; either an advanced class, regular freshman class, or worse, remedial. I decided that it would be wise if I cheated off somebody like Joyce whom I had thought was very bright, and unbeknownst to her, I copied every answer. When the results were mailed out, I was placed into the math zero and remedial English courses. I was livid. Of course, it was tough to tell Joyce that I was livid because I cheated. She never knew why I didn't speak to her for a year. She probably could have cared less anyway.

16.

Yussel did a lot of strange things. He was blond, almost white-haired, with a very fair complexion. He looked like an Albino. Yussel used to hang out at Queensberry Playground. He was a fair to poor athlete by our standards but he tried hard. He was a funny guy who enjoyed attention.

Yussel had great hair and was always combing it. It distracted attention from his complexion problems that he incurred from time to time. On "ugly days" when Yussel felt he looked weak, he would dress up in outlandish outfits which he had found in his cellar and would wear them to the poolroom. Yussel's mother never threw anything away and had accumulated enormous amounts of clothing in the basement dating from the '30s and '40s. Her son would wear unmatched shoes and socks, uncoordinated pants and tops, and colored Band-Aids on his face.

Yussel liked to wear different colored Band-Aids in class. He would put them all around his face and arms. It didn't go over big in high school, and he was eventually expelled from Forest Park for misconduct. It happend soon after they threw Steve Blumberg out for wearing red pants to school. As a matter of fact, on the same day Yussel was expelled, the Principal also dismissed two of our best athletes from school, Boogie Weinglass and George Burnham, for going over a high jump bar during lunch hour when there was no gym class in session.

17.

Charlie-Bo-Death-Straight-Twelve was named for his dancing ability—he danced like James Brown—and had a twelve-inch root. When he was 16, Charlie-Bo-Death stood on the corner of Park Heights and Rogers Avenue with a duffle bag and told everybody that he was joining the Navy. He stood there for two days and then went home to sleep. He went back to school the next day. Eventually he did join the Air Force shortly after marrying a girl named Marsha "Green-Eyes" who lived around Towanda Playground.

Bo Death entered the service about two years after his friend Arty, his best friend. While Arty was in the service, he asked Bo Death to watch his wife. Bo Death watched her all right, screwing her as often as possible. Before leaving for Tripoli himself, Bo Death did remember not to ask anyone to watch Marsha.

18.

Boogie was one of the most fascinating Diner and Northwest Baltimore guys to span the '50s through the '80s. His real name was Lenny Weinglass, the youngest of three brothers. There was Jackie, the eldest, and in the middle, Eggie, whose real name was Irvin. Their mother Nettie raised these boys around Towanda Playground. Boogie until the seventh grade attended the Talmudical Academy, which was like a full-time Hebrew School (instead of a regular public school). They very rarely spoke English at Talmudical Academy.

His brother Jackie became a clothing salesman, working in retail outlets and eventually pushing lines of men's clothes as a manufacturer's rep. And his other brother Eggie went to work in a wholesale clothing establishing. Jackie was a pretty righteous, stand-up kind of guy, a great athlete. (Now over 50, he can still play basketball and softball with the best of them.) Jackie supported the family for many years because he was always working one or two jobs. He always dressed well and this prompted Eggie, Boogie and a close friend named Jerry to continually sneak into Jackie's room as he was sleeping, and steal money and clothing so that they could gamble or wear his clothes. Only on rare occasions Jackie caught the guys and became convinced this was the only time that they attempted such acts. He considered himself far more hip than he really was.

Boogie was an excellent athlete in any sport he played. Perhaps he was best at basketball where he could leap as high as the blues and probably was as good as, or better than, most blues who played against him during that era. He was close to 6′ tall, lean, had a big nose and a d.a. haircut, and as much "balls" as any playground or Diner guy. He would fight anybody, no matter what size, and his quickness and skills usually won him most street fights. He was a colorful guy who would do anything on a dare or a bet, and would usually succeed at every crazy stunt he attempted. He was also a hustler, a gambler and what people then termed a degenerate, yet he was probably more of an anti-hero than anything else. He was very poor and most of his outfits consisted of jerseys and jackets which belonged to schools or teams he had played for, or whatever he could steal from Jackie.

Boogie sold blank report cards when he attended City College, and he once hijacked a streetcar out on Belair Road for a color play. Once, in front of Mandell's, he walked out into the parking lot and into a police car that was empty at the time—the police were at the carryout side of the deli—and took it for a joy ride. He didn't have a license.

Boogie originally attended Forest Park High School and played varsity sports in the ninth and tenth grades. He didn't attend classes regularly, and was not very concerned about what went on in the classroom. He was a major pain in the neck to most teachers, considering the fact that Forest Park's academic reputation was superb. He was following a long line of Weinglass brothers who could barely pass any course they took. If there had been classes on street smarts and daredevil stuff, I'm sure that Boogie would have always received straight A's.

One day when Boogie was in about the 11th grade [it's hard to tell because he repeated classes and grades from time to time], he was cutting school and hanging out on the athletic field during lunch. It's strange, but when a lot of guys would cut school back in those days they usually would end up hanging around the school that they were cutting.

We didn't have a lot of athletes during the late '50s at Forest Park, and athletic boys were at a premium. I recall having to play a number of sports, many of which I had no right to play, but had no choice. If you could run without falling down, the coaches insisted that you participate in sports as often as possible. For someone like Boogie, who excelled, it was vital in the estimation of the school guys that these great athletes remain in school.

George Burnham (who gave Fenwick his nickname) was an excellent lacrosse player who was also good in football and wrestling. He was cutting school that day with Boogie, and they were flirting with the girls during lunch near Bell Avenue where Frank the Candyman used to sell his wares. Gym classes used to come out in the fall and spring to work out, but there were no classes during this lunch period.

Boogie and George went over to the high jump bar and began to contest who could jump the highest. One of the gym teachers came out and caught them going over the bar when no class was in session. He didn't realize that they were cutting school, but felt that the crime of going over the high jump bar when no class was in session was heinous. He turned them into the Principal and they were both expelled from the school; a fairly harsh sentence by today's standards. What always befuddled me was that this same teacher who had Boogie expelled ended up being his basketball coach for the next two years at City College where Boogie was his best player. Burnham transferred to Edmondson High (in West Baltimore) for some unknown reason, and became the varsity quarterback, wrestling champ and an All-Maryland lacrosse player.

Anyway, Boogie telephoned his mother following his expulsion and she warned him not to come home. Jackie had found out and wanted to kill Boogie, who later tried to explain what happened, but to no avail. Jackie was also the only person of whom Boogie was afraid.

So, Boogie hid out at his friend Sambo's house until learning that Jackie was on the way over. Sambo informed Boogie of a "safe house" to go to until Jackie cooled down, and Boogie spent the next two nights at Kanky's, a middle-aged woman with a generous leg for high school boys.

19.

Sucker-punching was getting in the first punch when a guy didn't expect it. It also meant getting in the first punch when the guy did expect it. That was serious sucker-punching. There were certain guys, mainly Boogie and Bill McAuliffe, who epitomized the sucker-punchers of our generation of Diner guys. Neither was big, Boogie being tall and wiry and Bill medium and compact. They were also very rarely sucker-punched. (I recall one guy sucker-punching McAuliffe and McAuliffe not even flinching. He had a real hard head and it was like somebody slapped him with a feather. I knew that guy was in big trouble.) Everyone tried to emulate the sucker-punchers. Of course, not all of us were great battlers, and many a time we would miss a guy or bust our hand punching somebody and then have to run away.

Boogie's fighting reputation began to flourish after a controversial loss to a dangerous hoodlum, Gilbert Bones. Bones fought Boogie in

Harry Levine's poolroom once and Boogie went toe to toe for a while until Harry broke a pool cue over his back. Actually, Boogie was lucky that it was his last run-in with Gil Bones.

20.

Gil Bones was the ultimate "baddest" guy. It wasn't that Gil was physically imposing or rough, but because he was crazy and didn't bluff. If he said he'd kill you, he'd kill you. He was six feet tall, 185 pounds, with big forearms, and an ape-like walk which made him appear somewhat shorter. Gil's blond hair and pale complexion surrounded a beady-eyed but not unpleasant face which contorted when he was angry, evoking stark terror if you were his prey.

As a businessman, Gilbert Bones consumed other businesses. If a guy ran numbers, sold drugs, hustled hot clothes, etc., Gil would advise him to split the earnings. Nobody every refused him because his advice was backed with a gun to the ear. And people knew Gil would pull the trigger. Over the course of 15 years, it was estimated that he killed anywhere from 75 to 100 guys; not counting the people whom Gil beat up and left for dead, guys whose limbs were broken and their eyes gouged out. Actually, Gil was a free-lance assassin and hood who would "do" anyone, anytime.

He was insane. He was scary. He adapted the cowboy way of life to modern times. Gil's favorite line was, "You think you're tough? Go get your guns!" And then Gil would draw his from a shoulder holster. Other killers were terrified of him. They didn't want to die. Gil didn't care.

His main job was as a strong arm of the union. It didn't matter which union: teamsters, seafarers, longshoremen. Gil once pulled his gun and stuck it in Jimmy Hoffa's ear when Hoffa came to Baltimore in the mid-'60s to settle a dispute. He did it only to prove to Hoffa's bodyguard that he wasn't tough.

Sometimes he would even commit good deeds. Al Izella's son was buying dope from a guy named Pollock John near Patterson Park High School in East Baltimore. After repeated attempts by Al' to stop him, he and Gil Bones paid Pollock an unannounced visit one night. They caught him in the bathtub, beat the shit out of him, hung

him out of the third floor of his apartment, and then threw him
down the steps. Pollock John was busted up pretty bad\ and spent
two weeks in the hospital. About three months later, police found
Pollock John strangled to death with a coat hanger and assumed it
was Al's handiwork, but he had a legitimate alibi. No one asked Gil.

Gil never took no for an answer. If he heard there was a guy trying to frame him for something that he actually didn't do, Gil caught
up with him one night, tied him to a telephone pole, then repeatedly
drove his car in and around the pole until the guy confessed. After
the confession, Gil untied him, gave him a 20-second head start and
then ran him over.

Another time Gil was being interrogated by Captain Barroll of the
Narcotics Squad because he had supposedly sold drugs to Barroll's
daughter. He grabbed the cop and started to dive out the window
with him. They put Gil in jail.

Once, when he was in prison [he served several short sentences],
Gil was trying to behave so that the authorities would let him out on
an early parole. He improved his image by helping a blind prisoner
get around. One afternoon, it started raining in the jail yard and Gil
was getting soaked because the blind guy was slowing him up. Getting pissed off, Gil told the blind guy, "Come on, let's run for it, the
gates are wide open," and ran the blind guy into a brick wall. No
early parole.

Gil was finally sentenced to Patuxent Institute, the old Maryland
prison for the criminally insane. He fitted right in, killing two blues
who tried to stab him—before his surprising release 13 months later.

Many a hit man, including Patuxent's criminally insane blues,
tried but failed to kill Gil. The mob finally "hot wired" Gilbert,
forcing Gil's drug connection to sell him pure heroin. He O.D.'ed.

21.

Another classmate of mine at Forest Park was Bill McAuliffe. Bill
was a 5'8" semi-bleached blond-haired, blue-eyed, rugged looking
individual who did pretty well with the girls. He got in a lot of
fights, had a lot of guts, and was a reasonably good football player.
He also happened to get into so much trouble that many people

assumed that Bill and Boogie would never survive past 20.

I became acquainted with Bill in high school. I mean you had to be pretty friendly with most of the guys since, out of 460 students in my year, June 1960, less than 60 were boys. Bill and I would double-date, bang girls, and other normal things: cut school, start fights, smoke butts, drink cheap wine, etc.

I realized in my senior year in a chemistry class (which was so beyond me that it wasn't funny) that Bill actually knew what the teacher was saying, and he wasn't paying attention any more than I was. Bill had to apply himself somewhat, but he was still a very bright and articulate guy.

When we sat at Mandell's or in the Diner, we'd talk sports and girls, but there were times when a serious conversation would take place—rarely, and never between more than two or three guys at the most. It usually ended up with a guy exclaiming, "What are we talking about? This is a little too serious man!" That would be it, since you'd be embarrassed if guys knew you talked about politics, science, philosophy, and so forth, except that as we grew older, a lot of discussion centered around more than just sports and girls.

But back between 1957 and 1967, Bill's forte was fighting. He first came to the public eye with a startling one-punch kayo of Ray Blume as they strolled between the shop classes and the main building at Forest Park. The battle arose over something serious—Blume was kicking the bottom of Bill's chair in class.

Although Bill fought dozens of times, perhaps his classic efforts centered on a series of fights which was a vendetta even a Mafia Don would have been proud of. Bill was pledging a fraternity in high school and they were playing a softball game against another frat house. He ran out onto the field after a member of Sigma Phi's team slid a little too hard into the Alpha Phi's Pi's [Bill's fraternity] second baseman, spiking him badly. A guy named Herbert Mills did the sliding and he was supposed to be a pretty rough guy. Bill started an argument with Mills which resulted in a tremendous fight. He had Mills down on the ground about to finish him, when over came 14 Sigma Phi members who pulled Bill off and held him on his knees while Mills kicked him in the face, breaking his nose and blackening both of his eyes.

We didn't know at the time that Bill was not going to forget about it. For seven years, he methodically stalked everyone who held him down that day, along with the "kicker."

The first one he sought out was Mills, and although Bill didn't lay a hand on him, he intimidated Mills so that he didn't show his face around town for years. We were at a dance at Overlea Hall and Bill caught Mills leaving early. He followed after Mills who closed himself in his car and locked the doors. Bill proceeded to spit on the car, kick the doors, and yell every nasty name he could, but Mills refused to come out of the car.

Bill one day caught Sigma Phi's Bobby Kann cutting school from City over at Forest Park. Kann was a City track star and was standing by the front steps speaking to some girls. Bill rushed out the front entrance of Forest Park, pursued, leaped and caught Kann, whacking him down twice before Kann broke away and fled.

Soon after, Bill beat up two others at Mandell's and from that point on, for five years, nobody in Sigma Phi ever hung out at Mandell's or the Diner. They started to lean at the Suburban House [two miles north] and it became a pretty popular Sigma Phi routine, mainly because those guys and their friends were terrified to go anywhere near Bill's main haunts.

Over the next two years, Bill hunted down five more Sigma Phi's locating them at dances, parties, at synagogues on the High Holy Days, and on the streets where they lived.

Perhaps the guy Bill sought out the most was Don Gross, who just also happened to be dating a girl whom Bill liked. This made vengence against Gross even more profound, and he hid for a long, long time. There were occasions when Bill and I rode by Gross's house and Bill would throw a brick through his car window, or take a screwdriver and stab his car tires a few times. He did throw a hammer through Gross's bedroom window one night, but Gross wasn't there. Bill eventually got justice with everyone but Gross.

Seven years after the original fight, Bill went with Al Ezrine and me to Sigma Phi's Christmas Dance at the Alcazar Ballroom. Even though it was only a high school dance, it was *the* event during the Christmas break and everybody who was in Sigma Phi from the 1930s on, along with guys from other fraternities and friends, always attended this affair. There were usually about 2,000 people dancing to a big name band.

So here we were with McAuliffe, in the den of the lions—the lions being Sigma Phi, who were still terrified of Bill even though they assumed that all of his "enemies" had been caught and dealt with. Gross also figured all debts were squared, rationalizing Bill's crimes against his property were vengance enough. However, being ever so cautious, having avoided Bill for seven years, he surrounded himself at the dance with six or seven of his bigger friends the entire night.

Bill, of course, had confessed to me and Ez that he was going to get Gross that night, although I faked trying to talk him out of it. First, I felt kind of sorry for Gross; second, I thought that after seven years, Bill had done enough; and third, I wasn't going to bother Bill too much since I didn't want to get whacked out myself. Maybe Gross did deserve to get beaten up. After all, everybody else had.

Late that night Bill went downstairs where they checked the coats, and was pretending to comb his hair in the mirror. He had me and Ez stand to the side to watch. Gross came down and when Bill saw him waiting for his coat, he snuck up on him, tapped him on his shoulder, and, as Gross turned around, sucker-punched him. The punch struck with such force that for Gross twirled in the air twice, two full rotations, and then hit the ground out cold. Bill then casually took his coat, walked out, saying goodbye to Gross's girlfriend who was walking down the stairs, and went outside in front of the Alcazaar.

A bunch of Sigma Phi brothers, after seeing Gross, rushed out front as though they're going to go after Bill but hoping he was long gone. Instead, Bill was standing directly in front of the entranceway as they pushed through the doors. So, they faked-looking up and down the street a couple of times as though they're searching for someone else, and meekly walked back inside.

Gross ended up getting a tetanus shot. He thought the punch might have given him lockjaw. That night Bill's Sigma Phi vendetta ended.

22.

Barry Levinson was a very good-looking boy with an engaging personality. He had great hair [very important back then], an average build, and a handsomely chiseled face. He took a lot of sick days in secondary school which resulted in poor grades. Perhaps not paying attention in class, and writing his own sick notes, accounted for some of his low grades.

But Barry was very popular. When the senior class voted for the Best Looking Boy, he won it. Best Personality, he won it; he was even voted Second Best Athlete although he never played a varsity sport. He also won the cutest couple, alone.

Academically, Barry finished last in our class. He took courses like drums instead of physics and sat at the information desk most of the time doling out directions to visitors to the school.

Levinson was a happy-go-lucky sort. He mostly took it all in—leaning on a window, daydreaming at a desk, or sitting in a Diner booth digesting the ambience and the rhetoric, waiting for his moment.

When they played *Pomp and Circumstance* at Forest Park at graduation time, Barry was taking a test to see if he himself would graduate.

23.

In all there were three blue periods in my life: When I became a liberal Negro in high school in the late '50s; my moderate black period in the mid-'60s when I worked on Pennsylvania Avenue, the hub of the Negro commercial and entertainment sector of Baltimore before the riots of '68 and '69; and a conservative blue period when I coached, taught and administered at Morgan State University.

During the late '50s, when I first became a Negro, there weren't any references to being black, just shaded ones. One could be a different shade, either brown, gray or black. But black was used more in a derogatory sense then. For example, the Wilson brothers always described themselves as being cocoa brown, and there were other people who were described as different colored chocolates. Black didn't become fashionable until the '60s.

The Wilson brothers came over to Forest Park High and were among "the best and the brightest" who came out of the Negro junior high system in the late '50s following the desegregation ruling. Billy was in my year and his brother Rocky was a year or two behind. Rocky was a great basketball player and a really good looking kid. Word was that he was banging a couple of Jewish girls at school, which upset some people who heard the rumors, but actually turned me on, since you couldn't even rub up against those girls without having them crying rape. To picture them screwing Rocky was a kick and a half.

Rocky went on to basketball stardom in high school and junior college and then at Bluefield State. He sold insurance for a while after college and then went into the recording business as a manager. He had some pretty popular groups with which he toured Europe and Japan but, as with many others in the music business, he eventually changed careers. Rocky returned to selling insurance and is very successful today.

The Wilsons' mother, who became a school principal and has since retired, was a teacher back then and supported the household well. They had a nice home life and she dressed the boys stylishly well. As a matter of fact, I can remember borrowing and perhaps trying to steal some of Billy's clothes because they were the latest Ivy League fashions. Billy and Rocky had a great influence on the way I dressed and acted for a period of time.

Billy was in my class and he, Yussel and I became very friendly. That didn't help our academic record since by sitting next to each other we found it disruptive having to listen to a lecture or read a book. As it turned out, Yussel was expelled from Forest Park, and Billy transferred to City.

Bill became a talented musician and was the drummer for Jimi Hendrix. He was in his group when Hendrix died of a drug overdose in Europe. Billy returned to the States very despondent and became a drug addict himself. He eventually kicked his habit and has developed into a talented television cameraman and free-lance photographer.

Anyhow, for about a year it became fashionable, yet risky, to hang around and interface lifestyles with the Wilsons. But, it soon became painfully apparent that social relations, no matter how innocent, were at most embryonic; especially with the cold realization, in the form of Ben's knocking, that it was either go full-time blues or full-time Diner guys—there was no choice.

24.

Donnie Burger was a nice looking guy, solidly built, six feet tall with a square jaw. He had one fault: a very discernable twitch. His head would tilt up towards the right as his mouth opened, looking as if he was trying to bite off the side of his head. When he did this, his hands would move in an odd way, like rock singer Joe Cocker. It was unfortunate for Donnie in that most people who noticed it snickered. We thought it good knocking fun to imitate him, always behind his back since nobody wanted to get beaten up. Yet Donnie had an outstanding personality and witty side, but he was also a very sensitive individual who wrote short stories and poems when no one he knew was doing that sort of thing. He knew quite a lot about jazz and folk music. Donnie also had a violent streak and a reputation of being rough and crazy, prone to do off-the-wall things. Donnie's personality was an extension of his father's, who was a hustler like many of the Tin Men of that day.

When Donnie's twitch became more and more pronounced, his family took him to a number of doctors who prescribed various drugs to depress his central nervous system, thereby slowing down the affliction, producing an almost slow-motion twitch. What this did was make it more noticeable at times and started Donnie on the road to drug addiction.

Despite his twitch, Donnie pledged Mu Sig with Third and Charlie-Bo-Death in high school. During the late '50s, Mu Sig was not opposed to admitting popular young middle and lower-class men—a practice during this era to make the fraternity better. Earlier, it had been an elitist-spoiled brat fraternity.

Third and Donnie Burger became friendly in junior high school when they used to throw paint on each other in art class in order to get suspended and go home early.

25.

Everyone thought that Boogie's greatest skills were playing basketball, fighting and acting zany. They were wrong. Boog's forte was as a distance runner, a track star in the mile and two-mile run. He had tremendous endurance, the commitment and the physique. Boogie was extremely quick, especially his kick on the gun lap. Yet fate had other things in store for Boog. Every time it appeared he had a great future in track and would probably win a scholarship to college, he faced a new hurdle.

Two days before his first track meet at Forest Park, he was thrown out of school. He had been the starting catcher on the baseball team the year before, but because he could not get along with his coach, Old Andy (who also coached basketball), he decided to try out for the track team.

In high-top tennis shoes and long pants, Boog raced around the track in the quarter mile faster than anyone else in the Maryland Scholastic Association Conference—except for the two legitimate superstars of that era (1958–60), whose names no one remembered. Coach Martin of Forest Park was delighted by having a chance to develop a quality distance runner, and he had carefully prepared Boogie for a meet against the Johns Hopkins freshman team. Instead, to the coach's chagrin, Boog got thrown out of school two days before the meet. His opportunity to be a Forest Park track star vanished.

Two years later, when Boogie was established as a basketball star at City College, he went out for the track team. City, which had 10 times as many boys as Forest Park, categorized tryouts by days of the week—the sprints, the 100-yard dash and the 220 on one day; the 440 and the 880 on the second day; the mile and two-mile run on the third. Field events were scheduled on still another day. Boog was determined to try out for everything. He showed up every day, although he was working toward becoming a distance runner. On the first day, Boog did well enough running in the 100 and 220. On the second day, Boogie ran in the half-mile tryouts. He was leading the pack, when he slipped on a turn about 100 yards from the finish line. He fell hard on the cinder track, cutting up his wrists, arms and legs, and was rushed to the hospital where it required almost two days to get the cinders out of his skin.

Boog called from the hospital and asked the track coach if he can come back out and run in the mile and two-mile races. He was told emphatically not. It appears that the track coach's friend, the football coach, had taken a dislike to Boogie for selling football pools, and also for beating up two of his football stars at Doc's Pharmacy a week before. The football coach was no man to trifle with. He was a man of conviction, and he did not tolerate nonsense. His name was George Young. Today, he is the General Manager of football's New York Giants.

Although Boogie couldn't run high school track at either Forest Park or City, it failed to dampen his spirit. One could say that it drove him to become the first professional track star. Well, not precisely like a Carl Lewis, Sebastian Coe or Bruce Jenner, but professional in the sense that he competed for money.

It began one night at Benny's Pool Room where a Tin Man, Drake the Fake, thought he was conning Boogie with a "fixed" race. Unbeknownst to most, Drake had been secretly working out. He told Boogie that with a modest "spot," he could beat him in a distance run for $400. The course would be on Belvedere Avenue from Reisterstown Road to Park Heights Avenue, about a mile. To make it fair, since Boogie was five years younger than he, Drake would be given a head start at the Trolley Barn, approximately 300 yards.

Boogie agreed to the spot and convinced Benny to back him in the race. Benny put up $400 and promised to give Boogie $50 if he won. The guys poured out of the pool room to witness the historic event.

Although Drake had been in training, he was no match for Boog. At the half-mile point, Boogie had caught up with Drake. However, for smiles, Boogie didn't burst ahead but kept pace with Drake—first feigning exhaustion, then running backwards, taunting Drake. "Nice move, Drake. You sure conned me," Boogie said. Drake conceded the race and walked the final 200 yards to Park Heights.

Yet the evening's event was far from over. After Drake caught his breath, he made another bet.

"Double or nothing for the 50 Benny gave you, Boogie," said Drake. "We'll race a sprint down Park Heights to the Pimlico Bowling Alley. You spot me half the distance."

Boggie considered his decision for a few minutes before he

reluctantly agreed. The distance was 900 yards. Boogie reconsidered. "Drake, it's too much of a spot. Give me three-to-one odds, or forget it." Drake agreed instantly. He calculated he couldn't lose.

The race went swiftly. Fifty yards from the bowling alley, Drake slowed down to look over his shoulder when Boogie glided by holding a $50 bill in his hand.

26.

When Bux the Gripper got out of the Coast Guard, the first place he returned to was the Queensberry Playground. All of his friends were now either in college or working, and the only guys remaining were younger than Bux. He became a terror. He would approach people, shake their hands and grip them. His nails were always jagged and he would draw blood most of the time. Instead of running away from Bux, we swarmed around him like ants to honey. It was almost a subconscious suicidal wish to be around Bux. Deep down you knew if you were around him long enough, you were going to get gripped. Yet you had a lot of fun watching him grip other guys, egging him on, knowing full well that sooner or later Bux would turn on you saying, "You tried conning the Bux and now you're gonna get gripped!" Most of the time he gripped you around the shoulder, other times around the hands or wrist. The worst though was when he grabbed you in the fleshy part around the waist and dug his nails in deep, forcing you up on your toes, like a ballerina. You did anything Bux wanted you to do and there was no one to help you.

Occasionally, there were guys who challenged Bux. "Don't come near me," they would say, or, "I'll kill you. You're not gripping me!" It didn't matter, Bux would lull them into a false sense of security and then grip the hell out of them. He was so powerful and so terrifying that when he grimaced and screamed at you, you knew that no matter how badly you wanted to get back at him it would be a foolish play since he could probably destroy you. So you submitted to the grip and just waited for the time he gripped somebody else.

It was always amusing watching another guy try to avoid the grip and then seeing him gripped. Bux would literally stalk you down for weeks to grip you. One night, he forced Bob Litwin (a Philadelphia native, short, thin, scared, bright and articulate) and me into his car to seek out a potential grippee. We phoned a guy called "The Fan"* and said that we were coming by to get him and would honk the horn. Fan was terrified of Bux, but always warned that Bux better not fool with him or else he would smash a brick over Bux's head. As we approached the alley, Bux got out of the car and hid by Fan's corner house. As we blew the horn, Fan came dashing out to the car and Bux leaped out from the darkness and placed a serious grip around Fan's neck, arms, and hands. Fan squealed like a stuck-pig and his parents came rushing outside, but Bux wouldn't let go. He grabbed "The Fan" around the waist, got him up on his toes, and ran him up and down the alley a few times before disappearing into the night. We had instructions, of course, to drop Bux's car off at the poolroom and not to say a word. This was the terror of the Gripper.

Now, The Gripper was also the source of many legends and, whether accurate or not, guys swore they occurred. There was a new playground director named Mr. Witted, a black man who once roomed with pro-football great Rosey Brown at Morgan State College. Mr. Witted could punt the ball barefoot about 50 yards in the air and he was cat-quick. In our pickup football games, Witted would be on one side, and Bux would always be on the opposing team.

Bux, every now and then, would fantasize that he was different pro football players: Sometimes he would be Herm Clark, middle guard for the Chicago Bears. The instant he said it, he would rush out and tackle you—and he would grip you senseless. Sometimes he would be Gino Marchetti, the massive defensive end of the Baltimore Colts. You sensed when he was coming at you because he would get up on his toes in slow-motion as if he himself was a defensive end who had just gotten by an offensive tackle and would scream, "Here comes Gino." You knew it was all over. He would even chase you inside your house to tackle-grip you.

Anyhow, one day we were playing a touch-football game and had

----

*Perhaps the greatest sports fan of all times. He lived and died every victory and loss by our local teams and loved to discuss the teams, players, results, etc., ad infinitum. He was so biased in his rooting that he could never become an "expert" or "book," just a "fan."

our backs to the wall making a goal-line stand. Fortunately, I was on Bux's team at the time. Mr. Witted decided to run for the touchdown and Bux was determined not to let him score. As Witted took the hand-off and ran across the goal line, Bux threw his hands out and, instead of touching him, gripped him around the waist and tore a hunk of flesh out of him. Witted wheeled around pissed-off and threw the ball down in disgust, screaming and cussing at Bux. We called this the first spiked football, or the first ball-busting episode. Yes, it really happened at Queensberry and not Grambling College. Witted was incensed and banned Bux from the playground for a year. Bux came back the next day. Witted didn't say a word and bought Bux a Coke.

A lot of the guys thought they were tough. Some were pretty rough and would brag—when Bux was absent—that they had never been gripped, or that Bux had better not grip them. For some reason (I guess it was fate), no sooner did they say these things when you would see Bux an hour or a day later come up and grip them. They would just sit or stand there and take it. Sometimes they would pull away a little bit and Bux would give them a sort of scary look. That was the end.

27.

Naomi Ellen Cohen has just been reprimanded by the Forest Park Vice-Principal, Dr. Kramer, for coming late to school (for a change). It seems that Ellen (she dropped Naomi) was chronically late for school with a myriad of bullshit reasons for missing classes. The truth was that every morning she worked for her father down at the Mondawmin Shopping Center selling sandwiches and breakfast to construction workers. Her dad had converted a school bus into a lunch wagon, and usually Ellen Cohen looked disheveled since she had been working since 6:00 in the morning. Of course, her appearance was never very appealing since she was very heavy and did not keep herself immaculately dressed. Dr. Kramer sent her in to see Counselor Jerry Cohen. Cohen, no relation, liked Ellen and found her extremely intelligent but academically unmotivated.

The globular-built Ms. Cohen skipped another class and went to the cafeteria where she began telling some of her friends (fellow school choristers) that she would be a movie star one day. She had this strong dream, but she had not convinced the guys at a nearby table. They listened to the chatter and began knocking her and pelting her with food. However, the conviction in her voice made believers of some students. Although an accomplished member of the choir, she was not a better singer than Myrna Davis, whose good looks seemed more inclined to reach stardom than somebody like Ellen. But Ellen did have a magnetic quality. It was tough to put a handle on it, due to her appearance and the fact that when she got mad she could curse with the best of them.

The next evening, we were all at the new Northwest Bowling Alley about a half mile north of the Diner. Ellen showed up as I was telling Ben about her dream of becoming a movie star. Ben started knocking Ellen Cohen.

"Hey, toothpick, when can we expect tickets to your first movie? You fat toast!" Fortunately, Ben was standing behind a crowd of us and Ellen doesn't know who shouted the knock. Unfortunately for me, she thought that I said it and turned and sucker-punched me, knocking me clear off of my feet. Within seconds she was on top of me, pummeling her chubby fists into my covered face. Thankfully four guys were able to pull her off. I tried explaining that I didn't do it, while Ben continued knocking her from behind the crowd. She began cussing me out and everybody started laughing. I hid out for a week. It was an unfair fight; she outweighed me by more than 100 pounds.

28.

Among the epic gambling events, probably none has been more revered than the nine-ball pool matches for $1,000 a game between Swartzie and Drake the Fake, the premier aluminum siding hustler. Drake would shoot with one hand while Swartzie shot with both. It went on every night for four weeks at Benny's Pool Room, standing room only, during which time the major draw of this match-up was the knocking that went on between Drake and Swartzie throughout the course of each game. Drake was quite a hustler, but he could never out-hustle Swartzie. And Swartzie was only 16 years old then and Drake was pushing 21. Swartzie won the knocking battle for the most part, although it was closer than the bets. Swartzie must have salted away about $20,000 before Drake finally quit.

Of course this led to the next series of bowling gambling matches. Originally there were a number of older Diner guys who formed two-man teams and would bowl a series of games at the three major alleys in Northwest Baltimore: Forest Park Bowling Alley, the Pimlico Lanes, and the Hilltop Lanes.

The game was called 69-9 no count. Briefly, in this type of betting game of duckpins [the small balls and the small pins], the object was to score nine pins or more with only two balls. Anything less than nine meant that you received a zero or "no count" for the frame. You had to receive a score of 69 or more to win the 10 frame game. Teams were usually chosen up and they and the gallery bet on everything imaginable in the contest.

Swartzie would either book most of the action in the gallery or else wager on certain contestants. Every now and then, he would "fix" great bowlers like Bingle, a 60-year-old, nicknamed "The Oil Man," who always had grease on his arms and wore an Amoco Station jersey and an Amoco hat with a hairpiece underneath, usually awry. One time, Swartzie persuaded Bingle to throw a couple of matches (bowl under 69) and won a small fortune. There was another great bowler, a very fat guy who was called Orbit. Orbit would actually bounce the bowling ball up and down before he would throw it down the lanes. This was not helpful for certain people's nerves, nor to the alley floor.

A classic match occurred at the Hilltop bowling lanes, in the same Hilltop Shopping Center which housed Mandell's Deli and was across the street from the Diner. It was on the corner by Rogers Avenue and Reisterstown Road and only three blocks from where Swartzie lived. As a youth Swartzie worked as a pin boy, before the automatic pin-setters eliminated this occupation. At the end of the game, people would throw change down the lanes as tips for the pin boy. If the tips were less than a half-dollar, Swartzie would stand up and throw the change as hard as he could back at the bowlers. On this night, Drake was bowling and Swartzie was betting against him and booking the action. The guy who owned the bowling alley, Mel the Tailor, was also gambling serious money. He even closed the alley from Friday night through Monday morning so that only those in action could play.

The game was 69-9 no count, and Swartzie ended up winning $7,000 from Mel the Tailor. They then went double or nothing. Mel put up the bowling alley against the $7,000. He lost and Swartzie then owned the alley.

For two days, Swartzie just laid around "his" alley with the guys making a mess until Mel finally threw him out. Swartzie accused Mel of welshing on the bet and threatened that nobody would ever come near there again to gamble or to even use his bowling alley if he didn't settle the wager. So Mel decided to give Swartzie a $3,000 "take it or leave it" payoff.

Swartzie now was carrying around several thousand dollars he'd won from Drake and Mel when Bruce Hawk told him that before they could go out to a beer party at Chestnut Ridge (northern Baltimore County), they'd have to cop some liquor. The guys had been robbing booze in one house over and over again, up at the corner of Glen Avenue and Park Heights about a mile from the Diner.

They broke in as soon as it became dark outside. Swartzie just went along to see what else he could steal, but since he had a few grand in his pocket, he wasn't very interested. Hawk grabbed some liquor and was sitting around drinking when some lights flashed on outside. The guys scurried out the back door and drove over to the beer party.

Later that night, they returned and were hanging around the Park Heights area when Swartzie was stopped by a policeman. Earlier, they had stopped Hawk and took his name as a possible witness. Swartzie was pulled into the police car and was bluffed by the cops that they knew he was the thief who robbed the house. "Hawk had already given you up, Swartz. You don't want to take the fall alone, do ya?"

Since Swartzie and Hawk were only teenagers at the time, they didn't really understand the con game going on with the police. At the station house, the police booked Swartzie and confronted him with a story that Hawk was in another cell and was "singing." So Swartzie said, "Yeah, we just went there to get a bottle, not to rob the house."

As it turned out, during the sentencing, the judge dismissed the charges against both of them. Hawk, having some relatives with political clout, was let go. However, Swartzie was told that he must enlist in the Air Force immediately for five years. Swartzie figured that five years was a tad too much for just going along with a guy to burglarize a house for some booze. So he marched down to the recruitment office and continually failed the entrance test for the next two years. He finally convinced the court that he will enlist for six months in the National Guard when good and ready.

29.

For some reason, the Gripper would never grip twins Mickey and Rickey Wildstein at the playground. Perhaps it was because they were considered somewhat "loco" and as the blues and American Indians believed, it was considered bad luck to harm crazy people. Actually, the twins weren't totally nuts, they were just strange and difficult to understand. They should have been gripped.

They moved around Queensberry in time to play briefly for our 10-to-12 and 12-to-14 softball teams and both were considered solid players. The twins were bright, witty and very popular. But when they turned 16, something happened that caused them to become reclusive, keeping to themselves as much as possible. Mickey and Rickey were identical in physical appearance and mental and emotional demeanor, although Rickey was a bit more unusual than Mickey. The twins argued incessantly with each other.

They were fanatical baseball fans and, following the return of major league baseball to Baltimore in 1954, their emotional stability depended upon Oriole victories, which were few and far between in the late '50s.

The twins chose a favorite player and assumed the identity of that particular individual in stickball and softball games. At first they didn't mind playing with other guys or joking about their Oriole idols, but as time went by, they drifted away from our gang at the playground and only played against each other—games of violent confrontations.

Rickey "became" Gus Triandos, the slugging, plodding catcher of the Orioles, and Mickey "became" Bob Hale, the light-hitting platooned first baseman whose prowess as a pinch-hitter was legendary. Now I'm not saying that the twins fantasized becoming major league players, nor were they dreamers—they actually *became* Gus Triandos and Bob Hale.

They would only answer to those names, and even their mother had to call them Gus and Bob to get them to talk. It got so that they tried to legally change their names in high school and were, at one point, suspended for not answering to their given names in class and for signing Gus and Bob on test papers.

Their marathon stickball matches were continually marred by violent arguments that always ended each game. If, for example, after hitting a ground ball that bounced off Rickey's outstretched glove, Mickey, to enhance his batting average (or Bob Hale's) would call out, "Hit," while Rickey immediately retorted, "Error." They'd shout "hit" and "error" at each other, over and over, louder and louder, until silence enveloped the entire playground. At that point the game was either continued under protest or the twins stormed off the field arguing to themselves, or at one another, until they disappeared into their home behind the playground.

During their ball-strike, hit-error disagreements, I'd occasionally try instigating Bux to grip them back to this planet. Fortunately, for Mickey and Rickey, Bux would order Berdoff to grab me while I was summarily gripped and punched in the heart until my release. That brought me back to earth writhing in pain on the red clay of Queensberry.

The last I heard of the twins was a few years ago from Nat Smertz who told me that they were working, as supervisors no less, at the Probation Department. They had never married, but had changed their names again; this time to Kenny and Eddie. He said they dressed and acted like blues in tribute to their newest Oriole idols, Ken Singleton and Eddie Murray.

I still think they should have been gripped.

30.

Marvin Hillstein's father left home in 1952 to buy a pack of cigarettes and never returned. Ben would be up at the Diner entertaining a group of us when he'd suddenly wheel around and look up the street and scream, "My God, it's Hillstein's father coming back with a carton of L&M's under his arm!" This would always break up the guys, especially Hillstein.

31.

Neurotic Nat jerked-off without using his hands. It seemed strange that someone can masturbate against an inanimate object, but he had perfected this process to a fine degree. Now and then he got caught rubbing against a woman or an object near a woman, but he had learned to vehemently deny everything. He got this denial technique from his father, who taught him years ago that the more you deny something, people will sooner or later come around to agree with you. Nat remembered an example of this when, as a freshman in 1959, at the University of Maryland, Bernie Salgonik was caught cheating during a History 105 exam. Salgonik had the book open at his feet and was busily copying the answers when a proctor confronted him. Bernie leaped up, closing the book with his foot, and kicking it down about 13 rows, denying the accusation and insisting that the proctor had some kind of vendetta against him. He carried on so loudly that the proctor embarrassingly apologized, to the delight of the rest of the students.

To understand why Nat is so neurotic calls for a review of his upbringing, his family, and his relatives. Nat's father, Leon, who worked for the Federal Parole and Probation Agency, literally raised Nat as a civil servant or employee. From childhood, Nat had specific chores daily and was given an efficiency rating every six months similar to his father's government agency's. He was rated outstanding, good, fair or deficient in areas like school work, taking out the garbage, speaking during dinner, etc. Nat very rarely received an "outstanding" in anything and found himself constantly on probation as a family member.

Nat's father took his government job so seriously that he once docked an employee four hours of leave even though the employee had died. His justification was that he didn't receive news of the death until four hours after lunch, and, therefore, the employee's family lost a half-day's pay.

Leon was great at denying things. For years, he would go for French lessons twice a week, and would bowl in a league on another night. He would trudge out on Monday evenings at 6:00 with his

French books and then come back home by 10:00. On Thursdays, he would take out his bowling ball and return home at 11:00 P.M. Occasionally, he would come back home with a trophy. Years later, when Nat, searching for his father because of an accident at home, couldn't locate him at the bowling alley, he began to suspect that something was suspicious about his father's weekly "outings," especially since Leon had been in the same beginner's French class for over 12 years. Of course, at Nat grew older he understood that his father had a number of trysts with younger women. Yet, he couldn't bring himself to confront daddy. He knew that Leon would eventually convince him, through the denial technique, of his undying fidelity and devotion.

Leon was an internal security agent for parole and probation who relished his work and was both revered and feared by fellow employees. He never took a single day of sick leave in 40 years. Once, he was sent to Mexico to find out why so many welfare checks were disappearing or being cashed after people died. When Leon deplaned in Texas, he decided to take a bus to Mexico City to save the agency money. He fell asleep on the bus and when he arrived in Mexico City, all he had on was a t-shirt and his pants. His sport coat, shirt, tie, belt, shoes, socks and briefcase were all missing—stolen as he slept. Leon was arrested for vagrancy and put in jail for three days in Mexico City. (He docked himself three days comp time.)

A few years ago, Leon retired from the Government at 65 and began romancing a South American beauty when his wife was off in the Catskills with her girlfriends. Leon was taking pictures of his naked girlfriend on the stairs when his wife unlocked the door and walked in. "What are you doing here?" Leon exclaimed, "You're not supposed to be back until Saturday. It's only Friday night!" "What's going on here?" asked his shocked wife. "Nothing," said Leon as the girl ran upstairs looking for her clothes. Leon tried to put away as much of the incriminating evidence as he could: panties, bra, Polaroids. The girl came rushing down the steps again, she could not locate her clothes and ran out into the night. His wife again questioned, "What's going on here? I can't believe this. What's happening?" Leon replied, "Nothing, there's nothing happening." And he calmly dressed and went out into the night.

He located his girlfriend, still nude, two blocks down the street, took her home, and then came back an hour later. Once more his wife confronted him. She had already called both her son and her daughters and told them what had taken place. Leon asked why she would do something like that when nothing had happened? She asked about the pictures. "Look at these Polaroid pictures!" Leon took the pictures, looked at them and quickly slipped them into his briefcase. He also quickly slipped his girlfriend's clothing into the same briefcase and went upstairs. Leon denied, denied, denied everything, talking to his wife as if she had just awakened from a bad dream. "I don't know what you're talking about," he said, "There's nothing going on. The real question is, why are you home a day early? In all of these years you have never come back either early or late from anywhere you were supposed to be: Neither have I. What happened, was there something wrong?" She responded, "It was raining and the weather got bad and we decided to come home early. But what was happening here? What about the girl?"

"I don't know what you're talking about. Go on to bed, we'll talk about it in the morning," Leon said. For two weeks he continually denied the whole episode happened and, although Nat and his sisters knew something went down, a year later their mother was so totally convinced that the whole thing never occurred that she berated and chastised Nat and his younger sister Louise for ever bringing it up.

Leon rarely mentioned his own family and would never allow his own mother or father to be discussed in front of Nat or his sisters. Nat met his paternal grandparents on three occasions. Each time he had to sit with them for over an hour nodding his head since they spoke only Russian Yiddish, a language which Nat did not understand at all. No one knows what ever happened to Leon's parents since Nat has not heard from them or discussed them with his father for over 22 years.

Nat used to spend his summers in Wildwood, New Jersey, with his mother's parents who operated a fruit stand. People would continually come by and steal fruit or shortchange the grandparents. The grandparents never remotely considered the customers as thieves but always kept a wary eye on Nat who they believed was a crook. As a result of their accusations, Nat decided that he might as well steal from them and thus began his career of petty thievery. (Nat shoplifts to this day just for the thrill of it.)

His mother's side of the family was indeed very strange. Mrs. Smertz was one of six children. She had a sister who absconded with most of her parents' money. Following the death of her sister's husband, a refrigerator salesman who committed suicide after losing a huge sale of ice boxes to customers in North Dakota, this sister used up the rest of the family funds.

Nat's Uncle Wendell was a humanitarian doctor in New Jersey who treated blacks free in the '40s and '50s in Newark, and took care of a lot of charity cases throughout the state. He made an unfortunate error of marrying a shiksa which brought a curse upon him from his mother. She warned him that by marrying this shiksa his luck would change and something terrible would happen. A month later he was struck down with a very rare muscle disease, lost control of his body, and became a vegetable. He also was unable to speak and could only shake his head to say, "No."

Practically all of Wendell's savings were exhausted in order to buy a wheel turned by two men every hour to keep him alive. Finally, the New Jersey legislature passed a bill to buy him a rotating wheel that was similar to a "hampster wheel" which was manufactured for $24,000. Every hour it made a complete revolution. The legislature did this because Wendell was such a great humanitarian.

When Wendell took ill, his shiksa wife started "running around" and spending his insurance money. She would bring guys over the house and screw them quietly in the back rooms. He has been in the wheel for over 25 years and his wife still brings home young guys, only now she does them in front of him. He shakes his head "No" like crazy while they are there and she tells the guy, "Don't worry, it's an encouraging sign; he likes to watch!"

32.

There was a band of young men who during high school merged into a group called the Ten Boys. The Ten Boys were made up of guys dominated by the ULP fraternity, and to show their enlightenment even included a Gentile named Jimmy Reno. He happened to be one of the few non-Jews at Forest Park who lived in the area, was good-looking and did well with Jewish girls. He was their token goy.

Among the Ten Boys were Barry Levinson; Chucky Silver, who became a country and western songwriter; a guy called Schreevie, whose real name was Marvin Fribush (to this day nobody knows why he was named Schreevie, only that it fitted him because he looked like a Schreevie—even though nobody knew what a Schreevie looked like); Levinson's cousin Eddie Kirk, who smoked incessently and loved to drink; Miles Kirson, who was not in a fraternity although everyone thought he was; Stuart Baum, who was called The Wasp, and for a good reason, he resembled one; Barry Glickman, who went to Poly and the Maryland Institute of Art, was an early Bohemian, and is now a successful painter and graphics designer whose work hangs in museums and universities; Sheldon Wolfe, who was also in Mu Sig; and a couple of others who don't come to mind. Thirty years later, Diner guys still get a kick out of a difficult trivia question: *Name the Ten Boys.*

In the late spring of 1960, the Ten Boys and Bill McAuliffe decided that because they would probably end up working the summer in Atlantic City, they'd go there Memorial Day to check out employment possibilities. That's what they told their parents.

They were hanging up by High Hat Joe's, a small hot dog stand by the Ambassador Hotel, where most hip people from Philadelphia and New Jersey used to hang, and some girls walked by, all dressed up, on their way to a big graduation dance for Atlantic City High School. Instinctively the Ten Boys hit on these five or six girls who tell them, "Look, you guys can't go to the dance, but around 11:30, it will be ending and we'll be coming out, and if you want to get together, we'll do that."

So, the Ten Boys and Bill McAuliffe show up around 11:30 and they're leaning outside of the President Hotel against this window, sitting on a ledge. It sounded like a great dance with screaming and bottles being thrown out of windows. A couple of the girls came out with dates and told the guys that they were sorry but they couldn't go out with them later. Bill and the Ten Boys showed no concern because they knew there were three or four girls left who would be emerging shortly and who they figured for sure that they were going to score. Suddenly, out of nowhere, a mob of guys moved down the street towards the ledge, and then closed in around where the Ten Boys were leaning. The Ten were trapped, encircled with their backs to the window by close to 150 angry Atlantic City greasers.

Looking around, Bill asked, "What's going on?" without a hint of how this has happened. The leader of the mob came up to Bill and said, "Do you want to go a few rounds?" Some of the girls had obviously complained that the Ten Boys had bothered them. Bill feigned innocence and responded, "What do you mean go a few rounds? Fighting or drinking?" The leader retorted, "Fighting!" Out of the corner of his eye, Bill saw three guys start pounding on Schreevie, took this as a sign and sucker-punched the leader.

At this time, fearless Bill was in his prime, in great shape, and his sucker-punch knocked this guy's front teeth out. Because of the pressure of the crowd, the guy couldn't move, and Bill, his head down, just thrust into him, punching him as hard and as fast as he could. The crowd was so big that only a couple of people actually could come forward and really punch on the Ten Boys, and this gave them a small edge.

The leader was on the ground looking for his teeth and bleeding profusely, sirens started blasting, girls started screaming, and chaos reigned, sort of like a mini-riot. Seeing Miles and Schreevie running to the Boardwalk, Bill slipped into the hotel where the manager directed him to hide in the back.

Through the window, Bill saw Miles and Schreevie running back from the Boardwalk to help Barry Levinson who was lying in the middle of the street with 12 guys pounding on him. There was this one guy, well over six feet tall, who kept picking Levinson up, dusting him off, and letting everybody hit him until Levinson went down again.

Bill muttered to himself, "Oh, shit, I can't let Barry get killed." By now, Miles and Schreevie had joined the fight but were getting killed themselves, so Bill rushed out and sucker-punched the guy pounding on Miles. A big circle of 100 others now merged around this free-for-all. The now-toothless guy and his friends came up and started screaming at McAuliffe, "Hey, you in the red shirt, we're gonna get you!"

Just then the police arrived and the guy who had his teeth knocked out continued haranguing Bill, "Meet me up at the Boardwalk," and Bill cockily answered back, "Don't you think you've had enough?" The police began dispersing the crowd when this huge Atlantic City graduate in a white tuxedo approached and socked Bill in the eye, almost blinding him. Bill dove into his mid-section while yelling to the cops to come and get him because he can't see. The police shoved Bill in their patrol car to rush him to the hospital.

Meanwhile, Levinson, Miles and Schreevie were still encircled and crying out, "Hey, take us too!" But the cops sarcastically responded, "Go take a Jitney!" Naturally, it was Atlantic City High School, these are Atlantic City cops, and Bill and the Ten Boys were from Baltimore. Fortunately, during the confusion as the police cruiser drove Bill off past the crowd, Levinson, Miles and Schreevie sneaked up to the Boardwalk and raced back to their hotel.

At the hospital, Bill got his eye repaired and then he returned to the police station. He wanted to press charges against the guy who almost blinded him, but the police told him, "Well, it takes two to make a fight, and if you want to press charges, we've got to keep both of you in jail until after Memorial Day, which will be Tuesday. But if you drop charges, well, we'll forget it." Not wanting to spend the weekend in jail since he had come up to have fun, Bill had to let the thing drop and the police threw him out. He then had to find his way back to the apartment with one eye, where he found the Ten Boys licking their wounds, most of them black and blue.

Next day, the guys cautiously strolled the Boardwalk, fearing another attack from the Atlantic City High School grads and contemplating an early return to Baltimore. But to their surprise, overnight they'd become heroes. Some guys from Chelsea approached them and exclaimed, "You're the guys from Baltimore who beat up a dance!"

"Beat up a dance!" Levinson said, so sore he could barely walk or talk, "My God, we must be tough!"

Half an hour later, while browsing in a T-shirt store, fate delivered up the "leader," who had lost his teeth to Bill, behind the sales counter. He was in semi-shock as Bill grabbed him by the shirt and warned, "If anybody touches any of us, you're complete history." He punctuated this with a half-punch in the guy's Adam's apple.

33.

Third was worldly even in high school. He traveled across Falls Road, where the Gentile area began, and was befriended by many Gentile guys he had met while spending his summers in Ocean City, Maryland. In the '50s, there were maybe three Jewish guys who lived and worked in Ocean City in the summertime. Because of his non-Jewish good looks, and his way with women, Third was easily able to assimilate into the Gentile world. For years they thought

Third was one of them. Even the Jews began to think of Third as a goy.

As a result of Third's initial entree into "goyimdom," a number of Jews gingerly began to cross Falls Road, picking up girls at Ameche's Drive-in and taking them to the Pines (a make-out place for Gentiles). At the same time, a lot of Gentile boys started crossing the opposite side of Falls Road to date Jewish girls. And, peculiar as it may seem, the Gentile girls readily screwed Jewish guys and the Gentile guys just as readily screwed Jewish girls when neither was messing with his or her own kind, and everybody believed that the others were vestal virgins.

At the end of our senior year in high school, Sue and Third finally dissolved their relationship, and, although they would date sporadically over the next couple of years, it was finished. Sue enrolled at the University of Syracuse and stayed there for a year, occasionally returning to Baltimore and started to date Ford Lessans, the most eligible Jewish prince.

Third spent the summer of 1960 in Provincetown where he discovered how easily he could wheel upper-class men and women. He was introduced to marihuana and hashish.

There he met a very well-to-do young man named Seymour who claimed his mother was Isabelle Gardner, the renowned author of *Through a Glass Darkly*. Seymour convinced Third to sail with him to Europe in the fall. Third doesn't remotely know Isabelle Gardner.

Third first returned to Baltimore to try persuading any of his acquaintances to join him abroad. He went over to his frat brother Brosy's house where a bunch of guys were drinking red wine and listening to jazz. Third had brought back an ounce of marihuana from Provincetown and offered it to the group. Appalled and shocked, they threw Third out of the house, although Brosy's soon-to-be-brother-in-law Howard accused Third of passing off oregano as grass.

Disillusioned, Third tried contacting an Ocean City buddy, Mike Campo, to join him on his odyssey, and after several phone calls reached the Spice sisters. Mary Spice told Third that they're on the way to see Mike in Ocean City and they'll take him along, but first they had to make a stop in Northwest Baltimore.

The girls lived in Catonsville, in West Baltimore County. Carol Spice looked like Julie Andrews and Mary like Ava Gardner. They were street-wise beyond their years, yet looked and acted disarmingly innocent.

To Third's surprise, the girls arrived at Rogers and Park Heights Avenue on Vespa scooters and mysteriously announced that they must stop off at Bruce Hawk's house before leaving, planning to purchase some grass. Leery, due to both the public's (and the police's) attitude towards drugs, Third said little about his experience with marihuana or that he was holding an ounce.

Third was surprised. The connection everyone was waiting for at Hawk's turned out to be Donnie Burger. Big connection. He delivered a nickel bag to be passed among six people. Nobody offered Third even a drag.

Carol decided to stay with Hawk who promised better drugs later; and Mary and Third took off on the scooters for Ocean City. Just outside Annapolis, they stopped for shelter from the cold and Third produced his grass for a respite. After an hour, Mary and Third became enamored with each other and, after telling her why he was going to see Mike Campo in Ocean City, she confessed that she'd love to go to Paris. Third cancelled the Ocean City trip and told Mary to meet him the next Sunday in New York.

She drove the Vespa to New York and left for Europe with Third and Seymour. She and Third fell in love on the voyage. He had $21 and a one-way ticket, Mary $40, and Seymour three $10,000 letters of credit. Mary and Third advised Seymour that they're throwing their money overboard in order to begin fresh in France. Seymour then ripped up his $30,000 and tossed the pieces into the ocean.

Of course, being consummate hustlers, Mary and Third somehow left the boat in Le Havre with $1,000 cash.

Seymour had a prostitute friend living in Pigalle, who provided Third and Mary with drugs and contacts. Paris was an enlightening experience for the two Baltimoreans, but they returned in the spring. Mary moved to New York and Third played club lacrosse well enough to earn a scholarship to the University of Baltimore beginning September 1961.

Mary Spice was a free-spirit who just said and did what she wanted. If someone demanded more from her, she'd split. She was both open and real. Not a real hustler, but a kept woman from time to time. She was adventurous. I mean to get on a boat to Europe with Third after knowing him for two hours. . . .

Sister Carol Spice was cunning. She had a child from the first guy she ever slept with and was saddled forever with a guilt-driven responsibility to give the kid the best of everything. It seriously altered her ambitions and kept her in Baltimore, which stifled her.

34.

There was a point in our lives, either in our late teens or early 20s, when we realized we were never going to grow up, nor were we ever going to take life very seriously. Many of us didn't really understand what we were doing. For instance, whom we were hurting. Or if we were hurting anyone, we realized it and kept our mouths shut, because it wasn't cool to express feeling. But we did have a conscience. We didn't just consider women objects to be used for closet scenes or to be abused, and at the same time we didn't only look at guys in a knocking, sarcastic way or devote our lives to hurting people.

Male bonding and camaraderie kept us locked in another dimension, unable to face up to the realities of understanding both the past and present, or of even contemplating the future.

The serious student, the sensitive artist and the lovesick poet of our playground and Diner generation had to mask his true feelings to the guys, or exist as an outcast.

You hid your compassion well, or just denied it. To expose it you damage your reputation forever. Yet, there were instances of compassion: Taking up for a guy who was getting verbally or physically wasted, or not screwing a girl at a group sex scene who obviously had had enough (or talking her out of mass sex scenes). It however caused you grief. We weren't encumbered by passion and philosophy. Age brought compassion to some.

Many of us were totally selfish. Although we thought *we* deserved everything, we would use the term "deserved" with others in a sarcastic, negative way. For example, if someone had a good-looking date, received a good grade, or drove a nice car, we would yell out, "Deserved!" Even betrayal was okay. You could still get back in with the guys.

Why did many of us have this attitude? A chip on the shoulder, and inner-viciousness? Was it a first-born Northwest Baltimore Jewish son's syndrome, or a subconscious vindictiveness we'd somehow acquired?

When we were younger, we had to deal with our parents. We

were privileged by the way we were raised, although we didn't realize it. For example, our parents were pretty strict about curfews, but all they really wanted was to see us home safe. We knew that some Gentile guys never had to be home. So looking back, we realized that we were truly loved. Our parents wanted us to have it all, even if they didn't have it to give. Often we were told that they wanted us to have a better life than theirs, to have more than they did! Was this responsible for our arrogance, or the expectation that we deserved everything?

Perhaps one that incident typified the psyche of the first generation American son of the Northwest Baltimore immigrant Jew was the "dubs" story.

City was playing Dunbar for the 1959–60 Public School basketball championship and the right to meet the Catholic or private school's champs for the Baltimore City crown.

Victory seemed assured for City, which had the ball and led by eight points with 50 seconds left in the game. There was a timeout on the court, and in the City huddle the coach cautioned the team.

"Don't rush anything. Hold the ball. Only 50 seconds left and it's over."

Snyder left the huddle before it broke and hurried over to the scorer's table. "How many do I have?"

"Nine," answered Dunbar's scorekeeper, not even looking up since Snyder had made the same inquiry after every timeout.

City put the ball into play and began a deliberate slowdown offense trying to kill off as many ticks of the clock as possible. Twice Snyder had the ball at the foul line and each time he noticed exceptionally mild defensive pressure on him by Dunbar. On receiving a third pass, he turned to the basket and launched a high arching jump shot that tantalizingly circled the rim, but missed. The City players were dumbfounded at Snyder's shot and reacted shakenly to Dunbar's quick rebound, full-court pass and score to close the lead to six points.

The ensuing in-bounds pass by City, panickly thrown by John Angle, a 6'8" forward, was intercepted by Dunbar's All-State playmaker Charlie Leach, who scored a basket and was fouled in the process. Leach then made the foul shot and the City lead shrunk to three points. Incredulously, Angle (not the ball-handling guards) again put the ball into play, and Dunbar again intercepted it and scored. City's lead was now one and the Dunbar home crowd's cheering was deafening.

City's guards finally took the ball out safely and began dribbling away the final seconds of the game when Leach brilliantly stole the ball from a City playmaker. After one dribble, he tossed a desperation 45-foot shot that swished the basket to win the championship for Dunbar.

City was stunned. The dressing room was a morgue. Players looked for a scapegoat when Turns, who had quit the team weeks before, came into the locker room and approached Snyder.

Snyder had been given the goat's-role for taking a shot when everyone thought City would freeze the ball.

"Schnoo," questioned Turns, "Why'd you take that shot?"

"Why, for dubs, Turns, what else?"

"Dubs" was double-figures and in these days, double-figures, 10 or more points, in the scorecard section of the newspapers was the ultimate badge of athletic success in basketball, and major status among Diner, playground and poolroom guys. To Snyder, he *deserved* double-figures. Snyder's personal basketball goals overshadowed any team achievements. Yet as a defenseman in lacrosse, Snyder's prowess in an unglamorous position led City to two consecutive high school lacrosse championships. Figure it out.

35.

By the early '60s, we were sure about one thing only: we weren't sure about anything, particularly when it came to women or girls. We understood them, but we didn't understand them. Like most guys who were shaped by the '50s mentality, we had a parochial view of women. We couldn't relate to them, we had a fear of commitment, and we were fearful of losing the male bonding. We couldn't talk with most women on an interpersonal level. Girls of our age tended to treat us as juveniles or younger brothers and we could barely relate to younger girls.

We understood this much: Girls didn't talk about sports, fights, color-plays, smiles. . . . They couldn't stay out all night . . . They couldn't, or wouldn't, drive us places . . . They couldn't go to Atlantic City or Ocean City alone or without permission (which was never granted) . . . They never get high or drunk . . . They didn't hang-out . . .

There were a few girls who could hang out at the Diner and carry on quite a bit, but they never earned tenure for hanging out. It was a sporadic and short-lasting thing. We respected these girls who were independent, rebellious or had "balls," although sometimes we overtly knocked them. But we tended to treat them better than the other girls.

We dreamed to convert loose girls, fantasizing that our sexual prowess would make them into a one-man woman.

The guys really couldn't wait to get up to the playground, pool-room or Diner to talk about what they had done with a girl and how far they had gotten. Whether it was true didn't matter so long as you could somehow validate or verify your story, particularly if you could bullshit better than the average guy, as long as it wasn't someone's sister. We even bragged about girls we were seriously dating for a long time, or even considered marrying. It didn't matter. It was the status that counted with the guys more than any-thing. So, in spite of the fact that many of us had anywhere from one to four serious romances, relationships or affairs, and some of the guys married in their late teens or early 20s, we still had no understanding of women or relationships with them. We only thought we understood.

For some guys, dating or marrying a virgin or a girl whom nobody knew about, maybe from another town, meant status. You'd fear what the guys would say if you dated or married a "used girl." We didn't try to deal with behind-the-back gossip, we only wanted to spread it.

Yet as important as it was for us to date or marry a virgin, we never wanted to take out girls who wouldn't screw. We broke up long-lasting romances when a girl either refused to screw or when sleeping with her somehow ended the entire affair. Not necessarily the first time, but after a while.

Marriage truly brought fear into our hearts. It was as if the com-mitment, the guilt and concept of the Jewish family unit, was so strong that it was very difficult to even confront the possibility of divorce—which you thought about even before you contemplated marriage.

Yet on the other hand, the Gentile guys we knew treated marriage as if it were still dating. They came and went as they pleased, at least that's what we observed. They could stay out all night drinking and carousing with the guys from dusk to dawn without remotely recognizing their marital vows.

Paradoxically, we were in awe of bright girls in elementary and secondary school. They were always smarter than we were, and yet when we got to college we realized that we had somehow caught up, in spite of ourselves. We lost respect for women having any intelligence whatsoever, or having something to talk to us about.

It was hard to talk about our true feelings with the guys, about how you felt about women, aside from the physical or adolescent love affairs. Maybe you could confide your thoughts to your closest buddy or to a sister. But it was difficult. It was like talking about politics or philosophy at the Diner. If somebody caught you, you would be serious knocked and ridiculed. Years later we realized that most of the conversation at the Diner, the poolroom and the playground was philosophical anyhow.

Women were always secondary whether they became a key girlfriend, spouse or lover. They were basically good posts, but they never came ahead of hanging out, or being at ballgames.

Although he floated from being popular to becoming outcast, Third typified what many of us felt about but were afraid to express publicly. Third wanted to repel or turn people off, or to discover their weaknesses.

Third never fitted in with the blues with whom he grew up around Druid Hill Park. He never fitted in with the middle-class Jewish kids at the Beth Tfiloh Hebrew School. He only related to Bruce Hawk who was also a student there. He was an outsider with the elite snobs in the Mu Sig fraternity, although he liked Bo Death and Burger because they didn't belong either. Third never really wanted to be labeled. He was antagonistic for no apparent reason, and was literally and figuratively alone in Baltimore. Third was fully aware that he could always fall back on occasional color-plays and his treatment of girls—so much different than others—that it permitted him to fit in at any time he so desired.

Third always felt women were stronger and smarter than men. But he forgot to tell us.

The Sixties:
The Age of
Enlightenment

They scream your name at night in the street,
Your graduation gown lies in rags at their feet,
And in the lonely cool before dawn,
You hear their engines roaring on . . .
And get to the porch and
Look on Thunder Road.

—Bruce Springsteen,
"Thunder Road"

1.

It was only fitting that a new decade would signal our independence in the guise of high school graduation. Independence took on a number of meanings. It meant college, work, the Army (a version of independence), marriage (questionable independence), and even unemployment.

In a sense, it didn't matter what we did. We knew we'd make it. I don't know why we felt that way, as we drifted about, oblivious to the world around us. Somehow we really believed that everything would turn out fine. We assumed we deserved it. So why not?

But before independence arrived, some events in early 1960 occurred which tried to pull me back into the '50s: My Spanish teacher threatened to keep me from graduating, forcing me to seek out a tutor—a chain-smoking, no-nonsense divorcee, giving me my first feeling that domination is not my bag; my mother was carried from the Senior Farewell Assembly after fainting, having seen me with bleached greenish/orange hair from peroxide and a sun lamp that didn't quite work; I made a major mistake questioning McAuliffe's punching out of Sharon Satler at Alan Kaplan's party— he was aiming at her date, Bill said, knocking me out cold into Kaplan's bath tub, and after I'm brought to, Kap's insisting I owe him $6 for the torn shower curtain.

By the fall of 1960, Mr. Fisher, the Queensberry Playground Director, has departed and he's replaced by Mr. Witted, a black man. We've moved uptown and I'm in college at University of Maryland, but I come back occasionally to the playground to see the guys and play ball. Things are changing. Many of the guys now are in the armed services, working, in college, or married. I miss them. It's not the same. Worse than that, in two sports in which I excelled—one-on-one basketball and stickball—I am surprised and defeated by two of the younger players. "Completely Bare" shuts me out 1–0 in a stickball game, and "Playground Larry," a New York transplant, wastes me in basketball 10–4. And even more embarrassing for a college guy: I have to leave the playground in full flight to avoid the pincers of The Gripper.

2.

Fenwick and I had become very friendly with Snyder when we entered University of Maryland. Snyder was a member of ZBT Fraternity and a sophomore. Although he hadn't made good enough grades and was prohibited from attending fraternity meetings, he influenced the rest of the "Brothers" in terms of the incoming pledge class. Ben was in the same boat. It became necessary to seriously fake-blow these guys in order to get invited to "rush" ZBT. Many other Jewish freshmen from Northwest Baltimore were in a similar situation.

One afternoon, Snyder suggested that Fenwick and I and a rich guy, Arnold Potter, go to the old Bel Air race track for the day. Arnold knew not a thing about horse racing, yet to show off, he bet $100 a race. Fenwick ran out of money by post time for the fifth race. He volunteered to be the "runner" for the rest of the guys, placing their bets at the window for the remainder of the day. Fenwick actually held the tickets in his pocket until the race was over, for good luck.

By the last race, Arnold, who hadn't picked a winner all day, decided to bet $300 on a long shot that we all snickered over, figuring the horse didn't have a prayer of even finishing the race. From nowhere the long shot won and paid 40 to 1, which meant $13,000 to Arnold. Everybody was jumping and hollering, figuring that Arnold was going to treat everyone to dinner and maybe girls.

Fenwick couldn't locate the winning ticket and flew into a frenzied fit trying to find it, tearing apart his pockets, ripping his shirt and jacket, and crawling around on the ground picking at every torn and whole ticket left at the track. This drama continues until 8:00 P.M.—the track is now empty and dark—when Arnold, pretending it's "no big thing," said to forget it. Of course, he was dying inside. As we were leaving the track, Snyder, who was impressed at the extent to which Fenwick went to find the winning ticket said, "Too bad, you must really be upset." Fenwick replies in a whisper, "Upset my ass, I 'booked' all the schmuck's bets; I'm up $500. Dinner's on me."

3.

Donnie Burger also attended the University of Maryland and we became friendly. He had gone to City and so we were, at best, just acquaintances. At Maryland that year, the administration stiffened the eligibility rule concerning pledging fraternities. A student's high school grades had to indicate a 2.0 average, which Donnie and a few other popular guys couldn't meet. Yet, during the rush parties, the fraternities weren't aware of who met or did not meet the new criteria. So Donnie attended many such functions. I vividly remember a situation at the TEP House where they were giving a dinner for prospective pledges. Donnie was sitting at a table with a stalk of celery in his hand. As he went to bite it, he twitched, and shoved the celery stalk into his ear. This caused Bernie Salgonik to spit his food out and roll of his chair laughing uncontrollably.

As University of Maryland freshmen, we were at our craziest. You could take us out of the playgrounds and the Diner, but you couldn't take the playgrounds and Diner out of us.

Because Maryland had become so crowded, hundreds of trailers were brought in to accommodate the '60–'61 incoming freshmen.

It was a big mistake. Our crowd took over the trailers, terrorizing the inhabitants, and seldom attending classes. There was so little time for it.

Security was non-existent in the trailer park and anyone could jimmy the door knobs and open any room. We roamed the area from midnight til dawn brazenly walking in on unsuspecting students, banging the aluminum sides of trailers with logs to terrify sleeping freshmen, letting mean dogs inside, turning on showers, tying guys to their beds while they slept, and changing hours on alarm clocks. Very mature stuff.

The University finally nabbed us at the end of the first semester. Fenwick, Burger and I were among 11 guys singled out by the Dean of Students to be placed on disciplinary probation. While lecturing us, the Dean said, "Out of the six colleges and universities which I have been Dean of, you are the most vicious, crazy, demented group that I have ever come across!"

He didn't realize what a great compliment it was or how much we ached for this kind of success.

Donnie dropped out of Maryland after two semesters. He was typical of those of us who couldn't handle the social and economic pressures, and maintain academic standards. Donnie transferred to the University of Baltimore.

4.

You will remember Rifkin as the guy who Ben used to knock about his acne. Well, aside from his complexion, he was neither tall, nor dark, nor handsome. Yet he consistently dated the prettiest girls and went with them for longer periods than any of us. Everyone envied the way Rifkin handled himself with the ladies. What many people failed to understand was Rifkin's Law, how he acquired these women. Rifkin had staying power. He could go out every night of the week, often to the same bar, at other times to different bars. He stayed until closing time. He got to know the bartenders, the bouncers, the owners, and the guys in the band. Girls became used to his presence. Eventually they began talking to him. He symbolized security, especially if they didn't recognize anyone else at the bar. In addition, Rifkin had a great personality and was a great dancer. Whenever you went to a bar, you saw Rifkin. He was *always* there, either sitting at the bar or dancing. Great-looking guys would come into the bar and wouldn't get so much as a glance from the girls who were with Rifkin. Nobody believed it, yet it was Rifkin's Law. He could hang in, night after night, place after place. No one knew how he managed to work during the day. He dated and slept with girls whom everyone dreamed of, particularly the "Buddy Deaners." These were girls who were full-time committee members on the "Buddy Deane Dance Show"—Baltimore's answer to "Dick Clark's Bandstand." Guys used to come home after school, sit in front of the TV sets, and go bananas over these girls. And Rifkin had the best of them!

The opposite of Rifkin's Law was the "10 percent guys" like Synder and Fan. These were guys who would go into a bar and hit on a lot of the girls. Snyder's approach was rather crude. He would go down a line of girls sitting at the bar or standing on a dance floor and whisper to each of them things such as, "God, I would love to eat you," or "I wouldn't know what to do to get your soft lips around my root." Most of the time the girls would either scream, slap Snyder, walk away from him, call for the bouncer, or vomit. However, there seemed to be one out of 10 who would giggle, and

Snyder then knew he had her.

The Fan had a different approach. He was a real good-looking guy, but not too swift when it came to personality with the ladies. He would use one pitch over and over again. He would tell a girl how he had fallen in love with her the moment he saw her. He would get so maudlin that it made you nauseous. Most of the girls told him to take a hike. But there was always 10 percent, the one girl who would say to herself, "Oh my God, this guy is gorgeous, I can't let him get away," and Fan would be in. I remember one time a guy standing, listening to Fan, shaking his head, getting disgusted, and finally sucker-punching Fan and the girl he was wooing.

5.

"Trunking" was invented by Fenwick. He used to keep all sorts of clothing and other essential items in his back seat and the trunk of his car—old clothes, new clothes he could change into, lacrosse equipment, chenilled letters that he was supposed to give out when he was lacrosse team captain, and a Chicago Bears cape that he and Swartzie stole during a Colt football game.

Fenwick had this old black Buick which his parents had given him and which had no reverse gear. (One time he drove a bunch of us up to see Mt. Washington Lacrosse Club play some team on Long Island; a very harrowing experience to say the least.) When Fenwick would get frustrated, he would open the trunk of his car, jump in and slam it shut. He could get out, but you couldn't get into the trunk since he had the keys.

A group of us were at Fenwick's mercy to be driven into Baltimore and back to College Park during our freshmen year at Maryland. We never knew when we would be kidnapped, or "napped," which was Fenwick's terminology for keeping you occupied while he went down and visited dirty bookstores on The Block, got a haircut, or pined away outside of some girl's house.

We were returning to the University of Maryland one evening on Rt. 29 where Fenwick said he was going to take a short cut, and we became lost. It was snowing pretty heavily and the guys were knocking him, calling him Magellan and Columbus, and kibitzing quite a bit. Fenwick pulled over to the side and declared, "That's it fellas." He leaped out of the car and ran to the trunk before we could stop him. He locked himself in the trunk for an hour and a half while we stood freezing in the snow, begging him to come out. A fake-promise to get him a girl finally saved us.

Following Spring Break that year, Fenwick gave Neurotic Nat Smertz and me a ride back to College Park. Neurotic Nat had an exam at 8:00 the next morning and therefore risked going back with Fenwick rather than trying to catch a bus to College Park. Since Fenwick and I were rarely, if ever, attending classes during that period, it was no big deal whether we got back to school at six or seven o'clock that evening, later that night, or not at all. Neurotic Nat, of course, did not imagine this, figuring, like himself, we had to prepare and study for our exams.

We hit Rt. 40 and, schmoozing around, Fenwick said, "Well, fellows, if I turn right we head down to school, but if I turn left it's New York!"

I goaded Fenwick on, "I don't give a shit, go ahead and go to New York."

Fenwick replied, "You don't care if I kidnap you?"

"No, it doesn't matter to me," I said.

Neurotic Nat thought that we were joking and joined in, "Yeah, who cares?" Words that he would later regret.

Fenwick turned left and about 25 miles later, Neurotic Nat began to panic. I continued to egg on Fenwick, daring him, calling him chicken if he turned back. These were the wrong words to say to the "Wick." He could have cared less. Fenwick drove on as Nat became increasingly neurotic. Nat finally went into hysterics and tried to jump out of the car. We held him tightly between us.

About 55 miles out, Fenwick pulled the car over, grabbed Nat, shoved him in the trunk and closed it. Fenwick then proceeded to drive another 70 miles before we stopped off at Howard Johnson's. He came out and screamed into the trunk that he would let Nat out to go the bathroom and have some coffee if he promised to behave. Neurotic Nat gave his pledge, but once inside the restaurant he starts screaming and yelling. Fenwick gripped him (a la the Gripper) to slow him down and threatened him with a number of well-placed phone calls. This silenced Nat for a brief period. Unbeknownst to us, Nat scribbled on a napkin which he handed to our waitress that he was being taken prisoner to New York City when he had an exam at College Park. Unfortunately, the waitress thought it was funny and tossed it back on the table. At this point Fenwick grabbed Nat, carried him outside, and trunked him again.

Wick and I drove on until we were about 30 miles out of New York and realized, to our chagrin, that we didn't have enough money to visit there. We told Nat that if he promised to cool himself out and did the driving back to school, we'd turn around. We were exhausted anyhow, so we jumped into the back seat and fell asleep.

Nat drove all night. He tried to conjure up whatever images he needed to study for the exam that morning and it kept him alert. Finally, Wick and I were jarred awake when Nat, having dozed off, drove into a ditch off Rt. 1. We leaped up and pounded on Nat outside of the car, and forced him to drive on. We barely made it to his class at five minutes to eight. Nat received a "D" on the test and didn't talk to us for weeks.

Fenwick would trunk himself on occasion. If one of the guys had a girl who he wanted to make out with in Fenwick's car it became a sort of closet scene, henceforth known as a trunk scene. Wick had made a hole from the trunk to the back seat. These closet-like trunk scenes were difficult in his car since the trunk smelled so badly from the old clothes and Fenwick's sweat.

6.

The ZBT fraternity at the University of Maryland in early 1961 suffered a great schism between the blowers and the non-blowers. The blowers in this case were guys who "blew" Ray Altman; that is, they worshipped Ray from the beginning of his sophomore year. The blowers ran the gamut of freshman, sophomores, juniors, seniors, hanger-oners of ZBT, and dorm rats [non-aligned students]. There were various types of blowers. The serious blowers were Ben, Wayback and Scar, who did everything Ray wanted them to do and were always at his side. Then there were guys who were a step or two below mensches or main men who could have possibly had a couple of blowers, but who opted to be a semi-blower of Ray's. And there were even fake-blowers, too selfish to be real blowers, yet blowing at opportune times.

The guys who pitted blowers against non-blowers were Snyder

and Turns. Thus the frat house split up, about two-thirds became blowers and one-third stayed non-blowers. It didn't really matter which side you were on since independence was the only criterion for being a non-blower. It did, however, create a number of factional disputes that lasted 20 years. Perhaps the most interesting sidelight was that Altman never really suspected that he was the cause of the schism.

Sometimes we forgot that not everyone understood our lingo and often took what we said literally. One day, Fenwick saw one of our fraternity brothers brown-nosing an instructor outside the student union and screamed, "Duffy, I see you blowing that teacher!" Duffy turned to the guys, shrugged his shoulders, and yelled back, "Choice?" A negativism meaning, "Like I really have a lot of choice about this? He may fail me." Some girls from a sorority who overheard Fenwick's remarks ran back to the dorm and told everyone that Duffy was having a homosexual affair with his teacher. Thirty years later, a few still believed it. The words blows, blowers, etc. were used so often during thè '60s that it's amazing that most of the guys in Northwest Baltimore and the Diner were not considered an early gay activist group.

7.

Something almost unimaginable happened to Ben when he got to college. He started losing his hair, putting on weight. He discovered he couldn't compete academically with the guys, especially guys he knocked or guys whose friendship he desired. Although he continued to be funny, some of the humor like "Hi me!" was losing its touch.

He lasted about a year and a half at the University before flunking out. He transferred to the Junior College of Baltimore, until he realized that he couldn't cut it academically. He never returned to College Park.

Ben got a job selling records for Mike Richmond (who had previously dropped out of Maryland to get married) at Mondawmin Shopping Center which was now predominantly black. Ben got along well with the blues and his personality brought many of them in to buy records. Because of his friendship with Mike, Ben only worked when he felt like it and alternated days with Brosy who, when he wasn't high on drugs, was an extremely skilled record salesman and money changer.

8.

Much of the sarcasm and knocking at the Diner, while vicious at times and funny at others, was considered by a few to be destructive to the sensitive and the defenseless. Yet, sometimes it could be inspiring and helpful. Take the case of Bob Glick. In the late '50s, he was overweight, a poor dresser, possessed a koala bear nose, and had zero self-confidence. A lot of the guys, especially Moses and Hart, would consistently tell Glick, "Hey, you look good," or "Yeah, you've got a nice looking coat on," or "You're the Man, we knew it all along!" While they did this in a sarcastic vein, Glick began to believe it, since nobody explained to him that it was knocking. Glick believed so many of these fake blows that he became narcissistic, lost weight, and somehow got better looking, and started dressing smartly. He even became overconfident and developed a superiority complex.

Glick attended Baltimore Junior College along with Bill McAuliffe and Barry Levinson. His confidence helped him date the prettiest girl in the school, Betty Brown. The one problem with this is that Betty Brown was almost engaged to Freddie Betz, the younger brother of Ernie, the former "big man on campus" at Maryland. Freddie was the "Lord's" brother. He attended the University of Maryland at College Park and saw Betty only on the weekends, and then only on Saturday nights, although they had been dating for almost five years.

Betty's affair with Glick became serious enough that Betz heard about it and put out word that he was going to "kill" Glick.

Meanwhile, McAuliffe had become friendly with Betty in class, and somehow Betz got him and Glick mixed up. One Sunday morning, Betz arrived at McAuliffe's apartment unannounced. He shook McAuliffe awake and proceeded to vilify him. McAuliffe made himself coffee and casually listened to the threats. Betz was a fairly big, tough guy who it was rumored had never been defeated, even though he hadn't been in many fights. McAuliffe realized immediately that Betz had mistaken him for Glick, but remained silent and got dressed. Then he and Betz drove out to a vacant lot where they fought for about a half hour until Betz realized that he was in over his head. He stopped, shook hands with McAuliffe, and never issued any threats again. Glick now had Betty all to himself. All Bill had were scrapes and bruises..

9.

Fenwick fell in love with Natalie Wood around this time and decided he was Warren Beatty after seeing the movie *Splendor in the Grass*. He became obsessed with the film and memorized the words of every actor. He walked around the Fraternity House screaming, "Pride? I have no pride!" It's the line Deannie (played by Natalie Wood) speaks in a scene with Warren Beatty. Then Fenwick consoled Deannie as he assumed Beatty's role. After viewing the movie as often as possible in the Washington Metro Area, he convinced me to join him to see it at the Charles Theatre one evening in downtown Baltimore.

Fenwick had a new Nash Rambler and he conned me into chauffeuring him by promising me to pay for a hooker on The Block. We got a late start, for a change, and it looked as if we were going to miss the beginning of the movie. But, who cares, I'd seen it already and Fenwick had seen it at least a dozen times. Nevertheless, Fenwick *had* to see it from the beginning. He went bananas. I took a dangerous shortcut outside the city limits and picked up the Falls Road extension. I was flying along and it looked like we're going to make the movie on time, when a cop pulled me over.

Fenwick was furious. I was fairly mad too, since I already had a few moving violation convictions and two pending tickets. The cop decided to lecture us a bit before writing the ticket and we arrived 20 minutes late for the movie. Fenwick was beside himself. He copied down the cop's name and badge number and threatened to cause him serious grief. Then, we watched the movie, which was unintelligible because Fenwick was speaking everyone's lines throughout.

Despondent over these traffic citations, I let Fenwick drive his own car back. I was pissed since he didn't have enough money for a hooker, but still insisted stopping on The Block. He told me he wanted to get a haircut at William's, the only barbershop employing mental defectives. Actually, it was a ruse to pick up some dirty books. We got back to the dorms at College Park late enough to use it as an excuse not to go to classes. As it happened, we hadn't been to classes for weeks.

Fenwick told me not to worry about the speeding tickets. He'd talk to his father who he said was a "crack" attorney. The only thing "cracked" about Fenwick's father *was* his father, and rumor had it that he'd never practiced law or even tried a case. I don't even know if he was a member of the bar. I remember that my mother told me he worked in the University of Baltimore Law School library for a very long time. In fact, he sat home while Fenwick's mother ran a lucrative real estate firm and supported the family very well. To Fenwick and his friends, his dad had a very pompous, elitist manner, he was always preaching. Mr. F. was always accusing Fenwick of various nefarious deeds, such as reading pornographic material and self-abuse.

I figure Fenwick's father isn't going to do me any good. In fact, I didn't want him to even try to help me. And I knew there were these brothers named Abbrotzi who owned a gas station in a blue collar area of Baltimore who will "fix" a ticket for $20. With that in mind, I didn't broach the subject with Fenwick and presumed he'd forget about it.

A few weeks later, we're over Fenwick's house for dinner. Fenwick brought up the traffic ticket and his father scolded me, insisting that I shouldn't fix it. He couldn't believe that people fix tickets. Mr. Fenwick was either totally naive or just wanted us to think that he was naive. I insisted that the Abbrotzi brothers could take care of it for $20 and it was guaranteed. I'd done it before and I didn't want to lose my license. But Fenwick's father was adamant and grabbed the ticket from me.

I became wigged out at this, so Fenwick decided he is going to burn somebody to make me feel better. He found the police officer's address and phone number, and proceeded, for the next several months, to make obscene telephone calls, accusing him of adultery. He also sent gifts like Lazy Dazy party trays of food, and charged them to the cop, as well as restaurant tabs, etc. He created so much grief, that a year later the policeman and his wife split-up.

In the meantime, my case came to trial and I grudgingly went before the judge with Fenwick's father. In a fast "defense and verdict" traffic court, my "mouthpiece" began a lengthy legal discourse. He'd suddenly become Perry Mason. I wanted to disappear. The courtroom was packed and I was about the 50th case heard. Everybody else had gotten off, either not guilty, or with probation, and here was Fenwick's dad acting like it was the Scopes Trial. He brought up my driving record, which was terrible, and it was unbelievable that he would do it since there was almost no way of confirming past violations in the early '60s—before computers. I'm ill. But, it appeared that the judge may be lenient since he knew Mr. F. My elation soon evaporated as Fenwick's father, in his closing argument, spilled to the judge that I wanted to fix the tickets and how I had planned to do it. Here was Fenwick's father giving me up completely to a judge who'd get half of the $20 fix. I threw myself on the mercy of the court. The judge suspended my license for a year and sent me to driver's education classes for eternity.

10.

That summer in Ocean City, Bob Litwin took a liking to a young lady named Darlene, a first year nursing student at Mercy Hospital. They hit it off right away and dated about half a year. Not only didn't Bob ever make it with this girl, he even admitted to not doing it, yet he still bragged about her.

Bob claimed that Darlene, hoping to maintain her virginity til marriage, was the ultimate superstar at "dry-humping." Now remember, they weren't teenagers. She was so great that Bob renamed her Darlene Dry-Fuck, a name that holds to this day.

Other guys dated Darlene and verified her remarkable skills and visually contemplated how great she'd be when some guy finally brought Darlene all the way.

Remarkably, a Diner guy actually married Darlene Dry-Fuck a few years later, let her support him through college and graduate school, and then divorced her. He sadly admitted to the guys that she was a bum lay and that the only way he could make it with her was a dry-hump in the kitchen. The culmination of the act for real was unfortunately "Passadena" [forget it, or pass on it].

11.

Bux the Gripper occasionally gripped women, too. One time I was with a girl we called "Fine" who was sort of promiscuous. Bux found out about her making it with a lot of guys and also that I could get her kind of easy. He insisted that I fix him up. Naturally, I couldn't refuse for fear of getting gripped or punched in the heart, so Bux let me use his car for "our" date. I put him in the back seat, covered him with a blanket, and drove out to the Wellwood Softball Field. While I was making out in the front seat with Fine, a cop pulled up. It appears that while I was involved with her, my foot kept hitting the brake causing the back lights to blink on and off. Some neighbors complained and called the police. The cop pulled me out of the car and asked Fine and me for I.D.'s. He then spotted Bux in the back seat. Fortunately for us, Fine kept her cool. While we were trying to explain our presence, the cop received an emergency call on his radio and told us to leave the field immediately. Bux was more angry at me than at the cop, or at Fine. He told me I was in deep trouble. Fine asked what he was doing in the car and what was going on, and when I confessed that I borrowed his car and didn't realize that Bux had fallen asleep in the back seat, she accepted the story. (Fine wasn't real bright.) She asked me what else he had in mind, and Bux looked at me and told her, "Chip's going to take care of me like he promised," and Fine became very upset since she had heard of Bux's grips and heart punches.

I was now in mortal fear and I pulled Bux to the side trying to "worm" out, but it didn't work. Either he was going to make Fine or he was going to grip me. We drove out to Liberty Dam, a local make-out spot. Bux told me to wait in the car, took a blanket and went up the hill with Fine.

I got out of the car and wandered around, kind of relieved, figuring that Bux was going to score with Fine and not grip me. I happened to find myself unwittingly staring at a car full of dirtballs who questioned me about why I was up there alone. What was I going to do, make love to my hand? That kind of stuff. I had a smart mouth in those days and gave them a little shit back, and they said they were going to get me. I ran up the hill and told Bux that a bunch of these "dirts" from Reisterstown were coming to get us. Bux grabbed Fine and the three of us jumped into his car and drove off. The other guys chased us in their car about two or three miles down Liberty Road at pretty high speeds. All during this time Bux was screaming at me that I was really going to get it, but luckily I was in the back seat and Fine was up front. Bux started gripping Fine just to kind of relieve the tension and she started crying out and scream-ing at me. All of a sudden, Bux slammed on the brakes and exclaimed, "What am I running for, I'm the Gripper. I don't run from anybody!" He got out of the car and quietly said, "Now the hunted turns on the hunters," and he ran straight at the other car. The "dirts" slammed on their brakes and saw this madman rushing at them. Bux had a big wrench in his hand that he had pulled from underneath his car seat, and he smashed it into the side of their car. The "dirts" threw their car in reverse and took off, terrified, despite the fact that there were at least four guys in the car with their girls.

Bux returned to his car pretty satisfied about what he had done with these guys and gave Fine a playful punch in the heart, probably more or less to feel her up. She was at the point of hysteria, and I tried to calm her down. At this, Bux told her to bite me on the arm or he was going to grip her. She immediately started biting my arm as hard as she could and I had to sit there and take it. Then, we drove Fine home and prayed that she wouldn't tell her mother about what had happened.

I knew there was a lot of the night left and that I was in for some serious heartache. We pulled up at Benny's Poolroom and I jumped out of the car quickly. Somehow Bux stopped the car, locked the doors, and caught up with me about 10 yards from the door and yelled, "Whoa, Skinny!" He call me "Skinny" Chip based on an Oriole baseball player named Hal "Skinny" Brown. He gripped me something fierce. It was one of the worst grips I ever received.

We went up into the poolroom and I figured that my punishment for the night was over since I told Bux not to worry about driving me home, that I would get a ride. While there, I ran into Fred Savage, a wealthy guy shooting pool. Bux went over and introduced himself to Savage, who went to Mt. Vernon night school with me. Sometimes Bux could be deceptively suave and debonair and would kind of lull you into a false sense of friendship. He was talking to

Savage and being very nice. This guy obviously did not have many friends and he was taken in by Bux. As we were leaving the pool-room, Bux told Savage he must be rather strong because it looked like he had powerful arms. Now Savage was in no way strong. He was fat, about 5´9˝ tall, and weighed about 220 pounds. All flab. We went over to where "Sav"—as Bux called him—had his car. I wanted to leave but Bux said that if I didn't want to get gripped real bad, I should stay. He wanted Sav and me to arm wrestle each other. Well, Sav protested a bit but Bux had built him up so that Sav figured that he could probably take me. We locked arms on top of the car hood and then Bux announced that "the loser's gonna get gripped real bad!" Sav didn't know what a grip was and he thought he was going to have some fun.

As we started arm wrestling, Bux would go behind me and say, "Come on, Chip," and then he would go behind Sav and say, "Come on, Sav." While he did this he would grip me in the waist and grip Sav in the arm, and it would kind of give me more energy. Finally, I defeated Sav four out of five times. The only time I lost to him was when Bux gripped me so badly that I lost my strength and almost blacked out from a reverse heart punch in the middle of the back. Well, the loser, Savage, was gripped so hard that it drew blood all over his fat body. I just took off and ran down Belvedere Avenue as fast as I could. It was dark out. Bux was so happy to find a new guy to grip that he didn't even pursue me. He just screamed out that he would get me in the next day or two.

12.

At the Glen Avenue Fire House, not too far from the Diner, every Christmas the firemen would construct a beautiful nativity scene. It received press coverage all over the East.

Yussel decided for a color play one day to steal the Baby Jesus from the manger. One night we spotted Yussel running around the Diner with the plastic baby doll boasting, "Yeah, I stole the Baby Jesus from the Glen Avenue Fire House manger just for a smile."

The theft received headlines in the local section of the daily news-papers, which is enough to send police rushing around like the

Gestapo. It developed into a very shaky situation.* Guys began avoiding Yussel like the plague, and we had no idea what was going to happen. We keep begging him to return the Christ child. Finally, about two weeks later and just before Christmas, Yussel returned the Baby Jesus to the crèche with a note, "Forgive me Father for I have sinned," pinned to it.

13.

Barry Levinson had very little ambition after high school. He went to Baltimore Junior College, almost as an afterthought. He did not want to go into his father's carpets and appliances business. Barry soon dropped out of junior college and sold cars. Then he decided to become a lawyer. This ambition didn't last, and he found himself reading everything he could find about television and movies. He re-enrolled at Baltimore Junior College determined to receive an Associate of Arts Degree in Broadcast Journalism.

14.

Following our freshman year at the University of Maryland, Fenwick and I planned to join the armed services. It was the fall of 1961 and we figured that we will get our patriotic obligation out of the way. In addition, as a result of observing veterans at College Park, we were convinced that: 1) We'll come back bigger and stronger because we'll be older and more mature, and this will definitely be an asset in inter-collegiate lacrosse; 2) We'll definitely have more money in our pockets and this will help out

---

*Anytime something bad happened to a Church or Christian facility, my mother was sure that pogroms would begin anew. When I told her that Yussel had stolen the Christ child, mom hid my sister Nancy in the basement for two days as though she was Anne Frank.

economically, along with the G.I. bill to pay for school; and 3) We'll score better with girls. There was a fraternity called the Deke House* (next door to our fraternity, ZBT) and these guys did marvelously with the girls. Because of their "worldliness" as a result of the armed services, and their age difference, they interested every co-ed in sight. They could also hold their liquor better than any other guys in college.

So Fenwick and I marched down to the Army, Navy and Marine recruitment offices in Baltimore. But we were summarily dismissed by the recruiters since there was nothing much happening in the world at that time that would need our services; they had met their quota of enlisted men; and we should finish school and come back as officers by taking ROTC. They said the armed forces felt they were going to be in short supply of officers. Fenwick and I lamented over this for about a day and a half, and then forgot about it.

15.

Murray was a typical All-American boy. He was a scholar-athlete at Forest Park, achieving high grades and excelling in football and lacrosse. Clean-cut, energetic, and extremely polite, Murray was a definite "most likely to succeed" candidate. He was six feet tall, athletically built, had a crew-cut and looked like a West Point Cadet. He had a chance to go to the Naval Academy or other fine military institutions, but following graduation he decided to attend Drexel University because of their excellent math and engineering programs. Then a strange thing happened. After barely a semester of college, Murray dropped out and went to New York's Greenwich Village to live.

---

* The Dekes used to sit on the roof of their fraternity house and drink beer. One day, the Dean came by and ordered them to put their beer away and get off of the roof or they'd be suspended. The Dekes threw their beer away, stood up, and pissed on the Dean. No disciplinary action followed.

16.

Snooty, who pledged ZBT with me and Fenwick at the University of Maryland, was also in Mu Sig with Third, Bo Death, and Ronnie Berger. He was the epitome of the effete snob. Although he did not come from a great deal of wealth, his family was well-to-do and he reveled in the assumption tht he was much better than everybody else. He was about 5´10˝, good-looking, and had this aloof, elitist type walk. Not a true playground or high school athlete, Snooty excelled in country club sports. He wouldn't think of soiling himself by engaging in competitive sports with Playground, poolroom or public school players.

He received his comeuppance when he came to Maryland and had to be friendly with common folks like me and Fenwick, his new frat brothers. We tended to bring the worst out in everybody and Snooty was no exception, although he took a little longer to break down because he was such a snob. We ended up nicknaming him "Snooty." Unfortunately for Snooty, he lived in the freshman trailers and so we would do wonderful things to him, like break in and devastate his room, terrorize his roomate, "bad mouth" him to other girls by propositioning them on the phone saying we were him, and constantly remove all of the light bulbs in his trailer. Another time we told him we had to use his room for sex scenes with some sorority girls, and 55 guys came through the door, occupying the trailer all night. He found out two weeks later it was really only my roommate Krooper whom we had dressed up like a girl for a smile. After awhile, Snooty became one of the guys, and, like many of us, he even screwed up in classes in spite of being a pretty bright student. He was placed on academic probation every other semester for two years.

In his sophomore year, Snooty came down with mononucleosis and had to drop out of school. When he recovered, he began running to build himself up. Soon he was running 10 to 15 miles a day. The guys couldn't believe it until we tried to keep up with him on the track at a local high school or on Bonnie View Country Club golf course. He ran us into the ground.

17.

The last time Fenwick and I stayed at the Algonquin was during our sophomore year in college. Fenwick was visiting his girlfriend Gail from Silver Spring, a would-be model living in New York at the Barbizon Hotel.

Gail, a very pretty girl, was meeting with her agent that afternoon when she ran into Carol Lynley, fresh from her movie role in *Blue Denim,* and asked if she wanted to accompany us that night. To Gail's surprise, Carol Lynley agreed, but cautioned that the date be confirmed by 6:00 P.M. or she wouldn't go. Gail relayed this message to Fenwick.

Fenwick was a very vicious person. He loved to see people "win," Ben's jargon for losing. Wick got this perverted pleasure from seeing guys in jackpots. He thrived upon it, even with me, and I was considered his best friend. For kicks he would call the FBI and tell them I was a Commie spy. And that was only for openers.

Fenwick and I were off to see the movie *The Sporting Life* on 42nd Street, and he purposely forgot tell me about Carol Lynley, or that I'm supposed to call her, or even that I have a date with her. Carol Lynley was on the mind of every guy in America. We showed up at the Barbizon later and Gail chastised me for 10 minutes for humiliating her and not calling Carol Lynley and breaking the date.

I went nuts and started walking towards the Penn Station, swearing that I'd never speak to Fenwick again. He was in pursuit with Gail and Bobby Weinblatt, who had somehow joined us in New York City. Fenwick needed me as a friend. It would take years for any other human being to understand or befriend him. I finally acquiesced after Fenwick promised to give me 32 legitimate "blows," his car for two months, and $135.

18.

Swartzie, Jules and Harold left for Las Vegas with $8,000. They were sure they are going to make a major score, perhaps enough to attend UCLA. Swartzie's '51 Chevy provided the transportation. On the way, they stopped in Richmond, Virginia, where Swartzie hustled a guy out of $1,000 in pool to increase their Las Vegas bankroll. While motoring down Rt. 46 in Texas, the car threw a rod. A gas station mechanic advised them that the car was finished, but he'd sell them another one for $500. This "new" car, a late '50 model, would run forever, he swore.

The guys didn't figure that this was a literal statement. They couldn't turn the car off. It ran all of the time. The motor would not stop.

In New Mexico, upon leaving a motel, the guys decided to steal some linen just in case they needed sleeping material. Ten state troopers pulled them over after driving 20 miles from the motel, and they had to pay a $500 fine.

The three finally arrived in Las Vegas and checked into the Stardust where they quickly lost $2,000 the first night playing craps. Although they dreamt for months how they were going to take Vegas, things didn't go according to plan.

The next day, Swartzie and Harold decided to take jobs at the Showboat as bus boys. It appeared to be a good move—free jackets, bow ties, and free dinner before work. However, they found the work too tough and quit the next day. Jules, who had said that he would wait and see how the jobs went, was pleased that the guys had quit. For the next two days they proceeded to lose the rest of their bankroll. They were now totally broke.

Their attempt to sell the "run forever" car failed when it finally destroyed itself on the Stardust lot after catching fire. A distress call home to their parents yielded "return home" money and included an extra $150 which the guys immediately lost in a desperate attempt to break the bank.

So the three boarded a slow cross-country train, destitute. In the dining car, they'd wait for people to get up and leave so that they could finish any leftovers. They even rummaged through trash cans for half-eaten rolls. At a stopover in Chicago, Swartzie went through the phone booths looking for change and found eighty cents. He bought a submarine sandwich and cut it into thirds. It would be their last meal until Baltimore.

19.

Lon Angel, a borderline basketball and lacrosse player, disliked a group of beatnik Baltimore University students and bohemians. He ridiculed them, which wasn't funny, and picked on weaker members like Dan Gold.

A year earlier, Gold had attended National University in Mexico City to study archeology. He thought it would be a wise thing to do, hoping he would eventually become a writer like Jack Kerouac. But he found that the school was very conservative. He did not appreciate that a lot of the Mexican students whistled at him as he walked by them.

Gold was born to fairly wealthy parents. His father was a successful but very domineering lawyer. Although quite spoiled, Dan was accepted because of his gift for gab and trivia.

Angel had just broken up a radical discussion in which Gold was enticing some students to return the Hope Diamond to its owner—the ground. He was planning his strategy to steal it from the Smithsonian Institute and re-bury it in South Africa. He had great vision.

A few minutes later, in an English class with Gold and Donnie Burger, Angel walked by Burger's desk and said, "Hey Burger-Bits, how ya doing with the diamond?" To which Burger responded with a sucker-punch that knocked Angel over three rows of desks and rendered him unconscious. Angel was 6'8", kind of lanky, and had a reputation for being rough. Up until that day.

20.

Third heard about Murray's move to Greenwich Village and asked him to come to Baltimore and meet with some people whom Third considered very hip. He introduced Murray into this "in" scene in an apartment on downtown Charles Street, where 20 people are sitting around getting high. Murray began to lecture them and explain "The Community of Hip." His hair was now very long and he was wearing little round glasses. He concluded by saying, "You know you can live in New York free—in the Village you live free!" Dan Gold woke up when he heard this. He asked Murray if he's gay, thinking that the only way you can live free was if a guy was keeping you and you were gay, or if you hustled gays on the street. Murray assured him that was not the case. You do live for free in New York.

Murray had another adage, "New York City equals drugs." Third and Gold decided to leave for New York immediately. A facet of "living free" that Murray failed to mention was that he was living on a rice and beans diet.

Although Third did not need permission to go to New York, Gold's father would let him go only if he enrolled there in the New School of Social Research.

Claire was a hip girl who worked for *Vogue*. In addition to being quite stylish, she was a very tough-talking woman, whose father owned an airline. She had a Joan of Arc look. Her main quote was, "I don't know how to fight, but I go for the eyes." She had brown hair, was 5'7", and slender.

A few years earlier, Claire was in a hotel room in Spain with five other people including her husband, Shotgun Bill, a folk hero of expatriates at the time. The Spanish police raided the place and found a lot of marihuana and guns, and suspected that these people were there to attempt to assassinate President Franco. Claire took the fall for everyone and spent two years in prison, during which time she had a baby.

She met Third, Dan Gold and Murray at Dukes, an all-night place in the Village, where she was now an ultra-hip waitress. Claire took the guys to a couple of French movies, *Jules and Jim* and *Breathless,* which became big influences on their views of life.

21.

Fenwick just couldn't stand being gripped anymore. He couldn't bear the humiliating experience. One night, he came to the Diner and Bux was leaning against the window out front with a bunch of the guys. Fenwick figured that he was definitely going to get gripped since Bux had probably gripped everyone else already.

Fenwick was a big bluffer who fantasized that he could handle himself well, but really couldn't. In fact, he lived in a kind of fantasy world. As a student at the University of Maryland, Fenwick took a promotional picture of Jimmy Welsch, a half-back for the Colts in their glory years, and superimposed his own face on Welsch's body. He'd tell girls at Maryland and Montgomery Blair High School that it was a photograph of him. Once when Fenwick was staying in a New Orleans' hotel, he had the front desk page him as Jimmy Orr, another Colts football player. It never worked because no one ever came up and said, "Hi, are you Jimmy Orr? Can I have your autograph?" And no girls ever swooned: "You're Jimmy Welsch, we would like to take you on." But Fenwick really loved the ploys.

On this night, Fenwick resolved he was not going to take the grip anymore and, as Bux came out to greet him, he ripped off a car aerial and began swinging it back and forth yelling, "Bux, don't you come near me! If you do, I'll kill you. I've had it with your grips! I'll cut you to ribbons with this aerial!"

The Wick was swinging it about, and Bux feigned fear. The Gripper swayed back and said, "Easy, Fen. Just kidding. Just kidding. I wasn't going to touch you." Fenwick kept this up for a while as he saw he was playing to a big audience and that guys were awed that someone was actually standing up to Bux. He took advantage of it, which was a big mistake.

Bux went back over by the Diner window and let Fenwick hoot and howl and carry on, and then he said, "Fenwick, I'm sorry. You stood up to the Bux and you're a bigger man than anybody here. I'm proud of you. I'll never touch you again. I didn't know it bothered you that much. I was just having fun."

In a disarming way, he added, "Look Fenwick, put down the aerial. You stood up to the Bux. Come on in and I'll buy you a cheeseburger. I'm real proud of you. And maybe *you* and I will go around gripping other guys!"

Bux then thrust out his hand and exclaimed, "I wanna shake your hand, you proved you're a man."

Fenwick replied, "Nah, you're gonna grip me when you shake my hand." But Bux got serious and said, "I give you my word. This is it, you've got the word of the Gripper. I'm never gonna bother you again. You stood up to me."

Fenwick put down the aerial and, after a few seconds of thinking it over and figuring he had won a major battle, smugly went over and shook Bux's hand. He shook it, and kept shaking it, and then all of a sudden realized that Bux's hand was growing tighter around his wrist and his hand. As Fenwick tried to jerk away, Bux yelled, "Don't you ever, *ever* try to stand up against The Gripper again!"

Bux began gripping the Wick unmercifully and threw his left hand (his more powerful one) around Fenwick's waist and dug his nails into him, ripping skin and stuff out of his ribs. He marched him up and down the parking lot, forcing him to walk on his toes and squeal, to Bux's delight. Nobody ever stood up to the Gripper again.

On another occasion, one of the Ten Boys, Murray Kirschner, who had heard stories about Bux but disbelieved them, was sitting in the Diner and saw Bux come by. He told Bux he had heard about him and would like to meet him and wanted to shake his hand. Bux extended his hand. He'd never met the guy before in his life, and Kirshner was smiling and looking at people wondering what all the crazy stories were about. Suddenly, Bux squeezed his hand and pulled him out of the booth over the table and onto the next booth where he gripped him senseless.

22.

Swartzie and Boogie were casing the Embers Motel in Atlantic City on a Fourth of July weekend looking to pillage some rooms for "pin" money. Their surveillance uncovered several maids ripping off the rooms before they themselves could. Angry, Swartzie and Boogie robbed the maids' room where the women kept their street clothes and purses. The guys thought of themselves as Robin Hoods.

23.

In 1962, with nothing better to do, Yussel, Swartzie, Boogie, Jeff Hall, Hart, Shade, Barry Sell and Charlie-Bo-Death joined various arms of the military. Some envisioned it as a branch of Bennie's poolroom becoming a government agency.

Yussel and Hart took the Air Force entrance exam together. Yussel scored well but Hart failed most sections of the test, barely passing the section for cook, air cop and latrine cleaner.

Bo Death and Yussel enlisted in the Air Force; Hart, Shade, Jeff Hall, Swartzie and Boogie joined the National Guard; and Sell went into the Army.

After boot camp, Boogie, Swartzie, Hart, Jeff Hall and Shade were all assigned to a Guard Unit on Liberty Road not far from Bennie's. Our patriotic weekend warriors couldn't bear the Saturday and Sunday meetings and the discipline. It interferred with their poolroom and Diner activities.

Boogie became livid after a sergeant continued to heap verbal abuse upon him for untidiness. He knocked the guy out with a sucker-punch and was banished from all future weekend meetings. Other than that, nothing happened to Boogie, not even a court-martial. The other guys became jealous and sought to duplicate Boogie's rash feat.

Hart was short, stocky and muscular with kinky brown hair and a twinkle in his eye. Aside from Ben and Snyder, he was the most naturally funny guy at the Diner. His sarcasm was so finely tuned, it was often difficult to detect. Hart was in superb physical condition and well respected as a street fighter.

His buddy Shade was a tall, ruggedly handsome guy who was a former All-State football player and wrestling champion. Shade seldom got into fights, unless pushed to the outer limits of his control. Shade was basically selfish, and could not or would not take orders from anybody. He was just interested in doing "his thing."

Although Hart had enormous respect for the physical aspects of military life, he was the typical "Sad Sack" of the National Guard. He didn't make his bed, couldn't give his shoes a spit shine, dress properly, assemble or disassemble a rifle, or tie a square knot. Shade did it for him. They were both considered "goof-offs."

At summer camp, Shade often overslept and was punished for it. His punishment, fill water barrels with his helmet liner.

The morning of the punishment, Shade failed to show. The sergeant marched into the barracks, found Shade asleep, and tried to wake him. "I'm sleeping," growled Shade, "Don't bother me!" The sergeant strode out and brought back a lieutenant, later the captain. Shade's response was exactly the same. Finally, they summoned the company commander who stormed in screaming at Shade to roll out of the cot at once. From his prone position Shade responded, "Take a fucking walk!" Court-martial proceedings were initiated.

At the trial Shade, a normally mean looking guy, walked in looking sad and pitiful. He was facing serious stockade time.

Hart was Shade's sole character witness and, when called to testify, was a nervous wreck. He addressed the judicial hearings board. "Your honors, I'm used to speaking in my own way and not military talk. Can I use my own words?"

The judges agreed. Hart began a lengthy narrative. "I've known Shade all my life. He could never wake up in the morning, even under threats from his father. He's a great guy. . . ."

The judges and lawyers couldn't shut Hart up. He kept saying he was not finished and went on and on. It got so crazy that the M.P.'s were summoned and dragged Hart from the stand and the courtroom. He was still praising Shade.

The judicial panel was so pleased to be rid of Hart that they sentenced Shade to only two days in the stockade. Yet he still had to attend weekend meetings.

24.

Only three major scandals hit Northwest Baltimore between the '50s and the '80s, and two of them rocked the Jewish neighborhood early in the '60s. The first involved a half dozen peripheral Diner guys who were unaware (so they said) that a girl they had group sex with one spring afternoon was just 16 years old. It was not her first sexual marathon, but when her mother overheard her account of the experience to a girlfriend that evening, the girl altered the story a bit. Confronted by her enraged father, she said she was forced into it. Her dad immediately called the police and, within hours, all of the participants were arrested.

Although he was there, Neurotic Nat was not arrested, since he did not, in the legal sense, "cohabitate" with the young girl. It was not that Nat wasn't interested, but he was assigned last place in line. While waiting, Nat noticed that in the dimly lighted bedroom the girl resembled less an object of desire than a beached walrus. So Nat busied himself rummaging through the underwear of the mother of the guy whose house they used, losing all interest in live sex for that day. In all the commotion, no one complained about the underwear that turned up missing. God knows what Nat did with it.

An attorney was retained to approach the girl's parents with the real story and to negotiate a deal to drop the charges. But, the girl's father was still livid and decided to proceed.

Later, the girl confessed and her parents decided to negotiate a settlement. But it was too late. The story was leaked to the press and the judge refused to allow the charges to be dropped, insisting that it remained rape under the law.

A month later, in a jam-packed courtroom, the case was heard. Fenwick drove in from the University of Maryland and was joined by dozens of other guys to not only witness the proceedings but give support to the accused—all secretly thankful that they weren't involved.

But soon they come to regret their attendance at the trial when the defendants' lawyer dispersed the accused guys throughout the courtroom and insisted that the girl pick out the "rapists." While the bewildered minor dallied for what seems like an eternity in front of "innocent" guys, two of the real defendants almost escaped identification by lying on the floor behind the benches until she found them.

The half-dozen were found guilty and sent to Boys Reform School for six months. It was not the verdict or the sentence that hurt as much as the knocks that followed them for 25 years.

The second scandal occurred a year later when shocked Baltimore County police uncovered a high-priced prostitution ring operating out of a Pikesville Motel discovered during a mistaken drug bust. Five of the Jewish upper-crust's most beautiful married women, some for kicks and others for extra "pin" money, were running a call-girl operation catering to traveling salesmen. They had installed a two-way mirror in adjoining motel rooms and would take on who-ever "turned them on."

Like many other guys who'd heard about the new hookers, Neu-rotic Nat Smertz arrived in the ante-room disguised as an out-of-town salesman, and, following some spirited negative discussion among the women, was finally accepted as a customer. Nat nego-tiated his desires with one of the women, telling her that he wants to tie her up and spank her just a little before they have sex. The woman was a pampered "princess" who has only had missionary sex during her marriage and would allow foreplay with her husband only with her eyes closed. She freaked out at Nat's suggestion of bondage, then recognized him and threatened to tell his mother. Nat's ardor was seriously reduced by this threat and he went home celibate, less the money he paid up front. Nat later realized that the more guys who had sex with this woman, the less likely she would squeal on him. He told everyone he had a great time, and for awhile, the little sex operation did a land-office business.

The police, called to the motel for an unrelated reason, crashed into the wrong room, discovered the ring, arrested the women and transported them to the country lock-up. However, before the ladies are officially booked, the whole matter was quashed. But word leaked and instead of letting it die, their husbands forced the motel to take out a newspaper ad warning that "anyone caught spreading rumors of a prostitution ring made up of Jewish matrons operating out of a Pikesville Motel will be sued." Great move. This fueled the story for another 20 years.

The third scandal involved a vicious marital separation and divorce settlement in the early '80s. Sexy blonde Deena Wellbilt visited her husband in an intensive care unit following a severe heart attack and broke the news that she was leaving him. She informed him that she'd also changed the locks at their palatial estate in the valley. Dick Wellbilt, 12 years older than his spouse, survived a second coronary following Deena's visit. He subsequently hired a team of detectives and attorneys to place his estranged wife under 24 hours' surveillance, and to work relentlessly to keep her from stealing half of his vast fortune. The litigation would be difficult since Deena was very bright, with influential friends in high places.

The Wellbilts belonged to Jewishdom's fanciest status symbol, the Showboat Country Club, and Deena had been amorously involved for over two years with a couple of the members. This was not in itself scandalous since adultery was not unusual for hedonists belonging to S.C.C.; yet Deena, a gregarious type, had numerous male visitors to her home. Dick and Deena built the house together. It had an indoor racquetball court, sauna and steam rooms, an indoor/outdoor swimming pool, discotéque, etc., and was a gathering spot for Deena's friends following the separation. The private detectives staking out the home had a field day taking pictures, recording license plates, jotting down names, dates, and activities, and employing video tapes and well-hidden "bugs" to record conversations, etc. Money was no object, for Dick's vindictiveness knew no bounds.

Deena got wind of the surveillance too late to warn her friends. Between rumor, paranoia, and lovers of gossip the scandal exploded. Twenty-six prominent members of the Showboat C.C. were allegedly named as co-respondents in the divorce proceedings.

A rumor had it that the *Daily Record* and *Jeffersonian,* publications dealing with legal cases, decisions, zoning variances, "subpoenaed" adulterers, etc., was about to publish all 26 names. Supposedly the names also included women so the scandal reached epic sexual proportions. Innocent friends and visitors of Deena were mortified. The majority of them were "taped." Married men who visited to play racquetball or went over for laughs began to make excuses to their wives, thus bringing "heat" on themselves. Several club members, totally innocent, were so scandalized that their wives left them. Other guys who couldn't get a girl in Thailand or who haven't gotten amorous in years actually tried to *buy* their way onto the "list" or lied that they were *definitely* on it.

Neurotic Nat Smertz characteristically bragged too much that he had participated in all the goings-on at Deena's. Deena found out and confronted Nat at Miller's Deli on Reisterstown Road. Defiant to the end, Nat maintained he was a valued member of the Deena set. Deena became so enraged that she punched Nat in the chest as he calmly ate a hot dog. She then squirted him in the face with the mustard container. Nat proudly wore the mustard-stained shirt for two months.

Yet, when the case finally came to trial, not only was there no list of 26, but the judge would not allow tapes into evidence. Dick, on the advice of friends and associates, finally reached a settlement after three days of front page stories sensationalizing the case. Perhaps Dick realized that he would have no reputation as a stud if he exposed his wife as a raging nymphomaniac. The scandal went on through the entire summer of 1983.

25.

After leaving Forest Park in Baltimore, Fat Ellen Cohen hung around the D.C. area for almost a year before moving on to Manhattan to live in a series of rundown apartments, trying to start a show business career. She began as a folk singer in small Greenwich Village clubs. Then she sang as soloist with a number of different groups. Somehow she auditioned and was given a part in a touring company of *The Music Man*. She returned to New York to join a group called the Mugwumps, which included John Sebastian and Denny Doherty. Ellen fell madly in love with Denny and started following him around like a puppy.

26.

Rob Glick had an older brother named Sol who one day procured a couple of lovelies from lower Pimlico to take on some of the guys. They went over to Glick's place, and the guys, while waiting their turn, wandered about the house or sat on the front porch since it was a pretty summer day.

Forty-five minutes into the scene, a dozen motorcycles pulled up to the house and some nasty-looking "dirts" from Woodlawn led by a tough named Meehan approached the porch. It seemed they were also dating these girls and were extremely upset at the competition. Berdoff, the Gripper's protegé, stood in their way, but was immediately dragged onto the front lawn and beaten. Bill McAuliffe was sitting on the porch when three of the guys came running out of the house to see what the comotion was. These were no weak men: Snyder, Shade and Hart. But discretion being the better part of valor, they stood back and watched Berdoff being punched into submission. McAuliffe finally turned to the guys and yelled, "Come on, let's help Berdoff! Let's go get 'em," and leapt into the fray. Unfortunately, no one followed. The guys scurried into the house, hiding under beds and in closets. Meehan and his Woodlawn thugs proceeded to beat the hell out of McAuliffe and then departed.

Two months later, Bill was standing in front of the Diner when, to his surprise and delight, a car pulled up and he recognized a guy who dashed into the Diner to buy cigarettes. It was Meehan, without his back-up. McAuliffe walked over to him and said, "Hi, remember me?" Swiftly, Bill punched him three straight times in the face, got him in a head-lock, and then pulled him behind the Diner to an alley backing a number of row houses. Meehan was then dragged from house to house as Bill smacked him in the head repeatedly with the trash cans. Bill's vengence left a lasting impression on Meehan.

27.

During the summer, Ben would take off for Ocean City, New Jersey, and work in Somer's Point, about 20 minutes outside of Atlantic City. As I remember, it was only a three-sided pier with a few huge bars that drew big crowds during the summer months. Ben started as a bartender and occasionally worked the door at Tony Mart's. Eventually he became the key doorman and an associate bouncer. By this time, Ben had lost most of his hair, and had put on a good deal of weight. To alleviate the fat boy stigma, he began lifting weights and building up his upper body and arms. Ben had a lot of heart and never ducked a fight. By working in Somer's Point for the next couple of years, he developed quite a following, not only with guys driving up from Baltimore to hang around Tony Mart's and after-hour places, but also with a lot of locals from New Jersey, Pennsylvania and New York.

Ben coined the word "ticklers" to stand for guys who were extremely rough. For example, let's say a guy was a bouncer working at Tony Mart's. He was either a college football player or a street thug from South Jersey or Philadelphia. To tickle someone meant really blasting, knocking out, or punching someone senseless. Ben played off the word ticklers with sayings such as, "I saw this spade tickle this guy the other day," or "I heard McAuliffe really tickled some guy from Sigma Phi!" Sometimes he would scare a guy by telling him, "If you keep bothering me, I'm going to tickle your head!"

There's a classic story Ben told about when his band of ticklers (the doormen and bouncers at Tony Mart's) met their match one July weekend night. This bar patron was supposedly getting a little too obvious in his intentions with a local girl known to all of the guys at the bar, and he was told to leave Tony Mart's. The patron was about 6′1″ or so, weighed about 170 pounds, and wore wire rim glasses. He certainly didn't look tough in his plaid bermudas and knee-high brown socks. Ben started knocking the guy and called over to the bouncers, but the patron refused to leave. They threatened to take him outside and tickle his head. The patron surprisingly obliged Ben and the huge bouncers and walked out back of Tony Mart's.

On the way out the door, Ben grabbed a pool cue which he would use at times just in case a guy proved difficult as an opponent for five against one. He'd break it over the troublemaker's head or back. As Ben came through the door, he's shocked. Three of the four bouncers were already on the ground and the other was being rudely put away. The patron hadn't even taken his glasses off when he ripped the pool cue from Ben's hand, hit him with it, and then knocked him upside-down.

The patron turned out to be Terry Barr, an all-pro with the Detroit Lions. When Tony Mart, a real football groupie, discovered it was Barr, he heaped humiliation on Ben. He made him drive Barr around, fake-partying with him the rest of the weekend.

28.

Boogie was seriously dating Joanie, a very pretty and vivacious cheerleader from Milford Mill, a Baltimore County high school. They got married when she was 17. Her family had money and owned an auto parts store. They took Boogie in, hook, line and sinker. They gave him a job and rented them a little apartment, and Joanie's mother came over every day to cook, clean and make the beds. Joanie became a hairdresser and, within a couple of years, won every conceivable award in the field of hairstyling throughout the Baltimore-Washington area. Boogie dropped out of sight. He had a lot of money in his pocket, and didn't need the Diner scene anymore. The guys were disappointed, but they understood and left him alone. He began to gamble serious money.

29.

Ford Lessans was the '50s prototype of "Mr. Popularity." Tall, good-looking, great personality, rich, with a sports car. A great athlete too. He held the State 100- and 200-yard track records for over a decade. Ford was also an ex-Marine. He was married for about four months to Sue, Third's original love. Their relationship ended because of Sue's excessive spending and Ford's overreaction to it. When Sue would buy expensive clothing, Ford would retaliate by buying himself expensive clothes. She left him to pursue a business career in Washington and New York. Ford moved to downtown Baltimore near the Maryland Institute of Art, a big move for Ford, at least in those days, considering the Jewish guys' fear of *downtown*.

30.

It was August of 1963. Sell* was in Algeria in the Army. He sent a letter to England to Yussel in the Air Force, advising him that Bo Death is in Tripoli, Libya. Yussel, however, was already in Tripoli on temporary duty. He took the assignment to get some sun and go to the beach. He was the company clerk and he set up temporary assignments whenever he wanted to.

As company clerk, Yussel became a top dog in the black market by counterfeiting ration cards. At one point, he was under investigation by all three branches of Military Intelligence. It was one of the reasons that he decided to take a medical disability discharge from the service. The ration cards bought cigarettes, food, liquor, cigars, nylons, etc. He would sell these goods to the English for double or triple the cost to him. It was very inexpensive for armed forces personnel to purchase these with their ration cards. Yussel would sell the contraband as a huckster in Soho and in the Portobellow Road Market. He would carry a big bag over his shoulder, and knock on doors in seedy neighborhoods. He profited handsomely.

Anyhow, Sell's letter told that Bo Death was at the Tripoli Air Force Base, at that time one of the largest in the world. The letter was forwarded to Yussel and he called up Bo Death who was elated to hear from him and couldn't wait to get together. They ended up playing endless ping-pong games.

Bo Death hated Tripoli, as did most people. It was a horrible place to be. They couldn't fraternize because of the Arab situation; no families were permitted. Guys were going bananas because of the monotony. It was a drag. On one occasion Yussel and Bo Death met two Italian girls and double-dated with them and took them to the movies. They couldn't even touch the girls since the entire family followed them to the movies and to dinner afterwards. To make

---

* Sell was a Queensberry guy. He had long arms, was left-handed, a good athlete and nice looking. He was younger than most of us but dated older girls; and did such crazy things that he was accepted by playground and poolroom guys two years his senior.

matters worse, the American movie was dubbed in Italian with Arabic subtitles. Fortunately, the guys were high on hashish when they watched it, so it didn't matter. Unfortunately, they had to treat the girls' families to dinner and the movies. That mattered!

31.

"Trophy-banging" to Nervous Nat meant getting it on with a celebrity.

The history of Neurotic Nat's trophy-banging goes back to the early '60s when he discovered the famous stripper "Myrna the Body," on the beach in Atlantic City. A dedicated voyeur from early puberty, Nat was infatuated by strippers who used to play the circuit in Baltimore and Atlantic City. Myrna the Body was a touring headliner who stripped everywhere. Nat had seen her at the Globe Theater in Atlantic City, and at the Gayety Theater on "The Block" in Baltimore. Nat instantly recognized Myrna's body lying on the beachfront of Massachusetts Avenue. After two hours of getting up his nerve, he approached her and asked why she was checking baseball batting averages and taking notes on items from the sports page. Nat remarked that he had recognized her from her performances. She was his favorite stripper, he said.

Myrna was 6'1" tall and well endowed, particularly in her upper body. She wore a triple D bra. Myrna told Nat she was an avid sports fan, particularly a baseball fan. She followed several players whom she had known ever since they played in the minor leagues. (Later, Myrna confessed she had slept with many minor league players for the avowed purpose of following their careers after they went up to the majors, but she never screwed around with major leaguers.) Myrna had carnally known many of the present Oriole squad when they played for Rochester, because she had stripped at one of the clubs in that city.

Nat and Myrna hit it off immediately. They had several lunches and dinners together. As their friendship grew, she informed him that she preferred women but that she was kind of a sports trophy-banger herself. Although Nat begged and begged, she would never allow him to make love to her.

You know how people talk about where they were when President Kennedy was shot, and how they reacted that evening when the realization of his death hit them? Well, I can remember vividly where Nat and I were that night, and it is not an ordinary traumatic memory. Myrna the Body was in Baltimore to begin an engagement at the Gayety Theater. She told us that morning to arrange to have an early dinner with her and then go back to my house. My mother was away at the time. Later we would take in her show and meet her at a bar on The Block after an ice hockey game.

Myrna called us late that afternoon saying that to her dismay The Block was going to be closed for the rest of the day because of President John F. Kennedy's assassination, so we would probably have a late dinner and then could all go to the hockey game together. We picked Myrna up that evening and ate at Mandel's Deli. Following dinner, we paraded through the Diner for "blows" and then drove up to my place. We never did get to the hockey game.

32.

A very heavy snowstorm fell on the night that Fenwick and I double dated at the Alcazar for the Sigma Phi Christmas Dance. After the dance, Fenwick's car broke down, for a change, and we were stuck at a gas station on downtown Charles Street. We called the Diner knowing that even at two in the morning there'd be someone there to come down and get us. We spoke to Turko who was delighted to pick us up. He asked the Diner crowd who wanted to come along. Five guys volunteered since they had nothing better to do.

As they drove on, the snow got heavier. It was soon treacherous. Harold Goldsmith, nicknamed Oliver and later called just Ollie, was part of the ill-fated mission to Las Vegas with Swartzie and Jules. He was riding shotgun as they skidded on Mt. Royal Avenue towards Charles Street, "You'd better go easy here Turko, it's snowing real bad. This is one dangerous curve." Turko boldly replied, "Ollie, I happen to be one of the *better* snow drivers!" Moments later Turko lost control of the car and slammed into the front plate glass window of Luby Chevrolet.

We made frantic calls to the Diner. Bruce Hawk responded by stealing his cousin's car, which was scary since he didn't have a driver's license. He picked up Fenwick and me and our dates, as well as Turko, Ollie, and the other three passengers in the car in the Luby Chevrolet showroom. For months later, we referred to Turko as "The Better Snow Driver."

33.

Bill McAuliffe went to Baltimore Junior College and worked part-time as a Tin Man. He canvassed for aluminum siding salesmen. He also happened to receive straight A's during his two year stay and was rewarded with a scholarship to Johns Hopkins University, where he could complete his undergraduate education. His excellent academic effort at Hopkins resulted in his admission to Phi Beta Kappa.

34.

One night at a small folk music club in Washington, D.C., Ellen Cohen and the Mugwumps were entertaining. Recently divorced Sue, who was working on Capitol Hill temporarily, and dating boring guys from Harvard Law School, showed up at the club to watch the act. She knew Ellen from high school, but not well. Sue obviously was attracted to one of the Mugwumps, Zal Yanovsky. She met him and they dated for the next couple of months. She also became friends with Ellen Cohen.

35.

Boogie was $5,000 in debt to a bookmaker named Billy the Kid, a top dog in the Baltimore underworld. When Boogie couldn't raise the five grand, Billy the Kid advised him that he would arrange to have him killed. Billy had threatened the same thing from time to time. Boogie told his brothers-in-law that he was in a big jam. One said, "Don't worry, we'll report this to the Police Commissioner!" Boogie's naive brothers-in-law went to the cops and said, "We've got the name of a big bookmaker in town. It's Billy the Kid. He's threatening to kill our brother-in-law unless he comes up with five grand. So you'd better go out and arrest him."

The police chief calmly responded, "We *know* who Billy the Kid is, and we know what Billy the Kid does. But we can't do a thing to Billy the Kid until he kills Boogie. Right now no real crime has been committed. Also Billy the Kid will deny what you told us!" With this startling revelation, the brothers-in-law approached Billy the Kid to convince him to forgive Boogie's $5,000. After Billy the Kid stopped laughing, he informed the brothers-in-law that Boogie will still have to pay the five grand or die. The brothers-in-law implored Billy to consider negotiating the price down to maybe $2,500. "Fine," Billy said, "that means just Boogie's arms and legs will be broken."

With this information, the brothers-in-law reported back to Boogie that he was in real trouble, which was not news to Boogie. Moreover, Boogie's marriage wasn't going well and he began hanging around the Diner. We took him back.

One night into the Diner walked Harry Levin, a 65-year-old pool-room owner who had been known to shoot some people in his time, and Daddy-O. Harry also had worked for Billy the Kid, as now did Daddy-O, a hood and collector for Billy who relished torturing people and liked to play with knives. A bunch of us were "leaning" outside and weren't aware that Harry and Daddy-O had gone to the back of the Diner where they cornered Boogie by the dirty plates and coffee pots. Boogie promptly sucker-punched the both of them and threw Daddy-O through the plate glass window. Then Boogie hopped into his car (he still didn't have a driver's license) to drive back home.

Harry Levin and Daddy-O regained their composure, leapt into their car and pursued Boogie. They caught up with him a couple of miles later and cut him off. Boogie jumped out of his car as Harry Levin was going for his gun and he again sucker-punched both Levin and Daddy-O, leaving them dazed in their car.

When Billy the Kid heard about the altercation, rather than send out more henchmen, he embarrassingly called Boogie's brothers-in-law to negotiate a settlement. The brothers-in-law agreed to pay Billy the Kid $2,500, and Billy, in a face-saving gesture, then said that as long as Boogie lived he would never be able to place another bet. Unfortunately [or fortunately] Billy the Kid died a violent death soon afterwards. Boogie lived to place many more bets.

The brothers-in-law were upset by the gambling fiasco. Sensing this, Boogie quit the auto parts business and decided to become a hairdresser. He graduated from "Mr. David's" Hair Styling School and landed a job as a hairdresser, but he couldn't hack it. He hated the work, the bosses, and the customers. He was also worried that people would think he was a fag. So he quit.

36.

Third hooked up with a girl named Nancy from New York whom he'd met on Cape Cod. Her father owned a hotel in the Catskills and also manufactured a hair lotion. Together with Murray, Third drove up to the Catskills. Along the way, they drank some of the hair lotion trying to get high. Instead they got very sick. When they arrived, Nancy ordered the entire menu to fix their nausea.

37.

After Baltimore Junior College, Barry Levinson went to American University in Washington. Through an instructor, a program director at WTOP-TV, Barry got a job as floor director at the station. This impressive position paid $50 a week and consisted largely of moving sets around, making slides for backgrounds, and delivering cues. On occasion, he directed shows and sportscasts. Unfortunately, his schedule didn't leave much time for school work. While he could have eventually become a director with WTOP, he quit and resumed full-time study. He lived with Alan (Kaps) Kaplan and Richard Sher, near College Park. Every now and then, the guys made audio tapes of Sher, who has a great speaking voice, reading soft porno while Barry and Kaps improvised erotic sound effects.

38.

Kaps, who hung at the Diner (he had attended Forest Park High and was a ZBT at University of Maryland), was an anachronism among Diner Guys from high school until his junior year in college. He was an honor student, President of the Year, student body leader, and a member of all the major academic and class clubs; and he was also a three-sport athlete (cross-country, basketball and track).

But at some point in college, things changed and Kaps became more interested in partying, gambling and carousing. It wasn't that he didn't play around a bit in high school; he just masked it better.

Kaps and Levinson were close then, and since the farthest they'd been away from Baltimore by 1963 was Atlantic City, they decided to go to the West Coast to work that summer. They had a letter of introduction from Kaps' brother-in-law to work construction in San Francisco. However, at the party, before they left, they heard from

Mike Campo that the place to go was Lake Tahoe.

The guys answered an ad for a "drive-away-car" to Los Angeles. They took a bus to West Virginia to pick up the car—a station wagon loaded with furniture.

While going up a mountain in Colorado, Kaps noticed that the car was overheating and mentioned to Levinson that it should cool off quickly when they "fly" down the other side. But Levinson wanted to stop at the top of the mountain for peanut butter crackers, and despite Kaps' reservations, Barry was adamant about the snack. In addition, he was driving.

They pulled into a gas station and asked the attendant to check the car (they had "full" service back then), as Levinson went in search of the peanut butter crackers. When they returned, the attendant informed them that the car overheated because the radiator cap had blown off and cut the fan belt, which also severed the power brake lines. There were no brakes. If Barry hadn't craved peanut butter crackers, the guys would have been history.

Anyhow, the car was fixed and they delivered it to L.A. Then they decided to hitchhike to Lake Tahoe. Not realizing that the lake is 40 miles long, Kaps and Barry were dropped off on the North Shore at the Cal-Neva Lodge. (The North Shore only had the Cal-Neva for action, while the South Shore really hopped with more casinos and clubs.) They're told there were no jobs presently, but to check back, so the guys hitched down to the South Shore looking for work.

Barry tried for a job at a radio station but was turned down for lack of experience. The guys' funds were drying up fast. They decided to "pool" their money and play poker for a big stake to tide them over until they could get employment. Kaps and Barry were mesmerized by Tahoe—gambling in Nevada is legal! They were at Barney's, a poker place, and winning a few hands when they put everything they owned on the last one—and got beat. "Tap City." They're broke. So, they decided to hitchhike to San Francisco, but before leaving the Lake, they stopped back at the Cal-Neva. Their luck had changed—they were given jobs driving golf carts around, shuttling hotel guests to golf, dinner, registration, rooms, etc.

During their stay, the guys chauffeured around Sinatra, Dean Martin, Peter Lawford, Sammy Davis, Jr., The McGuire Sisters, and other stars. It was the "Rat Pack" days and Sinatra still owned the Cal-Neva Lodge. Levinson loved the atmosphere of the casino, the shows, the action, and especially the comedians. He watched every comic show performed in the lounge, night after night.

Kaps left in mid-season to go back to Baltimore because he missed his girlfriend, Marsha Blum, but Barry stayed until college began that fall.

39.

Every two months, Third returned from New York to hustle girls at Goucher College. He owed a girl $40 for about six months. When she finally confronted him, he opened his wallet and pulled out two tickets for the Sonny Liston/Cassius Clay fight, explaining, "Oh, I thought you wanted to see this fight, so I spent it on these tickets." The girl was shocked. "I abhor pugilism," she cries. "I don't want those tickets!"

"Fine," retorted Third, "We're even."

Unbelievably, Third also lived in a girl's room at Goucher. Most guys needed security escorts even to get through the gates.

40.

For Christmas, Burger and I decided to go down to Miami Beach, which was no big thing since every other Christmas or spring break, somebody would drive to Ft. Lauderdale or Miami. Mark Rudd had a new GTO and to share expenses we brought Fenwick along and Al Shimmelman whom Burger nicknamed "Schmar." This was no easy drive, since Rudd and Burger were high most of the time, bouncing between amphetamines and barbituates while breaking every speed limit for over 1,500 miles. And, if it hadn't been for being high on some grass myself, I probably would have had six coronaries. As it was, I sat in the back seat the entire trip. Unfortunately, Fenwick and Schmar were drug free and probably endured some very psychotic episodes during the ride down.

Burger disliked Fenwick and Schmar, and when we arrived in

Florida and found rooms at the ZBT House at the University of Miami, Donnie did a number on them.

We spent the day on the beach between the Fontainebleau and Mimosa hotels and ran into Dale Cole, whom we knew from Ocean City, playing guitar. He just arrived from Baltimore with Mike Campo, the Spice Sisters (Mary and Carol), and another girl who had stolen her doctor father's medicine bag. In their room off Collins Avenue, they had a huge jar of pills and another one of marihuana. This find turned into a great trip since we arrived with $10 in our pockets and returned with around $600.)

We'd lie on the beach while Dale strummed the guitar. Girl after girl would come by and sit around and harmonize while we buried their pocketbooks in the sand. It was a very rewarding experience.

An additional treat was that we were able to observe the Spice Sisters hustling older men at the Fontainebleau and at other stops in Miami Beach, and the girls shared their wealth.

One day, we strolled into a little bar-restaurant off Collins Avenue that had a pool table. It was around the corner from where the Spice Sisters had set up shop, and where we were all crashing. We were befriended by the owner, who calls himself "The Greek," and several shady characters who hung in the bar. We realized, after a couple of days, that there were some other patrons, newly arrived, who thought they were being cool and slick, but were quite obviously FBI and Interpol agents. Initially, we figured, "Drug surveillance—let's get out of here," but then we recognized two of the guys in the bar who were pictured in the Miami newspapers. They were Murph the Surf and Al Kuhn, prime suspects in the theft of the "The Star of India." What ensued was a very eventful New Year's Eve. Here we were, a bunch of semi-drugged pseudo-hustlers from Baltimore leaning on a bar and shooting pool with FBI, Interpol and Treasury agents, Murph the Surf and his entourage (which had grown to dozens), and God knows who else.

41.

Ellen Cohen reinvented herself as Cass Elliot and got jobs in nightclubs where Denny Doherty was now singing with two friends of his, Michele Gilliam and John Phillips. Cass begged the group to let her join in and harmonize but they keep putting her off, mainly for their amusement. Only after they all tripped on acid one night, did they realize that there was a great rapport among them. They formed The Mamas and The Papas. Within five months, the group's first hit, *California Dreaming,* had propelled them to stardom and Cass became the major force of the quartet.

42.

Yussel was back in London. He had a girlfriend who thought she was Yussel's only love, and she was very jealous. When a phone call disclosed that Yussel had gone out with someone else, she went green. Unfortunately Yussel decided to visit her the next day. After climbing two long flights of stairs to her flat, she opened the door and smacked him in the ear as hard as she could. He slipped and fell backwards down the stairs. Later, Yussel got a medical discharge from the Air Force. He suffered a 40 percent loss of hearing in his left ear.

43.

Ben moved downtown with some guys into an apartment across the street from the Maryland Institute of Art, a mecca of free-spirited artists and bohemians. Many of the students began hanging about the apartment, drinking and getting high. Ben met Carol, a student from Pennsylvania and they soon became romantically involved. Ben was obviously in love but, as a kibitzer, he couldn't admit his true feelings to the Diner guys. Soon after they began dating, he married Carol, and to save face he claimed, "I'm choice." Ben's jargon for no choice. He'd knocked her up. Also he said, "She's a penny. Sorry!" meaning she's wealthy and he's set for life. Too bad.

Although Carol was pregnant and came from a well-to-do family, Ben loved her because of her looks, personality, sensitivity and good nature. However, for image reasons, he couldn't and never did express his true feelings to the guys. Moreover, he constantly knocked Carol in front of other people, yet she, and everyone else, realized it was just Ben's way.

Ben and Carol moved uptown. Carol gave birth to a daughter in 1964. She was beautiful and made Ben very proud. Both parents helped the newlyweds financially as Ben bounced from job to job.

44.

Third decided to travel to Mexico for a few months. He flew into Mexico City and began visiting several expatriate American colonies. Although not financially able to conduct these site visits as a tourist, Third likened it to his trips to Ocean City and Europe, and he lived well on his wiles, scoring marihuana from the farmers and selling it on the go.

He made good connections, comprehended the Federales' (police) mentality, and came to the realization that he could maintain a fast life-style anywhere in the world in the illicit drug market as long as he was buffered and connected.

After much traveling, Third selected as his base of operation and Mexican home, the town of Ajijit—45 minutes from Guadalajara. Located on Lake Chappalla, Ajijit was a Bohemian artist colony. There were a number of Americans living there, including several from Baltimore. (Actually, during the '60s, as many as 50 Baltimoreans of my generation lived in Mexico, and most bought grass from Third.)

Perhaps the largest Baltimore contingent lived in San Miguel Allende, an American retirement settlement 7,500 feet above sea level in the mountains north of Mexico City. It looked like 18th century America and housed the Institute Allende Art School. Many drug smugglers lived or visited there under the guise of art students.

Third consumed a good deal of mescalin and LSD during his initial tenure in Mexico and considered it a year-long "out of body" experience. During his more lucid moments, he'd send couriers to

Manzanillo to bring back kilos of grass, and also engaged in travelers check scams. Usually, Third bought $1,000 worth of checks in San Miguel Allende and then would report them stolen in Mexico City. Doing this twice a year, without dealing drugs, was enough to live quite handsomely in Mexico.

Third met a Baltimore couple, the Butlers, whose San Miguel Allende mansion—which they rented for only $20 a month—included heavy wooden doors, a central court yard, several apartments and rooms with fire places, and hand-painted towels. They rented the place from the international movie star Cantinflas. (Twenty-three years later, my sister Nancy bought Cantinflas' townhouse in Beverly Hills.)

The Butlers later moved to San Blas, a fishing village on the west coast which was the first port before the growth of Acapulco. The town, 40 miles north of Puerto Vallarta, used to have a population of 50,000 but a malaria epidemic wiped out most of the people. When the Butlers arrived, there were less than 2,000 inhabitants.

San Blas was a haven for California surfers who visited the resort in droves. The Butlers made a connection with a local pharmacist and got strung out shooting Hicodan tablets. They'd sit on the beach all day, nodding out, watching the surfers, dolphins and porpoises frolic. They'd also collect a menagerie of local creatures including birds, ocelots, snakes, cats, dogs, tarantulas, and a heron and a snowy egret.

Third visited the Butlers in San Blas to score some Hicodan tablets, and arrived proudly bedecked in a floor length black suede coat. Following dinner and a sharing of drugs, Third retired fully clothed in a hammock in a room adjoining the Butlers. The birds of the household were nocturnal, and a couple hours after Third drifted off in a drugged stupor, he was awakened by loud screechings. Horrified, he saw snakes slither along the gratings and at the same moment the heron hovered over him and shit all over his floor length black suede coat. Before sunup, Third was on his way back to Ajijit.

45.

Levinson got tickets for Kaps and the Ten Boys to see Lenny Bruce entertain at the Lyric Theatre in downtown Baltimore. The audience was small and Bruce invited the guys, who are sitting in the back rows, to move up front. The guys laughed hysterically as Bruce plays mainly to them, yet Kaps didn't think he was funny.

46.

The Golds (Dan had married childhood sweetheart Devie) came down to Mexico to visit Third but couldn't find him. After driving around the town of Ajijit for hours, they finally stumbled across a priest who was wearing sunglasses in the middle of the night. Dan was shocked when the priest told him exactly where Third lived. They went to this hacienda, tapped on the back window because nobody answered the front door, and Murray appeared. Gold and his wife had to climb in through the window since the door was stuck. A big card game was in progress in the front room, with Third, the Chief of Police, and other officials of the town.

Murray showed Dan a guitar that he had made and said that he was going to give it to John Lennon as a present. He played it for a little bit and then they went into the cardroom to see Third, and within seconds, somebody came through the back window and stole the guitar. Gold and Murray rushed out and drove all over the town all night long; this after Gold had been driving from the States for days. They never did find the guitar.

Not only did Third have regular card and basketball games with the local officials, he also had certain women in the town who made him soup and orange juice. For a cad, a rouge and a tactless S.O.B., Third had a way of getting a lot of people to do things for him.

In addition, Third had no standards. Lots of people thought he just dated beautiful women but he didn't. Ugly or beautiful, it didn't matter to Third. He just wanted to take advantage, although he really believed he gave and received equally.

After two weeks, the Golds left Mexico, and upon their return to the States, were busted in El Paso for possession. Devie was caught with some grass in her purse which she unwittingly forgot to hide. Federal authorities, aware of their ties to Third, broke the car down three times but never did find a well-hidden huge cache of marihuana.

Unexplainedly, the Golds were never indicted—credit goes to Gold's dad. The car, however, was impounded and forever lost. Third was furious. Dan was always fucking up drug deals.

47.

In 1964, when Third was not attending the University of Baltimore, but I was, he played against us for the Maryland Lacrosse Club. We took turns letting each other score; throwing great fakes so that the other guy would fall down and make it look as if we were great dodgers. Third laughed too much, but did manage to score four or five goals. I was so excited at a chance to score so easily that I missed most of my shots, but still managed to collect two goals. Donnie Burger and Dan Gold sipped on cough medicine in the stands and cheered, "Come on Chip, come on Third," every few minutes, never knowing whether we were on the same team or playing against each other.

Third returned to Mexico after the lacrosse season and went to the Acapulco Film Festival where he met Brigitte Bardot and Jeanne Moreau, who were completing a movie called *Viva Maria!* After leaving Acapulco, he ran into Ava Gardner, who had been filming *Night of the Iguana* in Jalapa, a town across the bay from Puerto Vallarta—and stole her shoes. He said it was just a souvenir, but broke the heels one night while flamenco dancing in them while tripping on acid.

48.

The same spring, Snyder, Sandy Berman (a ZBT frat brother from Silver Spring) and I impulsively left town in Berman's brand new Chevy Impala and drove to Lake Tahoe in three days. We were looking for the ultimate job which Kaps and Levinson swore they found the previous summer. Berman's father was involved in manufacturing slot machines. He was our "in."

We arrived before the Western colleges' summer break to have a chance at good jobs. Because of his old man, Berman landed a job immediately as a Change Captain—a person in charge of change girls, who distribute money to customers who won tokens at the slot machines. A couple of days later, Snyder got a similar job, and by the end of the week, I was hired as a bar boy at Harvey's Wagon Wheel Casino, which was where we all worked.

At that time, Harvey's was the second largest casino in the world. The biggest was Harrah's, across the street. They were located in Stateline, Nevada. We rented a cabin in Stateline, California, on Ski Run Boulevard for a huge sum of $300 per year. I worked in the Polywog Bar, one of the nine bars in Harvey's. Harvey's was also the only place that had hotel accommodations and it was where most of the high rollers, entertainers and movie stars stayed on the South Shore.

The North Shore was where the Cal/Neva Lodge was located. It was there where Kaps and two of the Ten Boys were working. This was also the summer when Frank Sinatra's son was allegedly kidnapped from a motel diagonally across from Harvey's Casino, but on the California side.

Tahoe was the end of the rainbow. It was probably the most magnificent spot in the United States, or perhaps even the world. Winter or summer, it didn't matter. It was an unbelievable site. As a 21-year-old, I was making $100 bucks a week and a share of the tips from the bartenders which ranged from $200 to $400 a week— even then I knew they weren't giving me a straight shake.

To make matters better, most of the time somebody always bought me drinks or food, and the two Italian bartenders I worked with adopted me and really taught me the ropes and about life in Nevada. Furthermore, it seemed as if there were 10 girls for every guy. These were mostly California girls, although there was an ample sprinkling of European beauties. I loved the California girls. They weren't bright or demanding, and they must have started "swallowing" when they were young teenagers. I was in paradise.

My work shift went from midnight to eight in the morning, and if I didn't go with my bartender buddies into Reno or to Las Vegas, I would go to the beach and fall asleep. It was difficult to swim in the Lake because of the water temperature. The Lake was stone cold. Every now and then you'd see a body surface. It had been frozen for probably hundreds of years, or perhaps that's what the Mafia wanted you to believe.

This also was the summer of the topless bathing suits. Sheriff Byron, the Lake's lawman, took great pride in coming down to the Lake and guarding the topless girls so that nobody would come over, ogle them, or try to harass them. Sheriff Byron did enough ogling for all of us on the Lake and probably the entire state of California, yet nobody complained. Sheriff Byron, a big burly man with a full gray beard, was the enforcer who dealt severely with casino employees who cheated. If a card dealer or a roulette table operator was caught skimming, the Sheriff would take him upstairs, spread his hands flat on a table, and proceed to smash his bones with a baseball bat. The former employees didn't receive a police record, but Byron sure kept them from cheating.

Snyder's real joy was working as a camp counselor and athletic director at an overnight camp in Maryland. More than anything, he longed for this in spite of being in "paradise." He had a bad habit of sleeping late and being an irresponsible employee. Since we had traveled almost 3,000 miles, the management at Harvey's kept giving Snyder chance after chance when he would screw up in his job, which meant at least four times a day. Finally, he committed a series of cardinal sins. First, he failed to show up one day, then came late the next; second, instead of putting the safe which carried the prizes for the slot machines on the elevator properly, he forced it in just to get it out of the way, severely damaging both the safe and the elevator; third, Snyder blamed the damage on a change girl; and finally, he overslept the following day. This was the last straw. He was fired.

We weren't going to miss Snyder much since he promptly found another job on the North Shore, 20 minutes away. Kaps had gotten him employment downstairs at the Cal/Neva Lodge keeping an inventory of the food. Snyder felt as though he was living in an air raid shelter. He became claustrophobic and couldn't handle it. After two weeks, he joined a Ten Boys contingent of two who also couldn't stand "paradise." They decided to hitchhike back to Baltimore. I later discovered a letter to Snyder confirming that several weeks before, he had written the camp director in Maryland begging to return as a counselor. He had been accepted.

Snyder and the two Ten Boys knew hitchhiking to Baltimore was no piece of cake. After an entire day, they got as far as Reno, a 30-minute drive from the Lake. They decided to wire home for money for bus fare.

To his dismay, Snyder got dysentery on the bus. He was forced to beg the bus driver every few minutes to pull over. After several unscheduled stops, the bus driver balked. At one point outside of Nebraska, Snyder threatened to destroy the bus and the driver if he didn't stop, saying he'd defecate in the aisle. It was a hard four day trip, but Snyder finally became a camp counselor. His paradise.

49.

For a vacation, Fenwick, Dude and Matt Hammond went to New Orleans and then on to Mexico. They visited the border towns where there are many whorehouses.

Physically spent and feeling their oats as tremendous studs following a little tour of the red light district, they motored back to Baltimore. On the way, they stopped off in Washington to visit some of Fenwick's girlfriends whom he met at the University of Maryland. They were very wealthy young ladies who belonged to the finer country clubs in the Washington area. Fenwick discovered that one of the girls, Vanessa, was sunning herself at the Woodmont Country Club—perhaps the most elegant club. He drove over with the guys, telling them that they had to sneak in since Vanessa was only allowed one guest. They had to try to appear as if they belonged there.

"Be real low-key guys. Don't let them think that you're bums from Benny's Poolroom!" begged Fenwick.

At Woodmont, Vanessa advised them to speak softly, and to try and act classy.

Hammond worked in a grocery store in Mt. Washington near Fenwick's house, and was a gambling buddy of his. Dude was a used car salesman and sounded like one. He was a great knocker from the Diner, extremely sarcastic and very funny. Hammond was into screaming in the grocery store for the price of merchandise—which he had never memorized. It's hard to believe he later became a crack DEA Agent.

The guys remained cool, put on their bathing trunks, and meandered out by the swimming pool in an aloof manner.

While Fenwick was trying to impress his Vanessa with an account of his trip through Mexico (which was for cultural reasons), Hammond went over to the edge of the pool to sit down and dangle his feet in the water. He was not wearing an athletic supporter and unintentionally sat on his testicles. He began moaning very loudly and then started screaming, "My balls, my balls, I sat on my balls!" Club members were aghast.

Fenwick was enraged. He physically and verbally abused Hammond who was writhing in pain, grasping his testicles. The country club life guard, Fenwick and Dude swiftly picked up Hammond, whose hands were now thrust inside his trunks while he continued screaming about his balls. They carried him into a cabana. Within earshot of everyone, Hammond continued to cry out, even startling golfers on the seventh tee. After Hammond recovered, the boys were escorted out of Woodmont Country Club, banished as guests for life.

Hammond once dated the daughter of Hall of Fame baseball pitcher Hoyt Wilhelm, who pitched in the majors until he was 45. Wilhelm is best remembered for having the greatest knuckle-ball in the history of the game. He pitched a no-hitter against the Yankees while playing for the Orioles in the early '60s.

Hoyt objected to Hammond dating his daughter, and very rarely even acknowledged his presence. Hammond, a baseball fanatic, would always trail after Wilhelm begging him to have a catch. Finally, realizing that his daughter was becoming too involved with Hammond, Wilhelm agreed to have a catch. He gave Hammond a baseball glove and had him stand 60 feet away.

"Ready," asked Wilhelm.

"You bet. Toss it in here, Hoyt."

Wilhelm's knuckle-ball pitch was so difficult to catch that Paul

Richards, the Oriole manager, had a huge catcher's mitt custom-made for Gus Triandos. He still had trouble catching Wilhelm.

So here was Hammond, a novice, whose only association with baseball was playing step ball or whiffle ball against Fenwick. He always lost. There was no way Hammond could catch the ball. It hit him in the face, in the neck, in the sides, in his stomach, in his testicles, etc. Hammond tried not to flinch, but he fell over a few times and cried out a lot. After a half-hour, Hammond was black and blue and had to go home due to dizzy spells caused by getting struck by the ball.

On his way out the door, Wilhelm whispered, "Every time you come here, we're going to play catch until you stop dating my daughter."

Soon after, Hammond broke up with her. He feared permanent brain damage.

50.

When the 1960s began, so did my association with Bob Litwin. Bob was a short, nervous guy from Philadelphia who had just moved to Baltimore. He was bright with great-looking hair and very small ears. We were at College Park, attending the University of Maryland. Bob was one year ahead of me. Soon after we met, he helped me edit all the papers I needed. My sister Harryette used to help me, but she used too many big words. I was always questioned by my teachers about words like "paradigm" and "quotidian." Bob did such a good job I let him continue editing some of my papers for years, through two graduate degrees, one from Johns Hopkins University. At the Hopkins commencement, Bob showed up and tried to get some kind of special degree for helping me but was booed off the stage.

It wasn't hard to get Bob to do papers. In the beginning, I flattered him by telling him what a great editor and technician he was. Then I got him accustomed to free dinner, money, and dates I arranged for him with Gentile girls, who tied him up and made him do things to them. Every once in a while, Bob rebelled and refused to edit my papers. Then, together with Fenwick, we would threaten to call Nina Garp, whom Bob was dating, and tell her he had nude pictures of her that he was showing to her mother's friends at church. Bob dated Nina for a few years. I couldn't understand why. She was the thinnest, whitest white girl I ever saw. Eventually she went on a crash diet and lost so much weight she just evaporated. No one ever saw her again.

About this time, Bob met Gary Huddles, the only true idol of Diner guys, who would much rather look and act like Hud than be a mensch like Becker. Gary became Bob's sponsor at Maryland because he needed Bob to get him through Intermediate Spanish. The only Spanish phrases Hud knew were "When do I get my camera back" and "The ropes are too tight."

In 1964, Bob and Hud went to Maryland Law School, and Bob helped Hud again, even though Hud was two years ahead of him. Hud gave Bob all his law books, and in return Bob helped Hud with some of the more subtle points of law, explaining why torts weren't something you ate for breakfast.

Other guys were jealous of the time Hud spent with Bob, especially Nard Myerson, who tried to hang around with Hud and pick up his excess girls. Myerson was known locally as "the Judge." He failed the Bar Examination eight times. He lived near Bob and often drove him to law school. How they ever reached school was a miracle, since Myerson drove over sidewalks and knocked down trash cans whenever they were late, which was always. Myerson had a girlfriend named Corina who had dark skin and hair and always looked somewhat greasy. One day, Myerson was very late and, when he picked up Bob, he drove like a madman to Corina's house to finish an argument they had earlier that morning. He drove on her lawn and told Bob to come in with him. They found her handcuffed to a kitchen chair which she was dragging around with her. That's the way Myerson had left her.

51.

As funny as Ben, Snyder and Hart were, I thought that the most talented of all Diner and poolroom characters was Moses. He was tall and slim, always looked a bit over-tanned, and usually had a patch of his hair bleached semi-yellow.

Moses' forte was playing pool, and it was in Bennie's Pool Room where he sharpened an uncanny sarcasm and knocking ability which was supported by his talent for dialects. To the best of anyone's recollection, Moses had no formal language training. We all believed he was multi-lingual.

A skilled artist, he attended the Maryland Institute of Art on a scholarship and used to entertain us in the Diner with caricatures of the guys in funny situations, such as Hart in a tight, brief bathing suit, poised to dive from the edge of a toilet seat.

Moses had only one failing—an inability to handle his handicap. He was born without the three middle fingers of his right hand, and only had a thumb and pinky finger on it. Yet he could draw, shoot pool and function normally, or even far above normal considering his talents and his handicap. But Moses hid the handicap through such deft manuevers that only vague rumors of his missing fingers kept most of the guys curious enough to eventually find out the facts. Regardless of the weather, he always wore gloves or carried a scarf with which to hide the missing joints, and even while shooting pool he could camouflage it by keeping up a stream of sarcastic chatter aimed at other guys in the poolroom, or by using only his right hand to chalk-up the cue stick.

There were also cruel incidents. In Bennie's one afternoon, Moses came up behind Bruce Hawk while he was playing the pinball machine and placed his hands on Hawk's shoulders. "Ugh!" screamed Hawk, "Get that thing off my shoulder!"

I knew Moses five years before I was able to confirm his handicap.

52.

Bob Litwin's great love was folk music. For four years, he wrote a music column called "Platter Chatter" in the University of Maryland *Diamondback*. The column had a picture of him with a haircut so short that his head looked like a tennis ball. In his senior year, they took a poll. It turned out that no one had ever read his column in four years.

The best folk music was at the Folk Festival in Newport, Rhode Island. Bob went every July. This year, he drove up with Moses, who was trying to look and act like Peter Fonda, even though it was five years before *Easy Rider* came out and no one knew who Peter Fonda was.

One night, Bob and Moses went to Provincetown on Cape Cod. They were in a bar when someone goosed Moses. He spun around like a "dradel" (a Jewish child's top) and started screaming, "All right. Who goosed me? Who was it?" No one answered, but a lot of guys started smiling and looking affectionately at Moses. Turns out they were in a gay bar in Provincetown, and every homosexual in the place wanted a piece of Moses' ass. At least.

At the Newport Festival that year, Bob Dylan shocked the music world by introducing an electric back-up band, which violated the purists' idea of how folk music should be played. Litwin had a law school professor who went to Yale with Peter Yarrow of Peter, Paul and Mary. Peter gave Bob and Moses stage passes. After everyone booed Dylan off the stage when he sang "Like a Rolling Stone," Dylan came *back* on stage and did "It's All Over Now, Baby Blue." Moses, ever the chronicler of social change, told everyone backstage that "Dylan's career is finished. He'll never sell another record."

53.

Boogie's marriage broke up and he kicked around town supported, for a while, by his buddy, Obie. He had made a pact with Boogie when they were teenagers. Whoever had money could always support the other guy. This was great for Boogie back in the late '50s and up through the mid-'60s, since Obie always had money. He came from a solid middle class family.

54.

A letter from my mother arrived in Tahoe, followed by a panic phone call that the FBI came to the house looking for me. It seems that while I had a II-S deferment from the draft, by dropping out of college for a semester I violated the terms of the deferment and had either to enlist immediately in the service or re-enroll in college. Things were getting heavy in Southeast Asia, I was a little older and wiser, and I figured that I'd better place the military behind me for the time being. Maybe forever. So I returned home after taking a detour through California, Arizona, Mexico and New Orleans, and re-enrolled back at the University of Baltimore.

I resubmitted my II-S deferment and went to the draft board. Sable T. Reed, who was the head of that board and who had lost both of her sons in the first wave of the Korean War, was upset. It seems that Sable felt everybody should lose at least one son in what-ever war we had after what she had gone through. She experienced a whole lot of problems dealing with the Northwest Baltimore group which came under her purview since most of the guys were in no rush to enlist for front line duty in Vietnam. They did join Army Reserve and National Guard units. This was during that period when a whole slew of guys got married, when they learned marriage was major deferment. I never went to that extreme.

55.

Betty and Ford Lessans met and fell madly in love. A whirlwind courtship ensued behind Rob Glick's back, and shortly thereafter they married. Rob was devastated. The object of Diner ridicule at being snaked by an older guy (Ford was four years older), Glick moved even further downtown than Ford. He shed his pretty threads and became an early hippie, giving up his lucrative sales job to become a probation officer.

One evening, Ford was returning alone from the Mechanic Theatre's presentation of *Man of La Mancha*. He was so moved by the performance that he decided to walk home, humming the musical score along the way, reflecting upon marital bliss. He arrived at his lovely renovated townhouse to find the place empty. While he was at the show, Betty cleared out the entire house, and left a goodbye note. The marriage had lasted a little over a year.

56.

In 1965, Fenwick told my Uncle Albert at Reisterstown Road Plaza that I was a heroin addict. Naturally, Uncle Albert, who hated me, told my mother, who cried. I stopped talking to Fenwick only after I confronted him with the accusation and he confessed, "I don't know why I said it? I guess I did it for a smile."

57.

In April of 1965, while playing lacrosse for the University of Baltimore against Penn, Third became upset over my handling the ball too much. He took the ball away from me after sneaking up from behind while the opposing team looked on in disbelief. This really upset our coach.

Third was one of the very few athletes I ever saw play well while high on grass. In college he constantly got loaded before big lacrosse games. Once against Cornell, I tried it and fell asleep behind the bench before we even warmed up. Third scored three goals and two assists that day.

Third's tactlessness knew no bounds. Once, outside of the university on his way to lacrosse practice, Third passed by a heavy set policewoman in a squad car just idling in front of the school. He yelled at her, "Put your fat fuckin' arm back in the car!" The policewoman bolted from the car, called for assistance and took Third back into the school. He had to apologize to her in front of the president of the university in order to go to practice and get back on the lacrosse team.

Third probably played one of the greatest games I've ever seen by a midfielder against the University of Maryland. He scored five goals and three assists. We barely lost the game, 17 to 16. Our coach was new. He previously coached at a very fine prep school, but he had great difficulty dealing with lacrosse players at the University of Baltimore, essentially a commuter college. It was especially tough to coach Third and me since we had problems dealing with discipline and authority. Coach Mitchell came over and congratulated Third for a phenomenal game as Third stood up on the hillside crying. He consoled Third, "I think it's great, you really shocked me. You took this team loss personally in spite of having such a great game yourself, I'm proud of you."

"Proud, my ass," shot back Third, "Silverman just told me that there's a newspaper strike which began last night and that no one will ever see my stats in the paper. Imagine, scoring five goals and three assists," and he walked off bitterly.

Third was finally thrown off the team during a game with the Naval Academy for going up into the stands at halftime to flirt with girls. He took his uniform and equipment, sold it, and left for New York.

Third found out that his old high school girlfriend, Sue, was divorced, and working in New York. She began as a secretary and worked her way up quickly to a fashion coordinator for Jonathan Logan, a prestigious women's fashion company. One night, Third and Gold picked up Sue and her girlfriend Cheryl and took them back to their apartment in Greenwich Village. They were looking to get into a scene by getting the girls high on grass. But their plan backfired. The girls were so blown away on the dope that they curled up into the fetal position and fell asleep.

A couple of months later, Third visited Sue again while he was tripping on acid. He came in and began laughing hysterically. He thought Sue was very un-hip and didn't know what was going on, yet she knew, and dismissed him in an almost maternal manner.

A week later, Sue got a call from Joyce. It had been only seven year since they'd spoken. Sue had a falling out with Joyce in high school. They hadn't spoken to each other since 10th grade. Sue learned that Joyce was now divorced, had been teaching school, and recently had quit a job with WBAL radio in Baltimore. She wanted to start a new life in New York City. Sue, who figured a seven year grudge was extreme, decided that she will take Joyce out and then dump her. They went to P.J. Clarke's where Sue knew everybody, including the celebrities. She was extremely popular. She realized, after an hour, that she really liked Joyce a lot, and that Joyce liked her. They seemed much more mature than they did at 15. She told Joyce to get rid of the bubble hairdo and the "fat" clothes hiding her skinny body.

"Joyce, thin is in. Your kind of body is what people crave today." Sue had just resigned from Jonathan Logan and got Joyce her old job. Joyce held onto the new job for a week and quit to work as a secretary for an entertainment agency.

58.

Snooty and I became close friends when he began to date my younger sister, Nancy. Then one day he told me that he decided on a career in life. "I think that I'm going to be a Rabbi, Chip," he announced. "Nobody has even considered it from our group."

Snooty continued, "Not only that. If you're a Rabbi, the congregation buys your house and gives you a car and a great salary, and you're treated like a God. How can I miss? I am a God. Right?"

"Not quite Snooty," I said. "And what are the chances of your getting into, let alone graduating from, Rabbinical school? I'll bet you can't even speak Hebrew."

Snooty had an answer for that. "Well, I'm going to be a Reform Rabbi. It means less of a Hebrew background."

I dismissed the conversation, yet he sounded sincere, which was unusual for Snooty.

59.

Third joined Murray and Brosy on a journey to Antioch College in Yellow Springs, Ohio. They took acid for 25 straight days and then flew on to San Francisco. Third's main job there was to play softball. On the team was Bill Graham, the great rock and roll promoter, along with the Jefferson Airplane. Grace Slick, the group's lead singer at the time, was going with a guy named Rob whom Third later introduced to Claire, Third's former girlfriend from Paris and New York. Rob married her.

After a month, Third went back to Mexico and met up with Ken Kesey, the head of the Merry Pranksters. [Kesey wrote *One Flew Over the Cuckoo's Nest* and *Sometimes a Great Notion*.] He was a "beat" author who came to Mexico from New York with Shotgun Bill, Claire's ex-husband.

Third took Kesey to Mansanillo along with Neal Cassidy, made famous by Jack Kerouac's book *On the Road*. Later, Third sent Cassidy to stay with Brosy in San Miguel Allende where Cassidy soon died.

Third returned to Mexico City and began hanging around with the head of the local Communist Party named Diego Rivera.

Peg, a co-ed whom Third had met at Goucher and taken over her mind, followed him to Mexico. She spent a year and a half there, ingesting large quantities of LSD, hallucinating about her subsequent marriage to Third.

60.

Like Third, Burger did very well with Gentile girls. He was dating two or three who already had boyfriends in Northwood, an area full of some pretty rough customers. These guys discovered that Burger and some other Jewish guys were violating their women.

They put the word out on the street to beat up Burger and his friends. They went looking for Donnie, and three of them found his house one evening. Donnie already had left for the night, but these guys didn't realize it.

The leader of this group was Billy Rite. He banged on the front door screaming, "Come on outside Burger, you chicken shit. We're gonna kick your ass!" And a response from inside said, "I'll be right out." It wasn't Donnie, but his father who wanted to make sure the guys thought he was Donnie. Burger's father was a big burly guy. He made a charge, crashed through his own front door (which made little sense) and knocked two of the guys off the porch. He grabbed Billy Rite and bit his left ear off.

Throughout this period there was very serious involvement with LSD. The guys who were looking for Burger were indulging in acid. One night after the ear-biting incident, while tripping, they stopped by the Northwood sub shop. Billy Rite strolled in and ordered a whole Italian cold cut sub. He returned to the car, took two bites out of the sub, and had an LSD panic attack. He thought the sub took two bites out of him. He had a coronary and died right there.

In the '60s, a lot of guys died from drug overdoses. Criminal involvement as a result of drug deals was common, as were car accidents under the influence of drugs. There were a lot of funerals to attend. Wakes and funerals were a place to meet nice looking Irish and Italian girls, and the wake they had for Billy Rite was one of the best ones I can ever remember.

61.

Yussel returned from the Air Force and heard from Eggie that Boogie was despondent over his pending divorce. Eggie found Boogie in his empty apartment, totally cleaned out by Joanie and her parents when Boogie was at work. Eggie pounded on the door since he hadn't heard from Boogie for a few days. When nobody answered, Eggie broke in and found Boogie naked on the floor, wacked-out on barbituates. He didn't know where he was. He just wanted to get back with Joanie.

The depression lasted a couple of days and then Boogie decided to get back at Joanie. He and Yussel concocted a plan to kidnap the small poodle that Boogie and Joanie owned, which she took with her. Joanie was living with her parents in the Belvedere Towers, a high-rise complex in Northwest Baltimore.

Since Yussel and Boogie had nothing better to do, they conducted a surveillance for a week observing exactly when the poodle was walked. They realized the dognapping must occur inside of the building on the sixth floor. The two hid in a recessed entrance. The next day, they lay in wait for the dog's constitutional, peeking out periodically. It took them days before they chose the precise moment.

One morning, Joanie's 60-year-old father, dressed in a suit, was walking the dog down the sixth floor hallway. Boogie rushed out and grabbed the father, holding his arms, trying not to hurt him. The father was flailing away like a windmill and Joanie's mother came out with an umbrella trying to strike Boogie. Neighbors rushed out to see what's going on as Yussel ran down the hallway to snatch the dog. He missed on the first two attempts but then finally scooped it up, cradling the pooch as he fled. While running, the dog pissed all over Yussel's shirt and arms. Boogie released Joanie's dad and escaped with Yussel via the emergency exit.

Boogie took the dog from Yussel and they started running outside to screams of, "Stop those people! They're dognappers." The shouts came from Joanie's parents. There were renovations going on at the high-rise, and construction workers also gave chase to Yussel and Boogie.

The dognappers decided to separate. Yussel raced to his car, being pursued by Joanie's father, and drove down Falls Road towards Mt. Washington, the father tailing him, blowing his horn wildly. There was a tremendous amount of traffic at 8:00 A.M. and Yussel, figuring that he was going to get caught, pulled into a gas station and told police officers parked nearby that a madman was after him. Joanie's father drove up and ordered the police to arrest Yussel. They asked him where the dog was and that he'd better stop harassing Yussel. Yussel returned to Obie's apartment to await Boogie, who had jogged for two miles carrying the dog like a football.

But Boogie was in great shape and easily outran the construction workers. He hid every now and then, but finally got away, ducking the police cars cruising the neighborhood. The cops never saw him.

When Boogie got back to Obie's, he and Yussel called a friend and gave him the dog to take care of. But, they forgot about it for a few days and the guy ended up giving the dog away. It was never returned.

A month later, Yussel and Boogie received notice by mail to go to court. It was a "show-cause" warrant as to why they shouldn't be charged with dognapping. Luckily they were exonerated.

62.

When I still had one summer session to go in college, I became friendly with Jay Huff, an erstwhile rich kid who was in Mu Sig and later hung out at Mandell's and the Diner, but was not respected or liked by many of the Diner guys. He worked for a vending outfit that had candy machines, pinball games and pool tables throughout the city. He not only had a great salary but he also managed to steal six or seven hundred dollars a week. His boss never missed it. This placed him in a high income bracket, which I must say impressed the shit out of me. He dressed avant-garde and brought me to a store on Pennsylvania Avenue called the Piperack in the heart of the black district. He was one of the few white people who bought threads there. The clothing at the Piperack were the best you could buy in the Baltimore/Washington area. You would have to go to Philadelphia or to New York to buy equal, or better, quality garments. I asked the owner for a job. He hired me to work weekends.

63.

Following graduation, I began teaching elementary school, which was also a military deferment. On the advice of Donnie Burger, I immediately enrolled full-time in the predominantly black Morgan State graduate school which gave me additional deferment.

These deferments held for a couple of years, although every few months I would get a letter from my draft board. In a panic, I would try to explain myself to Sable T. Reed who, for some unknown reason, wanted my ass real bad. Don't get me wrong, I was very patriotic and very supportive of the Vietnam War, yet I would not have made a good recruit at the time, because I was more mature and not able to follow orders blindly.

Due to constant mechanical trouble with my car, Burger and I drove to graduate school together in his new Corvette. We were going to school at night and working during the day. I continued as a teacher and Donnie was a probation officer. It was amazing the number of probation and parole officers who were doing drugs or dealing them while engaging in this wonderful community service.

On the way to school, we would stop off at an apartment Donnie shared with a nurse from Sinai Hospital where he either did heroin or methadrene or a combination of drugs, or drank some cough medicine. It became a thrill-seeking and risky business from my point of view to go from his apartment to Morgan State in six minutes when it was actually a 20-minute trip. Going to school, straight and drug-free, introduced me to some serious anxiety attacks. After arriving at Morgan, Donnie would usually go into the bathroom and remain there for about an hour until the professor would send me to get him. I'd open a stall and find him slouched over with a needle in his arm, completely drugged out. Donnie got a lot of "incompletes," but continued to register for each semester.

Burger and I were writing a term paper called *Why People Take Drugs*. He wasn't convinced that I understood what real dope-taking was. So one evening on the way to graduate school, he urged me to fire methadrene intravenously to experience the feeling. Since I was curious with the effects of various drugs, I shot it and stayed awake three whole days. It was such a rush that there were times when I thought I could actually go into a ring with Sonny Liston. I called up Burger after the second day and asked him when it would stop, and he said, "Well, it could go on for another day, or maybe a couple of weeks unless you want to come down quickly. Would you like to shoot some smack?" I hung up the phone and went to the library, where I researched and wrote two term papers in longhand. Then I went home and typed them, even though I couldn't type.

64.

On my first day of teaching at Armistead Gardens,* I was shocked to find that my fifth/sixth non-graded class ranged in age from nine to 16. The genius of the class had an IQ of 108. I was approached that first class hour—after the Pledge of Allegiance—by an older guy who wanted to take a young girl out of the classroom. I asked him why and he told me she was his wife. It didn't shock me, because many of the people in Armistead Gardens were from the Carolinas, the Virginias, and Appalachia—transients who married young. The girl had just turned 12. I implored him that she still needed an education. He said that she has to be at home in order to watch the baby. I gulped and said that I thought it was the right thing to do. Next, another student wanted to talk to me. He was about 6´2˝ and weighed around 215 pounds. He was 16 years old. "Hey, Mr. Silverman," he said, "watch this," and proceeded to bend a bicycle handlebar backwards. He became the teacher's pet and was my main enforcer. I called him Sergeant at Arms. I had no further trouble in class, with the possible exception of the day Kenneth set fire to his desk, Mona became pregnant by her father, and Wayne slashed the Security Agent in the cafeteria.

65.

A guy who received probably as many grips as anybody was Neurotic Nat. Fortunately, he went to college and graduate school, stayed away from Bux for a long time, and was hired as a senior

---

* An East Baltimore community located in a highly industrial area which developed during World War II to house workers at the Bethlehem Steel and the Sparrows Point Shipyard. It was originally painted green for camouflage purposes and was never changed over the years.

management analyst for the Federal Parole and Probation Agency. One day in the file room, Nat was standing on a mini-ladder, reaching up, when suddenly he felt this excruciating pain. He didn't know what it was until he looked down and there was Bux, gripping him in the center of his thighs. Nat didn't want to drop the files because he could never find his information again, so he just inhaled a silent scream, almost passing out.

To his dismay, Nat found out that Bux actually worked at the massive Federal complex in downtown Baltimore. Bux decided that they were going to have lunch together every day and see each other at breaks. Well, Nat didn't want that at all but couldn't figure out what to do about it. Bux told him that if he didn't go along, he was going to grip Nat's father Leon, who was still working there. So, for about four or five months, Bux and Nat would go out to lunch and see each other from time to time during the day, and he would grip Nat or punch him in the heart as often as possible. The Gripper created further havoc for him by making threatening phone calls, telling Nat that he was going to grip any girls he dated, and even gripping some of Nat's friends and co-workers. Finally, Nat, already a massively neurotic guy, couldn't take it anymore, and he had become a total nervous wreck. He thought that he was losing his hair and fingernails, he began to dress sloppily, and he couldn't sleep. He devised a plan hoping to show Bux who was crazier. If it succeeded maybe Bux would leave him alone. At their next lunch, they were eating a sandwich in Bux's car and talking rationally when suddenly Nat screamed, "I can't take it anymore! I can't take it anymore!" He started gripping himself and threw his sandwich against the rolled-up window. He kept ripping at his arms and hands until he drew blood. Bux was so shocked by this act that he steered clear of Nat for the rest of the time he worked at Parole and Probation, which wasn't much longer.

66.

I was working on weekends at the Piperack. The Piperack catered mainly to blacks who had money in those days. They were principally gangsters, drug dealers and pimps. A couple of blues were major gangsters and dope dealers. Chief among them was Little Melvin, whom I'd known in high school and played softball against at the Towanda Playground. He happened to be a great softball pitcher and I thought him a nice guy, despite claims by both city and state police, FBI and Drug Enforcement officials that he was a notorious mobster. Melvin had lieutenants or henchmen, with very interesting names: Prospect, Pink Lips, Buffalo Man, and Sweet Cherry. Cherry was a pusher who was also a cough syrup addict hooked on Cheracol.

When Melvin came into the Piperack, Phil Kolodner, the owner, would lock the door and let Melvin and his henchmen roam at will, picking out clothing for which they would spend anywhere from five to thirty thousand dollars at a clip. They'd buy leather coats, fur coats, vests, assortments of sweaters and knit suits and pants.

Many design trends were set by '60s gangsters. For example, flare pants grew out of the continental slit. This was a slit in the seam where the cuff normally went, approximately a 2½-inch cut which created a flare in the pantleg. This cut was helpful, enabling a gangster to tape a big knife or a .38 revolver around his ankle without anyone seeing it. This style resulted in flare pants which later became very fashionable. The first two or three times I tried to measure a guy's seam, for cuffing purposes, and felt the gun and the knives, it proved somewhat disheartening and at first resulted in very rapid heartbeats. Pockets in fur coats also became the style, beginning when Melvin crudely cut a pocket in a $20,000 mink coat with a Swiss Army knife so that he would have a place to carry his gun.

Eddie Tucker was another gangster customer who rivaled Melvin right up until he was arrested and sent away. Phil Kolodner became so distraught at losing a client who was spending as much as $100,000 a year on clothing that he put up the bail money for Tucker.

There were other modish gangsters who kept the Piperack in business, even though Phil from time to time would declare bankruptcy in order to get money out of the shop and to avoid paying bills, as well as eliminating whatever partners he had brought into the business. Phil was a peculiar guy. Sometimes he gave me free clothes and bonuses, or sold clothes at cost. On days when he had a huge sale to one or two individuals, or what he considered an excellent day, he'd close the store and piss on the cash register for good luck. It was a messy superstition. I found it upsetting when he would ask me to ring up the next sale.

Phil's sales technique bordered on the ludicrous. Innocent customers would try on a suit that was a size or two too big. Phil would sneak around behind the customer and twist the back of the suit, exclaiming, "You couldn't take it a size smaller even if you wanted to!" He'd ask how much money the customer had, and when he took out his 80 or 90 bucks, Phil ripped it out of his hands. Phil would then pull the suit jacket off and tell the customer he'd put it on layaway, since there were six more payments to be made. Then he would usher the customer swiftly out the door, and lock it behind him.

After work, I used to go two blocks south to a place called the Casino. It was a great night club and was right across the street from "Mom's," which had some of the best food that I ever tasted. The Royal Theatre was nearby, where Sammy Davis, Jr., the Shirelles, Marvin Gaye and many other great black entertainers came to perform. They always ate at "Mom's."

The Casino was owned by a man called Little Willy, a former numbers racketeer and the alleged "main man" of all blacks. He once appeared before the Kefaufer Senate Committee investigating organized crime. Incidentally he is legitimate today. He paid the tuition for many poor blacks who had the ability to go to law school, business school, and medical school, and he backed others in businesses. He became the black Godfather in the area. He is now an important cog in Baltimore politics.

There always seemed to be four or five whites like myself, who people thought were crazy to frequent the Casino, except for the fact that we probably were safer there than we would be elsewhere. Usually Little Melvin would insure that I and my date or friends had escorts to go back and forth to the bathroom or if we wandered around the club. If someone black happened to be walking through the crowd and accidentally pushed us, he would end up with a pistol in his face for being too near people considered guests of Little Melvin.

One time, when Little Melvin was up before a circuit court judge in Baltimore, he was admonished before pronouncement of his sentence. "It's people like you, who peddle in the nefarious pond of slow death, that must be put away." I thought this was a classic remark, considering that the judge constantly was covering up for his godsons who were dealing and doing drugs much more extensively than anyone else.

67.

Now 0 for 2 in the marriages game, Ford Lessans gave up his career in his family's lighting business and cased locations for a health food store downtown. Shortly thereafter, he and Glick became friends. Betty would later marry a wealthy doctor.

68.

I really got interested in clothes at the Piperack and probably spent more money there than I was making. Nevertheless, I began to accumulate dozens of suits, sport coats and jackets, and various alligator and Cuban-heeled shoes. I also picked up so many of the black habits and sayings it got to the point where no one understood me, including most blacks.

During this period, from 1965 to 1968, a lot of white people started to hang out with blacks, go to their night clubs, and "blow" (flatter) the black athletes who were becoming the rage. This was especially true in Baltimore where the pro basketball stars Earl "The Pearl" Monroe and Gus "Honeycomb" Johnson of the Baltimore Bullets were performing miracles. The Baltimore Colts had Lenny Moore, and Bubba Smith was just on the horizon. And the Orioles were led to a World Series by Frank Robinson. Many of us were now hanging out at the Famous Ballroom to attend the Left Bank Jazz Society shows on Sundays. On Monday nights, we went to the Blackjack Club which all of a sudden had become one-third white when a band called The Echoes, which played at Hollywood Park and the Rhapsody, began to appear there.

The first date I ever had with my wife—after meeting her at the Lotus Inn during one of Earl Maget's eating contests—was when she offered to join me at the Blackjack Club for a Monday night dance session. I came home from teaching and graduate school, changed into my outfit as a blue, which is what I was at this time, and went to pick Lynne up. She was living at the Colony Apartments, a famous singles complex in suburban Baltimore County.

Unbeknownst to me, Lynne was being romantically pursued by her boss who was married, with a pregnant wife, and was in Lynne's apartment when I arrived. Wisely, Lynne decided to leave her apartment alone and meet me downtown at Rifkin's place. He was waiting with the Driscoll Brothers to ride over to the Blackjack Club. She flew out of the house because her boss had become drunk and was criticizing me. Toting a 16-ounce Budweiser can, he had purposely bumped into me a number of times in Lynne's apartment.

We sped across the expressway into the city with the boss in hot pursuit. He almost pushed me off the road in the rain, which was a drag since I had just bought a new Mustang with a tape deck and map lights. I thought I was the living end.

When we arrived at Rifkin's apartment house, I didn't see our pursuer and concluded that we lost him. I also guessed that guy was Lynne's estranged first husband. Not true. Lynne confessed to me that he was her boss, a former Lehigh wrestling champion. I began boasting that he was lucky not to be here, because I would have killed him. I prayed that he was miles away.

As we went into the apartment building, there were fire trucks everywhere due to a minor flood. Five to ten inches of water had flooded the lobby floor. Lynne sloshed to the elevator while I tiptoed in my beautiful new blue alligator shoes, houndstooth print slacks, and a beautiful suede/leather and lambswool knit plus my one and only blue "I Spy" raincoat. I treasured my outfit, and when Lynne's romantic boss came rushing in and almost knocked me to the floor causing water to splash on me, I almost went berserk. When "Mr. Romance" threw himself in front of the elevator and screamed, "Nobody is going anywhere!" he still had the Budweiser he was drinking at Lynne's apartment. I knew one of us was in serious trouble. And when he grabbed me by my "I Spy" raincoat and ordered, "Come on, you're coming with me, I'm gonna beat your brains out," I flipped. He was bending the lapels and pulling me through more water that was damaging my alligator shoes and houndstooth print pants.

There was no doubt that the guy was going to get sucker-punched, and it was just a case of when to do it. Only when I saw his head pass the glass doors on the way out of the lobby did I decide on the moment, and I suckered him as hard as I could. His head just kept rebounding off the glass as I hit him three or four more times. I might have landed seven or eight great punches in all. When you're in a fight, you just throw punches and pray that one or two hit. Well, this was one of those great times that every shot landed. The guy must have thought I was Muhammad Ali as he and I went down in a splash on the lobby floor. I grabbed him by the neck from behind and continued throwing punches around to his face. Of course, I was now lying in the water in my "I Spy" raincoat and was completely soaked. At the same time, I realized that I was awfully tired since, in a street fight, after you've thrown punches for about 30 or 40 seconds, you're exhausted; unless you happen to be a professional boxer, which I wasn't.

We rolled out through the door and I just kept praying to myself, "Please dear God, let this guy be dead or out cold because my arm can't swing anymore, and if he gets up, I'm Passadena!"

Fortunately, the police, the firemen and the Blake cousins were across the street and ran over and pulled us apart. I leaped up and threatened to have the guy jailed, and started screaming and yelling at the cop so hysterically that he wanted to arrest me. When the officer heard from Lynne that the fight had begun in the Colony Apartments in Towson, in Baltimore County, he informed me that it was out of his jurisdiction, and that I was to go back into the lobby and the interloper was to get into his car and leave. I insisted, however, that I get the guy's name and address from his license and wrote it down. Then I went back into the lobby where Rifkin and the Driscoll Brothers had just emerged and told me how brave I was. Where were they when I needed them?

We eventually got to the Blackjack Club and Lynne admitted that she was still a little shaken up over the fight, since it was her boss and she was concerned about losing her job. She wanted to compose herself so she went to the powder room.

My finger was now throbbing and I hadn't realized yet that I must have broken it against the guy's face. I was too busy telling people about this great fight and getting "blows." About 25 minutes passed when Hart approached and asked me to rehash the fight. He waited until I finished the entire story, which I had by now greatly exaggerated, and then told me that Lynne left in a car with Friner who had late-dated me. I was only semi-pissed since there was so much other action in the Blackjack Club that her absence didn't matter; I knew I would get back to her in the next day or so to cause both her and her boss severe grief.

The next morning, while I was teaching in school, I noticed that the little finger on my punching hand was about 14 shades of black and green. I called the principal to my classroom and informed her that while lecturing I had haphazardly smacked my hand against the chalkboard (we weren't allowed to say blackboard, since it was a racist term) and broke my finger. She bought the whole story and told me to have it examined immediately. Visions of Workmen's Compensation and sick leave danced in my head.

I went to see my family doctor and he told me that it was necessary to rebreak the finger and reset it. I assumed that he meant he was going to put me asleep or localize it, and while glancing around the room, he took out on of those small medical hammers and suddenly cracked my finger, rebreaking it and causing me to throw up and pass out. When I awoke and cussed him out, he responded by telling me how he had broken his fingers numerous times playing lacrosse, and was worried that I was becoming a sissy. I was too sick even to answer, and just let him bandage me. Later, I went home and slept for ten hours.

I phoned Lynne that evening and told her I was extremely upset with what had happened and that I wanted to call her boss. Either he was going to have to pay me off or I would tell both his father and his wife what he'd done. Lynne begged me not to. She said her boss hadn't come into work that day and to let her handle it. I acquiesed, and the next evening she informed me that her boss had come in, his face full of contusions and cuts, and that he was terrified to tell his father and his pregnant wife about what happened. He was willing to go along with a settlement. She advised him he would have to pay $800 for my broken finger and related trauma. She also told me how her boss couldn't believe how hard he'd been hit, and that in all his years of wrestling at Lehigh, which was a national wrestling power, no one had ever given him such a beating. Lynne added that I was a karate expert so that he wouldn't come after me. It was a great move on her part, because I knew her boss would have killed me in a fair fight.

Anyhow, Lynne announced that she is going to give me only $400 since she felt she was due $400 for having risked her job. I was surprised and a little upset that she was going to take half the money, but when I remembered that I was only going to ask for $200 to begin with, I agreed.

True to her word, Lynne gave me $400 that weekend. We celebrated the windfall at dinner at the Prime Rib Room and began an affair which culminated in our marriage three years later. It wasn't until a week after our marriage that Lynne confessed that instead of $800, she had really received $2,400 from her boss and had kept the $2,000.

69.

Within a five year period, Third had managed to become a top flight independent drug smuggler with contacts throughout most of the world. He has traveled, lived, partied, gotten high, and reveled in cities, farmlands and outposts throughout Europe, the Mid East, the Near East, the Far East, Mexico and North America. In reality, Third just wanted to have fun, and drug smuggling financed the fun.

Third took pride in the quality of drugs which he sold. He was not a major smuggler who rivaled organized crime syndicates, but a sophisticated connoisseur whose reputation as having the best dope soon came to the attention of Interpol and the FBI. But Third seldom, if ever, carried large quantities of drugs, employing instead various "mules" (people who carried drugs across countries and state lines) to make the drops and observing them from afar. His early connections and training in Provincetown, Baltimore, New York and Mexico seeded his worldwide distribution network.

This was quite an achievement when you consider that, during much of this period, Third was registered as a student/athlete at the University of Baltimore on a lacrosse scholarship, and he actually attended classes from time to time and participated in lacrosse every spring.

To understand how Third accomplished this dual role, it is necessary to review the nature of the University of Baltimore until the late '60s. UB was a commuter school located downtown with athletic fields in suburban Northwest Baltimore. It had an undergraduate program in pre-law and business and a night law school. Anyone could get into the college and admission to the law school was only 60 credit hours. Most students who attended the school also worked full-time.

No one cared much about academic eligibility for athletes or even checked up on it. And yet over the years, UB contributed the vast majority of legislators, elected officials, businessmen, lawyers, prosecutors and judges in Baltimore City and the State of Maryland.

It, therefore, was not difficult for Third to maintain current student status and lacrosse eligibility just by registering for classes—attendance wasn't necessary. On the average, Third went to classes and/or played lacrosse for a maximum of two of the eight-month academic year.

70.

Snyder, who took an extra year at the University of Maryland, finally graduated. He considered his options: work, graduate school, race track degenerate, or law school. He decided to become a dentist.

Although shy several credits for dental school, he re-enrolled at Maryland as a special undergraduate student to take the necessary requirements mandatory for admission.

The first class which Snyder took was a Chemistry I course and he was conscientious and proud of his new purpose in life. An initial set of notes was passed out by the instructor for the beginning assignment and, as Snyder looked it over, he knew that his comprehension of chemistry was just as remote as his understanding of Ancient Mandarian Chinese dialect. So he walked out of class, drove to Baltimore, and joined Turns at University of Baltimore Evening Law School.

Guys attended UB Law School for several reasons: they were guaranteed admission; they were turned down by the University of Maryland Law School; to pay tuition, they had to work during the day; or they just wanted a law degree in order to take the bar exam to get a higher paying government job. Very few were interested in the course content.

Turns was a real estate developer and had gotten married. Snyder worked for a Title Searching Company and "leaned" at the race track on a few afternoons. Neither attended law school classes with any regularity since it was unnecessary. Almost every student got an LLB degree and passed the bar exam after the first three tries, mainly as a result of the excellent three-to-six month Bar Exam

Preparatory Courses.

Nevertheless, certain courses were mandatory, with strict instructors, and there were some very interesting ones. Turns and Snyder seldom missed their Torts class taught by an impeccably dressed, well-tanned local attorney with a funny sounding name, Spiro Agnew.

The guys were impressed by Agnew. He never changed expression, kept the same posture, seldom looked up from his notes, yet knew if you were in class. And he never had any lint on his suits.

71.

Eating prodigy Earl Maget was a very complex person. Although he spent long hours plying his trade, he wasn't a true symbol of the American work ethic. He was self-employed, yet I'm sure his income tax return—if he ever submitted one—did not reflect his various money-making schemes. During the '60s, Earl was a freelance car "repo" man, pool hustler, card player, professional gambler, check "kiter," and door-to-door encyclopedia salesman.

Earl was seven years older than my generation of guys but hung out more with our group than his own. When "repopping" cars, he always took one or two of the Diner guys along. Car repossessing was done between 2:00 and 6:00 A.M. in order to avoid nasty confrontations. Banks, auto dealers and finance companies employed Earl who was considered a top notch car "repopper." Taking cars when someone slept was easy, but repossessing them from angry wide-awake owners was another story altogether. Once Earl was taking a car at 3:00 A.M. when the owner opened his upstairs window and aimed a shotgun. Calmly, Earl stood up, pulled out his wallet and held it up and announced he was the sheriff. He told the armed owner to bring the shotgun down at once or he'd have to arrest him, besides taking the car. Earl was so believable that the guy rushed downstairs, gave him the gun and thanked him for just repossessing his car.

Since Earl possessed the tools to impound cars, he sometimes stole the vehicles, "broke them down," and sold the parts out of state. He left this off his income tax return, too.

As charming as Earl could be, he was also a screamer. If things didn't go his way, he'd carry on something fierce, yelling and screaming like a spoiled brat. During one of Earl's tirades at a card game, he accused a burly guy of cheating him and wouldn't stop screaming. The guy sat still for a few minutes, and when Earl didn't let up, he reached out, pulled Earl toward him by his shirt collar, and punched him in the nose, breaking it. Earl stopped screaming, sat back down and continued to play cards with the guy silently for the next three hours while his nose bled and swelled up beyond belief.

When Earl wasn't screaming, he could charm the pants off you. A pleasant, reassuring look dominated his face which sat atop his 400-plus pound body. He didn't have a grotesque build. It was more like a Santa Claus image.

Earl's charm reached people in an honorable way—sort of like people sometime imagine "a man of integrity" to be, and this was exactly what Earl needed for a "check kiting" scam that he "worked" for almost two years. "Kiting" checks is basically using a large amount of money in an account at one bank as verification to cash checks at other banks, and then moving around that same amount of money from bank to bank to cover all of the checks. The only way to work this scam was to have "friends" or people in the banks who trusted Earl. He courted these friendships for months before working a scam. If the teller knew Earl, then he'd feel secure in cashing Earl's checks, of course after verifying the amount at Earl's key bank on a Thursday and giving him the weekend to cover the money. Earl would use the money for gambling and other scams until the following Monday when he'd have to cover the latest check he wrote. It's a little more complicated than that [I know the bank examiners can't wait for me to fully explain it], but at one time Earl, on paper, had over $200,000 in his accounts when all he really had was $10,000. An audit finally exposed his scam and each of Earl's tellers at the banks was fired.

No one could fault Earl's devotion to his family, however. He treated his mother and brother magnanimously, and whenever possible lavished gifts upon them. Sadly, Earl's brother Manny contracted cancer. When Manny found out he only had days left to live, he ordered Earl to the hospital for his death-bed wish.

"Earl," coughed Manny, his voice barely audible. "You've covered for me for years and I can't let you pay for my funeral. So this one's on Sol Levinson."

Sol Levinson's was the only funeral parlor in Baltimore for Jews.

After Manny died, Earl went to the funeral director and selected a top-of-the-line casket and service. He told the Levinsons that his and Manny's wealthy uncle from New York would pay for them and gave the funeral home a bogus name and address.

Sure enough, Earl's brother's funeral, one of the grandest held that year, was "on" Sol Levinson.

Earl's greatest challenge in the '60s was an eating contest bet that he almost lost. Several of the guys, tired of losing "eating" bets to Earl, researched foods and their qualities, and discovered that if an individual ingests too much ketchup he keep couldn't it in his stomach without repeated vomiting.

Earl took a bet that he couldn't devour a single bottle of ketchup. The size of the bet made Earl leery, and after sucking up one quarter of the bottle, he knew why. He became nauseated. However, he'd been nauseated before (during the Polish sausage bets two years earlier) and he soon overcame it, downing the entire bottle. Earl walked out of the Diner counting his winnings and smiling. He then zoomed home and vomited for the next 12 hours. From that day on, he never again used ketchup, or even looked at a tomato.

Earl was fond of using drugs, and one evening he convinced Jeff Hall, his eating buddy, to try some marihuana. After dinner, Earl, Jeff and four other guys met on the Diner parking lot, smoked a few joints of grass and then strutted across the street to the Crest Movie Theatre. Shortly into the movie, Jeff became paranoid from the dope and started telling people in the seats around him to leave. He didn't want them whispering or even being in the same theater. The patrons got scared and walked out, leaving Jeff completely alone to watch the movie. He fell asleep and didn't come out of the theater until the next afternoon.

72.

On the second date I had with Lynne at the Tom Foolery, a downtown Baltimore bar, her wallet was stolen. I had introduced her to a number of unsavory friends of mine, including Bruce Hawk and Marbles. Immediately upon learning that she had lost her pocketbook, she confronted them. They informed her that when Carol Spice had come over to have a drink with us, she lifted Lynne's pocketbook. I told Hawk to get in touch with Carol and that I expected the purse returned in 24 hours or I was going to give her a serious headache. The pocketbook was returned with Lynne's credit cards and money. Carol claims she found it in the trash dumpster at the Colony Apartments where Lynne lived. A clever ploy on her part.

73.

Barry Levinson returned to WTOP as a secretary in the promotion department, where he was responsible for grading and writing spot announcements. He worked his way up from 10 to 60-second spots, and later mixed the film, the voice-over and the music. He learned how to play with the intricate devices at the station and then moved to another Washington station, WTTG.

There, Barry did such an outstanding job that they wanted to promote him to administrator. He didn't want this job. He called home and told his father that he was going to Los Angeles to see if he can make it in the big time. Although his father was not thrilled with the prospect, he gave Barry a couple of hundred bucks and sent him on his way, figuring that he would be back selling carpet within a year.

74.

Lynne and I were dating sporadically and we'd go to movies at least twice a month. Newsreels were still shown in those days, and Lynne's comments started to peak my curiosity about her past.

One evening in 1967, there was a brief clip about a nuclear tank that the Army revealed and that they could have in service within a year.

"Christ! Could we use that in Vietnam," I said. Lynne whispered back, "The Army's had that tank for five years."

About a month later, we were at another movie and there was a newsreel concerning a radioactive cloud from an atomic test that had killed several hundred sheep in the far west during the past week.

"Lucky for the Army that only a few sheep were killed," I concluded.

"That's bullshit," says Lynne. "First, it happened several years ago. They've been keeping a lid on it. Second, it was 10,000 sheep. Third, several hundred people in Utah died. And fourth, if it hadn't been for a severe thunderstorm, many more people would have been killed."

As we're leaving the theater I asked, "How the fuck do you know this stuff? Or are you putting me on?"

Lynne informed me that her first job out of high school was with the Army at the Chemical and Biological Welfare Center at Edgewood Arsenal, near Aberdeen Proving Ground, about 25 miles north of Baltimore.

"I was secretary to the Commander. He looked like Gregory Peck. I had top secret clearance. You'd be amazed at what went on there. Just amazed," sighed Lynne.

"Amaze me," I deadpanned, "Amaze me."

Lynne began to tell me a story about how the Army tested innocent enlisted "volunteers" for experimental germ warfare. All sorts of deadly viruses and chemicals.

"These were human experiments and many soldiers died over a period of years. The deaths were listed officially as automobile accidents," she said. "And when there were a large number of deaths over a brief period of time, they became multi-car/multi-personnel deaths from a major chain-reaction accident."

Lynne continued the story by informing me that it came to the attention of a Congressional researcher that an alarming number of car-related deaths had occurred in the Aberdeen/Edgewood area involving soldiers. The accidents cost a great deal of insurance money to the government. Inquiries from grieving parents and spouses of the recruits were becoming embarrassing.

A Congressional Committee forced the Army to immediately institute an extensive Driver's Education program which they planned to monitor over three years. Driver's-Ed training began soon afterward replete with private consultants, films, sophisticated testing equipment, teachers at Edgewood. Everyone at the base was required to complete an intensified program and be retested twice a year.

The Driver's-Ed staff obviously did not have top secret clearance. Other Army personnel throughout the country with no top secret clearance read about the program and began reassigning personnel to Edgewood for Drivers-Education training.

The human experiments were seriously curtailed because of the high influx of people without top secret clearance involved with the Driver's-Ed program. As a result, the number of "auto-related" deaths dropped dramatically.

The Congressional Committee was so proud of its program at Edgewood that they made a major media splash over it and went to Edgewood for an awards ceremony. The result of the program was so astounding that the story commanded headlines. Top Army brass, "forgetting" the real reason for the decline in auto deaths, patted each other on the back for the brilliant success of the program, dismantled the Chemical and Biological warfare unit, relocating it to another top secret base. Edgewood was designated as its National Driver's-Ed Training Base.

I was mesmerized by the story. "Lynne, that is very interesting, but I'm afraid you're under arrest. I'm with the F.B.I. and we've been waiting for you to blab that top secret information. Come with me. We're going to my house where I'm going to interrogate you and then spank you severely."

Lynne stared at me and exclaimed: "You are sick!"

75.

Pick Dawson was part of Third's smuggling clique, although he usually just hung around Ibiza and didn't actually work with them. Pick told Third that he and Cass Elliot were lovers, that he was her old man, and that she covered for him, meaning that she took care of him financially in a jackpot, or trouble, situation. Pick told a story about ripping off a number of bathrobes and towels from a very famous hotel in London when he and Mama Cass were there. When The Mamas and The Papas returned to London, they were probably going to get busted.

Third went to Paris with Pick and they had a ball, twice being arrested and jailed for hassling cab drivers.

True to Pick's story, The Mamas and The Papas were busted when they re-returned to London for ripping off hotels. They received bad publicity just before leaving for Paris where they were part of a huge Jimi Hendrix concert. Third and Pick were staying at the same hotel as The Mamas and The Papas. Pick introduced Cass Elliot to Third, whom Cass said she had known well for years. Although Third vaguely remembered her as a fat chick who hung around downtown Baltimore at the Peabody Book Store and Martick's Bar (places where Bohemians and beatnicks leaned), he listened to her story for a while. He let Cass think that she also knew his twin sister. The girl had a similar name, but was older and not related to Third. After four hours of this charade, Third rudely told Mama Cass that he didn't know her at all, and that his sister was at least six years younger than he. He stormed out.

Later that night, Cass came to Third's room and apologized. They became very friendly.

76.

Neurotic Nat and his girlfriend Pam ran into Ford Lessans, after his separation, at the Tom Foolery Bar. They were feeling sorry for him and accompanied him to his now empty townhouse where they offered him some great hashish. He'd never tried anything stronger than scotch and soda.

After a half-hour of ingesting the drug, Ford continued to tell them that the hashish was having no effect on him at all. He offered Pam and Neurotic Nat a tour of the house and took them upstairs. While showing them the bedroom, he pulled a gun from underneath the pillow. Nat and Pam panicked and rushed into the bathroom, locking themselves in and hiding in the shower stall. Ford was actually in a somewhat nervous state and wanted to make sure that if he did get high he won't do anything rash. He emptied the bullets into one drawer, and put the gun in another. Nat and Pam peeked out of the door when they hadn't heard anything for awhile and observed Ford climbing out of the window. They grabbed him before he fell out.

"What are you doing?" they cry out. "I'm flying, I'm Peter Pan, and the Lost Boys are right behind me!"

Dope didn't do a thing to Ford. Neurotic Nat nailed the windows shut and stayed with Ford until four in the morning, when Peter Pan and the Lost Boys finally fell asleep.

This was his introduction to the vastly different culture to which Ford had come. He embraced it dearly by going a tad overboard.

77.

One of the other main places where many of the playground and Diner guys hung out (between 1957-67) was Harry's Barber Shop. It was located in Southeast Baltimore in a converted garage. Harry's customers included Tin Men, judges, lawyers, bookmakers, police, rich men, bums and degenerates. Among the assorted characters who hung out at Harry's were Rawhide, Jailer, Rainbow, Blackjack, Chink and Fast-talking/Fast-walking Frank. Harry was in his 40s and a former drummer on The Block, Baltimore's adult entertainment district. He had a great outlook on life, always happy-go-lucky, and was one of the best barbers in the U.S. in those days. (Later, when the unisex shops came into vogue, he lost most of his clientele, but this was Harry's golden era.)

His shop was always crowded, although not primarily for haircuts. It was a place for bull sessions. There were pinochle games and checkers, and other attractions. Many times, a guy would walk in for a haircut, see the crowd, flop depressingly into a chair lamenting a two hour wait, and be shocked by Harry telling him, "Next."

Not only did you get your haircut at Harry's but hookers were always available. Sometimes the girls came in such numbers that they would give "it" away to Harry and the guys, and, if the girls were "special," Harry would temporarily close the shop. Behind the barber shop in the same building was a room with a little cot on one side and a toilet on the other. The majority of hookers worked out of there. Sometimes when Harry closed the shop, the girls or the guys could sit in the barber chair and take turns "doing" each other; and many a guy got blown while his hair got cut. From time to time there were some reasonably attractive women hustling at Harry's but they were usually gobbled up and removed from the shop by a rich guy, or a sap who had fallen in love. These guys usually put the girl up in an apartment for a while. The shop regulars would get pissed off since the guy had absconded with a favorite.

The hookers at Harry's charged anywhere from $2 to $6 a trick. Every now and then there'd be a $10 girl who was a real beauty, on her way through Baltimore looking to pick up extra money.

Among Harry's regulars was Mat Delaney, the shop's resident philosopher and inventor. He was a brilliant guy whose mind had been damaged by alcohol. He always came up with the weirdest sort of inventions (an underwater umbrella was one of his best). Mat wrote angry letters to the city comptroller or the mayor. He felt there was blasphemy in Harry's, and he didn't like it. Although Delaney was a very interesting, crazy and sympathetic character, I can remember seeing him drunk in the gutter and a stray dog pissing on his face.

Years ago, Mat claimed to have invented stackable potato chips, backup lights for cars, air bags for car crashes, and other devices that he said people stole from him, or he was bilked out of by sharpie patent lawyers.

Mat also devised bionic germs to ward off muggers, and a way to move the Bermuda Triangle. He wanted to move it into the Black Sea to wipe out the Russian fleet.

There was a peculiar incident at Harry's once when a manufacturer's representative from Ohio came in for his monthly order of aluminum from the Tin Men of Baltimore. He was a straight-laced guy who always stopped by Harry's to get his hair cut and listen to the bullshit. Amazingly, he never expressed any interest in a hooker. This time, however, he overheard some glowing remarks from the guys about a girl named Sherry. He spotted her in the back just before the door closed.

Harry whispered to him, "That's Sherry, a lot of guys like her even though she's a little on the chunky side." This guy was no lightweight himself, weighing about 270 pounds. Harry added, "Say, if you want to get down, I'll cut your hair a little later." The guy hemmed and hawed and "reluctantly" decided he would go back and meet the voluptuous Sherry.

Harry sent in the manufacturer's rep right after the hooker's client came out. Fifteen minutes later, Sherry began calling to Harry softly, "Harry, could you come back here for a second." Harry answered, "Yeah, in a little bit." She said louder, "Could you hurry up please," and Harry angrily responded, "In a second!"

Finally Harry went back. Gasping for air, Sherry shakingly told him she thought this guy fell asleep on top of her and could Harry help get him off since he not only was crushing her but holding up business. Harry took a look at the guy and recognized something was seriously wrong. He quickly called in an off-duty cop named Chiller who was sitting outside. Chiller came back, felt the pulse, and told Harry the guy was dead.

Harry came out and announced to the shop, "I need your help fellas, we can't have this dead guy laying on top of Sherry!" So three guys scurried back into the very cramped quarters to try to lift the corpse off the hooker before the cops and an ambulance got there. They finally removed him, twisted him around, and propped him up on the toilet.

In the meantime, everybody was in a panic trying to dress the rep, since he had a "hard on" and rigor mortis was setting in. They finally got his pants up and zipper partially closed but couldn't find his underpants. As it turned out Neurotic Nat, who was there for his third haircut and hooker that week, stole his underpants so that he would have a souvenir of this bizarre incident. They decided to leave the rep with his pants down, as though he had a heart attack while going to the bathroom.

The police and the ambulance arrived and struggled to get this fat corpse out through the door and into a stretcher. As they were carrying him out, everyone saw the "hard on" and broke up. Meanwhile, Sherry the hooker was screaming for someone to go through the dead guy's wallet to get her fee. One of the guys in the barber shop threw his hands over her mouth because Harry didn't know who the police were and didn't want anyone to know what really happened. As they were leaving, one of the ambulance drivers asked Harry what he should tell the guy's wife about how he died. "In the saddle," Harry boasted.

78.

In February 1966, Boogie and Eggie decided to room together and rented a house behind the Diner. As a second thought, Boogie took a sales rep job in Atlanta, and Yussel moved in with Eggie. Eggie chose the top floor and Yussel set up shop in the basement. The house became a forum for bull sessions, card games, closet scenes and group sex.

Billy Joe was a weirdo from Harry's Barber Shop who liked being spanked and whipped. He became very popular at group scenes along with two hookers who periodically hustled at Harry's, and took turns whipping Billy Joe while he orally devoured the other.

The first night this bizarre scene occurred at Eggie and Yussel's guys haggled vociferously over prime seating around the bed. Snyder won the most comfortable and closest chair and the show began. Hooker Sherry, while drawing back the whip for Billy Joe's first lash, accidentally caught Snyder on the shoulder. Snyder didn't flinch, comically looking at the guys, raising his eyebrows. But on Sherry's next round-house blow, the whip caught Snyder across the face. He cried out, "Dibs!" and meekly vacated the best seat in the house.

79.

As a probation officer, Donnie Burger worked for the Supreme Court bench. He was wheeling and dealing with the clients, copping pleas for some and dealing with others. During his worst days as an addict, when he was shooting heroin every half hour, Donnie would invariably play in a six-handed pitch game at Yussel and Eggie's place. He didn't know that he was "in between," that is, being hustled in the game, because he was so wacked out all of the time. Every 30 minutes he would call a time out, pull out his kit, cook his heroin in a spoon, shoot up, then continue with the game. It kept Eggie and Yussel comfortably ahead in their rent payments.

80.

Boogie's new job was as a manufacturer's rep for women's clothing, traveling throughout the Southeastern United States. He was based in Atlanta and when he wasn't on the road, he played basketball for the Jewish Community Center and became quite popular. He accepted lots of dares, raised a lot of hell and got into crazy scenes with Southern belles. Boogie became a celebrity of sorts in Atlanta.

After a year, he and a friend decided to lease a store for a month and sell some of the cheap, unconventional clothes enjoying hippie popularity and made in Hong Kong. They figured to take a pop at opening a retail shop and maybe picking up some quick extra money. Boogie and his partner each put up $750, bought jeans and goofy-looking outfits from New York, rented a place on Peachtree Street, called it The Merry-Go-Round, and operated at crazy hours, from four in the afternoon until three in the morning, or from midnight to eight in the morning. They sold out of everything within a week. They quickly returned to New York, bought lots of crazy clothes, and sold out again. This time in three days. Boogie and his partner did outlandish things, such as dressing up like women or giving free clothes to the fifth black person or fourth oriental girl from Alabama, etc. They received coverage from the newspapers and TV. Within a month, they gave up their regular jobs and went into the business full-time. Shortly after, they opened another store across the street called Sexy Sadie's, selling shoes along with clothing. Both stores enjoyed meteoric success.

81.

Lynne was being hassled by a finance company because she had charged a lot on her husbands credit cards, just after becoming legally separated from him. Bo Death worked for a finance company at the time and I told him about the creditor's harassment of Lynne.

One night he came along on a date. While at Lynne's, the man from the finance company called her, hounding her about outstanding bills. Bo Death let Lynne talk for a few minutes and then he picked up the extension and forcefully said, "Do not hang up this phone. I repeat. Do not hang up this phone. This is Lt. Scanlon of the Phone Harassment Division of the Police Department. I repeat, do not hang up this phone!" Naturally, the guy hung up. He was terrified. Lynne never received another call nor ever paid a dime on the bill.

That same night, as we're driving over to Mandell's for dinner, Lynne related a story about Gary Sollors, a guy she'd also been dating pretty seriously. He told her that I was a heroin addict and said I had associated with Donnie Burger and therefore I must also be dealing drugs.

When we arrived at Mandell's, Bo Death and I excused ourselves, got Sollors' phone number, and went downstairs to the pay phone to call him. We knew he was studying for the Bar Exam and so the first thing that I said when he answered was that I was a little upset hearing the stories that he was spreading about me. Maybe he wouldn't like it if I spread some about him to the Bar Examiner's Character Committee.

Suddenly, Bo Death ripped the phone from my hand and told Sollors that he was Donnie Burger. He was livid over Sollors' accusations and threatened to kill him. Sollors was terribly upset and started screaming, crying and finally pleading into the phone, denying everything.

Finally, Bo Death (as Burger) said, "Look, Sollors, I'm not real tough, but I dig contact." At this, Sollors fainted.

After dinner, we walked past the Crest Movie Theatre and there, to his obvious misfortune, was Sollors waiting in line. He threw his hands back against the wall of the movie house thinking that he was going to be machine-gunned to death. We glared at him and continued walking slowly into the parking lot.

82.

Third used to fly into Bombay, buy 14¢ ruffled shirts, and sell them for $7 each in Paris and in Ibiza. While in Bombay one day, Third was walking the streets of the city when he was immediately attracted to the pungent smell of sex; a scent when you've been in bed with somebody all day, multiplied 20-fold. He was informed by a street peddler that he was heading in the direction of the Street of Cages where there are women who reside in balconies extended out over the street and which look like bamboo jail cells.

This was a red light district giving the illusion of "cages" hanging off of street lights. There, Third had quite a go with some Nepalese women. He said there was no big difference between women from Tibet and women from Nepal, but it sounded worldly to say, "Hey, I had a go at it with a Nepalese woman." Most of the time Third would smoke a lot of opium because he didn't want to think about any diseases these Streets of Cages women might have had.

83.

Donnie Burger had moved downtown and we parted ways after he launched into a career of heroin dealing. He was even in a series of life-threatening battles with other drug dealers who were always trying to rob each other. He became a patient in a methadone program, mainly to have methadone available to sell and/or get high on. He gave up his job as a probation officer and went on welfare and medical assistance. Yet he was making a bundle.

His girlfriend Slave really got off on abuse and Donnie relished abusing her. She finally got up enough nerve to leave him. Shortly after, Slave married and had triplets, but later got divorced.

Donnie had a crash pad on St. Paul Street. Actually, it was a "shooting gallery" for junkies, and the back room was loaded with televisions and lots of other stolen or traded materials that came from drug deals. He had a favorite motto: "It's not for $4.99," meaning that he'll never drop the price of heroin from $5.00 a bag.

The relationship between Ben and Carol fell apart due to Ben's inability to adjust to normal married life. He needed the adoration and attention of the guys, and was also frustrated by his inability to succeed in business. They divorced and Ben moved back downtown.

84.

In Los Angeles, Barry Levinson fell in with other out of work and would-be actors. For the next couple of years he worked with a small acting company, the Oxford Theatre. He studied acting, took part in production, and worked improvisational theater. He also had a part-time job in a delicatessen in order to support himself. Eventually he began appearing in some of the comedy clubs. It was during this period when Barry learned how to write comedy. He also met a bright actress/comedienne named Valerie Curtin and they began to date.

85.

Although it was obviously not civic pride that motivated us, many of the guys worked for the government, primarily as parole and probation officers. I became a school teacher because I couldn't pass the civil service exam for probation officer. I took it three times. I was going to pay someone to take it for me but got cold feet after a guy, whom Ben paid to take the insurance agent test for him, got caught. Glick and a guy named Waback were the first guys I knew who became probation officers. Waback got fired for falsifying mileage reports. His "do-good" supervisor followed him for days and caught him napping at home every day, all day.

Bill McAuliffe also became a probation officer to support himself during his doctoral studies. Following his Master's degree from Washington University in St. Louis, Bill returned to Baltimore to study for a doctorate at Johns Hopkins. He enrolled for a couple of courses in Morgan State's graduate school and took one with me during the second semester of academic year 1966–67. It was called "Migrations."

The course was taught by an African instructor named Opara, who was a very stubborn man. It provided an excellent mental challenge for me to be in class with Bill, a Phi Beta Kappa. I ended up with a higher grade than Bill's and it was my crowning achievement, along with receiving a Master's degree.

Bill was so pissed off with Professor Opara's method of teaching and his interpretation of examination questions that I thought he was going to sucker-punch the teacher. Bill showed great restraint.

86.

Cass Elliot's family was originally from Alexandria, Virginia, and they moved back there when she left high school in Baltimore. When Cass came into Washington from time to time, she always stayed in Alexandria. She learned that Third was back in the U.S. and called him to meet her in Washington. Third agreed but was not happy about it, for Cass was driving, and since it was her car, he was a captive. She wanted Third to drive but he insisted that he never drove girls around. Cass was very concerned about being accosted on the street by people. She's afraid that she might lose control of the car. This turned out to be a real concern because of her celebrity status.

As they drove around, they talked about Baltimore people. It was mainly about how people treated Cass back in high school. She told Third a story about some very wealthy, sophisticated, one-time high school sorority girls from Baltimore who came up to New York with their husbands when The Mamas and The Papas first hit it big. After the show, the girls came backstage to meet with Cass, and one of them, Mimi Seligman, greeted her like a long lost friend. Cass remembered how she had been treated with distain in high school because of her weight, and perhaps partly due to her gross behavior. She lashed out at Mimi, "You didn't know me then and I don't know you now!"

87.

Swartzie got married and soon opened a string of submarine and pizza shops—Two shops.

While Swartzie was running his sub shops, his buddy Jules was working for clothing manufacturer Bobby Brooks. Jules helps bankroll Swartzie in a real estate partnership to buy residential properties. Within two years, Swartzie bought 60 homes. He became an innovator in the real estate business. A speculator would call Swartzie about a house he'd purchased for $4,000 and offered to sell it to Swartzie for $4,200 in cash. If Swartzie liked the house, he would pay the guy with the money from Jules. He would receive a deed to the house, not a contract. Then he would take the deed to a savings and loan and ask to borrow $5,300. When they would ask for the contract, Swartzie would tell them that he bought it in a cash deal and all he had was the deed. The exact amount of the cash sale could not be confirmed. After settlement, Swartzie would end up with $500 or $600 profit. He also owned the house. He then offered prospective renters the house for $38 a week. The major city landlords were receiving $25 per week, yet Swartzie had a novel approach. "Mrs. Smith, we are a full-service realtor. We give you maintenance, electricity, plumbing, etc., etc. All you have to do is give us a $38 deposit, $38 for the first week's rent, and $38 from that time on and you will get full service. No other realtor will give you full service!"

Obviously Swartzie wouldn't deliver full service. What did it matter? He then cautioned the renter that if he missed one week's payment, the sheriff would put her on the sidewalk the next day.

One of Swartzie's major sub shop accounts was the Baltimore Orioles baseball team, because one of his stores was located near Memorial Stadium. Swartzie and Jerry, his partner, bet a great deal.

They believed they discovered a scientific way of winning bets on baseball games. It all depended on the number of Polish ham submarine sandwiches that Boog Powell ate. But the scheme didn't work and they lost more money. When they came home in the evening, they'd gamble until very late at night. They'd bet on particular "late" basketball or baseball games on the west coast. They'd send money to the "callee," usually a friend then living in California, so that he'd put his telephone near a radio in order for them to listen to a play-by-play of the game. Not only did their phone bill go through the roof, but they lost thousands. This didn't endear Swartzie to his wife. They are divorced.

88.

Murray began to spend a lot of time in Aspen, Colorado. He was shooting high dose levels of heroin, and was living in a teepee. Murray then was spiritually married to an Indian and his wife had a child soon after, but the kid had no Indian blood.

A couple months later, Murray returned to Baltimore, changed his name to Gyro, and started playing bass for a band at the Saytre House in Northeast Baltimore. An excellent "far away" bar.

The band developed quite a following mainly because of the lead singer, Jimmy Spore. He was to the Gentiles what Huddles was to the Jews, yet in a different way.

Third discovered Spore in Ocean City, brought him to the Diner, and they developed a solid friendship over the years. In high school, Jimmy had been an "A" student, class president of Calvert Hall High, and voted "most likely to succeed." He looked like a Roman god, had a silver tongue, and was irresistible to women. Yet Spore fell from grace. After high school he married his childhood sweetheart, who gave him a son. Then he just kind of drifted. Divorce followed, so did a serious drug addiction. He traveled throughout North America, paralleling Third's odysseys in New York and Mexico. Yet Jimmy was a winner. Any avenue he took usually led to success, legal or illegal. It was not surprising when he decided to become a rock and roll singer.

The key musician in the group was the saxophone player Jimmy

Lumes. Later he played with Mitch Ryder and the Detroit Wheel. Jimmy's girlfriend was one of Lynne's roommates. They used to go to the Saytre House often. One night after the bar had closed, Lynne, who was staying in her parents' house because they were out of town, invited the band over. Spore, Murray (Gyro), and Bruce Hawk (who was not in the band) decided to commandeer the place, and sleep there. Lynne was not too thrilled about that but didn't know how to handle the guys. She went upstairs and locked her younger sister Gail in her bedroom. It was standard procedure when Lynne lived at home as a teenager.

Spore got in Lynne's parents' bed and told Lynne, "You may lay beside me. Tonight's *your* night."

Lynne, who at the time would dearly love to make it with Spore, couldn't believe his approach and surprisingly passed on the offer. Spore, who is used to women falling all over him, became indignant and locked Lynne out of her parents' room.

Meanwhile, sister Gail watched from the upstairs window as Murray, in total darkness, took out the lawn mower, carved out a spot on the lawn, and went to sleep on it. Bruce Hawk was busy making phone calls to Mexico, Sweden and Morocco.

When Lynne awoke the next morning, she found the kitchen a wreck. Spore had attempted to cook brown rice. Murray was asleep in the bushes out front and came in to answer a collect call to Bruce Hawk from Tangiers. Lynne began to scream at the guys but her voice was drowned out by an impromptu band rehearsal that went on for hours. The band was very popular, but consisted of gypsy musicians. As soon as spring arrived, the group dispersed around the country.

Murray (no longer Gyro) returned to Aspen. He hadn't fired heroin for several months but decided to inject his old dosage. He promptly went into a coma and his wife couldn't wake him. She tried for days, brought in both medical and spiritual assistance, and then chartered a Lear Jet to take them to Johns Hopkins Hospital in Baltimore. The wife was constantly by Murray's side urging him on. "Wake up! Please, Murray, come back to me! Wake up!"

For weeks Murray didn't move, but then one morning he suddenly sat up at attention and announced, "I can't come back!" He fell back down in the bed and died.

89.

Jay Huff decided to start a vending business. Although he was very clever at robbing his boss, Jay wanted more. He convinced the tavern owners to return his boss's machines and to put in his own. Jay was very successful for a few months. He used his newfound money to buy a bar. It was located across the street from the state prison and was called *The Little House Across from the Big House.*

Jay was now drinking heavily. He also began to take speed. Eventually, he ignored the vending business, and began hanging out in his bar more and more. His old boss reclaimed his stores, and Jay's machines were thrown into the street. He was left the bar. After a few months, the drugs and alcohol took their toll and Jay lost the bar. He declared bankruptcy.

90.

Glick was busted for marihuana possession and distribution. He was caught with two pounds of grass. It's the late 1960s, so he got only a two year sentence. Being a probation officer didn't help his case.

On appeal, Bob presented testimony from psychiatrists who believed that he would "flip-out" if imprisoned. The judge bought it and changed the sentence to five years probation.

From then on, Glick became a macro-biotic obsessive, swearing total abstinence from meat, alcohol and drugs. Later he opened a health food store in Baltimore.

91.

Ez graduated from University of Maryland, married his college sweetheart and went to work in the family tire business. Because of brother Three-quarter Finger Charlie's aggressive leadership, the company grew rapidly. So did Ez's family. He had a son and daughter within two years.

92.

Dan Gold owed Third $8,000 for a hashish shipment, so Third decided to collect it personally in Morocco. Gold then lived in Casablanca.

Third was at his most powerful in Casablanca where he considered himself a member of the Junior Mafia, "Fast Eddie," as Gold called him. Third told Gold, "These aren't real Arabs here in Casablanca. They are fag Arabs." Third spoke to people in broken French and Arabic and presumed everyone understood him. If Third went to negotiate a price in the different markets, he would ask the Arabs, "How much?" and no matter what the quoted price, he would scream at them, "Fuck you!" He said they understood this. He once chastised Gold for a full week for overspending to purchase a bunch of beautiful masks for 35¢ apiece.

On a previous visit, Third and Gold were gambling at a hotel in Marakesh where they had spent two nights. The next day they paid the bill and boarded the train to Casablanca. Suddenly they were surrounded by dozens of guards and pulled off the train, which then was held up for two hours. The police told them to return to settle their hotel room bill. It seems that after Third paid the bill, he went back to the bar, had several drinks, and charged them to his room. It came to $7.00, yet Third argued relentlessly insisting the hotel call off the police, and finally paying the $7.00 as the paddywagon arrived.

Third showed up at the house of Gold and his wife, a huge mansion in an area called Ansa. There was no furniture in the house, although Gold had constructed a table out of cardboard. They argued immediately over the money that Gold didn't have, and never would.

So, Third and Dan went to Lebanon and met at a beach cafe in Beirut where they negotiated a fresh new deal, testing hashish Arab style, with charcoal in their pipes. As they were closing the deal, three Arabs tried to knife them. Fortunately, Gold overheard the word "Yehuden" (Jew) as the Arabs approached. They ran from the beach up into the hills and escaped. The '67 Arab-Israeli War broke out when they were in Beirut, and fortunately Third and Gold were evacuated.

93.

Levinson and Craig Nelson worked up a comedy routine which they performed in local night clubs. It opened doors and they submitted sketches to the popular *Lowman and Barclay TV Show* in L.A. where they were hired as writers. It was a tough job. There are only four writers to put together a 90-minute variety show each week. Eventually, Barry and Craig became writer-performers, creating a lot of their own material. They won a local Emmy Award the following year. The day after the Emmy Awards were announced, the show was cancelled, leaving Barry unemployed again.

In 1967, Mama Cass married songwriter James Hendricks (not to be confused with singer Jimi Hendrix). She did it as a favor to keep him out of the military.

94.

When the Baltimore riots occurred, I informed my mother that I was afraid of going down to collect the rents for the six homes my father had bought shortly before he died in the late '50s. They were rental properties in the worst sections of Baltimore. These houses were a losing proposition and were a tremendous problem. Renters would call the house day and night demanding that I repair their homes. My Uncle Albert was in charge of repairs and collections. But, the prick instead was ripping my mother off. That's why I took over.

One day, after the riots, I was on scenic Melvin Drive, a converted alley where the row homes had been built. They were clustered tightly together. I noticed some unsavory looking characters hanging around as I went in to collect the rent. When I came out, I saw five of them sitting near my car. Due to the bad times in the U.S., I now carried a gun, praying that I wouldn't have to use it. Yet I realized that a show of force was often necessary while collecting rent in Southwest Baltimore. I told these guys to move away from the car, but they didn't listen. I pulled my gun out of the holster. It wasn't easy and I was terrified. They began to back up and then ducked around by a side street, peering at me from around the corner. As I hustled to my car, they boldly began to come out. I shouted that if they moved again I was going to shoot, yet they kept coming. I guess they didn't believe me. I opened fire, emptying the gun, and then I leapt into the car. As I panically drove away, the car swiped the curb and several filled trash cans. By that time, I realized that I had wounded a brick wall, and killed the corner house.

I informed my mother that from now on tenants would mail in their rent checks. But before we set up a mail service, I would stop on Pennsylvania Avenue for assistance. Before driving downtown, Little Melvin would put two of his men in my car and we would all collect the rents. The henchmen, instead of protecting me, wanted to beat up on people. Anyone who gave me a weird look would get jumped. This did not work, especially when they beat one of our older tenants senseless. He had to pay doctor bills and couldn't afford his rent for two months. Finally, I found someone to buy the properties, but I had to pay him $3,000 to take the six homes off my hands. It was worth it.

95.

Swartzie and Jules began making loads of money as landlords, and prepared to invest in shopping centers and department stores, when they also decided to become bookmakers.

They had lost a lot of money gambling and were both divorced. Swartzie sold the sub shops and at first became a "beard" for two big bookmakers. A "beard" fronted for bookies when they needed a third party to bet with other bookmakers who had a game that they thought was a lock, or a "steamer" (a fixed game). Not many people across the nation were aware that in the late '60s and early '70s, the Kansas City Chiefs football team was suspected of fixing games. At the very last minute, Swartzie, as the beard, would lay a lot of money on a bookie betting either on or against Kansas City. This scheme worked well for a couple of years until other bookies sensed that something crooked might be going on. They took Kansas City games off the board.

In the meantime, one of the major "books" went to jail. Since it was Jules' Uncle Sid, Swartzie did him a favor and took over the business. When the "book" came out of prison, Swartzie handed him a quarter of a million dollars cash. As a result, Jules and Swartzie took over the major numbers and sports betting business in Maryland. Swartzie became a very successful high class bookie with a high class following. People were paid off immediately, no matter how big the bet.

They made money faster than they could count it. And they began to live in an extremely ostentatious lifestyle. Particularly Swartzie. The guys rented an enormous home in Greenspring Valley and set up shop.

96.

Boogie brought Bo Death, Obie and some "degenerates" from the Diner to Atlanta and gave them jobs. In spite of their weak work ethic, they all became fairly successful. Yet Boogie still had to fire and rehire them on several occasions.

Boogie's partner had difficulty dealing with Boogie's friends because their lifestyles were strange and they seemed more interested in taking some young girl into the dressing room for a quickie, or filching the till, shoplifting or giving away clothes in exchange for sex. Apparently their antics didn't dampen the success of the two stores at all. Boogie soon opened another store.

97.

In the fall of 1968, Eggie moved to a nice apartment downtown. Yussel got Elliot as a new roommate. An original hippie, Elliot had long hair and a beard, and constantly tripped on acid. He was totally psychedelic.

One afternoon Elliot was on a trip in his room after he took three tabs of acid. He hadn't yet met Hart, who was coming over to spend the day with Yussel. For a smile, Yussel cautioned Elliot that "Dr. Hart" is stopping by for a visit. He wryly explained that Dr. Hart was a brilliant physician from the old country who was also the Dean of the Hebrew College, Ner Israel. Elliot told Yussel, "It's cool. I'm straight. I won't embarrass you."

After Hart arrived and exchanged pleasantries with Yussel, he was introduced to Elliot who had barely managed to appear coherent. "Nu," greets Dr. Hart in broken English, "It is a pleasure to make your acquaintance, mine friend."

As they were shaking hands, Hart abruptly threw his arms around Elliot and began pumping up against his pelvis like a dog in heat.

The shock and the acid prompted Elliot to freak out and run to the bedroom, pulling the covers over his head. He remained under the sheets for 15 hours. Yussel and Hart were in hysterics with laughter.

98.

When I went to the Casino on Pennsylvania Avenue in the late '60s, the only other white guy I saw was Charlie Three-quarter Finger Ezrine. He had become friends with several of the Baltimore Bullets, notably Gus Johnson, and a guy named Jimmie Gilreath who used to be the roommate of Wilt Chamberlain at the University of Kansas.

He and Wilt had remained close friends. At a Bullet-Laker game, Gilreath introduced my sister Nancy to Wilt. Wilt became infatuated with Nancy and started a long distance phone courtship with her. This had my mother beside herself. One day, we were watching TV and I said to her, "Ma, that's the guy named Norman who calls Nancy on the phone. His professional name is Wilt Chamberlain."

"My God," replied Mom, "He's such a tall schvatsa. What's he want with Nancy?"

"You know, Ma," I deadpanned, "He makes a quarter million dollars a year."

"Well," Mom reflected, "She could do worse."

99.

I used to throw parties during my later blue period. There would often be 200 people packed tightly in our little row house near Reisterstown Road Plaza. The 200 included John Mackey, all-pro tight end of the Colts, and Gus Johnson, of the Baltimore Bullets, and if the Chicago Bulls were in town, they were there, too. Lou Alcindor, who became Kareem Abdul Jabbar, came to a party. So did Bubba

Smith. There were even some white players including Colts line-backer Mike Curtis, who was dating Lynne's sister, Pam.

One night, I invited Lynne, Curtis and Pam over for dinner. Lynne cooked the dinner, brought out a dozen pieces of fried chicken breasts and placed them near Mike Curtis, who obviously assumed that it was his plate. He devoured all 12 before we finished our salads. He then criticized us for being too diet-conscious.

Curtis relished patting you on the back very hard as though you were his buddy, not realizing his great strength. He almost crippled Lynne, Pam and me because his back pats were of the same velocity as "hits" that he delivered on the football field.

100.

For a couple of years, I became white again, even though I was now Assistant Dean of the Graduate School at Morgan State. The school needed a white Assistant Dean, since it was on its way to becoming, by 1970, the first totally integrated institution in the country, with 50 percent white and 50 percent black, an enrollment for which the Dean and I were solely responsible.

The Dean was a conservative black. He made Richard Nixon look like a liberal. So I had to act as white as I could. That's why I became white again. I stopped dressing like Johnny BeBop and Superfly, and went back to a semi-Ivy League look.

Later, I went into my third and final "blue" period in which I became a conservative black, like a black southern aristocrat, not much different from the Dean who came from the Charleston, South Carolina's black aristocracy.

Here's a piece of trivia. I was a research assistant for the Dean in writing, along with Frank Bowles, the last book that ever used the word "negroes" officially. It was a Carnegie Commission sponsored book entitled *Higher Education Among the Negroes,* which was eventually published in 1971. During the Dean's sabbatical, I served as Acting Dean for 11 months.

It used to amaze me, sitting in on meetings where the department chairmen decided who would teach in the Graduate School—which was an honor considering that a graduate school professor taught three courses instead of four or five. They also determined who would make tenure. Amazingly, the black professors and administrators openly discuss turning a teacher down on the basis of his shade and color. Not that he was white, but that he didn't have the proper shade of black. If an instructor were too dark, he had trouble gaining the respect and the support of the old-line college professors and administrators, unless one of them happened to be very black himself. I clearly recall someone who jokingly mentioned, "I'm not going to support that negro for tenure until he starts turning a little bit grayer."

I used to feel uncomfortable myself during the summer when, by tanning, I looked about as dark as any of the blacks who had been denied tenure at Morgan State. Thank God they knew I was white. It could have been my blue eyes.

I adapted to the Dean's style of administration and work ethic, and followed it to this day. He was an easygoing guy, very methodical and very hard working, yet he had certain biases which he had held on to for many, many years. He detested homosexuals, who were well represented at Morgan State. Their mere presence drove him into a frenzy. He had been a former baseball and basketball player. He was in the old Negro Baseball League, and had legendary stories to tell. He received his doctorate from an Ivy League school, no easy chore for a black man in the '30s.

The Dean worked in a nicely furnished office, and after he left work for the day I took it over. Since the Graduate School classes were mainly in the evening, it was my assignment to man the office. After 6:00 P.M. there were few callers. This worked out great because it gave me an excellent opportunity for little trysts with some of my favorite co-eds. One evening, I was engaged in a sexual encounter on the Dean's sofa, working away like a dog in heat when the door was unlocked and in strolled the Dean. We froze, unable to break apart while the Dean walked over to his desk for some papers. Never glancing our way, he casually walked out, locking the door behind. He never even mentioned it.

(The Dean was a great mentor and his philosophies about life, education, administration and writing have helped me a lot over the years. At 64 years of age, he also became a friend. Yet he had more of a father-son relationship with me, which I still cherish. He died a year after I left Morgan State to work for the State Health Department.)

Unbelievably, I was teaching *French Political Thought* in the graduate program at Morgan State when the professor for the course was away writing a book on Martin Luther King. No one else could instruct the course except me. By going full-time to graduate school in 1966–67, I had to take whatever class was available, so I enrolled in courses called *France Under the Republic* and *French Political Thought.* (A classic move on my part considering that I had "Breed" Hettle, a former Queensberry colleague and third baseman, take the second year French exam for me at the University of Baltimore in order to pass the language requirement.) In reality, I had no firm grasp on the subject, but luckily my graduate students were also completely lost.

There was a rabble-rousing student called Tiger (aka Clarence Davis) at Morgan State during the black militant movement in the late 1960s. I had recalled Tiger as a guy who hung out on Pennsylvania Avenue, and that he had a definite recollection of my association with a number of black gangsters when I worked there.

Anyhow, there was Tiger on the steps of Holmes Hall at Morgan State urging a crowd of nearly 300 vocal students. He's telling them how, "George Washington sucked the titty of a black woman. . ." He was trying to arouse the crowd during this pivotal period for many blacks. My office was in Holmes Hall, and I proceeded to walk toward the front of the building. The crowd gave me a wary look. Tiger* halted his rhetoric and silenced the crowd which anticipated a verbal if not a physical confrontation.

"All right, get out of the way so Chip can come through," he ordered. I parted the crowd as I passed up the steps right into the building as he gave me a bop. Never mind the militancy, he knew better than to fuck with Little Melvin's white boy.

---

* Tiger was the right man for the right season. He went from being an urban militant to a bureaucrat in Harford County to returning to politics in the streets of East Baltimore (where he grew up), and eventually winning a legislative seat in the State House of Delegates. He has become one of the brightest politicians on the Maryland horizon.

101.

The Mamas and The Papas have had four outstanding albums and had become popular internationally. Although most of the group was in it for fun, Cass was very serious, now caught up with "real" show business. She wanted gowns, hairdos, the whole shebang. Some bad vibes soon developed and the group dissolved during a tour of England.

Third returned to the States and was hanging out in New York, Virginia, D.C., and Baltimore. Again he heard from Cass Elliot, who had just come home. She was a tragic figure. She couldn't go anywhere since she was instantly recognizable and fans would constantly lionize her. She called Third to meet her in Baltimore and told him that her lover Pick was again coming into the U.S. via Canada. Cass also needed some dope, so Third contacted Bruce Hawk for a score. They met downtown in Hawk's apartment and got so high that they could barely see.

Then they went to Mee Jun Low's, a downtown Chinese restaurant located on the third floor of a building with a winding staircase, where patrons waited patiently in line on the steps to be seated. It accommodated only 15 people, so the wait was always long, but the food was good. Irene was maitre d' and waitress. She was married to the Chinese owner. To look Chinese, though she was American, Irene painted eyeliner from her eyes to her temples to give her eyes a distinctive slant. (Actually it was too distinctive.) She always yelled out her food orders to the *chef* and then would correct them. She never wrote orders down so she couldn't remember them when she left the table. No matter, the food orders never came out right anyway.

At Mee Jun Low's, Cass became violently ill from the dope and kept throwing up. Yet customers kept coming over to ask for her autograph while she was on her knees vomiting under the table.

102.

The guys loved to "bolt" from restaurants in New York and in Baltimore, i.e., leaving without paying the check. Third and nine other guys were at the China Clipper on Park Avenue in Baltimore. They ordered a lot of food and drinks. Not one of them had a dime in his pocket. Finally, they all left except for Dan Gold, Third and one other. They were nervous now because they were the only guests left in the restaurant and it was 3:00 A.M. Third called over to the waiter and asked for a box of cigars and the guys sat there slowly smoking, rising from the table and wandering around until they finally dashed out of the door. They made a run for Gold's car pursued by everyone who worked in the restaurant. They leapt in the car and started heading down the street, but their way was blocked by four Chinese guys trying to do a karate number on the car. Fortunately, the martial arts didn't work against a speeding Buick, and they made their escape.

Third's tactlessness hadn't improve. Third and some guys were returning to New York, so they let him drive. As Third stopped to pay the toll on the New Jersey Turnpike, he turned to the toll booth woman and said, "Thanks, cunt," in a very nasty way. About two miles up the Pike, five State troopers surrounded the car, aching to beat Third's head in.

For a time, Third worked at *Arthur's,* the famous New York "spot" owned and operated by Sybil Burton, the ex-wife of Richard Burton. She liked Third a lot and argued with her manager who wanted to fire him. The manager was furious because Third wouldn't wear a bow-tie, and had refused to change a light bulb. They finally let Third go.

Third had two New York City rules which he gave with cryptic instructions to Brosy and Gold. "Number one: If you're with me you can eat, but I'm not going to lend you any money to eat. Number two: You never wait for *anyone* more than 15 minutes."

Third hoarded money. He would put money in a sock and hide it away in one of his drawers and then, when he was broke and down and out, he refused to admit the money was there.

103.

Joyce's job, after leaving the fashion industry after one week, was secretary to the president of MGM. This led to the position of assistant to the producer, and later to associate producer of the *David Frost Show.*

She moved to California and caught on as the producer of the *David Steinberg Summer Show.* It took Joyce several years after a teaching career, and a divorce, to realize that she had the smarts to do what she's doing now. She had never made the effort to use her intelligence.

Sue occasionally visited Joyce in California. On one trip, she was asked out by movie actor Keir Dullea. She was ecstatic. Many years before, she had told her high school chums, while watching the movie *David and Lisa,* that "David" is who she'd like to marry someday.

Months later, Sue's dream came true, and she and Keir Dullea were married. But dream loves are fleeting. A year later they were divorced.

104.

Third went out to Los Angeles and visited Cass Elliot who had invited him to stay at her place in Laurel Canyon. It was a great scene, with many talented artists, writers and musicians hanging around Cass. Third stayed for three weeks. He was there mainly to oversee the transport of a load of hashish into L.A. It was his "watch."

Popular British folk singer Donovan was there at the time and he wrote a song dedicated to Mama Cass called "Fat Angel." Among the lyrics are "You will find happiness in your pipe" and "Fly Trans-Love Airways, it always gets you there on time." Third adopted this last verse and it became the telegram code which advised him when a drug shipment had arrived O.K. Donovan was mesmerized. He didn't realize there was that much hash in the world when he first saw 150 pounds of it in the living room.

David Crosby visited Cass from time to time. He was singing now with the Byrds. He just be-bopped around on his motorcycle and hung out there. Later, Crosby got together with Steven Stills and Graham Nash and began singing at Cass's home in Laurel Canyon. It marked the group's beginning.

105.

Snooty actually finished Rabbinical School in record time and got his first congregation in Wilmington, North Carolina. He also was running marathon races and even married a Baltimore girl.

106.

I completed graduate school, gave up teaching children, and was working as assistant dean of the graduate school at Morgan State. Graduation eliminated my deferments. I was now free bait for Sable T. Reed, who sent me draft letter after draft letter.

I enlisted the aid of what draftees thought was their support, the government appeals agent, not realizing that this guy was there only to break down your defenses, and get you to admit that you're fabricating a story and to turn on you during your appeal. I tried to strangle the guy at my first appeal hearing.

The dean of the graduate school and the president of Morgan State wrote to the draft board stating that it is vital that a white administrator remain at a predominantly black school, and that he be excluded from the draft, particularly at the advanced age of 27 years. Sable T. Reed cared less and sent me a notice that my appeal has been denied. I have only one more appeal before I am to report to Fort Holabird to be innoculated and sent to Fort Benning in Georgia, to learn how to die like a man in the mud in Vietnam.

I'm married with a child, which meant absolutely, positively nothing to Sable T. Reed. Finally, I went to my representative, Sam Friedel, a senior member of Congress on the Armed Services Committee—a very powerful and influential man. My father, until he died, worked as a volunteer in Friedel's initial election campaign, and each re-election covering over eight terms. My mother also always campaigned for him. My family never asked Friedel for a favor during his congressional career.

I laid out the scenario to Friedel, who by now was semi-senile. He sat and heard my story, sympathetically. He then gave me the following game plan: "Chip, what I want you to enlist in the service, go through Basic and go over to Vietnam. When you're there about six months, send me a letter telling me that you believe being in Vietnam works hardship on your family and that you can no longer support your mother and the rest of the family. *Then,* I'll try and see what I can do."

To make sure I've heard him correctly and hadn't had an LSD flashback (I never took LSD), I repeated the game plan Friedel had proposed. Then I asked him if he was out of his fucking gourd. He assured me that this was the way for me to proceed. I knew in my heart that this man had gotten 10 other guys out of way worse jackpots and had been compromised in his day, but he rose and dismissed me. I was having a fit now, but I left.

The next day at Morgan State College, I ran into sociology professor Parren Mitchell who had resolved to run for Friedel's congressional seat. There was now a large black constituency in the district which could give Mitchell a good chance of victory in the election, especially since another strong Jewish candidate, with a name similar to Friedel, was running.

About a week later, a Friedel politico put up a sign on my front lawn facing the elementary school where the vote takes place, reading "Re-elect Sam Friedel to Congress." I went into a rage, ripped the sign to shreds, and told the guy, "Don't ever just put any election sign up on my lawn without permission, especially for Friedel. I'm supporting Parren Mitchell!" Obviously this was heresy to the Jewish population of Northwest Baltimore.

I then requested that Mitchell give me a big sign to put on my porch showing that I was supporting him in the election. He thought me insane, describing what would happen if a black put up a sign in a white neighborhood. They would burn his house, or at the very least burn a cross on it. Mitchell asked, "Chip, are you doing the right thing? Do you want protection? Why not just work underground?" I was still kind of hot tempered at the time and I told him to have the sign up by tomorrow. It remained during the entire campaign. The neighbors were terrified I'd break the block.

The other Jewish candidate, whose name was Friedler, got enough votes so that Friedel and Mitchell ended up in a virtual tie, in which it appeared that Friedel won, but in a recount Mitchell was declared the winner.

I heard that some militant blacks called up Friedel and told him not to challenge the recount, to back out of the race and let Mitchell win, or he would never see the light of day again. I don't know if that really happened, and I really didn't give a shit. All I really knew was that the head of the Board of Election supervisors, a woman from the same political group that promoted Friedel, lost her job as a result of Mitchell winning the congressional seat, and that Friedel never challenged the results. Mitchell never forgot the risk I took to get him elected. Although I don't know how many votes he got in my neighborhood to begin with, I know he got mine and the rest of my family's because of Friedel's great advice that I go to Vietnam.

The week before I went down for my final draft appeal hearing, I drove to work in a snow storm and got stuck between Northern Parkway and Rogers Avenue. I had to walk to the Diner, the only sanctuary I could find from the weather. It was the last time in my life that I was ever inside the old Hilltop Diner. There were almost 100 people gathered inside ordering coffee and waiting for the snow plows to come through. They hadn't had such business in years.

I was explaining my draft problem to Donald Science. It was overheard by Joe Paper, who was a member of the Workmen's Compensation Commission. He was a former friend of my father's, and he told me that I should have been 4-F, or completely ineligible from the draft since I was a sole surviving son and the sole support of the family. He added that he'd mention this to a member of the Appeals Board whom he knew well. I didn't put much faith in Paper's statement perhaps because I was depressed at the time and was sure I was definitely going to war, which was very heavy now during the siege at Khe Sanh.

The day of my appeal, I was seated in a room with the entire Draft Board whose membership were mostly veterans from the

Spanish-American War plus Sable T. Reed. They were in a hurry to leave the meeting, because some Catholic priests and other anti-war activists were in the anteroom throwing blood on all the induction and draft records. They later repeated this in Catonsville and were dubbed *The Catonsville Nine*. Naturally, the Board was paying more attention to the ruckus outside than it was to my appeal.

When the Board finally went over my case, the man Joe Paper had contacted enlightened Sable T. Reed as to the fact that I should have been 4-F 10 years ago. Sable, acting bewildered and shocked, said that it just must have slipped her mind. She apologized for the error.

I was excused before I could strangle Sable. Everyone left through the back door as the police arrived to arrest the priests who were still pouring blood on the records.

107.

The '60s was an age of enlightment, discovery and enjoyment for my generation, regardless of the historical definition of the decade as an era of turmoil, anti-establishment, rioting and assassination. It never took on a serious vein for us until the very end of the decade. The old playground and Diner guys viewed the '60s as ending in late 1968.

That snowy, wintery day in 1968 at the Diner signified a major change in my character, attitude and outlook. Was I maturing? At 28, was I actually becoming responsible? Words like commitment and stablity had begun to filter into my consciousness. I had even bought an insurance policy.

What was happening to me? The rampant and flaunting drug use of my friends made me extremely nervous. The guys were bound to take a heavy fall. Youth was no longer a defense. Their other activities were becoming too hedonistic; and while I could identify and comprehend their cavalier attitude of at last achieving total self-indulgence, it was beyond sanity. I knew I had to break away, much as I disdained it, I grudgingly tramped into the '70s with a near total cut-off from the friends who had nurtured and sustained me for such a long time.

For many of the guys, late 1968 and the decade which followed brought highs and lows of such unimaginable proportions that it would take me until the middle '80s to fully comprehend it.

Something inside told me that I could no longer continue to be with the guys or condone their actions. Other realities tugged at my conscience. My sister Nancy got married (no, not Wilt Chamberlain, but amazingly, to a white classmate of Wilt's from Philadelphia). Mom had a severe heart attack and relatives were dying off at an alarming rate, especially Dad's family, who stopped talking to Mom after Dad died, but still insisted on her attendance at funerals.

The most sovering reality of the late '60s, which 20 years later still tortures Diner guys (and all Baltimoreans) worse than anything else, was the "New York disasters of 1969." The Jets, Knicks and Mets beat the Colts, Bullets and Orioles for three world championships. I can't go on. . . .

The Seventies:
A Period of
Individualism

Festival was over and the boys
were all planning for a fall.

—Bob Dylan
"Lilly, Rosemary and
The Jack of Hearts"

1.

Neurotic Nat and I drove up to Queensberry Playground. A big mistake. Although the Bureau of Recreation had renovated the playground by building a swimming pool, it still had an urban blight look. The remnants of the riots of the late '60s were still prevalent and our white faces produced serious stares. We were eventually chased back to my car and luckily escaped the confines of the playground.

2.

Towards the end of the 1960s, Bruce Hawk had established himself as a zany, risk-taking guy, rivaling Third and Boogie and probably surpassing them in terms of the jackpots he got into in a short period of time. Hawk was involved in some nefarious practices, involving both criminal and drug-taking activities.

During the early '60s, Hawk ran around with a lot of goyim, burglarizing homes. He got arrested, but family political influence and the fact that it was Hawk's first offense resulted in a suspended sentence. A few years later, he went to Florida where he met Boogie, who was selling clothes. They returned to Atlanta where Hawk began dealing pot and LSD. He was arrested in Dekalb County. While out on bond, Hawk got involved with a 17-year-old Southern girl he met and fell in love with. Later, Hawk got into a huge argument with her father who filed a complaint with the police. Bruce was busted again. His family hired a prominent Atlanta lawyer who immediately took Bruce to the airport after getting him freed on bond and strongly urged him to leave Georgia for two years at the very least.

On Bruce's arrival in Baltimore, he was arrested for leaving the state without permission, and was sentenced to Jessup Prison for three years. Jessup, nicknamed the "CUT," is a maximum state security prison for serious "blue" offenders. Hawk served nine months and was paroled.

During the nine month term, he was sent to the Sykesville Central Laundry Camp to work. He became friendly with a "blue" called Hooks. Hooks had spent four years on death row, but his sentence was later commuted to life imprisonment. He had already done 18 years. "Hooks" referred to the size of his hands which were twice as big as anyone else's. He could "waste" a man in seconds. Bruce and Hooks became great friends, primarily because Hawk was visited by various girlfriends who brought drugs into the prison. Hawk shared them with Hooks.

Hooks believed Bruce to be one of the craziest white boys he'd ever met. With Hooks protecting him, Bruce therefore had no trouble from the blues who liked to screw new white boys coming into prison. Bruce impressed other prisoners with the heart he showed playing competitive prison sports. Later, he got an award for being one of the meanest white flag football players in the Jessup Prison League.

3.

Nat got married in late 1968 for a month. He married Lorraine so that he could leave home. At 27, he found no other way to tell his parents that he was moving out. Lorraine looked like Jerry Mathers of *Leave It to Beaver,* except that she had blond hair and tits. She was, however, more neurotic, uptight and paranoid than Nat. They moved into an apartment following a honeymoon punctuated by numerous arguments and a fistfight on the New Jersey Turnpike.

Lorraine was very jealous and Nat felt he had to continue to make her jealous even though they were married. Nat believed she needed an edge to spark the marriage. He would allude to the fact that he still had girlfriends and that whenever he went out, girls always chased him. If Nat announced he was going out for 15 minutes and returned in 20 minutes, Lorraine would pack up and move back home with her unemployed electrician father who guzzled beer and despised Jews. Her father would then subject Nat to a terrifying interrogation before permitting Lorraine to return to the apartment. This is why Nat became addicted to beer. Today he can drink up to 14 bottles of beer a day. He said his confrontations with Lorraine's father that convinced him that beer-drinking was preferable to staring him in the eye, which caused Nat to hyperventilate and pass out.

In their fourth week of marriage, Nat told Lorraine he was going shopping for groceries at Slaters' Grocery in Pimlico. She screamed that she was sick and tired of his escapades and that if he went out, when he got back he would find her dead. Nat said if that was the case, he was going to buy a pound of calves' liver to bring back and fuck in front of her. With this remark, he stormed out the door.

When he returned he couldn't find Lorraine. He took the liver, for fear it would go bad, and put it in the refrigerator. When Nat opened the refrigerator, he found Lorraine inside and everything from the icebox was strewn on the counter. Hunched over and naked, she advised Nat that she was going to kill herself by first freezing and then burning herself until she went into shock and died. The initial step she said was to stay in the refrigerator for 20 minutes, after which she would proceed to jump into a hot tub of boiling water that was already in the bathtub. Nat told her it might work, but that the method would probably fail since she was such a loser. He asked her to move over and make room for the liver.

"If you do succeed," Nat said, "during my mourning period I'll have to have something to fuck other than just standing up and humping the casket."

He closed the refrigerator door and 10 minutes later Lorraine leapt out. She was blue and shivering and rushed back to the bathroom where she jumped into the boiling hot water, screaming in agony. Nat sauntered in and took a seat on the toilet to observe Lorraine, who was now lobster red and moaning. She maintained her composure, she did not pass out.

"Is your heart beating rapidly? Do you feel like you're dying?" asked Nat.

Lorraine just shook her head and cried that she had failed. Nat quickly added that she was a failure at everything, which prompted Lorraine to ask for a razor to cut her wrists so that she could bleed to death in the tub. All Nat could find were two injector blades which Lorraine grabbed and began using on her wrists. She did skin herself and shave her wrists (which were a bit hairy), but failed to end her life.

That was the end of the marriage. For his divorce attorney, Nat chose his friend Mike who had just passed the bar. He advised Nat that he would handle the divorce free of charge because they were such good friends. Actually, Mike the lawyer was one of the 31 roommates whom Nat had in three years at University of Maryland. He did a wonderful job handling the divorce. Nat and Lorraine had been making the same amount of money and were married for just short of a month. An excellent settlement was reached through crack attorney Mike. Nat was directed to pay Lorraine $9,000 and promise to see a psychiatrist for at least a year. If Nat remarried and had any children, they would go to Lorraine.

4.

Yussel moved downtown and shortly thereafter, Bill McAuliffe, who was at Johns Hopkins, became his roommate. Bill was conducting research for his dissertation, which was an attack on the widely accepted Lindsmith Theory of Euphoria. This theory was held if junkies continue to "fire" out of habit and fear of withdrawal, Lindsmith believed that they no longer could experience a euphoric high. Bill's dissertation intended to dispel the theory, and involved extensive interviews with heroin addicts, former Diner guys and Tin Men.

The apartment was not conducive to pure research and study, since Yussel's all-night parties and extemporaneous closet scenes interrupted Bill's academic world. At first, Bill threatened to beat up Yussel and the other participants, but eventually he just moved out.

5.

Eventually, Burger realized that the drugs were dominating his life. So he married the now-divorced Slave, adopted the triplets, and moved to a kibbutz in Israel with his new family. He loved Israel, became drug-free, and loved the three girls better than even a natural father could.

6.

When Hawk was paroled, he met a State Senator through his friend Saul Morris. He was hired as the State Senator's aide, principally because he could supply him with hashish. Since Hawk was receiving a paycheck from a State Senator, no one at the Parole Board could question his job.

Hawk traveled with Saul, Baby Blue and several other guys to Mailbu, California, where they visited Pick Dawson, Mama Cass's old boyfriend. Pick was living in Topanga Canyon, the home of the hippies in an area known as the Corral. It is also where Charles Manson's Family would live. Pick later became associated with the Family and is mentioned in the book *Helter Skelter*. Bruce dealed in hash in Topanga Canyon.

A few weeks later, he left California to visit a girlfriend in Detroit. After a couple days, he flew to National Airport in Washington because he couldn't book a direct flight into Baltimore. He called the State Senator who warned him not to come home. The police had busted Hawk's roommate and there was a warrant out for him.

The State Senator was an interesting man. He had a successful law practice and knew influential, wealthy friends in high places. He had the "Kennedy" look and was being groomed to run for Congress, and later, perhaps national office. But he was fed up with his marriage, and secretly planned to "leave it all" and travel around the world with his girlfriend. He advised Bruce to wait at the airport and invited him to join them on a world tour. Hawk couldn't believe it since he didn't have a birth certificate or a passport. The State Senator showed his pull. Within a day, he not only got Hawk's birth certificate but a passport as well.

That night they flew to London with American Express Cards and $20,000 in cash. During the next four months, they jet-setted around Europe, then through the Middle East, primarily Lebanon, and eventually to Pakistan. Hawk called Third from Pakistan and asked him where he can buy the best dope.

Hawk and the Senator's "master plan" was to score some hash, sell it in the U.S., and then return for more. Hawk naturally was the chosen one to go back and forth, and meet later with the Senator and his girlfriend in Nepal. They would then buy a boat and sail around the world.

Hawk returned to the States carrying a suitcase with a false bottom and 20 pounds of hashish. He looked like an Indian who had escaped from the reservation, over-tanned and wearing braids, as he went through immigration. When the custom's official checked Bruce's name against a specific code there appeared the alert "temporarily stop." When Hawk saw this, he chewed up the baggage tickets and swallowed them.

Hawk was taken to a room by custom agents who wanted to know where his tickets, his baggage, and the Senator were. There was suspicion of foul play involving the Senator, and concern over his whereabouts since he was presumed missing. Maryland authorities believed that Hawk may have been involved. Later when word leaked out that the Senator had just "split" for Europe, his name hit the headlines in many of the newspapers around the world. The customs agents eventually let Hawk leave after a series of volatile arguments. Hawk believed he had bluffed them out.

In New York City, Bruce called Pan Am, said that he couldn't locate his baggage ticket, and asked where they leave unclaimed luggage when people arrive from Europe. He's told and he returned to the airport but he couldn't find his suitcase. Upset, he went back to Baltimore by bus, but things are too hot for him there because of the outstanding warrant. He hastily returned to New York City and then convinced his parents to send him money under the guise of traveling to Israel to live on a kibbutz.

When Hawk went back to his Manhattan apartment stoned on heroin, he was nabbed by custom and BNDD agents, who brought him to their office and showed him his suitcase. They figured out what happened and convinced Bruce to confess. He was brought to West Street Station, and put in a holding cell for federal prisoners. This was the worst jail in the entire world. It was even hotter than it was in Karachi, Pakistan. Hawk had no bail because there was a "ticket" (warrant) on him in Maryland.

While in the lock-up, Hawk met all of the leading mobsters from Long Branch, New Jersey, a hotbed of organized crime. He got involved with one of the main hoodlums who became his secret partner in three-way gin. He and the main hoodlum cheated the other prisoners.

7.

Third's fall started when one of his couriers, Phil, was arrested at Kennedy Airport. Third saw it, ran to a phone booth and called Peg explaining what had happened, and ordered her not to take any calls from Phil no matter how urgent he says it is. Shortly thereafter, Phil the courier phoned Peg. He had already made a deal with the FBI and convinced her he hadn't been arrested. It was a total misunderstanding. She believed him and talked over the whole deal while the Feds taped the entire conversation. Third never forgave her.

Third then took off for Baltimore where his attorney convinced him to turn himself in. He did it reluctantly, and was placed in the Baltimore County lock-up in Towson. Third was wearing very fancy footwear and the jailer genuinely complimented him, "Nice shoes."

Third responded, "Yeah, you chump, they cost about a week of your salary."

His tactless diplomacy continued at a pre-sentence investigation when he was asked who he really wanted to be. He flippantly answered, "President." The lady investigator took a dim view of his attitude and recommended that Third be sentenced to seven years, because she felt he needed the time to cool off and learn some humility.

When Third got busted, everyone thought he would get probation. A woman called Superchick had two airline tickets to fly him back to Paris, where they had another drug deal going down. Third's connections and status were vital to its success. At this time, they were all making nearly $9,000 a month, and Third was having fun. But instead of being put on probation, he was convicted and sentenced to 10 years in prison.

Third did not understand the sentence which came under provisions of the since-repealed Youthful Offenders Act, and was essentially very lenient. Yet, he became so distraught that he downed nearly a dozen valiums and then tried to strangle his attorney and the Assistant U.S. Prosecutor.

He was taken to West Street Station in New York, the Federal Transfer jail. (Third was to serve his time at Lewisburg Prison.) Before reporting to lock-up, he asked to see Bruce Hawk who he knew was there. As Third was placed in an area to change to prison clothes, a couple of guys attempted to rape him. Hawk appeared as the prisoners were struggling to position Third. Being an old Beth Tifiloh Synagogue buddy, Hawk beat up both guys. The guards arrived and thought Hawk was just causing trouble, and put him in The Hole for a month. Bruce never said a word when he would get in trouble, or was punished during his time in prison. In jail, he lived by the code of the criminal.

8.

Despondent over the Colts' loss to the Jets in the 1969 Super-bowl, Fenwick, who by now had begun to experiment with drugs of all sorts, turned to PCP and began losing his mind, or at least what was left of it. He had apologized to me after I married Lynne. I had frozen him for five years, the longest freeze in the history of the Diner guys up until that time.

I later told Lynne that if Fenwick called to let him know that things are going badly. He must really believe that we were in a pathetic state, or he would make serious trouble, including firebombing the house. She asked me what kind of friend he was and I replied, "A true one, but very sick. Only your dearest friends will screw you!"

9.

Fenwick was terrifying at times. He could put fear into your heart and soul, but he could also frighten you into success. He did it to the "Knep."

Knep was Steve Knepper, a blond, heavy-set guy who used to hang out with Fenwick and me. I always found him at Fenwick's house when we were teenagers. Steve and Fenwick use to go one on one with each other in football, basketball, baseball, lacrosse, wiffle-ball or cards. If Fenwick won, everything was fine, but if the Knep won, it meant trouble—mental, physical or emotional hassles. It was almost worth the anguish to stay at Fenwick's home and watch him when he got mad. If you left, there was no telling what havoc he would cause over the phone with your family, friends, girls, school or job.

After Fenwick's brutal loss in wiffle-ball late one afternoon, the Knep had to do a chore for his mom. He left right after his big win.

Within an hour, Fenwick had made enough vicious phone calls to suspend Knepper from school, and got him slapped by his mother, beaten by his brother, barred from Mandell's deli, and threatened by the fathers of three girls. This was only the beginning.

That was enough for Knepper. He decided to work full-time after school rather than be subjected to Fenwick's tantrums. The Knep took a job with a large finance company when he was 15. By 19, he was vice-president of the firm, and by 24, one of the company's major stockholders.

My sister Nancy and I once worked in one of the "Knep's" finance offices in Ferndale (West Baltimore County). She worked during the summer and I was employed there part-time during college.

Knep's Ferndale office manager was Howard Kirk, Levinson's cousin. Like Barry's other cousin, Eddie Kirk of the Ten Boys, they were related through Barry's mother's side of the family. The real family name was Kirchinsky but it was shortened in the late '60s, even though they didn't have to go through Ellis Island. Barry said that Kirchinsky was originally a longer name, but was shortened when his family came to America. Longer than Kirchinsky?

Every now and then, the Knep would visit the Ferndale office to motivate his finance men, and I saw what made him so successful. He was the greatest phone-man of all time. Much greater than Charlie Bo-Death, whom I had believed was among the best.

The Knep would call someone who was behind in his loan from the finance company, and he had a "line" for everything. Once Knepper phoned this deadbeat who told him, "Hey, I'm broke. You can't squeeze blood out of a turnip, can ya?"

Knep answered, "But we didn't loan the money to a turnip, deadbeat!"

Knep's company was eventually sold, and with his profits, he began one of the first burglar alarm manufacturing outfits precisely when crime was rampant. His corporation made all kinds of equipment including home criminal deterrents. His success was fantastic. I believe he really went into the business to develop new ways to keep Fenwick from getting him!

10.

When Third arrived at Lewisburg Prison as a new inmate, he went around the cell tier introducing himself. "I'm Stewart Reichlyn from Mu Sig. I'm new here. Glad to meet ya!" One of the guys he gave his spiel to was a huge, black double-lifer who did nothing but lift weights all the time. He whispered to Third, "I left a gift for you on your bed."

"That's very nice," replied Third, not realizing that this guy wanted a piece of him. So Third returned to his cell and there was a Baby Ruth candy bar lying on his bed. He ate it and told the guy he really liked the gift, not realizing that it was prison acknowledgement that he was going to become the blue's "woman." The big blue flashed a big smile, winked at some other inmates and began to unzip his fly. Third now realized what was to happen and fled. This was the first in a series of rape escapes. Once he ran into the social worker's office. Another time he barely escaped through crowded corridors.

But one day he found the double-lifer in his cell and the blue said, "You're going to give it up now!" Third was terrified and, while figuring how he was going to get out of this, told the guy, "Okay but let's get undressed together." As the guy was bending over pulling his pants down, Third picked up a little desk in the cell and whacked him over the head until he was bleeding and out cold. The guards took the guy away to the prison infirmary. Later, the blue and his friends put out the word that Third was going to get cut to death, slowly. By this time, he had become the only white member of the football and basketball team in the prison, so he went to his teammates for protection. Since he was liked because he mixed it up with some pretty rough guys on the prison football squad, the team cooled down the double-lifer and his cohorts with serious threats of their own. Gold never bought the story and believed Third gave it up to the double-lifer.

Some years later, when Third came out to San Francisco to stay at the Gold's home, Dave put a Baby Ruth on Third's bed. As a matter of fact, every time Third would get frisky with Gold, he would recommend seven years.

11.

Barry Levinson was visiting Miles Kirson, one of the old Ten Boys, in San Francisco. One morning around 5:30, he was awakened to what he thought was screaming. Barry raced to the window and looked out to see Miles and his girlfriend Pat sitting on a hill. He thought they've lost their minds at first, but realized that they are only Yoga chanters. Barry quickly returned to Los Angeles.

12.

Boogie's friend Harold aka Ollie was very bright—what would be called an information "schnorer" in Yiddish. He liked to pick your brain for things, as opposed to real schnorers who usually just live off other people's money. It was very tough to embellish a story with Harold since he was quite perceptive and asked very difficult questions. When verifying or validating a sports victory or a sexual conquest, one needed to have all his "ducks in a row," or Harold's intense cross-examination would make you look like a fool.

Harold first became friendly with Boogie, Bill, Yussel and the guys at the poolroom where he developed a reputation as a shrewd card player, an effective pool shooter, and a fine ping pong player. Although he enjoyed gambling, he was a probability and statistics freak, as opposed to being a compulsive gambler. He *knew* when to press, and when to fold.

The guys considered Harold both intellectual and cunning. But what really impressed them was his ability to add rows of numbers in his head faster than a calculator. He won many a bet late at night in the Diner displaying this skill.

Eventually, Harold finished college and law school and went into the family's real estate business. Later, when he learned about

Boogie's early success with Merry-Go-Round, he decided to open his own Baltimore boutique with Obie's brother-in-law. All went well until they clashed over the color of the carpet. The deal fell through.

Meanwhile, Boogie supplied Obie and Sambo with fifty grand to open their own boutique in New Orleans. They called it the Red Balloon and the store was an immediate success. They opened up another boutique and bought an apartment complex in New Orleans and a house in Aspen.

One New Year's Eve weekend, Harold flew into Atlanta to meet Obie, up from New Orleans, and Boogie just for a good time. Harold flipped over the Merry-Go-Round concept. He approached Boogie proposing a partnership deal to bring in all of his real estate holdings plus an undetermined cash offer. Boogie accepted. He wanted to return to Baltimore anyhow. Harold paid off Boogie's partner who was ecstatic at leaving Boogie, because he could not endure Boogie's crazy friends.

The three stores adopted the Atlanta boutique's name, Merry-Go-Round, and the guys expanded immediately, opening stores in Baltimore and in Cincinnati.

Boogie developed a clever way of dealing with in-house theft, which often was costlier than shoplifting. He beat up suspected managers and salespeople. This violated their civil rights, but Boogie found it more reliable than giving them lie detector tests and firing them. If he felt they were thieves, he kicked ass. Word of this method spread so quickly that both confidence in Merry-Go-Round and profits exploded.

Obie began skimming Red Balloon boutique profits and flying off to Caracas, Venezuela, and Las Vegas where he eventually gambled them away. This and other crazy episodes severely depressed Sambo and he dropped out of society for a while. Obie's gambling habit resulted in the sale of the house in Aspen, the apartment complex, and the Red Balloon stores.

13.

Sadly, Slave didn't like Israel and decided to return to the States, which Burger didn't mind. But when she took custody of the triplets, it demoralized Donnie. He stayed on another two months, but couldn't bear the loneliness without the girls and reluctantly he returned to Baltimore. Within months, he was back dealing and using drugs, heavier than he ever had before.

Back with Slave and the triplets, he one day became very drugged-up. Donnie then was cruising at about 100 MPH down Resiterstown Road when a telephone pole leapt out into the road and wrapped itself around his car. Or so he thought. It was Donnie's last thought.

14.

Third served 11½ months in jail. With time out on bond and for psychological testing, the sentence covered nearly two years.

The day he came home, he married Peg. He considered it one of the terms of his parole. The marriage lasted 10 years, although they were seldom together for more than two months in any given year.

Mary Spice lived a fascinating jet-set life in New York City. She was involved in various affairs with wealthy and influential men. She eventually married an Irish writer and lived in an Irish Castle.

Third had just two legitimate job offers from his friends after leaving prison. I gave him the opportunity to be assistant lacrosse coach and attend Morgan State with Peg on an "other race" grant and Mary offered to send Third two Irish Wolfhounds so that he could begin a lucrative kennel in America. That seemed like too much work, so Third opted for lacrosse and school.

He took the grants, which provided him with pin money, never attended class, and he quit the team for a Provincetown summer.

Before leaving, Third went back to the Maryland Lacrosse Club with a vengeance. He was allowed to join only after a close team vote as to whether to permit a convicted felon to play.

The Maryland Lacrosse Club won the Southern Division Championship, led by a dynamic all-star midfield unit which included Third. A sudden-death overtime win over Carling Lacrosse Club propelled Maryland to the title. Third scored the winning goal. He left the field quickly before anyone could congratulate him. This was strange behavior for Third. When I asked him why he'd left so early, he said that he scored the winning goal with a stick he had stolen from the Carling bench during the first overtime period.

Third was knocked off his cloud as a result of his imprisonment. Jail broke him. The arrest was reported in the newspapers. It finished his social acceptance. Sue's father even sent her a clipping with an "I told you so . . ." letter. Third wasn't exactly Gandhi, and this affected his personality.

The fact that after prison, Third would "escape" to Provincetown, summer after summer, for another dozen years equated him with an old lifeguard.

15.

Mary Spice and Third's boat companion, Seymour, was involved in a number of interesting adventures which included designing the Rolling Stones' album cover for *Exile on Main Street*. Sadly, while Seymour was sailing his yacht through the South Seas, it was captured by French pirates, who wanted the boat for drug smuggling. They didn't need Seymour, so they killed him.

16.

Shade married Darlene Dry-Hump. She had an excellent job with great benefits at a top secret Defense Department Agency in

Maryland. (Okay, it's NSA.) The fringe benefits included educating your spouse and Shade took advantage, enrolling in college. Darlene supported Shade through undergraduate and graduate school. In appreciation for all of this, Shade divorced her and became a probation officer.

17.

Barry Levinson lucked out and was hired to write for *The Tim Conway Show* which had a 13-week run before being scrapped. He then went to England to write for *The Marty Feldman Show*.

18.

Cass Elliot decided to put out a solo album, and to work in Las Vegas for $40,000 a week, headlining a flower-child pop act. She had changed her singing style from rock tempos to slow ballads and had gained a new adult audience. The act was a flop.

19.

Nat returned from a trip to San Francisco and bought a new Corvette which turned out to be the last car he ever owned. He always believed that there was a conspiracy by car manufacturers to sell him one with oil leaks. There were no leaks. Anyone could look under a car during the course of the day and find at least a little drip of something. But Nat would consider that little drip as showing the breakdown of the entire transmission, oil, and brake fluid system leaking out of the car all at once. As soon as he located a drop, he would take the car back to the dealer and make him check every-thing. Once, after writing to the manufacturer's rep, he had the dealer take the entire engine out of the car, looking for the "leak." The guys in the service shop didn't seem to mind this work since Nat would always come by in the evening and brought them a case or two of beer. They found him both amusing and very crazy.

Nat strung a series of spotlights with four extension cords from his apartment reaching underneath his car so that he could run out in the middle of the night to check for a new leak.

20.

Ez was unhappy. He didn't like married life and was bored selling tires. One morning, he told his wife and children that he was leaving them forever and went off to New York.

Getting a bartender's job at Adam's Apple to support himself, Ez pursued a career as a male model. He was represented by a top modeling agency whose boss was a fairly attractive fortyish woman. In return for furthering Ez's career, she expected sexual favors from Ez, who was appalled.

"She's too old," Ez argued, who all of a sudden had become a man of high principles. He went to Baltimore briefly to see his kids. We ran into each other at a bowling alley.

"Ez, I remember you begging me to get you laid with an old lady of 65!" I reminded him. Naturally, he denied it.

"And by the way, Chip," Ez adds, "I've changed my name to Adam Allan."

"Atom, A.T.O.M.?" I innocently responded.

"No! Adam, A.D.A.M., you asshole!"

21.

Mama Cass was a frequent guest on TV shows, got her own television special, and later that summer co-starred with Ray Stevens and Lulu in a summer replacement for *The Andy Williams Show.*

A brief comeback try with The Mamas and The Papas failed, even though their new album made the charts.

22.

Bruce Hawk spent six months in West Street Station before he went to court, where he was sentenced to two years in Danbury Federal Prison. When he finished the two year stretch and walked out a free man, he was immediately picked up by the Maryland authorities. The parole officer and police took him to a Maryland holding prison.

Hawk was returned to Baltimore and assigned to what is known as the Diagnostic and Referral Center, which was actually the State Penintentiary. They shaved off Bruce's hair, and he was so livid over his haircut that during his hearing he attacked his parole officer. He was sentenced to another four months at Jessup State Prison and subsequently to the Central Laundry Camp where he renewed his friendship with his old friend "Hooks."

While in Jessup, Bruce was visited by the U.S. Customs people. His State Senator friend had returned from Nepal and had been arrested in New York for drug conspiracy. His photograph was on the front page of the *Daily News.* Hawk was to be the government's principal witness.

A few months later Hawk was removed to Federal Court in New York. Bruce had already completed his term and was technically "free," so he told the court that he "forgot the facts." The Senator walked with a "not guilty" verdict for hashish smuggling. Free and clear, Hawk went South and started hanging out in Washington, D.C. Later he moved to Florida.

23.

Vacationing at the Fontainebleau in Miami Beach, I ran into Swartzie. He had divorced a couple years earlier and was now a very successful Baltimore bookie.

Over dinner he confessed that he had temporarily closed down his business. There was too much "heat." He had been thinking about going into the drug business. He had a meeting the next afternoon with some young kid, a cousin of Rifkin's, who had a planeload of marihuana on the way from Bolivia. I tried to advise Swartzie about the public and law enforcement's *attitude* towards drug dealing, as opposed to gambling. He wouldn't listen.

I called Bruce Hawk that evening when I heard that he was working at the Diplomat Hotel in Hollywood, Florida, parking cars. "Hawk, I want you to explain to Swartzie about the dangers of drug trafficking."

He promised to join Swartzie at the race track the next day.

When we couldn't change Swartzie's mind at the track, we told him that Bruce would go along and test the marihuana to check that he wasn't being taken advantage of in the deal.

The young dealer met them after the races and they drove back toward Miami Beach sampling the grass. Its potency was devastating, but Hawk knocked it on purpose.

"You call this good shit," yelled Hawk, "I've gotten higher smoking toilet paper!"

"Stop the car," he ordered, "We're throwing this pseudo-dealer out now." Swartzie was pissed off [he didn't know what "pseudo" meant] and slammed on the brakes, pushing the shocked youth out on the 79th Street Causeway.

"Thanks, Hawk," Swartzie said apologetically, "I almost made a big mistake."

After parking at the Fontainebleau, Hawk got Swartzie to go inside. He said that he's got to make a phone call. Swartzie split, and 40 minutes later, Hawk was still in the back seat—catatonic.

The marihuana's effects were so strong he wasn't able to move for hours.

Before Hawk went back to Hollywood, he pulled out and shuffled what seemed to be a deck of cards. Actually, it was a stack of credit cards which he "found" in the glove compartment of the cars he had parked.

"Can you believe how fucking dumb people are? Leaving these in their glove compartment?" Bruce lectured. "Let me buy you something. A suit, television set, dinner? Take some cards home, please!"

24.

Snooty was promoted to a larger congregation in Madison, Wisconsin. I don't know how many Jews there were in Wilmington, or how many more there were in Madison but what did it matter? He was on his way to becoming a main Rabbi. I saw him one day when he was in Baltimore visiting his parents, running down Park Heights Avenue. He started to lecture me about my life style and spiritual fulfillment. I quickly reminded him of the few times he'd begged me to be with some very loose girls. He quickly reverted to the Snooty I knew.

Six months later, Rabbi Snooty jumped rope longer than anyone and got his feat into the *Guinness Book of World Records*. We are very proud of Snooty.

25.

Fenwick came to the house to see a Colts game, and Neurotic Nat also was there. Unbeknownst to me, Wick offered some dynamite grass to Nat who greedily took it. After two pulls, he fell to the floor screaming hysterically.

"What's wrong? I asked as I came into the room, and Fenwick said, "He's faking it."

"Faking what?" I shouted.

"I'm dying!" screamed Nat.

Wick confessed, "So there's a few flakes in it. Big deal. It's not going to hurt him. He's faking it!"

"You mean PCP? Angel Dust? Are you fucking crazy?"

"Don't worry," reassured Wick, "He'll be fine."

I threw Fenwick out of the house, and took Nat upstairs where he tried to leap out of the window. He told me to call his father immediately.

I tied Nat to the bed and kept him there six hours. He finally went home and only came out of the flashback six days later. I banned Fenwick from the house by refusing to answer the phone for months.

26.

While partying in Aspen, Swartzie became friends with a couple of hashish smugglers from New Orleans who invited him to visit them in Ibiza when he was in Europe.

In April, Swartzie took them up on their offer. After flying to Amsterdam, he rented a car and toured Europe. His reasons were twofold: to get away from the States for a few months, and to visit and evaluate as many discos as possible. When he returned in the fall, he planned opening a huge disco on the outskirts of Baltimore.

Swartzie got to Barcelona, and took the ferry to Ibiza. He met the guys from Louisiana, stayed with them for a couple of days and decided to rent an apartment. For the next two months, Swartzie relaxed on Ibiza, sailing, spending time at the villa of Elmyr de Hory, a new friend he met in Ibiza.

A retired art forger, Elmyr gave Swartzie an autographed copy of Clifford Irving's book *Fake!*, written about Elmyr. He told Swartzie that Irving was currently serving a prison sentence in Danbury, Connecticut, for the fake book "by" Howard Hughes.

Swartzie was unaware that, a few years earlier, Third had frolicked in the same places and was befriended by the same islanders, smugglers from Louisiana who happened to be a rival gang of Third's.

As Swartzie moved around Europe for a few months waiting for the heat on his bookmaking operation to cool down, Jules remained in Baltimore, very worried. In fact he was always worried. Whenever anyone hit the number or a big football bet, he would faint dead away.

Jules met Pat, Miles Kirson's girlfriend from San Francisco, during her transitional period after leaving the life of hippiedom. They fell in love.

27.

After he dried out, Jay Huff became a sidewalk superintendent, married and fathered a child. Within two years, he began to indulge again, now into much harder drugs. It led to a permanent separation from his wife.

28.

Perhaps the most insane time for some guys was the "McDonough Lane Epoch," when Yussel was then living with Ben and Rifkin out past the Beltway on McDonough Lane. For a brief period, the guys moved uptown and into more spacious Baltimore County. It was a scene of non-stop drugs, sex, the works.

They would party with black friends who were into heavy drug dealings. These were Superfly "blues" who wore white-on-white outfits. They would throw an ounce of coke out on the table for everybody to indulge in, believing it made them look cool. It did.

The caretaker of the McDonough Lane place was an escapee from the Spring Grove State Mental Hospital. His nickname was "The Magician" and he claimed that he was a male witch who could put curses on different people. He also would cook for the guys but they rarely ate. They feared they may have been cursed.

29.

Ez departed New York after a year of modeling and enrolled at Dealer's School in Las Vegas. It was a 10-week program and Ez, aka Adam Allan, lasted about four (he was a poor shuffler), before leaving for San Diego. He was having great trouble meeting alimony and child support payments. He cancelled them, rationalizing that leaving the ex-wife and kids a big new house was enough.

30.

Rifkin became Swartzie's chief lieutenant. Swartzie was now friendly with Maroon, a blue who ran a national marihuana distribution network out of Baltimore. Maroon was a small, slick, nice-looking dude who always wore a big Panama hat. He had two lieutenants: Half and Brute.

One morning, Swartzie, Rifkin, Half and Brute donned Panama hats, took an ounce of cocaine, hopped into a limo, and rode to the airport to take a plane to Mexico. The guys were dressed outlandishly. They flew into Dallas and continued on to Mexico City on a flight with only four of them on the plane. They danced and sang in the aisles, putting their hats on the stewardesses, as they flew into Acapulco.

On this trip, Swartzie had decided to "hit the plastic," meaning that he was going to deliberately use a specific credit card beyond its limit in order to bankrupt himself and ruin his credit. This was a result of a hassle with the bank that issued his credit card. They mistakenly repossessed his ex-wife's car, and it embarrassed him. He had already "banged" the card for a couple grand and was planning to hit the bank for another 25 or 30 grand in charges. Swartzie brought along $20,000 in cash, just in case.

Once in Acapulco, the guys checked into the Hilton, renting the two top suites. They partied and spent money like water, using Swartzie's plastic. They picked up every beautiful woman in sight and soon acquired a large entourage. Swartzie was buying dinners for up to 30 people every evening. The bar tabs ran as much as $1,500 a night.

The second day, their tour guide told them that he could get them some "Acapulco Gold" cheap. Swartzie ordered, "Give us $300 worth." This proved to be a pound. It was just for the guys and they used it liberally, taking their guide along to party. They threw a huge bash in their suites the next night. It just so happened that this was the same evening that Obie flew in to join them. He arrived in time for Swartzie's gala and couldn't believe his eyes. Two white guys and two blues, all in big Panama hats, in control of the City of Acapulco.

At eight in the morning, as the party was ending, Swartzie took a budding 16-year-old starlet out onto the beach to wait for a boat that was going to chauffeur the guys to some nearby island. After a three hour wait for the guys, Swartzie suspected trouble and went back to the hotel to find 40 Federales in the room. Rifkin, Brute, Half and Obie were being led away in handcuffs. Not being a shy person, Swartzie rushed in and demanded to know what was going down. The Federale chief said that the boys have been caught with marihuana and were being taken to the courthouse. Swartzie led the chief out to the veranda and offered him a bribe of $5,000, but the chief told him it was too late—although he thought about it for quite a while. Seeing that he could get no further, Swartzie packed up everything (including cameras and stereos) and strolled to the courthouse.

There they were all ordered directly to jail. Swartzie tried bribing other officials but failed. He was marvelous though—ranting and raving, and saying that he was the nephew of Joe Columbo, the Mafia boss.

"If you faggots don't watch it, a lot of people will die in Acapulco and all over Mexico!"

He acted like a wild man, but he was very calculating. Later, even Swartzie couldn't believe what he'd done. But he was on such a roll, he couldn't stop.

The guys were taken over to the Carsell Municipale, the Acapulco jail—a brick prison where 300 of the worst criminals in Mexico were imprisoned. There were only four toilets which were located in the center of the yard and emptied into the grounds. The place was filthy. The prisoners got slop food in the morning and slop food in the evening.

The guys went into the warden's office. Swartzie continued to carry on in such an intimidating manner about his uncle, Joseph Columbo, that the warden allowed him to keep his camera and personal belongings. Incredulously, Swartzie supervised the locking away of the suitcases of the rest of the guys. Rifkin and Obie were close to tears. The blues didn't know what to make of it. Except for Swartzie, they were sure they wouldn't be released from prison for years.

As the guys entered the prison yard, they were astounded to run into a Baltimorean named Pat from Hampden. Pat had shot a Federale in the shoulder during an escape attempt following his arrest for trafficking in marihuana. He had been sentenced to eight years in jail, and he explained to the guys that they probably wouldn't even be given a hearing for six months. Swartzie said that he didn't have the time to wait.

"I have to take my son to Disneyland next week. Don't worry, we'll be out by then."

While Pat was explaining that it would take at least four days to get an audience with the warden, two weeks to see a lawyer or public defender, and another six months for a hearing, Obie and Rifkin began crying. Obie hyperventilated and passed out.

Swartzie approached a guard and demanded in such a threatening way to see the warden that he got an audience within two hours. He walked into the office and told him, "Look warden, this is yours, this Franklin, a C-note, a hundred dollar bill! Every time I want to come up here to see you, I want to see you right away, and you will get a Franklin every time. I want to use your phone and I want to use the bathroom now, because I won't use that filthy hole in the ground. And I want to take a bath!"

He added, "If you help get me out of here, I'm going to take care of you. And I want to see that my boys are also having no problems."

Swartzie, as Columbo's nephew, was having a ball. The warden laughed at him while pocketing the C-note, and Swartzie phoned Jules in Baltimore. He told Jules briefly what had happened and to get hold of a girl named Pam whom he used to date and was now residing in Canada. She had lived in Mexico City and had connections with the local Mob. Swartzie then left the warden, telling him that he has to return the call the next day.

Back in the courtyard, Swartzie promoted a basketball game. The Americans against the Mexicans. His team won handily since the blues (Half and Brute) from Baltimore were on it, and were naturally better ball players than the Mexicans.

Pat from Hampden (a working class area of Baltimore) had taken control of much of the prison population, and since Swartzie was carrying his money with him, they were able to purchase certain cement slabs to sleep on, and rough guys to guard them so that nobody bothered them if they happened to shut their eyes.

Swartzie was perhaps the only guy in the history of the world who took photographs inside of a federal prison, where no one else was even allowed a notebook. He called guards out from their guard towers so that he could snap pictures of them posing with the guys. Rifkin and Obie continued to cry.

The next day, Swartzie laid another C-note on the warden. He called Jules and was informed that things were in the works.

"Pam is in Mexico City. We will try to work it out."

Jules added, "It will cost up to $50,000 to get out."

Swartzie instructed him that only Maroon should bring the money down and make the deal. He didn't want anyone doing a number on him.

On the third day, he called Jules again and was advised that the deal was completed. "Tomorrow morning somebody will arrive to pick up you guys and bring you to Mexico City."

Elated, Swartzie told the warden that they will be leaving soon, but the warden didn't believe him. He just laughed.

Swartzie went down to the guys who are still crying and informed them not to worry. He then snapped a picture of Obie relieving himself on one of the cement slabs in the prison compound.

The next morning, Swartzie was summoned upstairs and the warden, incredulous and wide-eyed, said that he and the boys would be picked up within two hours to be taken to Mexico City. Swartzie handed the warden money to bring food for everybody and to treat Pat and some of the prisoners he befriended to a huge going-away party. Swartzie went into the other room, took out his stereo and, as the guys walked in, was on top of the warden's desk dancing and singing. The others couldn't believe they would be going to Mexico City.

Two hours later, a large limo drew up to the gates and Swartzie, Rifkin, Obie, Half and Brute were escorted, bag and baggage, into the car for the drive to Mexico City. Upon arrival, they had to spend the night in the Mexico City jail and all five were put in one cell. The following day they were swiftly rushed to the airport, put on a plane, and told never to come back to Mexico again.

Before leaving the Acapulco jail, Swartzie told Pat from Hampden that he would return for him since he was such a standup guy. Pat knew he had eight years to serve and didn't want to believe Swartzie, but told him he appreciated the thought.

Swartzie took his kid to Disneyland the very next week. He telephoned Jules that he was going back to Acapulco with Rifkin to get Pat out of jail.

Swartzie arrived in Mexico City and discovered from the local mobsters that they can spring Pat for $50,000. Swartzie found the price excessive, but realized that it could be worked out. He returned to Acapulco and spent two weeks meeting different people until he made the right connection. It would cost "only" $25,000. He met a man whose father was the publisher of a Mexico City newspaper and they fixed a deal to release Pat.

Swartzie walked into the jail on his first day in Acapulco, wearing a white suit and a Panama hat and carrying a briefcase. The warden almost fainted when he again saw Swartzie.

Swartzie said, "I hope you've taken care of everybody. It's a good thing we got out too, or there would have been a lot of dead bodies, including yours."

The warden swore that he had been nice to Pat and had done all he could to get Swartzie out, but he could do nothing about Pat.

Swartzie partied like crazy with Rifkin for the next 10 days. Then he had to leave to go back to run his business because Jules was going out of town for a week. Swartzie set everything up by telephone and made sure Rifkin brought Pat out safely. When Pat got back to Baltimore, he rushed over to Swartzie's house and kissed his ring as though he were the Pope. As a matter of fact, the Mexico City papers wrote "These cinco (five) Americans who were arrested with a huge marihuana cache (a pound?) were led by the U.S. Mafia chieftain's nephew 'Swartzie' Columbo."

When Swartzie got home, Jules announced that he and his girl Pat were getting married. He was quitting the gambling business and they decided to begin life anew as import/exporters and live in Bora Bora in the South Seas.

Late that summer, Swartzie opened an expensive disco in Baltimore County. Despite the absence of a liquor license, the disco was a huge success, but residential and commercial opposition combined with constant police harassment, cut income and caused the business to fail. Swartzie lost many thousands of dollars.

31.

Mama Cass telephoned Third and told him to visit her at Sinai Hospital. Her leg had been injured. Cass could be a real bitch. She was often so tactless that she embarrassed Third who was the king of tactlessness. Mama Cass was overbearing and nasty with the nurses, but because of her celebrity status, they went along with her. Third came into her room and brought out some hash. They smoked in the hospital room for a long time.

Cass informed Third that, after her recovery, she was going back to the night club circuit, and would return to the Flamingo in Las Vegas. She was very nervous about this trip because a couple of years ago she had bombed out at Caesars Palace.

Later, Cass conned some nurses into bringing her hyperdermics with Demerol because of her pain. She "pocketed" a couple of them and later shot up Third with the Demerol. At five in the morning, the nurses finally asked Third to leave the hospital.

32.

For the past five years, Joyce had free-lanced as an associate producer for Alan King, Rona Barrett, some variety show specials, and Warner Brothers. She and Sue still were best friends and traveled extensively together when their work called for it.

Sue introduced Joyce to an acquaintance and they became partners, purchasing a property, the *Hardy Boys Series,* which they eventually optioned for TV. Later, ABC agreed to let them produce the *Nancy Drew Series,* and both shows became big hits. Joyce became the first woman to produce a continuing dramatic television series.

Sue married again, this time to an ex-pro football player who had had two unsuccessful previous marriages. His name: Don Meredith. He wanted to become an actor.

33.

Barry Levinson returned from England and again teamed with Craig Nelson and a man named Rudy DeLuca, writing nightclub routines before breaking through with *The Carol Burnett Show*. It was the best possible opportunity for Barry since he felt that Burnett was a great performer and there were all sorts of variety and comedies to write for her. He now could actually see how well the work he wrote was performed. It was an important experience. And Barry also won two Emmys in three years.

34.

As a doctoral student, Bill punched the lights out of Lindsmith's Theory of Euphoria. He interviewed many old-time junkies, former acquaintances, and other dope fiends in his dissertation, and was able to disprove Lindsmith. He won the National Academy of Science Award and was deluged with offers from major colleges and universities.

35.

After a year as a bartender in San Diego, Ez departed for Seattle following a close brush with death. One night, two blues in ski masks held up the restaurant where he worked. They severely beat up the night manager and roughed up Ez, threatening to blow them away with shotguns.

Ez remained in Seattle for six months before driving south to Arizona with an ex-firefighter.

36.

Hawk came back to Baltimore to go to a party for pro-football star Bubba Smith at Swartzie's new apartment. Yussel picked up Bruce at the airport and on the way to Swartzie's they picked up a hitchiking girl named Donna. She would become Hawk's girlfriend for the next dozen years.

Back in Baltimore, Hawk began to deal cocaine. He traveled between Florida and Baltimore to traffic drugs every two months. Bruce developed a minor drug network which included Earl Maget.

Without realizing it, Bruce was set up by an informant. The DEA had filmed Hawk and Earl completing a coke sale. He was not busted in Baltimore, but when he returned to Miami, he was arrested. There were so many charges against him by the Feds that he faced an easy 50 years' sentence. A three-time loser, Hawk caved in, realizing that he would have to work for the government to get out of this jackpot. The DEA wanted Swartzie and two brothers, suit salesmen from New York, really bad. Hawk, however, refused. He would not "turn" on any friends, but he offered other dealers to give to the Feds in return for his freedom. Hawk was then sent back to Maryland by the DEA to spend the summer in Ocean City.

37.

Barry had always wanted to write a screenplay. He lucked out when he was approached by producer Ron Clark (from *The Tim Conway Show*) who asked him to help with a film project that Mel Brooks was doing. It was to be called *Silent Movie*. While still working for Carol Burnett, Barry collaborated with Brooks and some other writers over lunch using a tape recorder at Factors' Deli on Pico Street near Beverly Hills. But they were so consumed by ordering food and eating that very few jokes are recorded. Instead, the tape consisted of ordering, munching and talking about eating.

Silent Movie was a real challenge, a 90-odd-minute movie without dialogue. It was a trip into the past. Nobody had done anything like it in 50 years and it took a great deal of time and motivation. Barry also got a chance to be on the set throughout the filming, which was unusual for a writer. It was Mel Brooks' idea and Barry felt the experience would set him in the right direction.

Following the success of *Silent Movie,* he collaborated with Brooks on *High Anxiety,* in which he also made a cameo appearance as a demented bellhop.

What were the odds that Norman Steinberg, class of '57, and Barry Levinson, class of '60, two guys from Baltimore's Forest Park High School, would collaborate with Mel Brooks on three of his greatest comedy hits—*Blazing Saddles, Silent Movie* and *High Anxiety?*

38.

Swartzie and Bruce Hawk left Ocean City to drive to New York. For Hawk it was strictly a business deal. For Swartzie it was strictly for fun. He was enamored with cocaine and had been promised by Hawk that he'd be able to score anywhere up to an ounce of coke. Like many "fast laners" of the '80s, there were those "connected" or celebrity types who became seduced by cocaine in the early '70s. Among them was Swartzie.

He had a connection who supplied him with pharmaceutical coke. At this point, he was out of the drug and wanted to score for himself, to share with some friends. He was in no way involved in dealing cocaine. He also did not know that Hawk had been "turned around" and was now an informant working with the Federal authorities. Hawk wouldn't give up any of his friends, but everyone else was fair game.

In New York, they met a big executive from one of the country's top fashion houses. Bruce was extremely well connected and knew everyone. They arrived and went to the gentlemen's suite at a plush, West Side apartment complex, where they "tested" some oustandingly pure cocaine. Swartzie was permitted to buy half an ounce and it made his trip. He was just having fun. However, Hawk informed the executive he wanted to purchase a kilo (2.2 lbs.) of coke, an exceptionally large purchase even in those times. The executive got on the phone and called Tennessee, arranging to score a kilo in four days. He passed all of the logistical information for the deal over the phone in the guys' presence and then hung up. He bid Hawk and Swartzie farewell and they returned home.

Four days later, a friend of Swartzie's informed him that a big fashion executive had been busted in Tennessee as he was about to leave for New York—caught with a kilo of cocaine. Right then it dawned on Swartzie that Hawk was an agent of the government.

He was both shocked and dismayed, but he also guessed that Hawk had not given him up and did not intend to.

When the Feds pulled Bruce Hawk in to find out what information he had, he would often be left alone in the DEA's private office. He'd pass the time ransacking the desks looking for things to steal, or else for information for his personal use.

One afternoon, while Hawk was rifling through the DEA office drawers, he came upon indictments of Swartzie and the two New York brothers. He phoned them, alerting them about the indictments. Short of leaving the country, there wasn't much time for them except to seek powerful legal help.

Swartzie was eventually busted when two young men from a hair salon with whom Swartzie shared his pharmaceutical coke tried to resell the same coke to a Federal agent. They were "turned around" also and fingered Swartzie. Of course, Swartzie could have "walked." All the authorities wanted from him was to give up his connection with pharmaceutical coke, or some big gambling figures. But Swartzie was not the type of guy to give anyone up and he refused to testify.

During his indictment and trial, Swartzie began an affair with a local girl named Rosie, and he married for a second time. His first marriage had lasted six or seven years. This one was more abbreviated. Swartzie's new bride was a serious junkie, a nice girl but addicted to heroin. Long ago, she had been introduced to drugs by Third. A sheltered Jewish princess until then, she went completely overboard. Swartzie found her paraphernalia one morning and had the marriage annulled after three weeks. The next day, he began a two-year prison sentence.

39.

Fenwick got into a beef with a man who was really bad news. This guy worked on The Block, got Fenwick laid now and then, abused his credit cards, and beat him badly in a drug deal.

Fenwick who now sold real estate, flipped out and threw a brick through the guy's window. The guy called the cops and Fenwick was grounded by his lawyer.

Wick was still smoking flakes (PCP) and one night decided to bust up the guy's house. He began wrecking lawn furniture, screaming threats and throwing stones at the house. Then he broke down the door. The guy feigned fear, lured Wick to his bedroom and shot him in the side. Wick went wild screaming, "Now I'm gonna kill ya!"

But we knew that Fenwick was a bluffer. It was a very stupid remark when the other guy had the gun.

So, the guy popped Wick in the back and killed him.

Wick went out in a blaze of glory just as he would have fantasized it. His death made front page headlines the next day in the *Baltimore Morning Sun*.

40.

Boogie and his partner Harold aka Ollie initiated a campaign to rapidly expand Merry-Go-Round stores. Harold's talent in fiscal and legal matters helped propel Merry-Go-Round into the forefront of jeans boutiques and stores catering to youthful trends. Boogie assumed the role of head buyer for the stores and his instincts brought Merry-Go-Round fast and enormous earnings within five years. Being close to the scene—and out all day and night, along with dating girls from high school—brought Boogie close to the kids, their wants, desires and aspirations just as they related music and clothes (music is blared inside and outside of the stores). This enabled Boogie to select the right styles and to predict future buying trends.

Bo Death assumed control of operations. It was his job to motivate, encourage, and harass store managers, assistant managers, and sales people on a daily basis by telephone. He also visited the stores. Bo Death was a motivator. This former finance company phone-man had great flair and spoke a lingo the kids could understand. He was still Charlie-Bo-Death-Straight-Twelve.

Past Diner and playground guys formed the backbone of Merry-Go-Round employees working in the warehouse and stores, and as area supervisors. Among them was my cousin Marv, who left a secure job with the Remington Sales Division to take over design and construction of Merry-Go-Round stores. Marv was on the road just about three weeks of every month. It led to a divorce.

Fortunately, for Merry-Go-Round, you could take Boogie out of Towanda Playground but you couldn't take Towanda out of Boogie. This gave him a unique jump on many other businessmen in the field of marketing and merchandising trendy clothes. By the mid-1970s, Harold's administrative and fiscal expertise and Boogie's street sense boosted Merry-Go-Round into one of the top privately-owned retail outlets in the country.

Boogie and Bo Death were still both divorced with years of partying ahead, but Harold had settled down. He married and had two children. His wife Rona was a former Queensberry Playground girl who, as Miss Maryland, was once a finalist in the Miss Teenage America Contest. Amazingly, Rona's mom was against her marriage to Harold, one of the town's most eligible bachelors. She considered him a degenerate because of his former association with Tin Men at the Diner.

Boogie also gave jobs to many of the Diner, poolroom and playground guys who either couldn't find work anywhere else or had been fired from other jobs, had troubles with gambling, drinking or drugs, were divorced, or had family problems. Whatever it was, Boogie never forgot the guys after they took *him* back after his ill-fated marriage and serious gambling problems. He gave them all a chance. If they didn't succeed, he would have to fire them, but he'd still feel guilty and ended up sending them money over a long period of time, to help them out with whatever payments they had.

But that was Boogie. Deep down, he was compassionate and good natured, even though some people thought he was merely a street hustler.

41.

When Swartzie went into jail, Maroon, the blue marihuana dealer, was about to marry a tall white woman who was a part-time hustler. The day before the wedding, his two lieutenants, Half and Brute, plus Rifkin and the fiancée all were around a small pond doing LSD when Maroon waded into the water with his hat on. He couldn't swim but he thought the pond was shallow.

Suddenly, he was attacked by a bunch of ducks who for some reason believed he was on their "turf." They had gone mainly after his hat. (Maroon wore his father's hat. It seemed that some years before his father had drowned with the hat on.) Brute, Half, Rifkin and the fiancée thought that the ducks were joking around with Maroon and that he was fake-screaming and yelling. He went under. After 15 minutes, Maroon still hadn't surfaced. The guys on shore finally realized that they were not really tripping and that Maroon must have drowned. They dove and brought him out but couldn't revive him.

42.

Mama Cass' second tour of Las Vegas was much more successful. She proceeded to take her nightclub act to San Francisco, Miami, Puerto Rico and London.

Sue and her new husband, Dandy Don Meredith of "Monday Night Football" fame and a promising TV acting career, were at the Fairmont Hotel in San Francisco one evening to watch Mama Cass Elliot as a soloist. It was a great show, and when Cass spotted Sue in the audience she did a little routine on Forest Park High School.

She then begged Sue and Don to introduce her to the Oakland Raider football player for whom she had fallen. She didn't have much time for courtship since she'd be leaving for England in a few days.

Cass had a problem with frequent vomiting, which could have been the result of on-and-off dieting. Her weight vacillated from 200 to 245 pounds. One late July night, she was in the London flat of singer Harry Nilsson, eating a sandwich in bed. She began to choke and vomit, and then passed out. She died from ingesting her own vomit. Many assumed her death was drug related.

Later, examining physicians discounted the choking theory and revealed that Mama Cass had died of "myocardial degeneration due to fat." The muscle of her heart turned fatty and just failed.

43.

I had a free and easy rein at Morgan State. I served as Assistant Dean for two years and Acting Dean for one. I also began a lacrosse program there.

Publicly I accomplished a great deal as the head lacrosse coach. We proved that the black athlete could play an elitist white sport, although the athletic director Earl Banks jokingly said, "For years they wouldn't let us play this game because they didn't want any blacks to have sticks in their hands during athletic contests against whites."

However, over five seasons we were ranked in the nation's "Top Ten" four times, and during 1973 and 1975 we went to the Division II National Tournament. We produced a number of All-Americans and were involved in what many considered to be the greatest upset in intercollegiate sports history—defeating the Washington and Lee University in Lexington, Virginia, where they had not lost a home game in four years or a regular season game in three. The year previous they were the NCAA Division I #1 ranked team. Their only losses in the last three years were in the quarter and semi-finals of the National Tournament; the same year, 1975, in which we beat them, 8-7, they defeated defending national champion Johns Hopkins in the quarter-finals of the Division I NCAA Tournament.

This was a great and heartwarming accomplishment for our kids, but in retrospect, if we had lost that game, we probably would have won the Division II title. As it turned out, the players became so enamored with themselves that they thought all they had to do was lay their sticks on the ground and they would win every game. But I wouldn't exchange that victory for anything. It stands tall in my memory. It can be equated to Morgan State beginning a football program today and five years later going to South Bend, Indiana to beat a #1 ranked Notre Dame, or going into Nebraska to beat the Cornhuskers. It was an incredible feat, especially since blacks had no tradition or adolescent training in the game of lacrosse.

When the racial composition changed in the Baltimore public school system, predominantly white schools that excelled in lacrosse or had lacrosse programs became predominantly black schools, while continuing to play lacrosse. The black students were good athletes, and a few schools even had good coaches who stressed fundamentals. I continued this technique at Morgan by extolling the philosophy of the great Naval Acadmy coach, Bill Bilderback, who in the early to mid-'60s had the longest lacrosse winning streak and NCAA Championship skein. He used athletes, usually players who excelled in other sports, and taught them basic fundamentals. He also implemented a vigorous conditioning program while, naturally, recruiting one or two excellent high school lacrosse stars as well. I adopted this philosophy and it worked well at Morgan State. I also utilized the "other race" grant in reverse by recruiting anywhere from one to four very good white players which proved beneficial; especially my goalie, a 5'2" kid with a heart about 10 feet tall. He was an All-American player and team leader who melded beautifully with the blacks.

Privately, coaching at Morgan State University was also a unique situation. Some players on my team disappeared, died, were shot or knifed. Dr. Larry Becker (a mensch) became a top orthopedic surgeon and he used to take care of my injured Morgan players. He knew they had no money to pay for his services. Some of the kids had Medical Assistance cards, others had nothing. I remember calling Becker one weekend about a lacrosse injury, and asked him if he could see the player right away. He obliged and met me at his office in a half hour. I brought in the player who had a bullet wound in his foot. Becker asked, incredulously, what sort of lacrosse injury this was, and how it had occurred. As it turned out, this young man had been playing basketball and a kid who wasn't chosen into the game came back with a gun and began shooting up the court. A bullet ricocheted off the pavement into my player's foot.

I had an equipment manager who decided to become the general manager and part-owner of the lacrosse team, even though you couldn't own a college team. He would ride on bus trips with nasal inhalants stuck in each nostril (maybe filled with cocaine?) insisting on chronic sinusitis.

When we would annually go to play Washington and Lee, the kids would normally try to stay up late, hanging in the town. One year, I insisted on a curfew. They watched dirty movies, went to sleep early and we were destroyed 16–4 the next day. After that, I let the kids maintain their lifestyle. They were allowed to go back hanging out all night in Lexington, ingest all varieties of garbage food, play basketball in the gym till three in the morning, and eat too big a training meal. Then they went out and upset Washington and Lee.

When the players saw "skin flicks," they used to ask the white players or me if we ever "went down" on women. Did we really eat pussy? When we responded in the affirmative, the players would go, "Ugh, ugh, that's sickening!" Most blues did not get into oral sex until the late 1970s.

Black guys really are supermen. I mean I had players who'd eat a steak sub (hero sandwich with extra onions) or a hot dog with the works before a game, or even at half-time, and then go out and play like gazelles.

We had a white player named Joe Alex who was an All-Maryland lacrosse and football player in high school. He was the first white player at Morgan State. He was called the Polar Bear. (Bears was the school's nickname). This guy either had guts or was insane, because being the only white playing in a black football league, of very rough, tough people, was brutal.

The only season our lacrosse team wasn't ranked in the Top Ten was 1972, when a lot of the kids who played for me signed pro football contracts and were therefore ineligible for collegiate sports.

When my wife Lynne would come to games, she would walk onto the field in her mini-dress and sit on the bench with the players. The opposing coach and players, for some reason, usually assumed that Lynne was married to one of the players. After the game they would come up and whisper, "Who's the blonde married to?" Naturally, I would pick out the biggest and blackest player, and they would respond, "Oh, okay. We won't say anything."

During one game, we had our first midfield in the game for more than five minutes which, if you understand the game, is a long time for lacrosse midfielders to run up and down on the field. Usually, a midfield stays in for two minutes, three tops. I started to call for the second midfield. At the time, I did everything from coaching and keeping score to lining the field and handled equipment problems. Ten minutes later, when the first midfields' tongues were hanging out, my wife came over to me.

"They can't go in until they're finished singing," she said.

I turned around and on the bench my players were harmonizing the Sly and the Family Stone song, "I Want to Take You Higher," and, naturally, the blues finished the song before they went into the game.

In the same game, Bernie Ullman, who was the chief referee of both the National Football League and the U.S. Southern Lacrosse Officials Association, came off the field to tell me that he was concerned about crowd control and why did I have people from the stands gathered around the bench instead of sitting in the stadium. I could barely contain myself. I asked Bernie how he expected me to coach the team, serve as trainer, equipment manager, scorekeeper and timer, *and* maintain crowd control. He laughed and never bothered me again.

Since I used a number of football players in lacrosse, and because Morgan State enjoyed a very fine reputation as a black college football power, many pro football scouts and coaches would come around in the spring. They were very curious about the game of lacrosse. John Madden, the former coach of the Oakland Raiders who is now a pro football analyst on television, used to hang around and watch practice to make sure that I did not keep blue chip—soon to be all-pro—Ray Chester on the team, since he had drafted him and was very concerned that players like Stanley Cherry were capable of breaking Chester's bones during lacrosse practice.

Stanley was one of my favorite players. He was 6′5″, weighed 235 pounds, and was mean and tough. He still is. He was the smallest and youngest of six children. Eventually, Stanley became a correctional officer in a prison. He was probably better than any defensive football player ever at Morgan, including all-pro Willie Lanier, except Stanley didn't kiss ass. He had a back operation during his junior year and was therefore not drafted. He signed as a free agent and played briefly with the Baltimore Colts and New York Jets before going with the fledgling and quickly defunct World

Football League where he was all-pro.

Stanley couldn't deal with or comprehend the politics of college and pro athletics. College politics struck in his sophomore year. He was the undefeated black collegiate wrestling champion, but the school refused to pay the $250 needed to send him for the NCAA championships, which probably he would have won.

He was traded by the Colts to the Jets because he observed the first pro football strike and the Colts management thought his allegiances were elsewhere.

I remember Stanley kibitzing during a ping pong match with a Morgan football player who was about 6'8" and 290 pounds. The guy grabbed Stanley and threw him against the wall. Cherry punched him so hard that it seemed as if the punchee's eye might have hit four walls and landed back into his head before he was finished off. Cherry was feared and respected totally while he was at Morgan State.

Stanley was a good lacrosse player who would hit (check) people so hard in practice and during games—legally—that you'd hear bones actually cracking. One time he was put out of a game against Dartmouth for unsportsmanlike conduct after he had already injured four players legally. The referees insisted that he was a health hazard. I played the game under protest, but it didn't matter.

Third used to assist me as a coach. Every year I fired him, or he would just take off and go to Provincetown for the summer. He wanted to be a friend of the players and party with them, but he also wanted to be Vince Lombardi, and these ambitions didn't mesh. Many of the players told me that they were going to murder Third sometime down the line. Once, after we played Hoffstra, on Long Island, Third demanded that the players from New York drop him off at the subway. So, the guys drove to ultra-rough Bedford Stuyvesant, screamed "Nigger" about 12 times, and threw him bodily out of the car.

Third got carried away with his role as my assistant coach at Morgan and, unbeknownst to me, approached athletic director Earl Banks and told him that he needed a raise. He wanted three or four more thousand dollars. Third was only getting $500 which I gave him out of my salary, which was only $1,500. Banks was incredulous.

"How can you turn on Silverman," he asked.

Third said, "Hey, I'm going to take credit for the team. Silverman is just an administrator."

Third didn't realize that 80 percent of coaching was organization, administration and planning. He thought coaching is just *on* the field coaching. Wrong!

Banks called me up the next day and informed me that he would drop the lacrosse program unless Third was fired. I sent Third a letter and fired him. We didn't speak for three years.

In the history of lacrosse at Morgan State, we experienced bias on several occasions. It was expected. Here were two white Jews coaching a black team! Yet, we always got a square shake from a referee named Larry Levitt, who was one of the old Diner guys and a contemporary of Snyder, Turns, and Ray the Mensch. Levitt was somewhat of a mensch in his own right. He had been an all-state selection in football, basketball and lacrosse. He was a real rough guy who grew up in a black neighborhood and was well respected. When he would referee the games, if he made a mistake he would change his call on the spot. No other referee would do that. Levitt's family also still owned a store in the old neighborhood. Many of my Morgan players lived in that neighborhood and hung out in "Levitt's," but if they ever gave Larry lip, they were told they couldn't come into the store for a week. There were Ivy League coaches who didn't understand this byplay during a game.

I used to motivate the kids by explaining to them that nobody expected blues to be any good, because it was an elitist game. I would also tell them that Jim Brown was probably one of the greatest lacrosse players, white or black, that ever lived. Because kids had great respect for Jim, who was a movie star at the time, his example served as a great incentive.

After we finished in the Top Five in the county in 1975, I retired and became white again.

During my time as a lacrosse coach, I moved from Morgan State University to the Maryland State Department of Health and Mental Hygiene. I first worked as regulations coordinator and hearings officer for the Secretary's office. After a year there, I transferred to the Drug Abuse Administration which had been created through emergency legislation to deal with the growing drug problem.

The public was very concerned about the drug abuse epidemic. The Secretary of Health, who has become a "media darling" by writing diet books and appearing on national television, decided personally to intervene in the drug crisis that summer in Ocean City.

Under the guise of tabs of LSD, drug dealers were selling a

"sunshine pill" containing strychnine to unsuspecting teenagers. It resulted in a couple of deaths and dozens of very ill kids.

The Secretary of Health, the Director of the Drug Abuse Administration, and I drove down to Ocean City one weekend to investigate the crisis and to formulate a prevention strategy. We decided to hire an airplane to fly along the beach towing a sign saying, "The Sunshine Pill Kills!" The media were alerted, and Sunday afternoon we were stationed on the boardwalk, among thousands of beach-goers that observed the event.

As the plane flew over trailing a huge golden sign, the Secretary, looking dandy and fine, pointed up at the sky boasting to the press of his strategy. The steaming crowds on the white sand looked up inquisitively as the sign fluttered. Just then the plane began to sputter, the engine stopped, and the sign became tangled up, and within seconds the airplane crashed headlong into the choppy ocean waters. Incredulously, cheers went up from the crowded beach.

We drove silently back to Baltimore.

44.

In Provincetown, Third picked up a young girl and took her over to his apartment with another guy. They convined her that they're going to give her some cocaine but that she had to go into the bathroom to get it. They cautioned her to take her clothes off before she entered to keep from getting wet. A pipe had burst. The girl went into the bathroom with just her panties on. As she bent over the toilet seat to do a line of coke, Third approached from behind, pulled her panties down, and jammed her from the rear. She knocked herself out banging her head into the commode and the guys thought that she was dead. Third fantasized he'd be going back to jail, forever. An hour later, the girl woke up and went home.

The next evening, Third was waiting tables at the "A" House, a gay restaurant where he had a job. There was a big party going on and the "boys" convinced Third to get up on top of a table and do a dance. The crowd got very wild since everyone was inhaling a lot of Amyl-Nitrate and a group of gays tried to rape Third, who had to fight his way out of the restaurant. Gold believed that the gays succeeded by offering Third a Baby Ruth.

45.

The ex-firefighter and Ez became entrepreneurs in Arizona in the fire-extinguisher business. Occupational Health and Safety Administration requirements left many businesses and hotels vulnerable to inspection scams. Ez and the firefighter randomly "inspected" businesses, refilling deficient extinguishers, and earned a couple hundred dollars a day.

One weekend, while climbing a mountain, eating magic mushrooms, and sightseeing around the Yuma sand dunes, Ez met a girl who convinced him to fly to Hawaii with her. They sold her car in San Diego for $700 and bought two one-way tickets to Honolulu.

46.

Neurotic Nat and I, in order properly to arm ourselves, decided to change our regular guns. I had a Walther PPK because James Bond used it in his films. Nat had a small Beretta. When we realized that these wouldn't stop an angry blue, we went out to Dave Yale's gunshop in Bel Air, Maryland.

The Dirty Harry movies were growing in popularity and we were mesmerized with the 357 Magnum. Dave Yale warned us that he'd better show us how to use it. We advised him that we were big boys and we knew what we were doing. We went back to where Dave has a firing range near his house. Nat put in ear plugs and took aim at the target which was only about 10 yards away. I took a look at the gun's size and moved behind a tree. Nat crouched down in the police position, aimed and fired. The reverberations knocked him back about five yards into the air. The shot missed the target completely, but not Dave Yale's cat, and blew off a side of his porch. Dave barred us as customers for a year. We didn't buy a Magnum.

47.

Snyder had an exceptional talent for promotion, particularly himself. He looked the part. We used to kid him that he looked like Soupy Sales or Jerry Lee Lewis. In fact he was a nice-looking, six-foot, well-built guy with the patter to match. He was ready to party in a New York minute, the kind of guy with whom others wanted to hang out. Women would do anything for him. But, they were always of a certain type: Submissive, attractive enough for maybe three dates and sex for most guys. But Snyder kept them around and allowed them to support him during cash-short times in between his money-making schemes, racetrack hits and self-promotions. Down times totaled 37 of his 46 years.

On a kibitz [joke] comparing great high school basketball teams, Snyder and I end up promoting two epic high school basketball games between 1974 and 1977 involving players who would go on to both collegiate and professional basketball stardom.

Snyder was living in Washington and thought that the 1973–1974 DeMatha High School team was the greatest thing since 7-Up. I argued that Dunbar High School, which had a winning streak of 39 straight games, was much better. DeMatha, whose streak went to 47 in a row, boasted players like Adrian Dantley and Kenny Carr, who went on to be all-pro basketball stars. Dunbar had a lot of kids from East Baltimore who seldom, if ever, even went to college.

We somehow promoted the game and filled three-quarters of the Baltimore Civic Center with 8,500 people at $4 a head. Surprisingly, Dunbar upset DeMatha, led by a player named Skip "Honey-dip" Wise who scored 39 points, 21 in the last quarter. This game put Baltimore basketball on the national map.

I was in Florida during the game and when I got back, I asked Snyder about the profits and what my share was. He told me that he had to give away most of the take to the city school system and DeMatha High. I knew that, but still thought I should be up a couple thousand bucks. Snyder told me he would get back to me shortly. Two years later, he gave me $200. He called it even, and complained that he lost $100 on the game.

In 1977, we promoted another basketball game, this one with West Philly High School, which was #1 in the nation. West Philly was led by Gene Banks, who also went on to become a standout in the National Basketball Association. Dunbar, undefeated for two years, was led by Ernie Graham, who later became one of the all-time scorers for the University of Maryland. Although the game was anti-climactic, West Philly won handily. We sponsored a slam-dunk contest involving high school kids that attracted some of the best basketball players in the country. Over 12,000 fans attended the game. Snyder and I made a good deal of money on this promotion. With his share, Snyder began a sports promotion business.

To make more money at a basketball game the following year, Snyder stationed Neurotic Nat at a side door to charge standees who wanted to see the game. Nat did very well for an hour, and pocketed lots of money. Then Nat noticed some teenage blues who had pried open a side door and gained entry. Nat left his post and began chasing the kids. Suddenly, the kids, four big young studs, said "Hey, what are we running from this squirt for?" and they started chasing Nat, who managed to escape behind the concessions, returning after the kids left to sell standing-room-only tickets. At this point a man from Civic Center management and a policeman came over to Nat and told him to join them in the main office. Snyder was paged on the P.A. system. They questioned Nat while they waited for Snyder to show up. Nat innocently told them he worked for Snyder. When Snyder arrived Nat repeated his story, emptied his pockets of money, and gave the cash to Snyder, who flung the money at the Civic Center guy and said, "Here, take your fucking money!" Everyone began yelling and accusing each other, except Neurotic Nat, who slipped out of the door, went to the men's room, and threw up.

48.

During the '70s, Boogie's reputation with women rose to dizzying heights. He couldn't miss. Moreover, he had the time, energy and funds to support his "lady games."

Snyder was dispatched to Atlanta for training as a claims adjuster and spent a week seeing Boogie. For seven days, Snyder found himself either in a closet scene or being invited to a "double-team" affair by one of Boogie's many girlfriends.

During the closet scenes, Snyder took copious notes and later revealed to the guys that one of Boogie's major techniques when screwing was to bang his feet up and down, sort of running horizontally. This was for maximum effect. The girl's perception was that he was pumping away non-stop for what she considered an eternity.

Boogie had become reacquainted with The Hair Garage Boys, Buzzy Kuen and Jon Salconi. In the early '60s, when he was an apprentice hairdresser, Boogie had met Buzzy and Jon. They were among the emerging non-gay hairdressing clique.

Anyhow, Buzzy and Jon began the first unisex hairstyling shops in Maryland and all over the east coast. Their stores expanded rapidly. Buzzy was on the artistic side of the business and Jon handled the fiscal and administrative end. Both had an immense following of women, for hairstyling and frolicking.

Buzzy and Boogie hung out a lot. They'd ride around in Boogie's chauffeured limousine dating girls between 16 and 36. They were an early Equal Opportunity duo. Women, regardless of age, race and religion, all were welcome into the web of their arms and charms. If one didn't get the woman, the other did. Their different looks, style, approach and "lines" made them almost impossible to "miss with the chicks."

Buzzy had jet-black, straight hair, a good build, and had an Errol Flynn look. And Boogie? Well, he was Boogie.

The guys attempted to change their names at one point. Boogie wanted to be called by his legal name, Leonard or Lenny for short. He felt "Boogie" wasn't respectful enough now that he'd become a mini-tycoon. Also that it didn't impress the parents of any WASP girls. Buzzy felt that his name was too young-sounding, so he chose to be called Chas.

I couldn't use Lenny or Chas after calling them Boogie and Buzzy for so many years. Yet most of the other Diner guys went along with the new names. Boogie later gave it up, but Chas made it official. When he left The Hair Garage and opened his own salon several years later, he named it "Chas."

49.

Third and Gold became publishers. They turned out two books. The first was by Hyman Pressman, the gadfly comptroller of Baltimore. The second was the *Maryland Children's Guide*. They lost a lot of money on the two books. Not only because publishing was an expensive endeavor, but also because they had a zero cash flow. They couldn't afford the overhead, and they were buying too many meals and making unnecessary long distance phone calls. Then Gold's brother stole the company's checkbook and wrote a lot of bad checks.

50.

When a few of his friends were busted, Hawk got in a violent argument with the U.S. Narcotics prosecutor for Maryland who had lied to him. The lawyer had promised Hawk that they would not prosecute his friends [like Earl Maget] but they did. They had everything on film. Earl was indicted, not only for cocaine trafficking but also for check-kiting, and was sentenced to jail for two years.

Bruce was one of the first individuals to come under the government Witness Program, or what was then called the Marshall Protection Plan. The word was around that there was a "contract" on Hawk and, although Hawk didn't seem to worry about it or even believe it, he enjoyed the idea of being paid by the Federal government, and to be relocated anywhere he wanted. He decided to "relocate" to the beaches off San Diego. At this time, the government essentially didn't know what they were doing, or even if there was a real contract out on Hawk. In fact, Hawk could have been killed easily had there been a contract.

Hawk finally went to trial for cocaine trafficking between Florida and Maryland three years later, and was given probation for his cooperation. Later, the government protection plan moved Hawk to Delaware where he got into a major hassle with his "protectors," and was thrown out of the Witness Program. Yet, Hawk finally convinced them to let him back in. He finally relocated to Florida where he went somewhat "legitimate," working for a while as a waiter.

51.

The fabulous success of the Merry-Go-Round stores expectedly bred their inflated egos and personality clashes, and Boogie and Harold drifted apart. They decided that only one of them could run the company and Boogie retired. But MGR really needed both of them, because the next year earnings began to drop. Several stores were shut down.

Harold and Bo Death took over as buyers, an area where Boogie excelled. Bo Death was needed in operations, particularly to monitor in-house pilferage, but the business continued to flounder.

During this time, Boogie was doing a lot of traveling, and having even more fun than he realized. He would play ball everywhere and seduced every chick he could find in California, New York, Aspen, Florida, Mexico and Europe. Although a lot of his main men kept score and warned him about the sales slump, saying MGR needed both Boogie and Harold, Boogie stayed away. He considered himself permanently retired.

52.

One night after a tough Oriole loss, Boogie's brother, Eggie, was in the Pimlico Hotel lounge when baseball star Reggie Jackson arrived. Reggie was in a foul mood and Eggie didn't help it when he began a Diner-type sarcastic knock of Reggie. Tempers flared and an altercation ensued. Jackson roughed up Eggie a bit before the "fight" was broken up.

A week later, Eggie sued Reggie for a million bucks.

53.

Earl Maget had legitimate prescriptions for Demerol and Delaudid. He mailed the pills down to Bruce Hawk in Florida. One day a package arrived and Bruce Hawk wasn't home. His girlfriend Donna picket it up and was immediately arrested by Federal agents. Donna managed to warn him by phone. Nothing ever happened to Earl or Bruce, but Donna had to go to court. The charges were eventually dropped.

54.

After Johns Hopkins, Dr. Bill McAuliffe became as Associate Professor at Harvard University. Later he was the youngest chairman ever of the Behavioral Science Department of Harvard School of Public Health. Not bad for a guy who wasn't expected to survive past 20 because of fights and lots of trouble.

55.

Boogie took up tennis, a sport that was never played on playgrounds in the 1950s. Within a year he became competitive with some of the better club players around the country.

Later, Boogie decided to become a professional boxer. He was 37 years old. He started training at Mack's gym, in one of the worst

Baltimore neighborhoods. To remain anonymous, Boogie bought a
beat-up old car which he drove to Mack's for his daily workout. He
developed quickly. After three months, he went three rounds with
Alvin Anderson, the ninth-rated welterweight in the world. He
stayed toe to toe with him. He got hurt, but he didn't go down.

56.

Obie got the best of it over the years, since he went broke while
Boogie became a multi-millionaire. Boogie was able to support Obie
in a way Obie had never remotely dreamed about. Not only did
Boogie bankroll the initially successful (but ill-fated) Red Balloon
Boutique in New Orleans, but he sent Obie around the world twice.
At the drop of a collect phone call, Obie would receive up to
$10,000 in cash to continue his travels. Obie told friends that he was
in the import-export business. But his chief import and export was
himself.

On Obie's second trip around the world, again courtesy of Boogie, he became a student of the Indian guru, Bagwan Shen Rajseesh.
The Bagwan's spiritual trip is "Don't deny yourself anything! Get it
out of your system." There were some large love sessions. This
lifestyle appealed to many Americans who followed the Bagwan's
teachings.

Obie became Swami Veet Giam. Bagwan's sect had to wear
orange robes and pajamas, and a huge necklace with a likeness of
the Bagwan. Obie shaved his head clean and spray painted it orange.

For the money Boogie was spending on Obie, the necklace should
have had Boogie's likeness instead of the Bagwan's.

57.

Swartzie served two years in Federal prison. He was paroled and
promptly resumed his career as a bookmaker. Somehow he seemed

taller and skinnier. He sported a Florida suntan. In time, he became one of the top ten bookies in the United States. We were proud of Swartzie. He had become the first really successful Diner guy.

58.

Neurotic Nat was unique. He could be frugal to the point of walking on the grass to keep from wearing out the soles of his shoes. Or, he could be extravagant by paying three $100 hookers during the course of a week. Hookers are Nat's passion. They have been so for over 20 years. Recently, he celebrated the anniversary of his negotiations with a prostitute 20 years before. At that time, he had had negotiations with 983 different hookers. On December 5th, his birthday, he was trying to reach the 1,000 hooker plateau. Nat had only 17 to go. Time was short. He missed by four. He was despondent for weeks.

Nat always had been very up front about his passion and could explain it rationally to anyone who cared to listen. He claimed he saved money over this 20-year period as opposed to the cost of being married. He actually totaled up the cost. He is additionally proud that he never caught a disease.

Nat got into some crazy scenes. Once, he had two hookers whom he agreed to pay $60 each to dress him up like a woman and position him outside of his bedroom door holding school books. The hookers would turn the lights out and hide in his bedroom. Nat would then start talking in a high falsetto voice saying, "I'm just a co-ed from Goucher going into a dimly lit parking lot. I sure hope there are no guys in here to jump me and rape me."

But sure enough, as soon as Nat walked into the bedroom, the hookers leaped out and pounced upon him. They'd hold him down. He would try to get away.

Nat once got into another scene at a massage parlor downtown—a place called the Roman Spa, where he found himself in an act of "equestrian training." A hooker stripped Nat and then put a little baby saddle on his back and taped a number on his side. She climbed on his back naked and whipped him on the backside while, on all fours, he paraded around a hot tub. On the third lap, Nat's knee gave out and the hooker pulled out a blank gun and threatened to shoot him.

Nat could turn around almost any situation so that it became a sexual one. A few years ago, a doctor ordered Nat to get more exercise. At 5′3″ and 148 lbs., he was overweight and out of shape. The doctor said he had the body of a 65-year-old in poor condition. Nat sent away for exercise ropes that he tied to a door knob so he could work out by pulling and lifting arms and legs for sit-ups, push-ups, and pull-ups. He discovered that it was a more pleasurable exercise if he tied himself to the door knob with the ropes and then had the hooker "threaten" him as he fake-tryed to get away.

Nat once was a trick pad, a place used by prostitutes, with two hookers on Park Avenue, unaware that the apartment was under police surveillance. He was lying on his back in the bed, handcuffed from behind, with one woman sitting on his face while the other was tantalizing him. Suddenly, there was a pounding on the front door followed by shouts of, "Police! Open up at once!" The ladies immediately leaped up, scooped up their clothing, and bolted out the back door.

Nat was petrified. His glasses were on the night table, he was handcuffed. He felt like a turtle turned on his back, and the banging on the door grew louder. He rolled off of the bed and backed his way to the door amid threats by the police to "Break it down in a few seconds!"

As Nat gingerly turned the doorknob with his fingers through the handcuffs, the police pushed the door, smacking him into the wall.

"Who the hell are you and what are you doing handcuffed?" the cop growled.

Although flabbergasted, Nat's mind raced for an explanation. He imagined the newspaper headlines and weighed his parents' reaction. Just then the hookers returned, pretending they were coming home from work. They accused the police of gestapo tactics, and demanded to see a search warrant. They pretended to call their attorney. The police regrouped and cited anonymous neighborhood complaints. Nat tried working on an excuse as he remained naked and handcuffed.

The police finally apologized to the ladies, even though they obviously pretended to believe Nat and the girls' excuse: a rehearsal of their Houdini-type escape act in a charity event. Unfortunately, they had lost the key to the cuffs, and went out to find a locksmith. "But why was he undressed?" the cops asked, as the hookers hastened them out of their house.

59.

I took my daughter Debi shopping at a discount store in Randalls-town. I hadn't seen the Gripper for 12 years. There he was wandering through a row of television sets in the store. Bux had opened an art framing store and was quite successful. The last thing that I had heard was that he was doing just great. According to Berdoff, "He could walk down the center of town and everybody still parted when he walked through!" As I saw him down the aisle, I turned to my daughter and thought, "Hey, you're 36 years old. What are you scared of?" My heart was racing and all I could think of was avoiding the grip and running out of the store. Yet something in the back of my mind said, "But you're 36 years old, Bux must be 40, why worry about him? Those were childhood days, he won't grip you now." Yet, I thought of the embarrassment of Bux gripping me in front of my 12-year-old daughter who looked up to me.

I quickly grabbed Debi and we left the store and ran down the street to an ice cream parlor. I told Debi I wanted to surprise her and get her some ice cream. Secretly, I wanted to get as far away from the Gripper as possible. We dilly-dallied in the ice cream parlor for 20 minutes. Even Debi seemed bored with the ice cream. She reminded me, "We have to get the tape recorder and bring it home to Mommy." I figured that by now Bux had definitely left the store, so I gathered up my courage and told myself that I was just being a wimp and walked back up the street.

Bux stood in front of the store watching me. My heart sank. I kept thinking of how to get out of the grip, and I reverted back to my behavior of years ago. I rushed up and introduced myself to Bux, shook his hand quickly, and started telling him about how Fenwick had been killed, how Boogie succeeded, and how Ez had moved to Hawaii. Anything to keep the Gripper off balance.

Well, Bux "nickled and dimed" me a little bit, said he was in Baltimore to visit his family, and that he planned to move to Pennsylvania to open a new business. I told Bux that I would definitely call him, apologized that I was in a hurry, and quickly went in the discount shop feeling relieved. Suddenly there was an arm on my shoulder, it was Bux. I figured, "Oh God, here it comes!" Instead, he just wanted my phone number, but I knew that could mean trouble. I gave him my a phony one. Bux shook my hand. He started to squeeze it a little bit, gave me a wink and squeezed at my arm some more. It was just a tease, to remind me that he knew I was conning him. Then he left.

60.

Anticipating even bigger payoffs, Snyder decided to promote a high school basketball TV game of the week and also a super-triple-header involving teams from the east, including one from the Dominican Republic. It was a pre-season extravaganza and it followed on the heels of the previous West Philly vs. Dunbar promotion. I tried to convince Snyder that this was not a good idea but he wouldn't listen. Fortunately, without my knowledge, he took on a silent partner, a black State Senator who thought that he was being slick in easing me out of the action and becoming Snyder's partner. What he didn't realize was that to be successful the games could only be promoted once every three years. The matchup was a terrible flop and they lost $20,000, which Snyder couldn't pay back. The TV game of the week also fell through. I lost just enough money to teach me a good lesson.

I confronted Snyder just before the triple-header games, "I know I'm no longer your partner and that you went into the deal with the blue legislator behind my back."

He tells me, "Choice. I couldn't do it any other way."

Later, he called me after the game, distraught. Instead of the anticipated 12,000 crowd sell-out, only 66 people showed up. It was a disaster and Snyder told me he felt so terrible that he wanted to jump from the eight floor of the Lord Baltimore Hotel. I couldn't muster up much sympathy; I encouraged him to jump. After that, we didn't speak for the next six years.

The State Senator had to pay back the guarantee both to the Civic Center and the Lord Baltimore Hotel.

61.

Bob Litwin and I went from very part-time free-lance writers for the *Baltimore News American,* a daily major paper, in 1976, to semi-part-time contributing editors for *Baltimore Magazine* in 1978. From an extremely small Chamber of Commerce publication, *Baltimore Magazine* grew to major status and increased circulation with the help of our trendy lists on the best and worst dressed, sexiest, and most powerful people in town, and our investigative pieces of prostitution, swingers, and drug abuse. We did this in our spare time, hoping to increase our recognition factor ten-fold throughout the city. We were no Woodward and Bernstein, but we knew what the public wanted to read, and we were actually far from serious about our new vocation.

The circulation crested on the "sexiest" list which sold out 35,000 copies and became a collector's item. It was controversial and done in the spirit of good fun, but readers actually took it seriously. So we invented a story about demographics and scientific surveys. The readership bought it. In anticipation of an annual "sexiest" list, people began to bribe us to be included on next year's list. As journalists of unimpeachable integrity, we considered accepting them.

The "sexiest" list included pictures of the 10 top men and women, and also included 60 other names by category. Hud made the Top 10. The supplementary list included Dr. Larry Becker, Third [as a publisher], Boogie, Harold, and Ben who was now a hairdresser's apprentice.

Ben unexpectedly appeared at my house one night around 11:00. For the next three hours, he entertained Lynne and me with stories, jokes and knocks. He thanked me for being put on the "sexiest" list, confessed that since the magazine article he had had offers from four girls and eleven fags. He wouldn't tell which of them he accepted.

Ben had a serious alcohol and drug problem. As the night wore on, his mood began to change drastically. He walked by our daughter Debi's room. She is the exact age as his daughter. Ben lamented that wedded bliss and a family could have been his if he hadn't screwed up his marriage to his former wife, who had since remarried.

Then Ben became extremely despondent and broke down. His despair lasted until dawn. Lynne got up and made us breakfast. Ben cheered up—putting on a clown's face once again. But later, the laughter subsided. I was worried about Ben. The drugs weren't the cause of his depression. They were his escape from it.

62.

Swami-chanting Obie visited Jules in Bora Bora, and Jules was ecstatic to see a fellow Diner guy, someone who could actually speak English. Until now, Jules had to bribe his help to play badminton with him. True to form, Obie overstayed his welcome—by about three months, taking complete advantage of Jules and Pat's hospitality. He ate them out of house and home, and literally took over the guest and the main house, with no regard for what Jules and Pat wanted to do. Finally, Jules told Obie he had to leave.

63.

Ben's world began to crumble. When he failed as a hairstylist, he got full-time work in Longfellow's Bar. Every now and then, one of the successful guys to whom he used to say, "Hi me," stopped in to shoot the breeze, leaving a big tip. Ben needed the money, but he couldn't handle the fact that these guys were leaving him big tips. He felt degraded and ashamed. It rankled him. He began to depend heavily on drugs and alcohol. Although Ben still had a lot of girlfriends and guys he befriended downtown, he longed to be like his buddies who had made it big. He ached for the old camaraderie. It finally ate on him so much that, against doctors orders to avoid drugs and alcohol, Ben overindulged. He died of a bleeding ulcer, but he really died of a broken heart.

64.

Boogie gradually realized that everything he and Harold had built up could crash, including his own security and that which he had planned for his close friends. Reluctantly, he came out of retirement.

Although the guys wouldn't admit that they were both needed, deep down everyone was relieved. Harold, now going through a divorce, decided to go into the savings and loan business, while Boogie took charge of Merry-Go-Round. Within six months, MGR was back making money. In addition, Boogie and Harold hired top quality people to replace them both when Boogie later returned to semi-retirement.

This was a complicated period in Boogie's life. He and Harold had a falling out. But Boogie's return began a new era at Merry-Go-Round.

65.

Things for Eggie were going great. Through his work with Boogie at Merry-Go-Round, he now owned a beautiful condominium in a plush Towson high rise, a new Mercedes, and more women than he ever dreamed of. He had settled his lawsuit with Reggie Jackson for five grand, and had a framed letter of apology from Reggie displayed on his living room table.

66.

Ez had been living in Hawaii for three years, supporting himself as a waiter, bartender, laborer and farm hand. For a brief period, he acquired a 1948 pick-up truck and did odd jobs on the island of Maui, living in the back of the truck which he had converted into crude living quarters.

He later moved down in the valley and was now living in a shack with a beautiful Oregon lady, her mother, and an eight-year-old son. They had no electricity, no plumbing. The place was infested with mosquitoes, large spiders, and continuous mud slides. Ez was dragging his leg along since it had been temporarily paralyzed from the sting of a large centipede, common in the Maui valley.

67.

Nat's mother was a superb wooden hanger-thrower. She had such dexterity that when Nat was younger she would give him a 10-yard start in the morning as he ran out the door. As he was hitting the doorsteps on the way outside, she would grab the wooden hanger and, in one swift motion, she'd hit him in the middle of the back. If there had been an Olympic event for wooden hanger-throwing, she would have won a gold medal.

Everything in the Smertz household seemed to revolve around the older daughter Norma, a pleasant-looking girl with glasses and braces, whose looks dramatically improved by contact lenses and dental surgery. Norma was a bright girl who went on to graduate with honors from Boston University. She married a successful medical supplies executive, moved to Chicago where she received her M.D. in psychiatry, and then did advance studies in sex therapy at the Johns Hopkins Sex Clinic.

Norma became one of the top sex therapists in the Midwest,

specializing in treating young boys or men who had trouble getting an erection or having orgasms. Norma became so adept at this job that she began to do turn-away business. She started a radio show on sex therapy, and became the advisor to swingers' clubs. Later, she admitted to Nat that she had gotten so carried away during one session when she manipulated a boy that she forgot her doctorly manners. This continued with her next three patients. Word soon got around the community high school, and teenage boys were almost breaking down the door trying to get therapy from "good Doctor Norma," at $80 an hour for a professional session.

Norma soon began hanging out at the Chicago version of Plato's Retreat, a swinging sex joint, and admitted to her brother Nat that she screwed half of Chicago's Lakeside during her "advanced lab work" on sex therapy.

Norma invited Nat to New York for a weekend of fun and to get together with their cousin Flo who had been divorced for a few years. She was one of two daughters of Mrs. Smertz's younger sister. Flo's sister had died of a heart attack on the sand in Acapulco and laid there for hours like a beached whale in front of her children who thought she was kidding. Flo had recently been dating Harvy Dreems, a porno movie star.

Nat was enticed to New York by Norma telling him that she would fix him up with one of her surrogate hookers named Melody from her Chicago sex therapy practice. Melody is a gorgeous Eurasian woman who is paid $500 an hour by Norma's sexually-impotent clients. Melody also works as a free-lance hooker for some of the big corporations in Chicago, making as much as $1,500 a night. So Nat went up for a weekend, and after lunch in Chinatown, he went to change in his hotel room when he got into a very kinky scene with Melody who knew just what Nat liked—garter belt, high heels, black nylons, and mild bondage. This was a gift from Norma.

Afterwards, Norma and her husband, Nat and Melody, and Flo and Harvy Dreems went out to dinner at Elaine's. After a few drinks, Nat got up to go to the bathroom and Harvy Dreems joined him. Dreems enjoyed the reputation as one of the most "physically" endowed stars of the male porno circuit. When he and Nat went into the john to take a leak, Nat found himself having trouble urinating as he watched Dreems' huge thing pour out a stream of water reminiscent of a fire hose. It seemed even larger than life as Dreems grappled with both hands trying to hold it steady.

When Nat finally returned to the table, his sister encouraged him to tell about some of his sexual exploits. Nat spent the next hour telling stories that had everyone in stitches. As a matter of fact, he was asked by Dreems to consider writing some porno screenplays for him because he found that Nat's imagination was superior to that of the writers Dreems had had for his flicks.

68.

Snyder promoted a "King of Capitol Hill" competition pitting Democratic Congressmen against Republicans. It was scheduled for a Sunday afternoon on CBS television, with a hefty payoff to Snyder likely.

He got a telephone call during the early promotion of "King of Capitol Hill" from a man named Hamilton Jordan who was interested in getting a competitor into the soon-to-be nationally televised event.

"Where's the Congressman from?" asks Snyder hurriedly.

"He's not a legislator, he's the former Governor from Georgia, Jimmy Carter," Jordan said.

"Never heard of him. Sorry, Mr. Jordan. Goodbye."

"Wait! Mr. Snyder! Jimmy Carter is going to run for President and this exposure could really help him," Jordan went on. "And once he becomes President, he'll participate every year. He's a good athlete. You'll make a fortune from the sponsors!"

Snyder attempted to suppress his laughter and said candidly, "Look, man, get serious. I'm looking for high ratings and can't risk putting some has-been Southern Governor in the competition who's got no shot at getting elected."

Jordan tried one more time. "We have done secret polls that show Mr. Carter can win the Democratic primary, but I can't say anything more about it. You're missing a great opportunity!"

Snyder was quiet for a few seconds and then said, "You know Jordan, name recognition might help my event, and I'd like to help the State of Georgia. Could you get me Lester Maddox instead?"

Jordan hung up. It took two years for Snyder to realize he blew a half million dollars on one phone call.

And the hefty payoff for Snyder's very successful TV production was eventually blown at the racetrack.

A few months later, Snyder started one of the early football handicapping radio shows called "Picking the Pros." It became quite a popular show and led to a late night television program at 1:30 A.M. with the same name. On his TV "Picking the Pros," Snyder was anti-Washington Redskins, although they were the area home favorites. Like most of us who were brought up on the Baltimore Colts, the Redskins were a no-no. Snyder reveled in knocking the Skins who were in a bad rut. They were underdogs against St. Louis and Snyder boldly predicted on his show that the Redskins would be destroyed and wouldn't cover the spread, or he'd never do another show. Despite Snyder's prediction, the Redskins won in a romp, but Snyder appeared on the next show anyway.

Later that week, he was approached by a woman in a bar who told him that she would like to get in a bet and could he help her. Snyder, thinking that seemed easy money, told her he knows a bookmaker and "books" her action himself. He later "booked" bets for other people she introduced to him. What Snyder didn't know was that they were FBI agents. It was obviously entrapment, but Snyder was terrified when they appeared one day at his apartment and told him that they didn't come to bet, just to show him their badges. Later they left. Snyder was subsequently indicted.

Instead of being low-keyed about it and dealing solely with the entrapment issue, Snyder went on Larry King's talk show to say that he couldn't understand why the U.S. Prosecutor's Office had gone after him with such a vengeance. He started knocking the U.S. Assistant Attorney General for persecuting gamblers. As a result of this, the prosecutor handling the case termed Snyder a "kingpin" of Washington gambling circles. This was like calling a "Sunday Preacher" The Pope.

The case came to trial and it appeared as though the judge was probably not going to hurt a small fry like Snyder. It was his first offense, still a minor case, and there were serious shadows of entrapment surrounding it. But, before the judge pronounced a suspended sentence, Snyder started knocking, "I'm not serving even one day, one hour, or one second no matter what."

The judge changed it to 10 days at the Federal prison farm. Snyder still didn't shut up. Snyder's attorney tried to hide behind the prosecutor's chair for fear of being disbarred because of his client's outburst.

69.

Obie began to preach about life and death. He was deeper into death since deciding to become a clinician working with the terminally ill. After a few days with Obie, those around him were probably happy that they were dying. Obie began preaching to Boogie telling him that he was living an unspiritual lifestyle. He once called Boogie at a time when Boogie was in bed with a girl. Boog was euphoric. Obie lectured him about Sodom and Gomorrah and spent an hour discussing it. Naturally, it was a collect call. Obie's travels were still being financed by Boogie's money. Obie was cut off for a month.

Obie went home and preached that the spiritual, not the material life, was the way. Yet for some reason he wasn't following his own dictum, because, for one thing he was driving a big yellow Corvette. I cornered Obie one evening in a disco. I had barely recognized him. He had on an orange Maharashi outfit. He had gained about 70 pounds, and was into some very hedonistic things.

I asked him, "Swami Obie, what is life?"

He looked at me and pensively answered, "Life is a joke. Lend me six bucks."

That was the extent of Obie's two years studying philosophy in the Himalaya mountains.

70.

Valerie Curtin is an accomplished actress and writer. She played Vera in the movie *Alice Doesn't Life Here Anymore* and has appeared on television and in legitimate theatre. She is bright and funny, and co-wrote . . .*And Justice for All* with Barry, winning an Academy Award nomination for best original screenplay. The basis for the movie was actually a legal hassle Barry had gotten into from what he thought was an inconsequential car accident. For legal background, Barry drew on some old Diner friends who'd become lawyers in Baltimore and learned about the horror stories associated with "Justice." With extensive research, Barry convinced director Norman Jewison to use Baltimore as the movie's location.

Not only was Barry able to get Jewison to shoot the Al Pacino film in Baltimore, but he also exerted his influence to cast some of the Diner guys as extras and, in one case, a speaking role for Donald Science.

Science gets the role of an attorney defending a sleazeball who mugged an old woman. You either saw Donald or heard his voice for a full minute and a half during the scene in which Pacino argues with the District Attorney out of court, upstairs.

Barry was only in town briefly during the shooting, but he made provisions for Science to be a technical assistant to Pacino, explaining the law to him. Furthermore, Science, as Barry's liaison, was able to get roles as extras for his wife, Third, Cliff Silbiger, a few other guys, and me.

We were scheduled for a scene in which Al Pacino and Jack Warden take off in a helicopter that eventually crashes in the water. Third and I showed up at the old Glenn L. Martin's Airfield at 6:00 A.M. on probably the coldest day of the year. It was 20° with a wind-chill of 30 below. Science informed us that we're going to be in a restaurant scene and to dress up in a suit or sport coat, and we complied.

Extras in a movie are treated somewhat like cattle. Although we thought we were "good things" when we arrived at the airfield, we found out in a hurry that extras are regarded as lepers. We were ordered to board the "Extras" bus and sit quietly. On the drive out, Third got high on hashish, exactly what we needed to deal with in our debuts.

I was seated next to Cliff Silbiger while Third is sitting with two pretty girls. The assistant director came aboard, looked around, and addressed Cliff and me with a nod, "You two, come with me real quick!" Our initial thoughts were, "Hey, we may have real good roles, everybody else is still on the bus." We quickly got off the bus and into a truck where they keep the clothing.

"Alright you guys, strip down and put on these outfits," barked the assistant director. He threw over two filthy mechanic's outfits which have probably been dipped in grease and dragged through every garage floor in America.

Then he said, "You guys will play two airline mechanics. You will remain outside during the entire shooting." I was astonished as Cliff starts to take off his clothes. "Hey Cliff, I ain't getting out of my clothes in order to get into this. It's too darn cold!"

Cliff began to put his clothes back on and, before the guy re-enters the wagon, we've put our outfits over our suits, looking now a little more chubby than most mechanics. The assistant director instructed us then to lean against a building and act as if we're talk-ing. A man is going to walk by us and point to an airplane. No one would hear any of this conversation because it takes place while Al Pacino is getting out of his car and into the helicopter flown by Jack Warden.

We spent four hours standing in the frigid cold pretending it was springtime. My hands and toes were completely numb.

It wasn't that tough for the actors. First of all, Pacino had a stand-in who got in and out of the car whenever they were checking the lighting. When they were ready to shoot the scene, a guy brings out Pacino who'd been standing inside of the building next to a space heater. Pacino had a fur coat draped around him and was walked into the car. Then, for the next minute or two, while they were shotting the scene, they remove the cape and Pacino pretends it's a nice mild day.

To film this nine second scene, it took several hours. Then, when they filmed Pacino and Warden in the helicopter, we still had to stand outside. When we saw the movie, we looked like blurs. I couldn't even freeze the frame on the video tape to find myself. On top of this, we were paid a whopping $60 before taxes for spending eight and a half hours in the cold. The "extra rule" means that it doesn't matter if your scene is over or not, you must be on the set the entire eight and a half hours. I needed this.

Two of these scenes had to be re-shot when Third decided to go to the bathroom. He got off the bus and walked through the area where they were filming our scene. I could have killed him. I was thoroughly frozen by then.

Finally they stopped filming. We got out of our filthy overhauls, and went to lunch—which was pretty good except that we had to walk through a swamp to get to the buffet. Next we remained another hours on the bus as they decided whether or not they were going to film the restaurant scene. Third was very cold and he picked up a jacket that was lying on the ground and put it on. It was a big warm green jacket. There was a pint of scotch in one of the pockets.

Third passed it around the bus as though the bottle was his. He left without returning the jacket. In the meantime, they finally let us off the bus, and put us in a room that was set up as a restaurant. Third decided to put on a little skit. He said he was really an undercover assistant director and conned some extras into performing a scene. This didn't increase our stock. With the missing jacket (which belonged to a cameraman) and the empty scotch bottle, we were telephoned that night and told that we were fired.

71.

Yussel got an invitation to a wedding. He never heard of the bride or the groom but decided to go. He read somewhere that Obie was involved in the nuptuals. Yussel was in Miami, buying cocaine, and he flew to the ceremony in Tampa. Obie, the Swami Veet Giam, was bedecked in white and orange and performed the wedding ceremony before 400 guests. The bride was pregnant and the groom was Catholic. The church will not sanction the marriage. But Obie did.

72.

Swartzie's second wife, to whom he was married for a week before he threw her out, was named Rosie. She was a former Jewish princess who unfortunately came under the influence of Third and Bruce Hawk during her vulnerable early years and took a turn for the worse. She became a big drugger and a friend of many a drug smuggler. Later, Rosie wandered throughout North America and Europe.

In the late '70s, she ended up living with Rifkin, who started his own drug trafficking business and became a major coke dealer in South Florida and Jamaica.

He had become cold and paranoid and lived on a huge estate outside of Miami in what was known as "Drug Dealer Lane," or
"Cocaine Row." Although it was a beautiful place, they were virtual
prisoners since Rifkin trusted no one. He had extremely tight surveillance and security, like in the movie *Scarface*.

After a year, Rosie took her daughter, from a previous marriage,
and went back to Baltimore.

73.

As much as I "lived" the '50s and '60s, I saw the '70s from the
viewpoint of an isolationist—chronicling the activities of the guys
from afar—because I was concerned with my own career and my
marriage, family and home.

Not speaking to a number of the guys, for sometimes as long as
four years, in retrospect, I was trying to fit a square peg into a
round hole. I wanted the guys to fit into my scheme of things, which
was greatly changed, rather than appreciate them for what they were
and to accept their failings.

During the course of the '70s, I had become a government
bureaucrat serving primarily as the Deputy Director for the Maryland Drug Abuse Administration. This was an agency responsible
for drug treatment and later included compulsive gambling—two
areas with which I was familiar.

In 1975, I received an MPH, Master's in Public Health Degree,
from the Johns Hopkins University's School of Public Health and
Hygiene. Hopkins was considered the finest public health school in
the country. Here was a prestigious program that primarily admitted
physicians who sought careers in the public health sector. I was in
great, even visionary, company. There were courses in Epidemiol-
ogy, Biostatistics, Quantitative Analysis—words which playground
and Diner guys couldn't even spell—but after a month of classes
when my study group and fellow M.D.'s began copying my work, I
knew we were in trouble. When I discovered the number of
anesthesiologists who were getting high . . . well.

The '70s closed out with Mom getting her first coronary by-pass
operation in Madison, Wisconsin, where Snooty was the main rabbi.

Sister Nancy and spouse moved to Beverly Hills, and Sister "Just" Harryette was contemplating divorce after 20 years, and self-imposed exile in Arizona.

The approaching decade would evoke the pangs to reinstall some of the camaraderie of the '50s.

The '80s would reawaken our intense playground and Diner pride in the accomplishments of buddies who made their "bones" by hanging out night after night: Boogie and Harold's retail business success; Professor McAuliffe's research efforts; Barry Levinson's depiction of us in films, and his genius at writing and filmmaking; Swartzie's "bookmaking" life; Third's nomadic and wildly improbable escapades. . . .

7

The Eighties:
A Time for
Discovery

And as I still walk on I
think of the things we did
together, while our hearts
were young.

—Del Shannon,
"Runaway"

1.

The red clay of Queensberry Playground is no longer visible as
"Just" Harryette and I drive quickly along the back alley of
Queensberry Avenue. "Just" Harryette has somehow convinced me
to accompany her to visit our old house on a nostalgia trip.

"My kids want to know their roots and I promised them pictures," says "Just" Harryette, as she parks in the middle of the block and begins snapping photographs.

I'm lying "low" in the car praying that we get out alive as curious neighbors and street wanderers begin to surround "Just" Harryette. This area, considered the hub of the Cylburn/Pimlico region, according to Federal statistics is among the Top 10 criminal impact areas in the country. There have been two known double-murders in our old house during the past five years.

The blues probably think "Just" Harryette is a bit touched as she asks them to pose in front of the steps of the house.

2.

Forty years after my paternal grandmother died, the wanderings, which had subsided after both grandpas passed away, continue and now I am the proverbial playgroundman or Dinerman (Baltimore's Everyman since most of the playground and Diner guys were Ashkenazi Jews of East European or White Russian descent) traveling under duress, and my wife's threats, on a bus ride through the Negev Desert in Israel on a mission of God. Well, actually with the Jewish National Fund (JNF) Mission touring Greece, Egypt and Israel on an eight day, one night forced march to elicit guilt and contributions.

Let me qualify my stand before some of my paranoid brethren and sistren (who read anti-Semitism on the back of cereal boxes) accuse me of inciting mass crimes. I'm very proud of my Jewish heritage and am a devout believer and supporter of Israel. There!

My wife Lynne, who works for the JNF, finally convinced me to take a trip to Israel amid my fears of bombs going off in crowded marketplaces and Arab terrorists throwing me out of a hijacked airplane. Lynne is a beautifully sexy, aggressive and ambitious former Gentile from Eastern Baltimore County (my older sister still refers to her as Sarah Shiksa) who converted to Judaism while we were dating, and has since embraced Zionism like it was Richard Gere in *American Gigolo*.

Not being the sort to back down to anyone, Lynne can be a bit argumentative from time to time. Therefore, we establish an over/under bet for the trip at "30," as the number of arguments she will get into, with most bettors going "over." This "line" was arrived at by Las Vegas bookies based on Lynne's A-type personality and anticipated confrontations with New Yorkers, as well as Greeks, Egyptians and Israelis.

The smart money looked safe when, between take off at Kennedy Airport and six hours over the Atlantic, Lynne was on a roll with eight solid arguments and three mini-hassles. These are highlighted by: 1) a nasty finger-pointing episode with the owner of Kropnick Travel Agency for arbitrarily switching the tour from the Mina House to the Heleopolis Sheraton in Egypt, culminating in Lynne tactfully twisting the guy's finger while calling him "an asshole" to the total applause of the tour group; 2) a hassle with two stewardesses and a steward over the inability of Lynne's seat to go back properly and her insistence that it be repaired immediately— she got so pissed that she continued to slam back in the seat until it broke in the recline position, bruising and imprisoning an old immigrant Greek woman for over an hour; and 3) Lynne's verbal attack on an influential judge's 66-year-old partially senile wife for parading around the plane 12 times in a see-through negligee which she changed into because, "It's nighttime and my bra and girdle were strangling me."

The final few hours of the flight were uneventful with Lynne and me having to fake-listen to the members of the JNF mission, including a guy from Texas who kept telling us how wealthy he was; a Kansas City Jewish funeral director (probably the only one) telling business jokes; and two 80-year-old brothers who asked a million dumb questions and reminded me of the Wildstein twins from Queensberry Playground.

We arrived in Athens, the first leg of the trip, about as fresh as week-old chopped liver. Thirteen hours in the air, in cramped seating, wasn't a lot of fun if you've got gas pains and have to stand in line at an always-occupied restroom to break wind in private. But the trip to Israel was amazing. I quote from my diary:

> The object of our mission to Israel, and similar tours, is to visit the Israeli settlements sponsored in part by JNF throughout the country. By the second day, I felt we had visited one too many settlements, and by the fourth day, I know we had been to 10 too many settlements! But, it's good for guilt, and greater for the ultimate build-up

for guilt on the next to last day; the visit to the Memorial to the Holocaust. Believe me, even Hermann Goering's heart would have melted from this mission.

Since we never finish dinner before 11:00 P.M., due to the endless speeches by ministers, generals and JNF maven, and we begin daily tours promptly at 5:00 A.M., I'm averaging about 2.5 hours sleep a night. Great vacation. The worst part though is arriving late at exotic ancient cities like Tiberius with its beautiful spas and baths, and leaving early, thus missing everything but speeches, settlements, bus routes and box lunches on farms.

Lynne's boss is constantly calling meetings with JNF staff to talk about how they're going to "hit up" these people for donations. Thank God I'm not at those meetings or I'd only average 30 minutes sleep a night.

We called our daughter Debi last night and she showed great concern over our well-being. Not once did she ask where we were or how we're doing. She did, however, try to get out of going to school, avoided talking about a deficiency slip in English, and hurried off the phone to watch "Mork and Mindy." A chip off the old block. Lynne's mother did manage to put us at ease by telling us not to worry much about Debi's ear infection, the burglar alarm going off last night, or the dogs running away; everything would be fine.

Tomorrow morning we have to be out of Tiberius by 5:30 A.M. (that late!) because we're going to tour the Golan Heights where they say you can see the eyes of the enemy. I can't wait for that; I need to see the enemy that early. I mean this ain't like Park Heights, Liberty Heights or Shaker Heights; the Golan is a serious heights. Being tired and constipated and having to deal with Arab terrorists and hostile armies just beyond the hill is real reassuring to Diner and playground guys who had trouble dealing with "drapes" (greasers).

Israel has only one country club, but it's restricted. No Jews allowed. Just kidding. It's funny though; there's a group of people called Druse who serve in the Army, guard the border and are great fighters, but are discriminated against. None will ever be Chief of Staff or have any big title or responsibility. I can just see the sign at the Israeli Country Club, "No Druse, blues or dogs allowed."

After the Golan Heights, we stopped at the ruins of one of the oldest synagogues. While we're there, the Hadad, the Lebanese Christian Militiamen, were having mortar battles against the PLO. The shelling sounded very close until we turned to find it was only the 60-year-old Baltimore insurance man still farting nervously from his security check run-in at the airport.

Here's some disturbing news for goyim. Remember in the song "Michael Row the Boat Ashore" where it said, "the Jordan River is mighty and wide, hallelujah"? Don't believe it. It's a very weak and tiny river. Amazingly, the widest part might have been 10 yards and it moves real slow. What a shame. We also visited where Jesus walked on the water and surprisingly, there were a lot of rocks, and at low tide even I can walk on the water by walking on the rocks. I sure hope that this doesn't hurt any ecumenical efforts.

By the way, Israel has a national rule that soldiers have to be picked-up if they're hitchhiking. I ask Lynne that if this was the law in America and she saw some blue with a rifle hitchhiking on the New Jersey Turnpike would she pick him up and she said, "Passadena!" (No way!)

One thing that Egypt and Israel now have in common are beautiful modern hotels with toilets that seldom flush and, if you don't take your shower really early, the water is either cold or doesn't run.

On Friday, we visited the Gaza Strip and heard some great Bedouin stories from one of the heads of the southern district involved with the planting of forests, vegetables and fruits. The Bedouin is a very interesting person. He has been blessed by God to pick pockets as well as pick up dialects and languages very easily, and he can speak Arabic, Hebrew, English and anything else that comes his way. The Bedouin also has no idea of how to measure time and distance since, by constantly wandering in the desert, he could go crazy worrying about the time with the weird desert days and nights. But he can interpret distance by, for example, explaining that it will require smoking three cigarettes to reach a certain place. Obviously, non-smokers will perish in the desert.

The toilet paper at the kibbutz sure wasn't Charmin. It was really rough like sandpaper, yet they told me that it used to be worse and that most people traveling in Israel usually bring their own. No wonder the Israelis are an angry people.

The Israelis I've met can't understand my paranoia over being in their country with hostile armies at their borders and daily infiltration attempts by terrorists. They tell me that it must be horrible to live in American cities with the muggings and murders. I tell them they're nuts. What about all the terrorism? And I'm told there were only four murders in Israel all last year . . . and four murders a night in East St. Louis! Maybe I'll move to a kibbutz.

3.

Merry-Go-Round had now expanded to over 250 stores. Boogie and Harold were considering going public. They were self-made multi-millionaires.

Boogie decided to give boxing up when word went out that he was the Merry-Go-Round co-owner. Boog's feared that too many people at the gym would want to put the touch on him.

Speaking of putting the touch on Boogie, it got to the point where no matter what he did for people or what he did for charity, it was never enough. He eventually bought condos in Florida, Aspen, New York City and Ocean City, Maryland, and became more or less reclusive, letting his attorneys and other close friends handle the "schnorers," or those really in need.

Merry-Go-Round partner Harold remarried a girl named Beth and they have a son. Harold became a force in donating and raising funds for Israel and various Jewish charities. His savings and loan business became a rising star in Maryland's banking industry, and he has been involved in profitable real estate and development ventures, as well.

4.

Eggie came home one evening after a date in Pikesville. He was thinking of an upcoming trip to Jamaica while his Mercedes was breezing around a hair-pin turn by Suburban Country Club, a few blocks past the city line. Eggie lost control of the car and it rolled over twice before crashing. He never came out of a coma and died a week later.

5.

Following ... *And Justice for All,* Barry and Valerie remained busy with their screenwriting, creating *Inside Moves, Best Friends* (based on their courtship), and *Unfaithfully Yours.* Valerie continued acting in the theater, and became one of the stars of the television series *9 to 5.* She and Barry also worked on *Tootsie* along with other writers who opted for money rather than screen credit. No one figured it to be a hit.

Barry had always wanted to do *Diner,* and while Valerie was appearing on stage in San Francisco, he began writing the script. It had finally come to him, the whole *Diner* treatment, and he wrote it in less than four weeks. Barry showed it to producer Jerry Weintraub (*Nashville, All Night Long, Cruising,* etc.) who got MGM to buy it almost immediately. The movie, budgeted under $5 million, was to be filmed in Baltimore. It was Barry's first opportunity to direct—a goal of all screenwriters, who are never really satisfied with the way directors interpret their work.

For years, Barry used to share old Diner tales with Mel Brooks, who encouraged him to write a movie about it. But Barry could never quite get the connection he needed to tie all of the funny stories together. Then one August day, it came to him. He understood how little *we* understood about women, and that our male bonding, our camaraderie, was really responsible for our inability to understand women. This was the tie. It finally made sense.

6.

Lynne brought our daughter Debi to the *Diner* set. Debi was sulking because she had been grounded and can't go to the STYX concert tonight.

Debi was the only person in Baltimore who didn't want to be in the movie *Diner*. Nothing or no one could alter her hair style for any reason, and it was a '50s period film.

Paul Reiser, who played Modell in the movie, referred to Debi as "Young Deb," and, when it began to rain, he took her into the trailer with the rest of the actors. "Young Deb" found a sympathetic ear from the youthful cast as she complained to them of her grounding, and Kevin Bacon told her that they'll have their own concert. So Reiser turned out the lights, Tim Daly turned up the radio, and Steve Guttenberg, Kevin Bacon, Mickey Rourke and Daniel Stern flicked their lighters on and off.

7.

Hawk was again involved in drug dealing in Fort Lauderdale. His partner was busted for coke trafficking by a Miami Vice cop who let Bruce off the hook when he could have also arrested him. Hawk later was befriended by the cop when the latter needed coke to impress the girlfriends of some major Cuban dealers whom he and his partners wanted to bust. Hawk showed them how to 'cut' (with adulterants) cocaine and also gave the cops some quaaludes. It helped the officers make a major "pinch" and they become real pals with Hawk.

Then Hawk got busted by his Florida parole officer for having 500 "ludes." The Miami Vice cop friend came forward as the main character witness for Hawk who, because of a probation violation, was remanded to the Federal prison in Lexington, Kentucky for 13 months. Hawk didn't mind this. A five-year probation was a restriction that he couldn't handle. So he does nine months in Lexington and the remainder in a halfway house.

When he went back to Florida, his Miami Vice cop friend had become a homicide detective. He phoned Bruce to tell him that he has two K's (kilos; 2.2 lbs. of pure cocaine) and he needed to turn them into three. He asked Hawk how he can do it. Hawk couldn't believe it. This guy was among 10 other homicide cops who were ripping off drug dealers and selling their coke. Bruce often would get high with these cops and watched as they made a fortune in South Florida.

Back in Baltimore, Hawk couldn't get into the drug scene because his friends were also doing the same kind of drug dealing and he didn't want to go to prison again. So Hawk left for Texas and got a legitimate sales job. While he was in Texas, a call came from his Miami cop friend, now turned dealer, who said that he and his fellow officers were under surveillance and were going to be busted. The cop would like to do a "Serpico" number and needed Hawk's advice.

With the help of Hawk's "Serpico" friend, nearly a dozen homicide cops were indicted, and massive publicity preceded their trial. The cop begged Bruce to be a character witness for him and Hawk flew in from Houston. This was a major media event in South Florida and Hawk believed this to be a closed-door trial. However, the proceedings were on television and Hawk became a media darling with his name in print all over the newspapers. He couldn't handle it and left, never knowing the fate of his buddy the cop.

8.

Since no one else had ever done lists before in Baltimore, Bob Litwin and I became known around town as the Listmakers, minor celebrities, but a big deal in our hometown. We were interviewed on radio and TV talk shows and were written about in the papers. We hoped it would last for a long time, and it did. We recognized by the reactions to the early lists that the key to continued, broad interest in them and in us was a recognition factor. So we started including people who were bona fide Baltimore celebrities—media types, politicians, even a schmuck with a following in certain parts of the city. Everybody was a good sport, regardless of what list we put him or her on. Well, maybe. After all, it was a special kind of publicity, and we were never really mean to anyone. "All in the spirit of good, clean fun," we used to tell people. Well, maybe.

One of the best "sports" we met was Oprah Winfrey. She came to town from Atlanta to do the evening news, then co-hosted a regional TV talk show based in Baltimore. She—and her outfits—generated a lot of attention. She was a perfect choice. At first we put her on one of our newspaper lists as one of Baltimore's worst-dressed women, and the tag line we wrote for her was that she was "Harpo spelled backwards, but she dressed like Groucho."

A couple years later, when we had started doing lists on nighttime TV, *Evening/P.M. Magazine,* we put her on our list of *best*-dressed women [she was a big local star by now]. Every person on the list would be interviewed for A-roll [audio voice-over] and also filmed [B-roll/video] modeling clothes, at work, or at play. Oprah was a pleasure to interview and to "cut it up with." She suddenly took over our show. She had turned the tables on us and was conducting her own interview. "Chip and Bob, you amaze me. Everyone says women are fickle—but you two. C'mon, explain how I made the jump from worst dressed to best dressed in only a couple of years!" "Easy," we told her, "You went from K-Mart to Macy's."

9.

Neurotic Nat's career at Parole and Probation had been on a see-saw. When he first began working, his father was still employed there so Nat tried his hardest, climbing up the grade level ladder very fast. When his father retired, Nat resolved that he was no longer going to be ambitious since for a guy his age he was making a great deal of money with low expenses. All he needed was money for his apartment, food and hookers. He also had become friendly with people whom he had trained years before, but had now sur- passed Nat and had become high-level managers. Nat kept these guys amused.

Nat was befriended by a local columnist who encouraged him to use his creative talents on radio. Through media contacts, the columnist got Nat part-time work which Nat parlayed into a radio talk show. He becomes successful very fast. His ratings continued to climb and he soon became a frequent guest on other television and radio shows. The notoriety gave Nat a new-found respect in himself. He started dressing better and even let his hair grow and changed glass frames, but he refused to wear contact lenses.

Although Nat's neurotic behavior has shifted and his recent dalli- ance with the media has enhanced his recognition and confidence, it's no wonder that he always stayed out in the Diner lot. When the movie *Diner* was filmed in Baltimore, Nat refused to shave or cut his hair to look "fiftyish" unless he was given more than an extra's role, and even when he was offered a small part he chickened out. When he hosted a local radio special on the movie, he faked illness to leave early so he would not have to mix with the old Diner gang. And he refused to see the movie because . . .

10.

Diner became a critical and box office success, and served as a catalyst for the careers of several then-unknown but very talented young actors. The film was nominated for many film critics' awards in the United States and Europe and included an Oscar nomination for best *original* screenplay for Barry.

With Barry directing *Diner* and Valerie doing television on different coasts, their relationship began to deteriorate. After seven years of marriage, they separated.

Originally, *Diner* didn't test well, did poorly in Baltimore, and was almost dumped by MGM. Only Barry's perseverance and pressure from New York critics who loved it forced its release nationally.

Many Baltimoreans couldn't relate to *Diner* because they tried to identify too much with characters, locations and attitudes, instead of just enjoying it as an amazing comedy/drama.

I heard the goofiest remarks during the world premiere showing: "Why's it called the Fells Point Diner and not Hilltop? Boogie would have never dated a married woman. . . . I don't remember Shreevie getting married after high school, and Fenwick was *never* that good-looking!"

17.

Following Nat's divorce, he struck up a liaison with a young lady who also worked for Parole and Probation. She did not have the academic background of his first wife, but, in terms of being neurotic, she had more extensive credentials, and better legs. Bonnie was divorced and lived with her three children, a dog named Marvin and a slightly weird brother. The brother eventually got a job as a sweeper at the zoo through some political influence, but before that he would always hang around the house "protecting" his sister. One time, Nat was making out with Bonnie on her sofa when the brother appeared at the top of the steps screaming. He rushed downstairs threatening to murder Nat and leaped on the sofa as Nat rolled off. The brother ended up on top of his naked sister. Nat took off in his underpants, dragging his clothes out the door and down the street. The dog pursued, not as an attacker but as a protector, and Nat never forgot the show of concern on its part.

In later years, when Bonnie ran off with another guy. Nat dog-sat for Marvin in his apartment. While Nat was at work most of the day, he left newspapers spread over the apartment except under the dining room table, a spot where Marvin defecated for four straight days.

12.

Barry went to a film festival in Dallas for *Diner*. He was feeling great, pumped up from by the plaudits he was getting for the movie. Since he'd seen the film over 100 times, Barry paced in the lobby during the showing. There he was approached by two statuesque women.

"Mister Levinson, what a pleasure! We love *Diner*. We've seen it twice!"

Barry thanks them. He couldn't help admiring their beauty and began to small-talk them. The women were stewardesses. They appeared extremely friendly and the conversation turned more personal.

"We'd love to take you back to our apartment," one said in a slight Texas drawl, "and fuck you silly."

Now Barry was awed by their offer. While the discussion went on, he began reflecting to himself. "Hmm, here I am on top of the world. I'm making money, the critics love *Diner,* there are tons of offers for me to direct more movies, I'm single again, in my prime at 39, and in front of me are two gorgeous Texas stewardesses (only Dallas Cowboy Cheerleaders could be better looking) waiting to screw my brains out. But I just read a *Time* magazine article about the herpes epidemic. Let's see. It said there could be as many as 30 million women with herpes. Most women with herpes are between 17 and 28 years old. Now, if there are 110 million women in America and the vast majority are either over 38 or under 17, then these stewardesses, who must be around 25, must have a 95 percent pop at having herpes. I'm at my all-time peak and I've gotta 'T.D.' this offer?"

"Sorry girls," confessed Barry after this agonizing thought. "I've got a dinner meeting after the film and then I'm leaving town." Feeling sorry for himself now, Barry amusingly thought, "Maybe I'll turn gay," until he remembered a *Newsweek* article on AIDS. "These are difficult times."

Levinson flew back into Baltimore from Texas. He never acknowledged residence in California. He considers himself a Baltimorean, receives the *Baltimore Morning Sun,* calls often about the Orioles and Colts, dines at the L.A. restaurant, "The Maryland Crab House" and, although he owns three homes in L.A. and has been there for 17 years, confesses, "I'm only visiting California."

He cut me the Texas stewardesses outcome and we had a lengthy discourse on herpes. Barry feels that herpes is either a religious or communist conspiracy. I concur. "God felt there was too much sex going on and had to slow it down. But if there is no God, then it's the Commies who must think too much sex is not in the best interests of the State."

We called Professor Bill McAuliffe for a scientific viewpoint. "It's the pill," replies Bill. "Before the pill, girls were afraid, and so were guys to a large degree. Since the pill, girls have gone overboard enjoying sex. Sex has become a national epidemic . . ." Bill went on and on, injecting biostatistical and epidemiological data. We agreed with Bill. We don't want to get beat up.

We considered talking to Boogie who'd been involved in so many scenes over the years, but easily guessed his answer, "I'm immune. It matters! Later!"

13.

Yussel served on and off as a probation officer for a dozen years. Occasionally he'd go to a psychiatrist and get approval for an extended sick leave for "stress." Then he'd travel and goof off for months at a time.

Although the State tried, it could not fire him. He never married, drifting from relationship to relationship, becoming more deviant in his sexual behavior and abusing drugs.

Yussel became infatuated with cocaine, not only for the "high" but for the easy access to women. He graduated to free-basing coke and became a paranoid schizophrenic. To support such an expensive habit ($2,000 a weekend), Yussel began dealing heavily. He was busted, later convicted, and sentenced to prison, an unusual sentence for a first offender who has a documented addiction history.

During the trial, the Federal prosecutor referred to the defendant as "aka Yussel," attempting to sway the jury that this case was a continuing criminal enterprise and major conspiracy. Like Yussel was *The Godfather,* when it was a nickel-dime case. Yussel's attorney argued, to no avail, against the prosecutor's use of "aka Yussel."

"Your honor," he pleaded to the judge, "Yussel is his Yiddish name, that's all!"

"Overruled," shouted the judge. "It's still an alias!"

14.

Glick eventually married and he and his wife became seriously involved in "est." Then his wife fell under the influence of commune people, who convinced her to leave him.

I ran into Glick outside Colonial Village Pharmacy. He told me about his marital breakup, and then broke down. I comforted him as best I could. Reluctantly, he later accepted his wife's defection and swore off being an "est" follower.

Still looking for spiritual fulfillment, Glick decided to become a Yoga trainer, influenced by Obie's advice to travel to India to study the craft from a master teacher whom Obie had recommended.

Obie left for Aspen to join Boogie who had just split up with a Florida girlfriend. Boog really liked this girl, Pepper, and Obie's attempts at cheering him up didn't work. The boys' relationship had been deteriorating for a while and the pact between them had worn Boogie a bit thin.

When they went to buy ski jackets (on Boog, of course), Obie's cost twice as much as Boogie's, and the pact becomes null and void.

15.

Third was working as a food and beverage coordinator for the Mosconi Convention Center. An article appeared in Herb Caen's nationally known column in the *San Francisco Chronicle* criticizing the center for the misspellings of five entrees for dinner at a fancy reception. Third allegedly was responsible. He had spelled filet mignon, mingnonia, among other selections. He denied it. "I am not guilty—it was a dumb secretary."

Recently, Third had married for the second time. He went to Boca Raton for the wedding and immediately alienated his fiancée's entire family. He had already hassled her mother on the phone, lamenting that her daughter wasn't ambitious, or worked hard enough. As it was, her daughter was married to a very successful lawyer the first time around, and now she was marrying Third. Smart move!

The wedding almost didn't occur. When Third went to pay his hotel bill, he was told that it was $30.00 more than what he had been told on a confirmation telegram. So Third announced that he was going up to his room to get the confirmation, but the hotel clerk told him, "It doesn't matter. It's $100 per night and not $70."

Third insisted on bringing the telegram back, and the clerk coldly repeated, "It doesn't matter." Third demanded to see the manager who reaffirmed, "It doesn't matter."

Third then announced, "It doesn't matter to me either. I'm not going to pay the bill!"

The management called the police and when they arrived Third reiterated, "It still doesn't matter. I'm not going to pay the bill."

Just then his fiancée appeared in her wedding gown and started screaming in the lobby as she watched the police hurrying Third away. Swiftly she paid the entire bill with her American Express card, but Third's response was less then enthusiastic. He thought for sure this was God's way of telling him not to get married, and insisted that she not pay the bill.

16.

My mother advised me of a death notice in 1983. (She keeps me up on obituaries every day of my life.) Jay Huff had died. Cause of death was an embolism. Rumor was that it was related to his drug and alcohol abuse. He was destitute at the time of his death.

17.

Swartzie married for a third time. He put on a lavish wedding reception. The cost per guest was staggering. Among the bill of fare were tins of very expensive Beluga caviar for each guest. Alas, many of Swartzie's guests were not familiar with the finer things in life, shoving the tins aside; some even used them as ashtrays.

18.

Shade couldn't handle the rigors of being a probation officer. He actually had to work a couple of hours a week. He left and kicked around for a while, needing this period of his life to reflect upon what he was going to do with the rest of it. He eventually began a home improvement business, à la the Tin Men, and joined forces with the great siding hustler, Vincent Aldo.

19.

Hart worked mainly in his father's poolroom until the latter retired and sold the business. Then, Hart moved in with his parents and lived in a reconverted closet. It was fairly small, but Hart didn't complain. He was out of work for a brief period, some seven years, and then went to work for his younger brother who owned a sports handicapping service. Hart answered phones and doled out information which subscribers paid for, such as who was going to win a certain football, basketball or baseball game, or horse race. He proved to be an accomplished phone man, relishing this new work, and he became fairly successful although he didn't overdo it, working only three nights a week. The rest of the time he either slept, ate or worked out at the Jewish Community Center. (Why did he like living in the closet? Was there a connection?)

20.

My wife, Lynne, aside from working 90 hours a week, decided to go to college to become a lawyer. Naturally, Third decided to tell her his philosophy of college and work.

"School is only for social life and playing ball. Work is for dressing up in suits and ties and sports coats and walking around downtown. Unless you can spend a couple of thousand dollars on new clothes every three months, continuing to work makes no sense."

Third quit his job at the Convention Center a week later.

21.

Jeff Hall was a nickel-dime bettor, strictly small-time. He was in Atlantic City at the blackjack table playing what is called third base—the far left seat at the blackjack table. A "preferred" customer was playing first base, the first right side seat of the table, and losing heavily; he was also blaming his losses on the way Jeff was playing third base. He continues to berate Jeff and talk to him about playing blackjack, and Jeff said, "Hey, I can't help it, that's the way I play!" The guy became so abusive that he finally tried physically to get Jeff to leave the table. Jeff resisted and, in the course of the scuffle, punched the guy over the table into the pit where the pit bosses stand to observe the games. "Security" rushed over and took Jeff into a holding room to discuss the altercation, along with the preferred customer. While there, the preferred customer broke away from the security officers and, while Jeff was sitting down, the customer punched him in the face, busting his nose and bruising his eyes. The casino, immediately realizing their liability for what happened to Jeff, made him an offer of $5,000 to settle as he wiped the blood off his face. Not really thinking too clearly, hearing about an easy $5,000, and knowing what he could do with it while still in Atlantic City, Jeff signed a release. He took the $5,000 and proceeded to lose it all the next day.

Jeff went back to Baltimore and told the story to Earl Maget and another guy named Marty. They decided to keep the story confidential and work out an elaborate scam to fool Benny, the owner of Benny's Poolroom which has now moved from the Diner area into a more exclusive neighborhood further north in Pikesville. Benny still has the first dollar he ever earned, has never gone for anything, and considers himself as good a hustler as anyone around because he never went for any bizarre deals over the four decades he ran the poolroom.

Earl drove to New York to see a prestigious law firm and asked to meet the managing partner. While he was waiting, without an appointment, Earl realized he'll never see the top lawyer. He asked the secretary for some travel directions. Earl told her that he had to leave very shortly for Baltimore, but he had a major accident case. He wanted to discuss it with a lawyer. Could she loan him some paper so that he could write it up for her to deliver to the lawyer? The secretary gave Earl directions, an envelope and some stationery, and after a few minutes he left for Baltimore.

Earl was in the poolroom the next day engaged in a conversation with Marty and another fellow discussing Jeff's minor melee in Atlantic City. There was no word that Jeff settled the case. Just gossip that the casino initially offered him a quarter of a million, and that on the advice of a lawyer friend, Jeff proceeded to New York where he was advised by a major legal firm that he could make anywhere up to $15 million as a result of his law suit. Earl and Marty continued talking about this every few days near Benny and then walked away.

Later, about the second week, Jeff went to Benny asking his advice as to what he should do. He showed Benny a letter (which Earl had typed) from the law firm. The "attorney" had written that Jeff should be extremely quiet about what has happened; that there were a number of people involved, including the Mayor of Atlantic City and organized crime figures; that he was never to mention that his law firm was representing Jeff. The minium the case was worth was $5 million (if they settled quickly) but that he could earn as much as $15 million if he waited a year.

Jeff informed Benny that maybe he should just settle for the quarter of a million. He was upset because the lawyer called and told him that he needed upfront money immediately in order to make some initial payoffs of $50,000. The money was needed to pay off the mob, the Mayor of Atlantic City, and some other Gambling Commission officials. Jeff was glum because he was broke. Benny, who felt that he has a once-in-a-lifetime opportunity, told Jeff, "Don't worry. I'll give you the money if you'll sign over half of the final settment."

Jeff balked at his offer. He thinks 50 percent is too much. Later, Jeff let Benny convince him that he should do it after Benny agreed to cover all legal fees and payoffs down the line. Benny swiftly got a customer who was an attorney to draw up the proper documents which Jeff eagerly signed. Now Jeff had more money then he had ever had before and he was going to Atlantic City and gamble heavily, eat out all the time, treat the guys, leave tips beyond belief, and have the time of his life. Periodically, he went back to Benny for additional money for different payoffs and different fees for the lawyer. (Naturally specified in letters on the firm's stationery and typed by Earl.) Eventually, Jeff took close to $400,000 from Benny.

By coincidence, during this period of time, the Mayor of Atlantic City was actually indicted, and so Jeff went to Benny again, saying he needed more money to bribe the new mayor. Benny, who'd been reading the Atlantic City articles in the newspaper, actually believed this was going on and again dug into his pocket.

On the sly, Benny called up Jeff's lawyer and got the answer that was mentioned in the letter; that is, they were sorry but they can't discuss any of their clients, standard operating procedure for any legal firm.

In the meantime, Jeff took some of Benny's money and bought his own poolroom with Earl. He had also given Earl and Marty a portion of the money because they were part of the scam, but he spent most of the money himself, living a wild and crazy life. He even tipped the people who work in the toll booths on the way to Atlantic City.

One day, Jeff was screwing around in the poolroom with a gun he had there for security purposes if the place was being robbed. He was a little juiced up, and although he knew the gun was not loaded, he was just scaring people by pointing it at them. One guy finally yelled at him, "Cut it out, don't be crazy. I don't need this shit.

You're going to have an accident!" Jeff responded, "Hey, there's nothing in here!" He turned the gun to his head and pulled the trigger. Nothing went off the first time, or the second, but the third time a bullet, which must have been lodged in the chamber, went off and Jeff blew his brains out.

Jeff was rushed to the hospital where he was pronounced dead. The word got to Benny fairly quickly, and a few hours later in the early morning, he drove to Sinai Hospital where he demanded to see Jeff's body, not believing that he was dead. Benny had to lie about being Jeff's father in order for them to let him into a room and show him the body. Heartbroken, Benny went outside crying, not over Jeff's death, but over the fact that he had invested almost $400,000 in the law suit.

Regaining his composure, Benny realized that he might still be entitled to the money because he had the sign-off from Jeff that he got half of the "purse." He decided to drive up that morning to New York. The four-hour drive took him to the prestigious law firm where he rushed in, demanding to see the head lawyer. Naturally, without an appointment, the office staff would not allow this. But Benny carried on so and was in such a state of despair that they eventually got the chief attorney to speak with him. He repeated his statement about confidentiality and Benny told him he is aware of this because it was in Jeff's letter. The lawyer denied writing the letter, telling Benny that it was a fraud. Benny figured they were trying to scam him and beat him for half of Jeff's money; that they were going to keep it all. He was physically forced from the building, and returned to Baltimore still believing the story.

22.

A chorus line of a New York dance troupe snaked around a crowded wedding reception at the Woodholme C.C. in Northwest Baltimore County on that beautiful June night to the Broadway tune "The Best of Times." And in the dance line, bedecked in black sequinned jacket and top hat, were Boogie and Pepper. They were married an hour earlier in a ceremony that included: a spontaneous ovation as Boogie walked down the aisle; Ralph, Boog's trusted

black chauffeur for nine years as best man; and a tête-à-tête between
Boogie and his mother Nettie while awaiting the bride under the
canopy.

"What are you doing here?" she asked.

"God if I know," said Boogie, who'd waited almost 20 years to
remarry. He'd lived with Pepper for almost three years now. Yet he
was not easy to live with.

The reception was the biggest and the best ever thrown in Baltimore. The food was beyond description, the bar champagne was
Dom Perignon. The entertainment, which included the original
Shirelles, was eye-popping. Every half-hour, the dance troupe performed a Broadway hit which involved audience participation, and
the guest list included dignitaries in from Florida, Aspen and New
York, along with a contingent of playground and Diner guys. The
recently married and proud father Bo Death was there, having taken
early retirement from Merry-Go-Round, Obie (still philosophizing),
Glick (who offered a free Yoga lesson to the newlyweds as a gift),
partner Harold, Sambo, Altman the Mensch, Science, Zug (my
cousin Marvin, a Merry-Go-Round V.P.), Lou from the Coast, . . .

This crowd was genuinely happy for Boogie, and the energy
throughout was a high, both physically and metaphysically.

Pepper, Boog's pretty bride, was from Tennessee, and one of her
neighbors, never before out of the backwoods, was overheard on the
telephone explaining the festivities to a caller back home:

"These Jewish weddings are something! They applaud the groom,
a black dude's the best man, nobody has a real name, and every
half-hour they perform some ritualistic number with these hyper-
dancers. Must be some hidden religious meaning to it. Jews hide
their emotions publicly. Privately, you see, it's mobbed in the john
where people crowd into the stalls and cry a lot. I heard them all
sniffing real bad."

23.

Barry Levinson called to tell me he'd just completed a TV pilot of
Diner for CBS. He asked me if I'm interested in being a story consultant for the series, if it's picked up by the network. Naturally, I

agreed. What a break!

CBS had spent over $10 million for 16 pilots to find a situation comedy that it could place in a time slot against *The 'A' Team*. The *Diner* set has been recreated (for big bucks) on the MGM lot. With this outlay of cash, I grew optimistic and began counting up my accrued annual leave days from my 18 years working for the State of Maryland.

A month later Barry phoned back. "I've got good news and bad news. The good news is that CBS loved the pilot."

I breathed easier. "That's great, but what's the bad news?"

"The bad news is also that they loved the pilot."

This deserved an explanation as I began to hyperventilate.

Barry continued, "If the pilot is too good, then the network executives don't feel that the masses will understand the humor, or accept the show. So they want me to put in a laugh track, which it didn't have, and girls with big tits."

He paused, "Since I've got creative control, I'm not doing either. I'm not going to prostitute the show so it rivals those idiotic sitcoms the network thinks the masses cry for. So anyhow, it doesn't look good for the series or your new job. But, you might want to call up Joyce who is head of comedy programming at CBS and see what she thinks may happen."

The next day I phoned Joyce and reported the predicament. She was sympathetic. She reiterated the executive's desires—a laugh track and big tits—and added that although the fall season was out of the question, perhaps it would go as a mid-season replacement.

I began to get optimistic again.

Soon after, Barry began directing *The Natural* starring Robert Redford; Joyce was lured away from CBS by an offer she couldn't refuse to be a major executive for Home Box Office; and at Barry's encouragement I started writing this book as the result of background work I'd done in anticipation of the *Diner* story consultant job.

24.

It was fall. I went to the airport to pick up my daughter. I saw Bruce Hawk at the ticket counter and called out to him. He turned quickly and told me to keep quiet; he was pulling an airline ticket scam and was on his way to Kenya to meet some new friends he had made in Florida. It seemed that a guy he met in Miami was trying to set up a charter flight, a camera safari, into the Kenya jungle. Ever since Hawk saw the movie, *Greystoke, the Legend of Tarzan,* he wanted to go to Africa. His new friend couldn't get enough people for the charter but intended to go anyhow, letting Bruce tag along since he had promised (money upfront) to pay for the car rental throughout the trip which came to $400 a week.

The Hawk, his new friend, his friend's wife and their six-year-old son departed a few days later and landed in Nairobi. It was a great trip. There were many state parks to visit and in each state park, a Holiday Inn, a Hilton, lodgings all the way down to inexpensive places with few amenities. They stayed at the plush resorts on the Indian Ocean for $7 per day. It was at these places where they would cop "a finger or an arm," an African drug term for grass.

As they were driving along, the new friends got mad at Hawk, accusing him of stealing their money. Hawk was really concerned, since they were in the middle of the jungle, and he insisted that they immediately conduct a strip search of him. They declined and became so icy to him that they wouldn't let him play with their six-year-old, who really liked Hawk.

The next day, the couple seemed a little warmer towards Hawk as they drove to a small town outside of a village to trade in their rental car for a jeep. Hawk went into the store to buy some sodas and when he returned, the jeep was gone. All he had on was a tee shirt and shorts. His money, the plane ticket, his passport, his clothes—everything was in the jeep. Hawk couldn't believe it. This wasn't happening to him, so he waited for a couple of hours and finally realized that he has been abandoned.

Pitied by a Kenya worker from the gas station who befriended him, Hawk was taken to his village and introduced to his family.

Hawk was flipped out and somewhat dazed. He called the American Embassy in Nairobi collect and waited 20 minutes for them to accept the call.

The Embassy informed him, "You're 200 miles away and we can't pick you up. Why don't you take a bus?"

Hawk was in a town called Mitito-Andei, some 200 miles north of Nairobi. Freaking out, he got in a huge argument with the Embassy people since he had no money with which to get back. Finally he borrowed money from his new-found friends in the village and took a long bus ride to Nairobi.

Hawk finally arrived at the Embassy and was sent over to the police station. The police didn't have the sophistication of American law enforcement because they couldn't locate the people, or the car, who'd stranded Hawk, so he returned to the American Embassy where he was told they'd get him a bed at the "Y." He freaked out again and carried on so much that the Embassy allowed him to call his office in Texas and several friends in Baltimore who might wire him money. It wasn't like Western Union, and to get money to Africa, it had to be sent via the State Department in Washington and then put in a diplomatic pouch and routed to the Embassy in Nairobi. There were only two flights out of Nairobi every week and the last one just left.

Hawk convinced the Embassy to call one of the hotels in Nairobi to put him up for the night and, to the delight of the Embassy staff, Bruce Hawk left the building. Hawk has not been heard from since.

25.

Recently, I ran into one of Hawk's old girlfriends whom he called from Kenya for money and she was very worried about him.

"Chip," she said, "Isn't where Bruce is in the part of Africa where there are wild animals?"

"Yes."

"And doesn't that little green monkey that they say is the cause of AIDS live there?"

"Yes."

"Suppose Hawk gets bit by one of those monkeys?"

I tried to console this budding scientifically nescient young girl by explaining my own theory of the AIDS epidemic.

A lot of blame has been passed around as to the cause of AIDS and I think I'm onto how it originated and who's behind it. It's the condom or rubber manufacturers. They controlled the market until the '60s.

Then came the pill and the I.U.D. and women went wild. Promiscuity was at epidemic proportions. Suddenly new strains of gonorrhea appeared and the medical community was forced to discover and manufacture stronger penicillins to combat V.D. Yet, sexual contact continued rampant, women felt protected and safe with the pill, and the rubber industry went into a decline.

Things were so bleak by the dawn of the '80s that several condom producers decided to turn to germ warfare. They invented the herpes virus and unleashed it upon an unsuspecting public. And even with cover stories in every major publication professing that millions were infected with herpes, promiscuity was still rampant and herpes victims learned to cope. Yes, sales in rubbers did slightly increase, but only briefly.

Thus, the rubber-makers resorted to the doomsday virus—only to be released among the population if the business seemed about to bust. AIDS was spread to the populace—if you caught it, you died. Pure and simple. It wasn't even like cancer, where you have a chance. Physicians, epidemiologists, researchers and top government scientists came forward and announced that the only safe sex was with a condom. Two condoms for anal sex and one condom for regular and/or oral sex. If in doubt, wear rubber gloves when fondling a stranger. Better yet, a full wet suit.

Does the public finally understand that the condom industry means business? Yes. After they killed off huge portions of the gay community and the I.V. drug users, rubber sales have skyrocketed. Stocks are causing a run on Wall Street. Promiscuity is frozen. Husbands and wives are now faithful.

26.

Snyder conjured up another promotional extravaganza, "The Battle of the Corporate Stars." It became a success and after a number of years the show got on TV on ESPN. It pit top corporations against one another in major cities with the final championships in posh resorts. It was all an extension of the "color war" process at the overnight camps where Snyder worked in the '60s. Network TV was now interested in the show and it led Snyder to become a mini-entrepreneur earning more money than he every imagined.

27.

Boogie and Pepper moved to a large Aspen, Colorado ranch. Pepper needed to be busy, so the two of them opened up a men's and women's high style fashion store. In the meantime, Pepper became pregnant. As Boogie awaited his first child and someone to carry on in the tradition of the playground and Diner guys, the store became wildly popular and he opened another.

It was Boogie's zaniness and guts that made his reputation as a tough guy, and was also responsible for his success at Merry-Go-Round. Over the years, an interesting phenomenon took place. Harold's reputation, intellectually, fiscally and corporately, became so impressive that the guys began speaking in awe of Harold's prowess as they had of Boogie's image. Guys boasted of putting Harold up against any corporate wizard in the country and betting in his favor. And they'd probably win.

With other tycoons and entrepreneurs around the nation, Harold was in another league. Just as he mesmerized guys in the Diner with his fiscal abilities, he came out of negotiations and acquisitions with his opposition feeling as though they had been hit by one of Boogie's sucker punches.

28.

The Earl Maget of the 1980s was still involved in scams of all sorts: gambling, drugs and "check-kiting." He went to jail briefly again, but bounced back stronger than ever. Over the next couple of years, Earl bought a poolroom, but became distraught over Jeff Hall's death. He went on a serious diet, losing 150 pounds. In 1985, Earl died suddenly of a heart attack.

29.

At 4:00 A.M. the phone rang. It was a collect call from Malaysia. Third decided to chat. Since he was "between jobs" in San Francisco, he said he needed a vacation, so he split for the Far East.

"I'll be sending back cheap artifacts that will reap huge profits in San Francisco and New York galleries. Do you want to invest in a golden opportunity?" Third asked.

Bleary-eyed, I declined his offer and advised him to confine collect calls from the Far East to the afternoon and evening hours. Ignoring the comment, Third proceeded to discuss his itinerary which started in Hong Kong and moved to Thailand for a few weeks. Malaysia, his current port of call, came next and would be followed by tours to Bali, Australia and New Zealand before he returned to San Francisco.

"Once I establish an import connection in the States, I'll go back to Thailand. I may live there for a couple of years. It's a great place, like a huge drugstore and whorehouse," Third said.

"Isn't it dangerous?" I ask. "It's close to Vietnam, Cambodia, Laos . . . and Third, what about you being an American Jew . . . there could be Libyan hit squads."

"Chip," Third snapped back, "everybody here is on a good time. Remember Sheldon from the Ten Boys? Well, he lives up in the

Northern Providence near Chiang Mai, and he even married a Thai woman. When I visited him last week, he was leaving for the Mekong Delta. He's been in the Far East for years, and he isn't an Arnold Swartzenegger type."

I was awake now. "Christ, Third, what does he do? Spy for the government?"

"No, asshole. He's a gem exporter, and the only time he ever had a confrontation was once in India. He was riding in a train section with the lowest people on the caste system there and they threw him off the train for looking too prosperous!" Third barked.

"Did I say that I'm meeting Pick Dawson in Bali. He's been hanging out in Goa," he said.

"Third," I concluded, "This call's getting free. Lose my number until you get back to California."

30.

A bunch of guys who worked with Neurotic Nat Smertz in the Probation Department urged him to join them at a new dance club in Baltimore County. Even though Nat was exclusively into hookers, no dating or hugging, and was very fearful of rejection, he agreed to go out to Club Wurlitzer one Friday night. He did have an ulterior motive. His supervisor, Martin Hersh, was always at the club and Nat, currently in line for a promotion, wanted to impress him.

Hersh was slightly weird. He seldom showered or washed and secretly was called Martin the Bathless. He did, however, spray himself with lots of baby powder—too much actually, and the powder was usually all over his clothes. Hersh owned a nasty pit bull that'd been with him for almost 15 years. The dog's name was Sniffer.

Nat showed up at Wurlitzer's. He was nervous at first, but the free buffet, '50s and '60s music, and pretty girls seemed to calm him down. Later he was introduced to Hersh's latest girlfriend, Moana, an associate professor at an all-girls college. Nat was impressed— first by being privileged to meet the boss's woman but also by being taken into his confidence. He told Nat that he had a suite across the street.

Nat had several drinks and was feeling quite loose. He approached a pretty blond Amazon wearing a tight-fitting, beige, see-through mini-dress and long, red, very high-heeled boots. She was about 6'2", built great, and rough talking—and, although Nat was at least a head shorter than her, they danced a few numbers. He obviously amused the Amazon. With his alcohol-induced confidence, he invited her to join him in a little tryst across the street. He figured that by bringing her over to Hersh's suite, he'd impress the boss.

Surprisingly, the woman accepted and told Nat a bit about herself. Known as Tilly the Toiler, she was a GLOW girl—a *G*orgeous *L*ady *o*f *W*restling, and was quite a celebrity in her field.

Nat and Tilly went across to the suite and banged for minutes on the door until Hersh opened it. Nat pulled his far-from-elated boss aside and begged his forgiveness, and the use of his pad.

"Look, asshole," whispers Martin the Bathless (whose odor almost knocked Nat backwards), "use either the living room or the kitchen. Be outta here in an hour, and leave $30 on the table for your half of the room. . . . If my girlfriend hears anything, you'll never see a promotion!"

Hersh went to the bedroom, brought Sniffer out to the living room and went back to sleep. Nat and Tilly the Toiler began kissing in the kitchen. Tilly had lifted Nat up on the counter and was seriously necking with him when they heard growling. The dog went berserk. Little Sniffer's dick shot out, his eyes bulged, and he made a growling beeline for Tilly.

Just as Sniffer's snout made for Tilly's groin, she shoved Nat toward the refrigerator and began to fight Sniffer off. They rolled and pitched over the kitchen in a vicious bout as Nat lay wide-eyed. For what seemed an eternity, the lady "wrassler" and the pit bull, locked in mortal combat, fought—from the kitchen to the living room to the foyer—and then Tilly's superior strength surfaced. She grabbed the old pit bull's jaws, pried them apart and then yanked back with all her might—killing Sniffer. Sniffer was 105 years old in a dog's life, so his jaws weren't as strong as your average pit bull's bite.

Sniffer's blood was all over Tilly and the foyer as Nat, Hersh and a shaken Moana stood in shock at the ungodly sight. Tilly casually picked up her purse and, turning to Nat, said, "This has been a blast, but it's late and I've got a match in St. Louis on Sunday. See you guys around someday."

As Tilly the Toiler walked out the door, Moana grabbed her things and was gone seconds later, her screams echoing off the hotel hallways. Martin the Bathless held Sniffer's dead body in his arms as he looked at Nat.

"Well, Smertz, is there anything you've got to say?"

"Yeah," said Nat meekly, "Do I still owe you the $30?"

31.

Levinson was always secretive, but some of his experiences with the entertainment business made him almost uncommunicative, for Hollywood and the movies are synonymous with treachery and deceit. Scripts, ideas and stories are a constant prey of rip-off artists, and originals like Barry are prime game. After being burned a couple of times, Barry rarely offered up information to anyone in Hollywood or at home back east. Before the guys in Baltimore knew he was married, he was already divorced. Before the guys saw Barry as an overnight sensation with *Diner,* he'd already written several hit movies.

And so it came as no great surprise that following *Diner* and during *The Natural,* another well-kept secret was being kept: Barry's romance with the eternal Jewish boy's dream—the beautiful, blue-eyed, blond shiksa.

Her name was Diana, a Baltimore/Washington-based model who worked for the casting agency Barry used for *Diner.* Diana had met Barry briefly during the filming, and when she later moved to California, they renewed their acquaintanceship. They began to date, and a couple of years later they moved in together.

Barry and Diana's romance blossomed. Her personality and charms fit neatly into his needs, and he was enamored by her frankness and openness, a surprising contradiction for "Mr. Covert Himself." They married shortly after *The Natural,* and during the filming of *Young Sherlock Holmes* in England, Diana gave birth to their son.

When the guys heard that Barry, over 40, had a child, they figured that he'd give his first born a secret name—had to be either Sherlock Levinson, Young Levinson, or Quick Watson Levinson. So the ultra-confidential Barry named the boy Sam.

32.

When Yussel got out of jail, he drifted once again. He didn't know what to do with his life. He was still involved with drugs. After a few months, he enrolled in a drug treatment program as a result of his parole, and at some point he began working, selling food out of his car in affluent neighborhoods. Yussel surprisingly became very successful. One day he reluctantly went to a Narcotics Anonymous meeting. It changed his life. After a couple of weeks, he stopped drugs altogether and attended as many meetings as he could, even encouraging other guys to attend.

Yussel then channeled his energies into business and became so successful that he had a number of people working for him. He bought a new house and car, and was considering franchising his company. And he finally married.

And Obie could have sulked around and felt sorry for himself after Boogie cut him off (well, okay, he did for a couple of years). . . . He finally his got his act together and was fast becoming a very successful insurance salesman. And he finally married.

33.

I only saw Neurotic Nat once more—down at Fell's Point, an old-time funky little community by the Inner Harbor. Nat was at Kim's, a Korean second-hand shoe and repair shop. Kim made a deal with the morgue that when some well-dressed guy was killed, Kim would get his shoes. Nat, as preoccupied with death as anyone, was a regular customer. He was in the back of Kim's, trying to jam his feet into too small a pair of classy Nunn-Bush loafers, when he pulled a muscle in his back. Nat fell down, and was unable to move without screaming. Two guys carried him out on a board toward a jeep when I saw him. Nat just twitched and tried to smile when he saw me . . .

"Nat, I'm sorry to see you like this. But I need to know something. You've never loved and you've never had a compassionate, meaningful relationship with a woman, yet your obsession with hookers has provided you with an envious lifestyle that even a lot of the guys have begun to take notice of."

Nat groaned and blurted out, "Get to the fucking point, Chip. I'm in serious pain!"

"Well," I added, "I know that one of your reasons is that you don't want to hug a woman after you've made love, but why else have you never gotten romantically involved?"

"Jesus Christ, you asshole," cried Nat, "I never wanted to end up like Richard!"

"Who?"

"The guy in Joni Mitchell's song, 'The Last Time I Saw Richard.' I mean Mitchell's a broad and *even* she understood."

Nat was gently lowered into the jeep as he waved me over and whispered, "Listen to the song and thanks for the sympathy, schmuck."

I drove home, found the album, played the song and finally realized Nat's fear:

"Richard got married to a figure skater,
and he bought her a dishwasher and a coffee perculator.
And he drinks at home all night
with the TV on and all the houselights left up bright."

34.

Barry came back to Baltimore to write and direct *Tin Men*. It starred Danny DeVito and Richard Dreyfuss and became one of the Top 10 movies of the year. The Disney studio was so excited about Levinson that they made another deal for him to direct Robin Williams in a movie called *Good Morning, Vietnam!* Williams' career as a movie star has not been exactly phenomenal and nobody at Touchstone Films saw this movie making any kind of big money. Barry's

attitude was always to take the negatives and turn them into positives, so he took a crew to Thailand to film the movie which went
on to become a huge box office hit, grossing over $100 million.

When Barry came back to the States, he called me up one night at
about 2:00 AM in Ocean City, Maryland. He'd been thinking of
maybe coming right back to Baltimore, although that was not his
"M.O.," since he usually waited two movies to come back to do a
"Baltimore" story. Barry also informed me that he'd read my
manuscript while flying from Thailand to America, and that he
really loved it. It made my day. It made my night. I couldn't go
back to sleep, and I was up for the next 48 hours.

While Barry was still thinking about his next project, his agent,
Mike Ovitz, who also represents Dustin Hoffman and director Sid-
ney Pollack, got Barry involved in trying to sort out some problems
with a movie called *Rain Man* starring Hoffman and Tom Cruise.
The more calls Barry got about *Rain Man*, the more his interest
perked, and when Pollack became the fourth director to back out of
the movie, Barry's wife, Diana, encouraged him to do it.

Several directors nixed *Rain Man* because they felt it was "just
another" road movie, the theme was difficult, Hoffman could be
hard to work with, and there were a number of scheduling and
budgetary problems. Barry again turns the negatives into positives.
He wants to do a road movie, likes the theme of autism, doesn't find
Hoffman difficult, and he's never come in over-schedule or over-
budget. Levinson does get sidetracked a bit when the filming begins
in Cincinnati. Diana gives birth to his second son, Jack.

During the last stages of the filming of *Rain Man* in California, I
fly out to lecture on cocaine and visit my sister, Nancy. I take her
up to the shooting of the final scene of *Rain Man* where Barry is
also playing the part of the psychiatrist who has to make the deter-
mination as to whether autistic Dustin Hoffman can live with Tom
Cruise. Nancy is in seventh heaven. She can't believe where she is.
While we're waiting for the shooting to begin, she takes a look at
Tom Cruise, who has a hairdresser and makeup artist hovering
around him trying to fix everything on his body. Nancy whispers,
"Who're they kidding? I'd be around him no matter what. There's
nothing wrong with him. He doesn't have a hair out of place." She
adds, "My God, look at his face. He doesn't even have any pores.
He's absolutely gorgeous." Dustin Hoffman comes over, and Barry
introduces us. Hoffman likes Nancy, and why not? She's even
shorter than he is.

About a month later, I'm back in California, this time with Snyder, while he's doing his West Coast version of the "Battle of the Corporate Stars." Barry invites us over to see a rough cut of *Rain Man*. We're mesmerized. The film is phenomenal. Barry, of course, is nervous, as he is for all films. He figures maybe it could be a critical success, but doesn't know if it will make any money. Danny and I feel that it's unbelievably great and tell Barry, but he just looks around and shakes his head. . .. *Rain Man* becomes the box office hit of the year. It received Golden Globe Awards and four Academy Awards including Best Picture and Best Director!

35.

Before Kaps, no one took pictures at parties. In the mid-'60s he used my camera at parties in my house. A small row house that held 10 people comfortably, but during the parties, 150 fanatics squeezed their way in.

Kaps eventually parlayed his photography into a job teaching video at the Antioch College in downtown Baltimore, a few years after he graduated from the University of Maryland.

A student of Kaps pitched him the idea to do a documentary on the life of Harold Clurman. When they realized that the documentary was eligible for federal and private grants, Kaps and the student formed a partnership and left for Los Angeles in 1976.

For the next 12 years, Kaps took the low road to video stardom whereas Levinson had taken the high road, and supported himself by means of various grants, supplementing his income with odd jobs selling tax-shelted investments in cattle, diamonds and housing, instead of being a waiter as Barry had been.

Harold Clurman was the founder of the Group Theatre in the 1930s. He introduced Method acting to Broadway theater, and changed the whole direction from the melodramatic to the realistic style we know today. He taught Lee Strasberg, Stella Adler, Elia Kazan, etc., and they became teachers who motivated other teachers. Kaps' Clurman documentary spanned the 1930s through the 1970s.

Interestingly, he initially had difficulty getting Hollywood and

Broadway celebrities to participate in the documentary but after Clurman's death in 1979, most agreed to honor him.

So Clurman's students and Arthur Miller, Karl Malden, Meryl Streep, Roy Scheider, Joan Hackett and others all appear in Kaps' documentary. His film is fast becoming a national treasure since Clurman, Lee Strasberg and Joan Hackett all died shortly after they appeared in the documentary, although some in the business consider Kaps and his associates the "jinx crew." If you're in the Clurman documentary, there's a good chance you'll not survive its air date on PBS for which Kaps is still waiting.

The American Library Association publication, *Choice,* said that Kaps' film "will be a classic. Its place in the education of young theatre students is assured."

Of course, Kaps regards his documentary like *Gone With the Wind.* He called Levinson one day to ask him for a favor. The world premiere of *Good Morning, Vietnam!* was scheduled on the same night as the screening of Kaps' documentary at his synagogue. Kaps wanted Barry to change the premiere date so that it didn't conflict with his screening. Barry apologized but said that he couldn't buck Disney (Touchstone) Studio. Kaps was upset.

36.

In semi-retirement in Aspen, Boogie decided to build an upscale clothing store and restaurant and named it Boogie's Diner. He spent a couple of million dollars and opened during Thanksgiving weekend of 1987 on prime land near Aspen Mountain. The store was an overnight success. On the first floor, Boogie sells very expensive yet very "with it" clothing. The cheapest items are Boogie's Diner teeshirts that sell for $25. Jackets go for $700 and boots for $2,000 and $3,000 a pair. There is memorabilia throughout the store, including Elvis' Corvette. Upstairs, overlooking the store, is a small diner, a replica of the diners of the 1940s and 1950s. Even the waitresses dress and act in the old style. The food is cheap, yet as tasty as any in Aspen. Celebrities flock to Boogie's Diner: Martina Navratilova, Barbra Streisand, Don Johnson, Rob Lowe, and many others.

When the store was about a month old, Donald Trump and his wife, Ivana walked in. Trump was infatuated with Boogie's Diner. He asked Bernie, the manager, to introduce him to the owner as soon as possible.

Boogie soon appeared and met Trump who expressed tremendous interest in the place. "We can replicate this all over the country. I can see this in two or three of my places. You and I will be partners!" Boog listened to the pitch and told Trump that he could be interested, and perhaps they could talk about it later. So Trump asked Boog to call his secretary and was about to give Boogie his secretary's name and telephone number. Boog drew back and said to Trump, "Whoa, Don. I think we're getting off on the wrong foot here. I don't call secretaries." Trump apologized, gave him his personal number and told Boogie that when he's in New York next month to please give him a call.

A few weeks later, Boogie was in New York and phoned Trump from his apartment. Trump was pleased that Boogie called, and he told Boog that he would now turn him over to his secretary so that they can arrange a time to meet. It was a Friday night and Trump would like to meet with Boogie as soon as possible on Saturday. However, Boogie again balked, "Don, here we are getting off on that wrong foot again, I don't talk to secretaries." Trump regained composure and told Boog that he will go out to the office and see what time they can meet. It was obvious that Trump wasn't used to walking around his secretary's desk and filling in dates and times on his appointment book. Over the phone, Boogie could hear the rattling of papers and waited for a considerable time before Trump got back. Trump said, "Boogie, how's nine o'clock sound to you?" Boogie responded, "Nine o'clock Saturday night sounds great to me, Don." Trump said, to Boog, "I meant nine in the morning." Boog was aghast, "Don, I rarely get up before noon. There we go getting off on that wrong foot again." Trump laughed and told Boog that the latest he could meet him is one o'clock that afternoon, and Boogie agreed.

Boogie showed up looking for Trump at 1:00 P.M. the next day. He was wearing jeans, boots, a jacket and a tee-shirt. When he got off at the floor where Trump's office was located, Trump's bouncers attempted to throw Boogie out since they didn't believe a guy dressed like he could have a meeting with Donald Trump. They asked him, "Who are you looking for?" And Boogie responded, "Trump." "Sure," the bouncers said, "everybody wants to see

Trump. Get lost." An altercation almost broke out, but Trump arrived and ushered Boogie into his office. As they discussed options and plans, Boogie wondered to himself, What do I need Trump for? Although Trump has billions of dollars and ideal locations, Boogie isn't really planning for big expansion. He built Boogie's Diner for fun, he has money and contacts, and he's put enough Merry-Go-Round stores over the country that he won't have too much trouble finding developers if he wanted to expand."

So Boog asked Trump why he needed him as a partner. Was Trump going to work food upstairs, or retail downstairs? How much of the buying was he going to do? Boog went on and on. Trump didn't see himself doing anything except providing status, locations and money. Boog didn't see the advantage. He thanked Trump, but said no thanks, and departed.

A few months later, Boogie decides to let Merry-Go-Round (which had grown to over 600 stores) handle the Boogie's Diner expansion, and in 1989, the second store opened in Chicago.

37.

Barry was in town recently researching a new Baltimore story. We met for breakfast at Miller's Deli on Reisterstown Road. Miller's is about two miles north of where Brice's Hilltop Diner was located and has, since the early '70s, become the replacement for the Diner. Modern day Tin Men and the likes congregate there from dusk until dawn.

And even though many of the Diner guys have become enormously successful, our treatment by the management is still the same.

While Barry and I were sitting at a table bullshitting, the owner told us we had to leave unless we ordered something. Indignant, I told him who Levinson was and he screamed back, "I know who he is, he's Irv Levinson's son. So what, he's still got to order!" And Barry Levinson dutifully ordered a toasted bagel. It was just like old times at the Diner.

38.

So here I am descended from an illiterate carpenter, a shiftless capmaker, active and passive drug addicts, a couple of crooks, a pair whose names were changed faster than a Muslim pro basketball player . . . my father and his four brothers all died of heart attacks before 50 . . . thank God my parents were honest (a trait they didn't completely inherit). They must have been left by Gypsies (in Pinsk?).

If that's not enough, I'm afraid to get my wisdom teeth pulled, I'm getting shorter every year; the Diner is now a "blue" liquor package goods discount joint; Queensberry Playground is now part of the Top 10 criminal impact areas in the country; everytime I have trapped gas, I think I'm going to have a massive coronary, and my wife says I live in the past. (So maybe Minsk wasn't so bad.)

Live in the past? I don't think so. Sure, I love to bullshit and reminisce about the past with the old gang, but that to me is minor nostalgia. I'm very happy with the present, unlike some guys who'd love to be transported back in time to Forest Park in 1959. It's when they peaked and they've never been able to adjust to today. Now that's living in the past! Besides, we did tend to over-exaggerate the good old days—if not, they wouldn't have been "the good old days," although ours were better than most.

Of course, I wouldn't mind going back in time to correct or improve on a couple of instances—like with the pretty blonde shiksa I'd been trying to make it with for a month in the summer of '63, when I finally got ready to score in the Islander Motel in Ocean City and I couldn't get hard; or at a 1958 closet scene when I came too fast with this fat chick from South Baltimore and was soundly booed by the girl and three guys watching from a window (I guess ejaculating on contact would be considered too fast) . . . or . . .

39.

Murray, Burger, Ben, Fenwick, Mama Cass Elliot (nee Ellen Cohen), Jay Huff, Eggie, Earl Maget, and Jeff Hall are dead. Only Jeff and Earl lived past 40. Third, Yussel, Swartzie, Earl and Bruce Hawk all served (some) hard time. Only Yussel kept out of jail 'til 40. The others were indicted before they hit 30, and drugs were the common denominator in mostly every death and indictment except for a few (to the best of my knowledge).

Barry lives in Malibu, Boogie in Florida and Aspen, Bill in Boston . . . Snyder and Turns in Washington . . . and last we heard, Third's in Thailand, Bruce Hawk's in Kenya, Jules is in Bora Bora . . . and Ez is somewhere in the South Pacific.

They still come back, drawn by some of the guys. (I wonder where the Gripper is?)

What touched us wasn't the prose of Leon Uris, the commentary of Russell Baker, the politics of Spiro Agnew, the Broadway successes of Ken Waissman, the operatic bass of Spiro Malis . . .

What touched us was the grip of the Gripper, the sucker-punch of Boogie, the sarcasm and wit of Ben, the euphoria of Burger's cough syrup, the nomadic escapades of Third . . .

It was the camaraderie—foreign to our kids and today's youth—a never-to-be-recaptured era, moments framed in time; gone, along with the playgrounds, poolrooms, street corners, alleys, Diners. . . .

Appendix A

Aluminum Siding:
Annals of the Tin Men

The rear of the Diner was normally occupied by the Tin Men. They were older men who mainly sold aluminum siding, although hustlers from different variations of the home improvement business were among this group which also included degenerates and derelicts. They were mostly confidence men and free spirits whose lifestyles consisted of gambling, drugs and booze, good times, very little work, and getting in and out of "jackpots" (trouble). "Anything Goes" was the motto of that era of the aluminum siding business, before the consumer advocate and Home Improvement Commission days.

Fake was purposely missing the tree with the pears he was throwing, imitating Yankee ace Whitey Ford. At $2.00 a bullseye, the farmer was already up $14.00 and, although normally a pessimist at heart, even he had to agree that this was his lucky day. After all, he'd already convinced this "big shot from the factory" to redo his home, practically free.

Earlier that afternoon, Drake the Fake (or just Fake), Vincent Aldo and Bill McNally had pulled up to this rural farm and set up a tripod with a camera to photograph the home. Eventually, out of curiosity, the farmer and his wife came out and asked what was going on. Vincent pretended they were a minor annoyance and briefly advised them that their house was being photographed by *Look* or *Life* Magazine as a "before" house, in a "before" and "after" advertisement for Reynolds Aluminum siding. The "after" house he said was to be a neighbor's home a couple of miles down the road. (Naturally free of charge). The siding guys continued to ignore the farmer and appeared engrossed in their photography to such an extent that the farmer and his wife actually begged them to use their home for the "after" picture.

The aluminum siding business began in Baltimore in the early '50s. A guy named Sol Kantor arrived in Baltimore from Pittsburgh with 20 salesmen and six families of carpenters and started "selling tin." This was basically the sale of baked enamel aluminum for the exteriors of shingled or wooden houses. (In those days, they didn't even try to sell trim; 99 percent of what they sold was siding. The owner of the house had to purchase the trim himself. Some siding guys would provide the owners with paint to use for trim.) Many of the completed siding jobs were terrible since the mechanics and carpenters were butchers, save for some from Pittsburgh, and once the job was sold, no one involved in the sale or workmanship gave a damn about the finished product.

At first, the guys from Pittsburgh would drive into Baltimore on Sunday night, work Monday through Thursday, and then go back to Pittsburgh. This became tradition and today most guys in the home improvement business only work Monday through Thursday, with paydays still Thursday night or Friday morning.

> On payday, the men took a number at Sol's place to get paid, just like in a bakery shop.

> Sol Kantor had a partner named Bernie from Pittsburgh who put up money to spread the siding business into Baltimore. Sol and Bernie would play head games with their salesmen. Sol would come on soft, pretending to give a salesman a big advance, while Bernie would scream not to give him a dime, bellowing, "He isn't worth anything."

> The whole key to status among Tin Men was how much you were on the "sheet" for to Sol. The sheet represented how much money you owed Sol. You were a big man if you owed Sol more money than anybody else since the sheet indicated how much guys were producing or selling. Sol would advance them half of what they were generating before he actually received the money from the banks for approved credit applications. He was the middle man and all he had to do was make a few phone calls and that took care of everything. He also warehoused the materials enabling him to amass even greater profits for himself.

> When the Tin Men sold a job, they would say they got lucky, but Sol said, "You only get lucky when you work." Another expression was, "The hardest door to get into was your own car door," meaning that

you only needed to go to work in order to earn money in this field.

As the business spread, the Pittsburgh group moved their families to Baltimore and started hiring local guys, many who were called "maggers." Maggers did what was known as "magging," selling linoleum floors in black or lower class neighborhoods. They would buy a 10′ × 10′ roll for $20, re-roll it to look huge (40′ × 30′ or bigger), knock on doors in poor areas, and sell the linoleum for kitchen floors or anything else at escalated prices. Normally they sold to the elderly, widowed and senile. Maggers began working for the guys from Pittsburgh whose base of operation became Northwest Baltimore. By 1958, maggers and other hustlers left the Pittsburgh group and started selling siding on their own. (Rodney Dangerfield was an aluminum siding salesman years ago and Lionel Stander, from TV's *Hart to Hart,* once worked as a rep for a major aluminum manufacturer during the period when he had been blacklisted by Hollywood. He frequently dealt with Baltimore Tin Men at the Diner.)

As a young man, Sol Kantor was a respected prize fighter who fought highly-ranked boxers in New York's Madison Square Garden.

After a couple of years selling tin in Baltimore, he was making so much money he often paid his salesmen $500 a week *not* to work. He needed the free time for some of his more licentious activities such as gambling. Had it not been for these excessive habits, Sol would have been a multimillionaire.

Sol Kantor and the Pittsburgh group used to hang out at the Pimlico Hotel (not a real hotel but a very fine restaurant/bar near Pimlico Race Track). They ran up huge tabs, drinking and eating there all of the time. They wrote in big tips on their dinner and bar checks. But, at the end of the month, as soon as they had sold a few jobs, they immediately paid off their tabs. (Sol Kantor became so spoiled that he actually bought his groceries at the Pimlico Hotel/Restaurant, an expensive luxury.) However, when the Pittsburgh group finally left Baltimore to begin selling further south, they stuck the Pimlico Hotel for the last month of tabs. The owner was not so much upset with what they ate and drank that month, but with being stuck with such an awesome amount of tips.

When Kantor and company left Baltimore, they moved to Charlotte,

North Carolina. Historically, Tin Men were responsible for breaking neighborhoods, though not in the racial sense. Their families wanted to live together in the same areas, and they created so many problems partying, carousing, arguing, etc., that people moved away as soon as Tin Men moved in.

Baltimore Tin Men evolved into a far more slick and professional sales force than the Pittsburgh group, and became the benchmark for the siding and home improvement salesmen who followed them.

Tin Men were a special breed of born hustlers with tremendous cunning. They weren't like the early home improvement guys. They were used to earning a lot of fast, big money and had to know how to ask for $3,000 rather than $300. That's why a lot of maggers and small-time hustlers eventually dropped out of the business. They couldn't cope with asking the higher prices.

One time, Vincent and Eddie "D" went to a house where two fags were holding hands, wearing earrings, and carrying on like dogs in heat. Vincent began to talk sweet, graphically describing the siding process: "The siding is blown on . . . It slides in easy from the rear . . . They put it on with under-suction . . . and, we are going to send out our most handsome mechanic." Vincent then told Fake to send out a good looking mechanic, but Fake, not knowing what they're talking about, sent over this 350 pound slob, and the fags cancelled. Vincent then had to rewrite the deal, convince Fake to hire two young boys, naked to the waist, to put up the siding, and throw in free pink shutters.

New technology in aluminum siding since the '70s produces a maintenance-free product. However, when sales began in the '50s, the siding was sold as a maintenance-free product which it was not, and today most of those jobs with a baked enamel siding that were completed in the early years have faded to oblivion. As a matter of fact, there are home improvement companies today that will also resurface or repaint the siding on the old jobs.

The siding business developed as a partnership of three groups: the banks, or the financial end; manufacturers like United States Steel and Reynolds, who supplied the aluminum siding; and, the Tin Men who were the salesmen on the street. These three combined to make a unique force.

The original sales pitch, called "the model home approach," was the promise of a "free" job; that is, the tin men promised to cover the exterior walls (the asbestos or wood shingles on a house) for free, predicated on the premise that the dwelling would be used as a model home. The sales pitch was based on the phony concept that the siding would create a dream house. As the new house, or the first job on the block, any jobs that came after would supposedly result in residuals, bonuses, dividends or commissions for the homeowner. The salesmen would even give away money to the customer and say that it was upfront payment for the first few jobs that they were sure to sell based on the homeowner's new dream house. The give-away money was added on to the final price. Final price? Yes, the "free job" somehow contained a charge, plus some additional minor charges. Plus extras.

Most Tin Men never told people that it was *really* a free job; they would always imply it. They sold the job basically on the dividends (commissions, residuals, etc.) and that the job would eventually liquidate (pay for itself), and then as they handed over the predicted first few dividends, they would say to the homeowners, "Now look at all this money. Leave it in the cookie jar and don't let your wife buy a mink coat with it. Just hold on to this money!"

Vincent Aldo had these scams where he'd either whisper, "We would like to give you the job free, but Johns Mansville ruined things years ago and now there is this law that says you must pay for the above labor and materials. And that's all we're charging you," or he would shout out that: "Government regulations prohibit giving away free jobs, so you just have to pay for labor and materials. However, because this is a once in a lifetime job, we normally include a handsome profit for us, and you can't blame us, but since this is a sample house (only labor and material costs), you won't have to cover the profit!"

The average actual cost of the jobs back then, including labor, was around $1,000. The homeowner's price of about $2,400 allowed for an $800-$900 commission divided between the salesman (closer) and the canvasser.

There were, of course, variations of the "free job/model home" approach but it basically went like this: The canvasser would knock on a door and say, "Hello, Mrs. Smith. I'm with Reynolds and we're thinking of putting up siding on your house. It looks like your shingles need work, and we're just going to select three or four homes in the Maryland area. Fortunately, yours has been chosen as a sample home." And he might also say, "I'm not a salesman! I'm here strictly making a business proposition. Today I am not selling! I am just trying to get my boss in because he selected your house . . ."

The canvasser then added, "We're going to take pictures afterwards to use for national advertising." He'd then "fake beg" the homeowner to give them permission to use his name in the national ad, and then announce that the top man was outside. "My boss is in from Pittsburgh for the day." (Of course, the boss would be sitting outside in a beautiful Cadillac convertible.) The "closer" was dressed to the teeth and acted as though he was either the company owner or the manufacturer's rep. He'd enter the house and explain the materials needed, show pictures of the siding, and talk about all the guarantees. At that point he'd say something like, "We're only going to charge $3,000 since your house is a sample house, and we're sure it will get us so much business that you are going to receive $100 per home for every person in this neighborhood who sees your house and decides to buy." Then he'd hand the people anywhere from $300 to $500 up front.

Upfront payments or dividends, also called "bonuses," were not given out at the beginning of the pitch. Bonuses were given as a last option to people who became skeptical. On the way out of the door, in order to save the job, the closer would go back and offer the bonus money. This was after he'd have already thrown in a new roof (it cost $500 and would be included in the final price), storm doors with people's initials, triple-track-storm windows, and/or shutters—all to entice the sale.

A lot of closers would present a letter to the people on stationery that they had stolen from Reynolds or Alcoa. It would read, "This will introduce Mr. Brown, a representative of this company and he has the authority to give dividends," and would be signed "the President."

"Here," he would boast, "This is for your first four payments. That's how sure I am that this area will be a boom neighborhood for us!" They had this working stiff eyeing $500 in cash which he probably hadn't seen before. (Remember, this was an era when $500 was really something.) It was a huge amount of money and the homeowner couldn't wait to sign. He believed that he would never pay for the siding job or that he would pay only a little. The salesman did say, however, that if he couldn't sell enough jobs, then the homeowner *might* have to make a couple of payments. "I can't promise you, Mr. Sucker, that you're not going to have to pay anything; but I can promise you that you'll only have to pay a small amount. And here's that $500!"

> One of Vincent Aldo's favorite variations of the model home approach was: If a homeowner said he had lived in this house 17 years, Vincent would respond, "Gee, I'm sorry, but the policy says you have to live in the house for 18 years before I can bring in the MAN; but, on this day only," he'd add, "I'll make an exception because I like the type of people you are!" Then he'd ask them three things: (1) "Would you object to our taking 'before and after' pictures of your house?" (2) "Would you object to us bringing over 'doubting Thomases' after the job is completed?" and (3) "Would you object to recommending a product that will give you good service?" If they answered yes to those three things, Vincent brought in Fake to close. Then he would tell the customer, "I'm not going to promise you that Mr. Big (Fake) will select you . . ." If they begged a little bit, then he "tried" to convince Fake to choose these homeowners.

Tin Men never asked the people if they would mind talking to the head man from Pittsburgh. It was always, "If you people qualify, he might talk to you." It was always the "man from the mill" or the "man from the factory" who was setting up locations with this brand new material throughout the country, and was a very important figure. If people bought the story, the Tin Men sold them the bomb.

> Canvassers were also called "qualifiers," that is, salesmen who could identify if the homeowners were "goons" (qualifying as "marks") or "mooches." For example, Vincent Aldo would go up to a home, and if a guy was tall, he would throw down a match box or a piece of paper and say, "Here, put your name and address and telephone number on that match box." If the guy bent over and picked it up, Vincent knew he was a goon. If it was a real short guy, Vincent held the paper up real high in the air and asked him the same thing. "Put your name, address and telephone number on this." If he reached for it, the guy was a goon. Mooches were people who had fake animals or fountains on their lawns. This identified them as marks.

> Other times, Vincent would say, "All right, look, clean your house up. I'm here with Mr. Big and he may come in any minute!"

Sometimes he would add, "After you clean the house up, you'd better have a glass of water out because Mr. Big's got bad kidneys!"

If the customer had other notes (car loan, doctor's bills, etc.), the closer would suggest combining the bills and remark, "We're going to incorporate all of your bills into one payment. You'll only have to write one check a month for everything. Don't worry about your other bills." At that time, the maximum financing term for siding jobs was around five years. The people who signed the note seldom bitched to the bank even though they never received the bonuses or commissions that the salesman promised. Before they signed, they were told that the bank would give them a coupon book for making payments until the salesman sold other jobs, and when they sold other jobs, the homeowners would have their payments taken care of.

Since there was no Home Improvement Commission in Maryland until the mid-1960s, the salesmen could get away with anything. With no consumer advocate or consumer protection agency, Tin Men could promise or say anything, and nothing would ever come of it.

The siding business grew rapidly and dozens of groups appeared, all competing for the big and little dollars. Some guys had only one small crew while others formed big companies with anywhere from five to 25 crews on the street. Each crew contained two to four men. While some companies became legitimate, most of the others' practices went from questionable to very crooked.

The composition of siding crews was never really stable because guys drifted in and out of the business. It was a field that anybody could sell in. Guys might have a regular job, leave it to go hustling tin, return to their regular job and then probably get fired or laid-off; then they'd return to selling siding.

The salesmen and canvassers came from everywhere. Tin men could work with a guy for three months and then never see him again. It was just a hustle. They were born salesmen who went through life selling—the product could be aluminum siding, encyclopedias, books, vacuum cleaners, magazines or religion.

The quintessential Tin Man was Drake Gemora. He started hustling tin for a "kibbitz" (a joke) and eventually became the top man in the field to emulate.

At the age of 17, Drake the Fake, or just "Fake," was considered the greatest carpet salesman ever to hit the east. That same year, his father gave him $3,000 to start the siding business. Aside from a natural cunning, Fake also profited more than his competitors at selling tin because he had his father's money behind him. Thus, he could finance any "bad paper" that a bank or loan company wouldn't take. But Fake still got a thrill from sticking banks with bad credit applications. Fake not only caused savings and loan institutions to fail, but he once stuck Reynolds Aluminum with $100,000 worth of bad paper. He had 22 jobs in Havre de Grace, Maryland, that he said were all good, and he told Reynolds to call the credit union there to check on the pending deals. Naturally they did and the credit union said all the deals were approved. What Reynolds didn't know was that Fake owned the credit union and Fake answered the phone inquiry. (Drake also stiffed places like Chase Manhattan Bank.)

In the carpet business, Drake was great at the "bait and switch" con. He would sell people carpeting for $99 with a simple, direct sales approach. The bait was the cheap price.

After the customer signed a contract, Drake or a salesman would say on the way out, "By the way, you do have a real good vacuum cleaner don't you? This carpet will shed and you will have to vacuum it three to six times every day." Naturally, the purchaser would go bananas over this, but then Drake would add, "Of course, there is another carpet that we have which is a step upward, a little more expensive, but I think we can give you credit for your signed contract." And then they would bring out this beautiful piece of carpet which by that time the person was eager to buy. That was the switch.

Fake also used the bait and switch approach initially when he started hustling tin. After selling a customer some cheap siding, on the way out he would say, "Well, I do have to inform you that if you don't own a ladder you'll need one because this siding will rust. Now in order to prevent it, it has to be rubbed down twice a day with kerosene, and you must have a six foot ladder. So, I have to warn you about this!" The customers, who Fake knew were primed to buy, were dumbfounded by this. But Fake would then add, "I do have this other siding sample though which is a step up from what you have just bought. We'll give you credit for it and I'll throw in free shutters because . . ."

Drake the Fake's crews were made up the whackiest guys around and his sales pitches were legendary. For example, his canvassing techniques were classic. If Drake found someone standing outside on their porch either looking around, doing a little work, or just staring up at the sky, he would drive up onto the lawn of the house, jump out of the car and ask, "Didn't the guys leave the siding?" Naturally, the man on the porch was bewildered and then Drake proudly explained that this house was one of the 18 model homes chosen in the State of Maryland for siding, and the owner had to pay only for labor and taxes. "Something is definitely wrong," Drake would add. "Work has to begin immediately so it will be finished when *Look* Magazine comes out to take pictures." This always hooked the people, and from there it was very simple to sell them the siding deal. Of course, many times the "taxes" Fake added on when the people signed the note were in the hundreds of dollars.

It was great to grab people outside of their homes, cutting their lawns or on the porch. It showed that they took pride in their house, and once a Tin Man got into the house, he would talk to the owner about how nice his place was and why it was selected. Soon the homeowner was joining in and knocking certain neighbors for not maintaining their properties as well as his.

If Drake was canvassing and closing by himself, he would wait until a door opened and then just walk right into the house, exclaiming that the pictures on the wall were beautiful. He talked about the pictures and how pretty their kids were, and just change the subject from one thing to another for over an hour. Finally, as if by a miracle, he somehow got back to selling siding to these people who thanked him profusely after he sold the job.

One time, Eddie "D" and Vincent Aldo were out canvassing a black neighborhood. They couldn't get in the front door of this one house because the steps were being repaired, so they went around to the back. This family kept their insane son outside in the yard. He was 21 years old, huge, and grunted a lot. They didn't want to send him to the black state mental institution at Crownsville so they kept him in this huge reinforced orange crate. He looked like a big gorilla in there. He would make all of these sounds like he wanted to kill everybody, and people had to tip-toe around him. Eddie and Vincent finally got in the house and sold a deal to the family.

Next day, they went back to Fake, and informed him that the family cancelled the job. Vincent couldn't believe it and he told Fake, "Come with me. We're going back to make them take this deal!"

When they reached the house, he told Fake, "Look, we're going to have to go around the back and sneak by this guy who's kept in a big box." Fake thought Vincent was hallucinating and didn't believe him.

But, sure enough, there was this blue (Tin Men jargon for blacks) in a cage by the back steps. The people didn't want Fake and Vincent to come in because they were afraid they'd buy the deal again, and they couldn't afford it. The blue in the crate is going "umph, umph," and finally Vincent went berserk and pushed the crate and the blue over, and then burst into the house; but the people still wouldn't take the deal. Meanwhile, the caged blue was over being stunned and wouldn't let Fake and Vincent out of the house. They finally slipped out the front window at night during feeding time of the "crate man."

To avoid cancellation after a deal was closed and to keep competitors away, the Tin Men resorted to "spiking" a job. The guys might paint the side of the house, rip off the shingles or rip up the roof.

The home improvement business today has what is known as "the three day rescission." If the homeowner decides he does not want the job, he has three days to cancel it. But back in the late '50s and early '60s, Tin Men could begin the job an hour after they wrote it. The salesmen would spike jobs in several ways: (1) If he wrote a job in a house at 9:00 P.M., he'd say, "Let's go outside, I think maybe we ought to start here," and would take bright red paint and write on one side of the house, START ON THIS SIDE FIRST. Well, nobody was going to cancel after that. (2) Sometimes they went outside and said, "Okay, we'll need to take off this whole bottom row of shingles here and take them back to the lab for tests." Naturally, if a house had no bottom row of shingles it looked ridiculous, so the owner was not only going to keep the siding deal, but have them begin right away. (3) The closer would say he needed to check something on the side of the house, and, after taking a crow bar out of his car, he'd rip off maybe six or seven panels. The large hole that appeared in the side of the house was so conspicuous that the homeowner demanded immediate repair. Therefore, the next morning at 7:00 A.M., the Tin Men were there with their crew. While the family was still sleeping, the carpenters would bang on the walls putting up this aluminum siding. (4) Another way of "spiking" was to drop off the material on the lawn immediately, even if they couldn't begin the job for a week. (Today, home improvement men "spike" a job if they're running behind schedule by dropping off the material all over the lawn and putting up one square yard of siding. This secures the job and they have legally started the work.

One way that Vincent Aldo used to spike a deal was to rip off either the storm door, kitchen door or screen door as he left the house and exclaim, "Oh, this slipped off, we had better take it in and have it checked also!"

> There were these two Italian brothers called the Squirrel Boys who not only sold siding, but roof jobs as well. As soon as they completed a sale, they would "spike it" by going upstairs and ripping off a section of the roof. Once they did it before one of the worst storms ever to hit Baltimore. The customers called the Squirrel brothers at 1:00 A.M. and said that water was pouring in all over the house. The Squirrel brothers had to drive over to the house and bale out water all night long. They brought in the carpenters the next morning to put on the roof and added on an emergency call fee of $300.

Financing jobs was almost as tricky as selling "tin," especially since the majority of deals were made in lower-middle class settings. At first, Tin Men had to go to a bank and get a commitment for the money before they could actually begin work on a house, then back to the bank with signed forms from the homeowners for approval. (Occasionally a bank gave "paper" or approval in advance so the salesman could take a credit application, and a note for the people to sign, without returning to the bank.)

If the bank turned the deal down, the salesman had to go to a place like the Second Mortgage Company which would take bad paper (a very weak loan application). The mortgage company would take 30 percent of the deal, and, as long as there was enough profit in the job, the siding salesman accepted it. Let's say they had a $1,500 job and the bad paper was for $3,000. The Second Mortgage Company would only give them $2,200. This was called "discounting a job." Sometimes the Tin Man had to rewrite the "paper" into a covenant or a deed of trust that included the home, and, since the customer was being given extra money, he didn't mind signing anything.

If the homeowner didn't like the job that was done on the house, or if he couldn't afford to pay, he was in no position to complain to anyone. The banks or the loan companies back in those days could take away the house when the customer couldn't meet the note. (No one actually lost his house; well, maybe a few people, but usually the loan companies and the bank would make arrangements to get the note paid off. If it was really a problem, the people went to the Better Business Bureau or raised a stink with the bank.)

> Once, Vincent went to Southern Maryland (a favorite siding area) with a guy called Mr. Fisher, whose pitch was to come in and flash a plane ticket, proving he was ready to return to Pittsburgh. After making the deal, Fisher would announce, "Here's what areas of Maryland I'm going to give you as dividends when we sell them. I'm going to give you Crofton, Charles County, and the southern tip of Prince George's County." The customer started insisting that he also wanted Monkton (a wealthy "horsey" area for the gentry) but Mr. Fisher refused to give it to him. Vincent was there and he couldn't believe it. The homeowner demanded, "That's it, I don't want the deal unless I get Monkton," but Fisher declined. Outside, Vincent yelled at Fisher. "What are you crazy? Why wouldn't you give him Monkton?" Fisher responded, "I just couldn't give him Monkton. I thought it would really help the con if I did that." Next day, Vincent returned and gave the customer Monkton, Hawaii, and Park Circle (one of Baltimore's first integrated areas), and closed the sale.

Although it seemed as if the Tin Men were at the mercy of the banks (God forbid someone should have shown mercy on the homeowners), this was not necessarily true. Drake had the edge when he dealt with the business-type, Ivy League bank executives because the siding guy was sharper. The bankers couldn't handle con artists mainly because they had never been exposed to them.

Anytime Drake tried to sell the second mortgages or bad paper to the banks, he never let any of his canvassers come along. He was very secretive. Drake spent a good part of the day going to different banks to convince them to buy the weaker loans. Sometimes siding company owners cultivated "hooks" in certain banks—guys they paid under the table to assure the approval of some bad loans.

When no banking or lending institution would approve bad paper, the siding guys turned to friendly loan sharks. One was Poor Louie Sussman, who now owns one of the biggest home improvement companies in Maryland. Poor Louie got involved in the late '50s with the aluminum siding guys who came to him to borrow money. They would borrow $800 from Poor Louie to do a job and would give him back $1,000 a week later. He was financing their business, a precarious practice since these guys went through money very quickly.

Actually, it wasn't too precarious for Poor Louie since he enjoyed
a reputation as the toughest Jew around, and the wrong guy to fail to
repay a loan. Poor Louie's fights and exploits were legendary and of
epic proportion.

There was the time Poor Louie found out that a restricted swimming
club called Beaver Lake had put up a sign that read, "No Jews, dogs,
or niggers allowed!" All Louie did was shave his big barrel chest and
paint I AM A JEW on it in red. Then, wearing only a bathing suit and
one of those Viking hats with horns, he burst through the club gates
at a Fourth of July picnic and ran rampant on the outdoor furniture,
raining disaster on any picnic-goers who tried to stop him. The sign
was removed.

Lou was so tough that when he was 15, he beat up a professional
fighter called Clancy, nicknamed the King of Pimlico. Once, when
Louie was in high school playing basketball, a guy in the stands
started calling him Jewboy. Louie just leaped into the stands where
he heard the slurs and proceeded to beat up the entire crowd.

Poor Louie was six feet tall, about 240 pounds, strong as an ox, and
extremely agile for his size. He excelled in basketball, lacrosse and
particularly football. However, his voice was soft and high-pitched,
and it gave certain over-confident individuals a false image of Louie
as a passive teddy bear. One such individual was the great University
of Maryland center, and later pro-football star, Bill Pellegrino. Pellegrino was the BMOC (Big Man on Campus) at Maryland when
Louie arrived as a freshman on a football scholarship. Late one afternoon, Pellegrino and his entourage entered the cafeteria and proceeded to break in line ahead of Louie, playfully advising him that,
"Rats (freshmen football players) don't eat until the Man does!" Poor
Louie insisted to Pellegrino that when it came to food (a subject very
dear to him) he could not accept second class citizenship. But all he
received was a shove. That was Pellegrino's second and last mistake.
Louie sucker-punched Pellegrino in the stomach so hard that he not
only doubled-over in pain, but he embarrassingly lost his lunch (and
probably breakfast) on both the cafeteria floor and some of his loyal
followers.

Louie dropped out of Maryland and later attended the University of
Baltimore where his rock 'em-sock 'em lacrosse play as a defenseman caused the U.S. Lacrosse Association to change its face-off rule.

To briefly explain, at the beginning of each period and after every goal, the opposing team's center midfielders face-off like in ice hockey. The old rule allowed everyone to go after the ball following the whistle which included the attack and defense player who were 20 yards away. By the time they arrived at the face-off area, the ball was usually in someone's possession or rolling toward the other team's goal area. However, Louie was so quick he got to the face-off midfielders before possession, and their rapt attention on the loose ball allowed him to throw vicious body checks on unsuspecting midfielders. This caused a rash of serious injuries. After two years of this mayhem (all legal), the Lacrosse Association changed to the current rule which states that until a midfielder gains possession, the attack and defense players must remain 20 yards off behind a res-training line. It's known as the "Sussman (or Lifesaving) Rule."

Occasionally, Louie would get drunk and drive out to very rough ethnic, redneck or Gentile areas at two or three in the morning. He'd blow his horn for ten minutes, climb atop the car roof, and loudly challenge all comers. Needless to say there were always challengers, usually three to six rushing Poor Louie, but alas, they were soundly trounced.

Back in Poor Louie's era, every neighborhood boasted its roughest guy, but even they grudgingly admitted to Louie's prowess, with one exception—"The Rabbit." Rabbit was from East Baltimore, a former Golden Gloves boxer, a strongarm on the docks, and the head bouncer at the Surf Club, a popular night spot where many tin men congregated. Rabbit and Poor Louie were the acknowledged two toughest guys in Metro Baltimore for over a decade and efforts were always afoot to get them together for the ultimate fight. Unfortunately, the fight never came off until both guys were well beyond their prime, and Rabbit was declared the winner in an anticlimactic, short-lived and unspectacularly pathetic event (over a girl).

Rabbit's fighting reputation almost went nationwide when he supposedly backed down the late, great heavyweight champ of the world, Rocky Marciano. It seems that during a brief stopover in Baltimore, Marciano and his chauffeur went to the Surf Club (to see Dizzy Gillespie entertain) where The Rock proceeded to bypass the line of patrons waiting outside. Rabbit was working "the door" and, not knowing it was Marciano, stopped him at the entrance and told him to go to the end of the line. An argument ensued during which Rabbit was advised by a patron that it was in fact "the" Rocky Marciano. But Rabbit by then didn't care, challenging the Champ to go out back and fight it out. Cooler heads prevailed and Marciano decided to leave, but before he departed he promised to meet Rabbit the next night and had his "seconds" remain to determine a site.

The setting for "The Fight" was a dimly lit industrial area located on the outskirts of Little Italy, and two of Rabbit's buddies lurked in the darkness behind him. The buddies (currently matriculating in prison) supposedly were armed and ready to do battle with Marciano and his seconds should the Rabbit go down in defeat (a likely outcome, although the gutsy Rabbit was considered the consummate streetfighter). But the Champ never appeared, or even left an excuse. In all probability, more important matters or appointments prevailed, along with fear of lawsuits and publicity unbecoming the world champ.

But Rocky never appeared, and that was the bottom line. To this day the Rabbit, still fit and quick at 57, wears the badge as the only guy who ever backed down Rocky Marciano. Supposedly.

After certain of his men closed a deal, Drake would have to go to the home and perform what was called "cooling out the mark." He employed a closer named Norty Osborn who would give away anything. Besides money, he would give the homeowners all kinds of deals and goofy things. Drake had to go back to the house into a very adverse situation after the mechanics had begun the job. The people realized that not only had they overpaid but all they had to show for it was a signed contract and maybe some bonus money in the form of a (bogus) check. In "cooling out the mark," Drake would attempt to straighten out the deal and make it seem reasonable. This was very difficult since Norty had promised the world to the buyers, then swore them to secrecy.

Norty Osborn, who worked for Drake, was constantly accused of being a give-away artist. He practiced the old "model home" scam where he would draw a map for the customers showing their home in the center of his sales area and telling them that any other deal that his company made within this radius would result in a $40 reward. He would then write out an enormous check for the other deals ahead of time and give it to the homeowner.

Norty was very secretive about what he promised when he was closing a deal. He seldom told his crew, and very rarely would he even tell Drake, who was his boss. Drake would then have to come back and find out what Norty had promised, get the check back, and then convince the people to make their payments. To aluminum siding guys, being a "freebee" artist was a knock on their salesmanship. Of course, Tin Men all had their own version of the old model house story, but they loved to accuse everyone else of being a give-away artist.

The majority of tin men "cooled out the mark" at the front end, that is, at the culmination of the sale. As insurance to keep people from phoning to complain about payments, on the way out of the door the closer would add, "Now look, I need assurances that you can afford $50 per month just in case . . ." That took the heat out of the job, not like the guys who gave jobs away.

First, Drake would ask to see the original contract. He looked at it for a second and then ripped it up right in front of the homeowner; this contract which had promised money and everything else. Then Drake rewrote it. He had this tremendous ability to confront highly volatile people. Invariably he fabricated a story that his salesman either had died the day before or been fired. He got the people on his side by confessing that he was sorry he had to fire a salesman with a wife and four kids, but the guy shouldn't have made promises that he couldn't keep. It usually took Drake about an hour and a half. He was great at talking around the customers on a different subject, and getting off on tangents; yet somehow he came back to the point and finally just beat the people down. In the end, the homeowner actually thanked Drake when he finally left with a new signed contract.

In those days, some people couldn't afford to put siding on their whole house, but this didn't deter the Tin Men. They would sell a job to put siding on only one, two or three sides of the house. It looked ridiculous but the siding guys didn't really care. In the end, all they wanted to do was sell the job. There were some guys who occasionally tried to get the mechanics to put the siding up well, but most of the time the workmanship stunk. The reason was that it was a new industry, things were being promised that couldn't be delivered, and most of the mechanics or carpenters didn't know what the hell they were doing. Also, without regulation, no one really cared, and once they got a guy's money, the deal was "history."

The mechanics were mainly from the Hampden and Falls Road areas, usually from a big family group, and many intermarried.

They were rough-looking, uneducated and extremely unskilled carpenters. In those days, the siding was very difficult to bend and even a decent carpenter did a super-poor job on these homes.

Every day was the same to the siding salesman who continually cruised the streets. He might have had a fixed area for a week or two and then had to find a new one. Everything depended on getting lucky and finding a mark. It was a routine involving no planning, taking a ride, smoking a few joints, relaxing, getting something to eat in the afternoon, and "hitting" a few houses.

Siding guys worked initially in the Harford, Belair Road and Essex sections, all Gentile areas on the far east side of Baltimore Metro. They looked for a little square house, hopefully one-story. Another real good area was Glen Burnie in West Baltimore Metro. Tin Men were looking for a believer, with a family, and on a medium income (upper-lower or new middle class); people who were unsophisticated in their buying habits or their understanding of business. The guys never sold Jewish people because they were non-believers. They never sold to white collar workers as a rule in the beginning, strictly looking for Bethlehem Steel areas, those who had jobs at Sparrows Point shipyard, blue collar workers, or farmers. And it was always considered bad luck if relatives or neighbors were around when a sale was in progress. They had a way of souring the deal.

Many Tin Men were flipped out on "uppers" (amphetamines) all the time. They called the pills "door knockers" and used them to talk for seven or eight hours straight without stopping. They went to homes at 11:00 or 12:00 at night and pretended to look for and retrieve a pamphlet they'd left on the porch during that day. They'd start rapping to the resident and sometimes sold jobs that late at night.

Siding salesmen got up around 11:00 A.M., had breakfast at the Diner, and then sat around to bullshit for awhile. If the Pimlico Race Track was open, they would go for three or four races and leave about 3:00 P.M. They'd start hitting houses until around 5:00 or 6:00 P.M. depending on whether or not it was daylight savings time. The preferred work schedule was just three hours a day. Of course, if they had an appointment, they'd go back at night. The entire workday took about four hours, 16 hours per week maximum. The only Tin Men who worked on Fridays and Saturdays were legitimate family men and they were scorned by the majority of their peers. They were not considered the traditional hustling siding salesmen.

Most siding guys were into the race tracks, gambling and marihuana, and they wanted to party all the time. Seventy-five percent of the salesmen and canvassers got loaded while in the business, and many siding teams consisted of one junkie and two pot heads. They were very fast livers who wore flashy clothes, had new cars, and were either divorced or single. Some of them were former drug addicts or current heroin addicts. A number had been in jail for minor offenses. They weren't self-motivated salesmen but were always looking for the easy way out. Aluminum siding to them was a legal con game.

There were few if any college graduates among them. Their average age ranged from 20 to 35 years. Much of the time they discussed women, gambling and getting high. Many liked to play cards or shoot pool between 11:00 A.M. and 1:00 P.M., and when they came back from work they continued to play from seven at night to three in the morning.

The one thing these guys did best was to bullshit—either the customers or one another. They could talk on any subject, whether they knew about it or not, and loved to argue. Tin men were always procrastinating about going to work that day and debated about it for hours. They never even knew if the main guy on the siding crew would show up at the Diner. Mainly, they told siding stories, which most of the time were greatly exaggerated.

As Tin Men drove around, they spoke of different deals that they had made. They were fascinated with conning people, and pulled off these sales jobs through great lies. One of the cons they referred to was the "freebee" when they accused and ridiculed one another of being give-away artists.

Tin Men vilified guys who sold only to blacks or in very low class neighborhoods. The reason they bad-mouthed these guys was because blacks and low class whites, while the easiest people to sell to, basically realized that they could never afford to pay for the siding or anything else, and the salesmen also knew it. However, this type of Tin Man was selfishly looking for an advance from the company for the sale before the credit application was turned down, or before the buyer lapsed in his initial payment.

The guys visited bars frequently. Norty was a drug addict and alcoholic who eventually O.D.'ed, and many of his discussions were about who had died yesterday or the day before, or who was very sick. These eulogies revolved around junkies more than anyone.

Drake and other siding owners leased Cadillac convertibles for many of their closers, since that type of car impressed people and was one of the keys to a sale. When the guys weren't working, they'd pull up in the Diner lot or maybe somewhere else out in the county in these Caddies and either lie on the hood of the car or sit in it with the top down and try to get a suntan. Lying in the sun was a very important part of their work day. They would also "hit on" women whenever they could, driving up and girl-watching at the local high schools, colleges or shopping malls. Most of the time, girls would come over and speak with the Tin Men because of the flashy Cadillacs.

Perhaps the most important thing that the guys talked about was how they were going to get money from their boss on payday. They discussed getting advances and would sit and brag for hours about how much they thought they'd be able to collect. Tin Men always tried to get at least $100, whether or not they had closed any deals. They would meet Drake for hours in the Diner, in one another's car or office and haggle over how much money they should be getting, what they deserved, and finally what they really needed.

There were two types of offices. One was the traditional kind like Drake's on Reisterstown and Belvedere Avenues, not necessarily in an out-of-the way place, but somewhat off the beaten path. There was no display sign saying "Aluminum Siding" or "Home Improvements," and visitors were discouraged. The office was for the salesmen to congregate, bring in their jobs, and be paid. A second type of office was casual—in a guy's car, on street corners, or in eating establishments.

Back in those days, the Diner was really the main place where Tin Men leaned. One siding company owner, who died recently, was named Pomerantz (also called "Palmer" or "Posner") and he actually made his office in a Diner booth. Occasionally, Palmer's other office was the hood of his car. Palmer died a millionaire, selling jobs mainly from guys or canvassers freelancing on their own, or who owed money to their closers. He also bought a lot of jobs from the "Forty Thieves."

There was a group of drapes (greasers) from Southwest Baltimore called the "Forty Thieves" who operated in rural areas outside of the city as pseudo-siding salesmen. They used the same cons on isolated homes, carrying siding books and samples with them. However, they did this as a ruse, since they were actually looking for an empty house to burglarize. If someone was home and they actually sold a siding job, they would turn the job over to a middleman (like Palmer) for a small profit. As a result, the "Forty Thieves" caused true Tin Men problems with the police from time to time.

To make extra bucks or get out of debt during Christmas, the guys would hustle fake jewelry, phony diamonds, or bogus Canoe Cologne and Chanel #5 (it looked like Canoe, smelled like Canoe, and came in the same type of bottle; only problem was that two days after it was opened, the scent evaporated). Watches were another thing the guys "moonlighted" to make extra dollars, along with sweaters, ties, collars, etc. Rich Honkofsky originally got into this business in college by hustling sweaters. They were V-neck sleeveless, and at that time, in 1961-62, no one wore sleeveless. The popular choice was the Perry Como type. The sweaters were made of very strange fibers which the sun faded into nothing after a few hours. Rich purchased these sweaters for $5 each and put a $39 to $49 price tag on them. He then sold them for $15 to $19 and earned anywhere from $200 to $250 on a weekend. Additionally, the sweaters were very volatile, going up in flames if they came too near a cigarette.

Some Tin Men were so successful with these "wholesale" hustles that they left the siding business and did it full-time. For instance, there was a guy I portrayed in the movie *Diner* who sold clothing and other items from the trunk of his car on the Diner lot. Using a very cautious and paranoiac approach, he gave the impression that everything in the trunk was "hot," which was not true at all. He usually walked guys out to the lot one at a time, looking over his shoulder, taking his time unlocking the trunk and closing it every time a car drove by or someone walked out. He'd say things like, "These just came in the other day. Don't say a word to anyone or they'll put me away forever." He loved to use expressions like, "If I'm lying, I'm dying; these coats were smuggled out of East Germany" or, "This sweater is made from a rare sheep that has been extinct for years." He would emphatically tell us Diner guys that the price was not negotiable and then proceeded to negotiate the price for at least 15 minutes. We always were told were getting the deal of a lifetime. I remember buying a raincoat from him for $35 that I saw one week later in a department store for $24. Yet the next time I saw him, I bought a pair of binoculars I didn't need. He was just so slick that he made everything seem believable and a steal.

If siding guys didn't make a sale for a week, they'd tend to go broke for long periods of time. There were always some guys who didn't pay their rent or couldn't make car payments. Their cars were always being hidden from repossessors, and their constant borrowing from loan sharks made them go even deeper in debt.

Many car repossessors were tough customers, big and strong, but the repo-man feared most by the Tin Men was an American Indian woman named Mona who was an expert motorcyclist. She seldom performed her work in a clandestine manner—instead she almost invited interference from the late-paying car owners. Mona was an accomplished knife wielder who also utilized a straight razor, and her presence clearly meant "bye-bye" to the car. Mona's sexual preference was women and she had little regard for men. On her upper arm, she proudly wore a large tattoo that read LOVE SUCKS.

Probably the funniest thing the Tin Men debated was how a job should have been pitched. Most of these arguments centered around jobs that were lost, although from time to time certain guys like the Aldo brothers vehemently argued over a sold job.

Vincent and Freddie Aldo lived around Towanda Playground. Vincent was a tall, well-built guy (forever lifting weights) who had real slick black hair and a devilish look on his face. Freddie was the short, squatty-set type with a cute monkey-like face. The Aldo brothers were known as good athletes, and were such tough guys in a fight that many considered it suicidal to go against them.

One Monday, Vincent and his brother went out canvassing, made a great score, closed the deal, and earned $1,500 each. They took off the rest of the week and just hung around the zoo looking at the animals, buying all kinds of junk food, and arguing about the deal. They got into three different fist fights during that week at the zoo discussing the proper way to close the deal (in addition to beating the hell out of the zookeeper for trying to break up their second fight over by the polar bear pit), even though they had each made $1,500!

Freddie soon left the siding business and became a very successful bail bondsman while Vincent became a legendary Tin Man working with Drake for years and later as a free-lance home improvement salesman.

Vincent Aldo and a guy called Breeze were considered two of the best Tin Men in the country. They worked not only the Maryland area, but 30 other states as well.

Breeze was a tall, handsome man who spoke in a smooth whisper-like fashion. His younger brother, Maische, also sold tin. Over the years, Maische and his wife were involved in hundreds of car accidents—mostly fender-benders, employing dozens of lawyers. (Ironically, Maische and his wife died in an automobile collision years later in Texas.)

Breeze called everything and everybody, "Triple-A beautiful, gorgeous, doll-face," whether it was a man or a woman. Depending on the situation, he would go for sympathy by limping, begging, etc. He'd even show them scars.

Guys like Breeze were "trust" men. "You trust me, I trust you." He also had sayings for his canvassers like, "Rain, hail or Yom Kippur, get a fresh one."

> Breeze was always giving people free paint. (To cover up siding jobs because there was no trim.) He'd tell the customers that he was going to send over a painter whose costs were very reasonable. Breeze did this because his father-in-law was a painter. He was also an idiot. One time some people called up and cried, "Hey, the painter painted our towels inside of the house," and Breeze calmly responded, "There will be no extra service charge for towels."

Breeze once forgot to bring a contract out on a job and went into the bathroom where he put some toilet paper in his pocket. He pulled it out when he finished closing the deal and told the homeowner that it was a new type of stationery. On top of this, he offered the same customer five bonus books (which would have been like $500) if the guy let him date his daughter.

> In Virginia one time, Vincent and Breeze went to this house where these "blues" lived. It was around 10:00 P.M. They pitched their story and the black guy says, "Excuse me a minute, I have to go to the bathroom." He goes upstairs, and a half hour later he still isn't down. Vincent says to the black's wife, "Hey, I have to go upstairs, too." So he walks up the stairs, opens the bathroom and the "blue" is in there taking a bath. Vincent exclaims, "Hey, are you ever going to come down?" and the guy answers, "No!"

It turned out that Vincent could not measure anything, although it took Drake about 10 years to realize that. Vincent used to go outside of a customer's house and act as if he was measuring the square footage; then he would walk back into the home and confidently announce a figure. Drake and the homeowner actually believed he had done some serious arithmetic. Sometimes his guesstimates were close, but many times Vincent was so far over the estimate that Drake almost lost money on the deal.

> Eddie Levin was a very bright guy who thought he was two different people. (He also used to hear voices all the time from the other guy he thought he was). Eddie'd go out, write a job, and then put in a voucher for $900 apiece, for him and this other guy he thought he was. He always tried to get the other guy paid. Once, he tried to pull this number on Fake and Vincent, and Vincent told him that he had already paid the other guy for both of them. It drove Eddie absolutely up a wall and he argued with himself for days after.

Some Tin Men stood out more than others, not necessarily due to their salesmanship but because they were such characters. One of the characters was Marty the Humph, who was an excessive, compulsive, neurotic individual. His head shook a lot and he also used to twitch as if he was trying to bite his ear off. What he would do was "humph" a lot, kind of breathe and make funny sounds while talking. He also had false teeth that he took out when he was speaking to the guys in the Diner. Real appetizing! He had a funny walk, sported a disheveled hairdo, had been in Spring Grove State Mental Hospital more than once, and was on tranquilizers a lot. Everybody thought it amazing that he could even sell a job. Yet he had this great approach of sometimes spending 30 minutes to an hour at a customer's door discussing any subject and sooner or later he would get in the house and actually sell a job.

> Before Danny Cohen started pushing tin, he used to sell furnace jobs. He would drive to homes in rural areas where he knew a kerosene stove was used and he would tell the owner, "Look, instead of paying all of this money for kerosene, you should buy a new oil furnace, and then you won't have to purchase kerosene all of the time. And what about the danger of kerosene?" Naturally he had great horror stories about how kerosene had caused fires and killed and maimed families and small children. Of course, he failed to tell the customers that they still had to buy oil for the furnace.

Jay Polite was an ex-carnival barker who used to work the "carney" circuit. His pitch was to drive up to a neighborhood, jump out of the car, and start talking real loud about what he was going to do, how he was going to transform this old neighborhood into a modern one, and how his national company was going to use this block as an example. All residents would eventually come out, listen and talk to Jay. He was a fast talker who could excite a crowd and the entire block would stand around and watch. He eventually ended up selling the whole street, like Robert Preston in *The Music Man.*

As a teenager, Jay traveled with the carnivals working with a guy called Freddie the Loon, who also became a Tin Man. They broke in together at Carlin's Amusement Park. Jay was great at guessing people's weight and age.

Once, Jay and a siding crew were at Timonium Fairgrounds goofing off and waiting for the racetrack to open. They were watching a young man trying to work the "Guess Your Weight and Age" concession. The kid couldn't get anybody to play. So, Jay made a bet with the guys that within three minutes he could have 50 people gathered around him guessing age and weights. Sure enough, Jay grabbed the microphone from the kid and began pitching to carnival goers. He skipped over to an overweight, homely woman and barked out, "Hey miss, with those beautiful legs you can't weigh much more than 130 pounds, and I'll tell you what, if I can't come closer than one year of your age, I'll give you anything on this prize shelf!" In five minutes, there were 100 people packed around the stand. (It cost $1.00 for the guess and no prize was worth more than 30 cents.) The kid was sick when Jay finally left for the track.

Jay Polite could size up a customer better than anyone. His knack was assessing the maximum amount of money the homeowner could afford and get approved by the bank. It was uncanny, but minutes into the deal, way before the people even filled out the credit application or anything else, he knew how much money they were good for. He knew when it was appropriate to sell a job for $1,000 or $4,500.

Jay Polite had what was known as the "shove people" method. He would go into a house and back slap and shove the homeowner on the shoulder. He'd keep talking to him saying, "Hey, I've got this great deal for you, Buddy," and whack him, "My Buddy here, My Pal." Whack, whack, whack! Pushing and shoving.

One of the best canvassers on the market was a guy named Little George. He was quite short and had slicked-back greased hair. He

talked very softly, was a dynamite salesman, and a dapper dresser.
He was also known as Dancin' George. He danced cross-country
marathons. Little George frequented the Left Bank Jazz Society
dances in the Famous Ballroom and usually stayed in one corner
dancing for two or three hours non-stop either alone or with a
partner. He had total energy. He also screwed a lot of the lonely
married women whom he canvassed.

> The Duke was considered one of the all time Tin Men. His territory
> was Maryland, Pennsylvania and Ohio. He was also called "The
> Crip" because he would act like a crippled guy and ride around in a
> truck with a wheelchair like *Ironside*. There was nothing wrong with
> him, but he would have the canvasser say, "My boss is here. He's in
> a wheelchair and must leave right away." They would wheel Duke
> out of the truck and into the house. The homeowners felt sorry for
> him. They loved the Duke and he never had any trouble closing the
> deal.

> Another guy named Smiley used to come into a house with his hand
> contorted for the old "crippled-hand story." The only time this didn't
> work was once when he went in to the house of some guy who was a
> disabled Korean War veteran and said, "Hey man, look at this! Do
> you think it's easy to sell like this?" And the guy retorted, "Hey, do
> you think it's easy to live like this?" as he pointed to a huge hole in
> the middle of his forehead.

> Smiley was also called Mr. Ceiling. Every time he went into a house
> he never looked at the people; he always looked up, talking to the
> ceiling.

Many Tin Men were good card players and it rubbed off in their
salesmanship. Ely Goldberg was an excellent poker player whose
forte was bluffing the other players. He would go to old, black-
owned row homes downtown and sell trim for their houses or for
gutters on the front of the house. When Goldberg started pitching
the blues in their home, he'd let a $5 bill slide out of his pocket to
the floor exclaiming, "This must be yours!" Naturally, the blues
always agreed. This proved him to be an honest guy and he sold a
lot of trim based on guilt.

There was another card-playing siding guy called "The Counter"
or "Count." He was a gin rummy player who was supposed to be
great at mentally knowing every card and point in a game after his

opponent had drawn a couple of cards. There were challenges for this guy all over town. Only problem was he lost every big match. While he was still mentally counting the cards, his opponent would lay down gin. He was a better canvasser than closer.

Some of the nicknames of other Tin Men were Sam Spade, Abe the Konk, and Jinx. Jinx ran around with a black cloud over his head. He also drove a cab. On time, Jinx was caught leaning by his cab with a joint of marihuana. He told the judge that in all his years as a cabbie he never had an accident or a problem because the marihuana calmed him down. The judge, who was only concerned with the drug charge and was about to grant him probation, revoked his license for his admission of driving around high and sent him to jail for a year. That was how the name Jinx began.

By 1963, homeowner complaints against aluminum siding salesmen were rampant. Local and state legislators were so deluged by constituent grievances against Tin Men that legislation, swiftly passed and signed into law, immediately set up the Home Improvement Commission to regulate and license the industry.

In actuality, the Home Improvement Commission was created by the crises brought about by Tin Men who went into home improvements other than siding. Such improvements as electrical, plumbing and room additions, things that really created enormous problems with shoddy work, were potentially life threatening and dangerous to homeowners. Siding deals, no matter how bad the finished product, never drew the backlash one might have expected.

The Home Improvement Commission cancelled out bonuses, freebees and the sample-home con.

Many of the guys became legitimate, abiding (almost) by the Commission, others quit and drifted towards less publicized scams, and some continued hustling tin the old way until they were eventually charged, fined and blacklisted from the business.

Breeze stopped selling tin in the late '60s and drifted into narcotics distribution. A series of medical operations had left him with an almost continuous scar from his neck to his ankles. Breeze's numerous maladies—cancer, heart disease, diabetes—allowed him to acquire large quantities of prescription synthetic opiates (Dilaudid). Thus he began a lucrative illicit drug trafficking business which helped to finance his gambling habit.

Recently, Breeze died, and at his funeral he was eulogized by surviving Tin Men who rehashed some old Breeze stories and updated the fate of the legends of the golden age of siding . . .

Sol Kantor moved to Virginia Beach and instituted a mortgage brokerage scam, selling the same mortgage to different banks—until he was indicted, convicted and sentenced to 15 years in prison. The day Sol was to begin serving time, he and his family disappeared. Some say they're in the Bahamas, others say Israel . . . and . . .

After Drake's home improvement license was revoked, he ran gambling junkets to Atlantic City, and also started selling second mortgages at inflated (but legal) interest rates. His second mortgage practices created a series of scathing newspaper articles condemning the activity and resulting in proposed legislation to closely monitor the business and tighten the regulations . . . and . . .

Jay Polite was caught in a Federal cocaine conspiracy which led to the indictment of 20 other guys. It was assumed that Jay informed and was in the government Witness Protection Program; but a local bookie, just released from jail, swears that he saw Jay in a Midwest Federal prison . . . and . . .

Appendix B

Northwest Baltimore's Famous Graduates

Almost three decades later, the moment is still evergreen in Kenny Waissman's mind.

It was in the cafeteria at Forest Park High School where Waissman was a teenage kid with a brush haircut. He was introduced to a girl named Ellen Cohen, who had a globular build and an arresting dream.

"She told me she was going to be a movie star," Kenny Waissman remembers. "I still remember it, because the way she said it, the conviction in her voice, made me totally believe here."

It's overheard at adjoining lunch tables by raw sophomore students Joyce Heft, Carrie Robbins and Barry Levinson.

As high school anecdotes go, the unbelievable part comes later.

It comes when Kenny Waissman, class of '58, grows up and marries another Forest Park student named Maxine Fox, class of '61, and they put together an incredibly successful Broadway show called *Grease,* based loosely on their days in high school. The *Grease* sets and costumes are designed by Carrie Robbins, class of '60 . . .

It comes when Ellen Cohen, class of '59, grows up and reinvents herself as somebody called Mama Cass Elliot, forms a group called The Mamas and The Papas, and helps revolutionize pop music in the 1960s . . .

It comes when Joyce Heft, class of '60, becomes the first woman to produce and create a network television dramatic series, *The Hardy Boys* and *Nancy Drew* . . .

It comes when Barry Levinson, class of '60, writes and directs the critically acclaimed movie *Diner* . . . and in 1989, becomes Forest Park High's first Academy Award winner for *Rain Man.*

And when you talk about Forest Park students of the 1950s, that's just openers. The road to show business might be paved with broken dreams, but its starting point was that high school at Eldorado and

337

Chatham avenues.

And, for an astonishing number of those students, the dreams were anything but broken.

Consider a few students from the 1920s through the 1960s other than Leon Uris and Spiro Agnew:

Hal Timmanus, who ran George Wallace's strong presidential campaign, was a 1936 grad, and Bernie Ullman, a classmate of Agnew's, was the Chief Referee of the National Football League.

Not known as a great athletic school, Forest Park did have its moments. Perhaps its most famous graduate to achieve stardom in the field of sports was Bob Scott who graduated in 1948. He became the legendary lacrosse coach of Johns Hopkins University, guiding them to seven national lacrosse championships before he moved on to become the school's athletic director.

Another illustrious alumnus of Forest Park who also attended Johns Hopkins was Dr. Robert Kershner. Kershner graduated in 1932 and was considered one of the fathers of the space age—his face adorning the cover of *Life* Magazine in the early '60s.

But sports, politics and science were not the major fields where Forest Park graduates excelled. It was the performing arts. It began with 1929 grad Thomas Beck who appeared with Alice Brady in the early Broadway success *Mademoiselle,* and then acted in the movie *Heidi.* Next came 1935 graduate Alan Schneider, the famous Broadway director, and the only person ever to receive the Tony and Obie awards in the same year, 1962-1963, for his brilliant staging of Albee's *Who's Afraid of Virginia Woolf?* and Pinter's *The Dumb Waiter* and *The Collection.* His directing efforts are too numerous to mention here, but he also received the New York Drama Desk Award for outstanding direction for the Broadway show, *Texas Trilogy.*

A young classmate (he was only 15 or 16 at graduation) of Schneider's was little Irv Feld. He parlayed an entertainment career into the ownership and producer of "The Greatest Show on Earth"—Ringling Bros. and Barnum & Bailey Circus. Feld was also the president of Madison Square Garden.

Deborah London, class of 1939, at one time produced and performed for five dance companies known as the Deborah London Dancers from Quebec to Caracas, Venezuela. Aside from dancing in swank New York clubs such as the Sans Souci and La Conga, she appeared professionally in *Oklahoma!* and was also a choreographer for CBS-TV in the early '50s. Ms. London started five musical theaters throughout the United States. Now an instructor who lectures on dance throughout the country, she is also on the Board of Directors of the ultra-prestigious American Dance Guild in New York City.

In 1940, Robert Weidefeld graduated, shorted his name to Weede, and became the famous baritone of the San Francisco Opera Company. He was also a Tony nominee for his performance on Broadway in *The Most Happy Fella*.

Another Forester who received international plaudits in the field of opera is bass-baritone Spiro Malas, class of '50. Malas was discovered by music teacher Genevieve Butler in a woodshop class and has since become the leading bass-baritone of the New York, San Francisco and Chicago Opera Houses, along with the Metropolitan an other international opera houses.

But these famous grads only greased the skids for the students who would attend Forest Park during its halcyon period from 1957-1961. We begin with the class of 1957. Dave Pelovitz changed his name to Paulsen when he appeared on Broadway in a major role in Chekhov's *The Three Sisters*. He toured with the play to England and continued his role when it became a movie. Paulsen then worked in *Second City* with David Steinberg and Robert Klein, was an ice skating clown in Europe for a while, wrote the lyrics to an Israeli show on Broadway, *To Live Another Summer, Pass Another Winter*, that lasted about five months, and then entered television and movies. His movie credits include writing and directing the thriller, *Schizoid*, and writing *Diamonds*. Currently, David Paulsen is one of the three story editors for the hit TV series *Dallas*, for which he writes and directs many of the episodes.

Jay Tarses began his career with his friend Tom Patchett as a comedy team in nightclubs and on television shows such as Johnny Carson. They went on to write popular television series such as the old *Bob Newhart Show*, the *Mary Tyler Moore Variety Show*, and *Open All Night* (in which Tarses appeared from time to time). Tarses subsequently created the Emmy-nominated TV series *Buffalo Bill* and *The Days and Nights of Molly Dodd*. He has also written two movies, *Up the Academy* and *The Great Muppet Caper*.

Another classmate of Tarses, and still one of his best friends, is Norm Steinberg. Steinberg's career began as the writer of the David Frye *I Am the President* and *Radio Free Nixon* albums, for which Steinberg won Grammy Awards. Norm next went to Hollywood where he co-wrote *Blazing Saddles* with Mel Brooks, Andrew

Bergman and Richard Pryor. He wrote the TV series *When Things Were Rotten* and later won three Emmys for writing the *Flip Wilson* television show. Recently, Steinberg wrote the Luciano Pavarotti movie, *Yes, Giorgio,* the box-office hit *My Favorite Year,* the Michael Keaton gangster spoof, *Johnny Dangerously,* and the TV series *Doctor Doctor.*

Still another '57 classmate was Ann Hams Weston who had roles in the movies *Splendor in the Grass* and *Pity Me Not,* and is today the very successful producer of TV movies such as *Forbidden Love, Miss All-American Beauty, Country Gold, Split Shift, Teenage Sexuality, Getting Physical,* etc.

The class of '58 included Ken Waissman who, along with 1961 Forest Park graduate Maxine Fox, created and produced *Grease,* one of the longest running shows ever on Broadway. *Grease* was loosely based on some of Waissman and Fox's memories of their days at Forest Park, and the set design revolved around many Forest Park yearbook pictures from the '50s. (Waissman and Fox gave John Travolta his first Broadway role, and were also instrumental in discovering Jeff Conaway and Marilu Henner of *Taxi.*) Following *Grease,* Waissman and Fox produce *Over Here, Fortune in Men's Eyes* and *Miss Reardon Drinks a Little.* Subsequently, Waissman independently produced two critically-acclaimed Tony Award-winning Broadway plays, *Agnes of God* and *Torch Song Trilogy.*

The costumes designed for *Grease* received a Tony nomination and spurred the career of Carrie Fishbein Robbins, Forest Park '60, who went on to win Drama Desk Awards for costume design for *The Iceman Cometh, The Beggars Opera* and *Over Here.* Her Broadway credits also include costume design for *Agnes of God, The First, It Had to Be You* and *Frankenstein,* along with *Molly, Yentel* and *Broadway!*

1958 also graduated Murry Sidlin, former resident conductor of the National Symphony, assistant conductor of the Baltimore Symphony, and presently conductor of the New Haven and Long Beach Symphonies and musical director of the Tulsa Philharmonic. He is also host and conductor of the PBS series "Music . . . Is," and the Emmy Award winning "New Haven Symphony Orchestra."

1959 produced the talented Margie Margolis who went on to become an NBC News reporter and TV talk show hostess of the syndicated *Two Plus You Show.* Margolis has also authored the best seller *They Came to Stay* and the novel *The Girls in the Newsroom.*

The class of '60 was the pinnacle of this period of graduates who would go on to achieve major recognition and stardom. There was a little known school choir singer Ellen Cohen. She changed her name to Cass Elliot, helped form, and sang with the pop group The Mamas and The Papas, and then went on to become a very famous solo singer.

Joyce Heft Brotman was an associate producer of TV specials for Alan King, David Frost, Rona Barrett and David Steinberg before she became the first woman to produce and create a continuing television series, *The Hardy Boys* and *Nancy Drew.*

The class of '60 also included a young man named Barry Levinson. His early credits include television's *The Marty Feldman Show* in England and, upon his return to Hollywood, he won three Emmy Awards for writing *The Carol Burnett Show.* During this period, he also co-wrote *Silent Movie* and *High Anxiety* with Mel Brooks. Later Barry teamed with Valerie Curtin to write *Inside Moves, Best Friends* and . . . *And Justice For All,* for which he received an Academy Award nomination. Levinson independently wrote and directed the critically-acclaimed movie *Diner,* for which he received yet another Oscar nomination. He also directed *The Natural* starring Robert Redford, *Young Sherlock Holmes, Tin Men* and his Oscar-winning *Rain Man.*

Alan Holtzman was Forest Park's class president in 1964, his senior year. He became a film editor after he journeyed to Hollywood, with credits ranging from *Battle Beyond the Stars* to *The Amsterdam Kill.* Subsequently, he directed and edited the movie thriller, *Forbidden World,* which won the Paris International Festival Science Fiction Best Film Award. Additionally, Holtzman penned a novel called *Ticket to Boydom.*

In the late '60s, Forest Park produced two oustanding rhythm and blues singers: Otis Dammon Harris, who sang with The Temptations, and Billy Griffin, who replaced the great Smokey Robinson with the singing group, The Miracles.

But Forest Park didn't enjoy a monopoly on these promising students or the creativity and vitality that would eventually reap them success. Two other high schools, Douglass, located in Northwest Baltimore, and City College, attended by many residents of Northwest Baltimore, also contributed.

City College is the third oldest public high school in the United States, and its former students have made significant contributions, at both the national and international level, since the turn of the century.

Between 1900 and 1919, City College produced such individuals as world-renowned Johns Hopkins Professor, Abel Wolman, considered to be the father of water purification; former Secretary of the Air Force, Stuart Symington, who became a U.S. Senator from Missouri and Democratic Presidential nominee; and baseballs' Johnny Nunne, who managed the New York Yankees and Cincinnati Reds, and is in the Hall of Fame for completing an unassisted triple play while playing for the Detroit Tigers.

The 1920s was a busy era for City College graduates beginning with educator Dr. Norman Hackerman, the current president of prestigious Rice University; pharmacologist John Krantz, who developed the process for the buffered aspirin; internationally-known and revered sculptor Ruben Kramer, whose works adorn many public locales; tennis great Eddie Jacobs, and former owner of the Baltimore Colts and Los Angeles Rams, Carroll Rosenbloom.

Also graduating in that decade were noted historian and Princeton professor Eric Goldman, who was an advisor to President Johnson and has written acclaimed works such as *The Crucial Decade* and *Rendezvous With Destiny*; the infamous Alger Hiss, whose trial for treason is still hotly debated; legendary movie and Broadway star Edward Everett Horton; and the world's greatest concert and jazz harmonica player, Larry Adler.

Nationally-acclaimed Baltimore Mayor William Donald Schaefer (currently Governor of Maryland) graduated from City in the late '30s, a decade which produced such luminaries as Hugo Weisgall, a world-renowned music composer; World War II poet Karl Shapiro, whose works are mandatory reading in poetry classes in most colleges and universities; New York Yankee pitching great Tommy Byrne; Charlie Eckman, most remembered as the prototype modern basketball referee who also coached the Fort Wayne/Zolner Pistons to two National Basketball Association world championships in the '50s; and anti-feminist author Dr. Edgar Berman.

The '30s also graduated former Maryland Attorney General Bill Burch; former Governor Marvin Mandel; and famous television personality and Emmy Award winner, Garry Moore, whose real name was T. Garrison Morfitt.

Since I've already mentioned outstanding 1940s graduate Russell Baker and dropout Leon Uris, I'll jump to the '50s which opened the decade by graduating former Maryland Senate President and current Lieutenant Governor Mickey Steinberg.

Perhaps it was the mood of the 1950s that fostered yearnings for entertainment. '57s Dave Jacobs left City for New York where he wrote ten books, then moved to Hollywood where he first created the enormously popular TV series *Dallas,* and followed by creating the highly rated *Knots Landing.* A classmate of Jacobs, noted character actor Harvey Jason, has appeared in most major TV series and a dozen feature films; and 1958 graduate Stanford Blum was a TV sports director, a movie actor in *M*A*S*H* and *Two Minute Warning,* and later founder of an image identification management firm with major celebrity clients. Also graduating in the '50s were *New York Times* reporter and author Myron Farber; *Los Angeles Times* editor Tony Day; and novelist and TV writer Alan Goldfien.

The 1960s introduced successful football players such as fullback Bob Baldwin, who played for the Baltimore Colts; defensive back Willie Scrogs, who became the head lacrosse coach at North Carolina University, leading them to two national championships in the early '80s, and halfback John Sykes, who also played for the Baltimore Colts. End Tom Gatewood starred at Notre Dame and was its first black All-American before going with the New York Giants, and quarterback Kurt Schmoke became the first black State's Attorney for the City of Baltimore and now its mayor. They were all coached by George Young, a City history teacher in the '50s and '60s who's now the vice president and general manager of the New York Giants football team.

The '60s also graduated former Speaker of the House for the Maryland Legislature and now Congressman Ben Cardin; and Brian Avnett, who became one of the music industry's top personal managers.

Until 1956, there were three segregated black Baltimore high schools: Dunbar, located in East Baltimore, which sent a small percentage of their graduates to four-year (mainly black) colleges; Carver Vocational, a trade school, the location of which very few really seemed to be aware, and Douglass which bordered the Mondawmin Shopping Center in Northwest Baltimore and boasted attendance of many black intelligentsia who matriculated to numerous black and white colleges and universities.

Over the years, Douglass High produced some very illustrious and nationally recognized graduates and students.

Perhaps the most honored and respected alumnus who got into his share of trouble as a teenager was a 1925 graduate, Thurgood Marshall. He was often punished for deportment and, as a result, had to memorize the Constitution of the United States in the basement of the school. It obviously had an impact; Marshall became the first and, so far, only black Justice of the Supreme Court.

World renowned entertainer Cab Calloway, who graduated from Douglass in 1928, fondly remembered Thurgood Marshall as a "Straight 'A' student all the way."

But Marshall's academic reputation didn't motivate Cab Calloway, whose flamboyant lifestyle inspired George Gershwin to pattern the role of 'Sportin' Life' in "Porgy and Bess" after Cab.

Ironically, the role of Sportin' Life in the original cast of *Porgy and Bess* was played by another Douglass grad and Calloway school chum, the legendary Avon Long. Much later, Long co-starred in the Broadway hit, *Bubbling Brown Sugar,* and he was also seen in the movie *Trading Places.*

Equally ironic was the fact that Ann Brown, a classmate of '29 grad Avon Long, played the female lead of Bess in Gershwin's immortal *Porgy and Bess.*

Bill Kenny also attended Douglass High and went on to form and sing with the world-famous Ink Spots.

But, entertainment wasn't the only field in which Douglass grads excelled. Educator Lillie Mae Jackson became nationally known as "The NAACP Lady" and was in the forefront of the civil rights movement. The new head of the national NAACP office is another Douglass grad, Enolia McMillan.

Carl Murphy became the publisher of the Baltimore *Afro-American,* which developed into one of the largest and most influential black newspapers in the United States; and Dr. Herbert Frisbee, a former Douglass alumnus and later a teacher of Cab Calloway and Thurgood Marshall, achieved international fame as an Arctic explorer and war correspondent.

An *Ebony Magazine* article on the 100 most influential black Americans once listed three Douglass graduates: Justice Thurgood Marshall; Hank Parker, Treasurer of the State of Connecticut; and Congressman Parren Mitchell, nationally considered a hero of the poor and minorities.

In the field of athletics, Douglass produced standouts such as football star Albert Johnson, who played with the Houston Oilers; all-pro tight-end Raymond Chester of the Oakland Raiders and Baltimore Colts; and Pan-Am gold medal track winner Clifford Wiley.

But it was a strong music and drama program which gave Douglass students a chance to display their talents, and such talents they were: popular singer Ethel Ennis; the late actor, Bill Elliott, who also discovered and married singer Dionne Warwick; international concert singers Veronica Tyler and Juneta Jones, and television star Damon Evans who played Lionel on *The Jeffersons.* Howard Rollins, who starred in *Ragtime, A Soldier's Story* and TV's *In the Heat of the Night*, attended Douglass but later transferred and graduated from Northern High across town.

The current Baltimore City School Superintendent is '37 Douglass grad Alice Pinderhughes, and the '50s Jack Noel, the second black jet pilot in the Air Force, was also a Douglass alumnus.

Quite an array of multi-faceted talents emerged from what many used to consider an inferior institution with inferior students. This misconception is made even more glaring since I've only included nationally recognized names and withheld numerous successful business people, legislators and educators.